Nc
Say

D0581056

A pity beyond all telling
is hid in the heart of love
W.B. Yeats

No Way to
Say Goodbye

Rod Madocks

Five Leaves

No Way to Say Goodbye
by Rod Madocks

Published in 2009 by Five Leaves,
PO Box 8786, Nottingham NG3 5GA
www.fiveleaves.co.uk

ISBN: 978 1 905512 57 7

Five Leaves acknowledges financial support
from Arts Council England

Five Leaves is a member of Inpress
(www.inpressbooks.co.uk),
representing independent publishers

Typeset and design by Four Sheets Design and Print Ltd
Printed in the UK

Prologue

You went up the five steps of the hospital gatehouse lodge. Up the five steps then goodbye to the world boyos.

There were two nurses waiting for me there who took me from the prison officers after signing for me. They had blue uniforms and peaked caps in those days and they brought me down a corridor to a big, bare room where there was a tank of water like a paddling pool. There was a strong smell of chlorine and disinfectant. I'll never forget that smell.

There was a man in a white coat sitting at a desk. A doctor. He sat for a long time reading my notes in silence as we waited. Then he went through my things which I had brought: papers, letters photographs. He ripped these up in front of me and threw them into a bin and said, "You won't be needing these here."

He was a doctor for God's sake. I was told to strip and they tossed my clothes away saying, "You won't need these either," and I was handed a blue boiler suit to wear. I began to protest but got a slam in the mouth and lost my front teeth. They then pushed me into the pool, to disinfect me, they said.

And that was my start in the hospital. I was there eighteen years. They took everything away.

The things I could tell you. If the staff didn't like a fellow...

Patient R. Recounted to the author 1997.

PART ONE

1986

Chapter One
A Night in September

She came home for the last time as day was closing. I know that much. It was a Thursday evening in September, and it had rained after a long summer drought. There were puddles in the uneven asphalt of her street; car doors were slamming and homeward footsteps sounded in the darkening gullies of the city. I know also that she changed out of her work clothes and she put on washed-out jeans, slightly long in the leg, with frayed edges on the hems and she slid into some old Dolcis flats with no socks so that you could see her mauve-painted toenails. Then she went out again, taking a small, folding umbrella. It was ten past eight in the evening. The air was warm and moist, and snails had come out on the paths in the lamplight by the front gardens bordering her street. She took the four-minute walk to the Paradise General Stores on the boulevard where the last of the homeward traffic was splashing out of the city. The shop had a sign advertising a drinks brand which cast a violet shadow onto the wet pavement and the glass door rang a bell when it opened. Rachel must have grasped that worn, brass door handle when she left the place and it is the last thing I know that she touched.

In those days surveillance technology was limited, but the store had been raided some months before, so the owner, Mr Dhaliwal, had mounted a camera on the wall above the till taking shots at five-second intervals on grainy black-and-white Betamax tape. Rachel appeared in three of the blurred images. In the first, staring up at a shelf of goods, fingers touching her lips in a familiar gesture of uncertainty; in the second, at the counter, looking down at her purse where the angle of her cheek could be seen against the dark mass of thick, spiky hair. In the last one you could just make out her shoulder and the shadow of a moving arm as she headed for the door.

As far as we can tell she bought a packet of rice and a roll of cooking foil, put these into a plastic bag and then stepped out beyond our sight. This grey picture was our last glimpse of her. The owner's daughter, Manjit, vaguely remembered serving her and recalled no significant conversation. You could also see Manjit in two of the pictures, standing with her back to the camera. You wanted her to run after Rachel and pull her back from the doorway, but she remained unmoving, barely altering her pose in the blurry video images.

Rachel's return journey should have brought her along sixty yards of lit boulevard, down a darkened passageway through a municipal shrubbery and then another right turn and a short walk below high, shadowed buildings back to her front door. I walked there five days later, retracing her steps and that journey she should have made. I came back there many times thereafter, especially on September nights, standing under the big plane trees where the leaves reached down to the lamplight, looking out at the arched doorways in the old buildings along the boulevard with their dark entrances. I would pace out Rachel's route again and again under the glow of the street lights, with one lamp seeming always to flicker, throwing my shadow over the silent shop fronts, the hoardings with their adverts for student club nights and the battered metal bus-stop shelter with its green hooded roof.

What else was happening in the world on that day and on that Thursday night? I know now that a great fire burned in Yellowstone Park, consuming 1,000-year-old trees; that the Shroud of Turin was declared a medieval artefact; that uranium radioactive dust, blown out by the destroyed Ukrainian nuclear reactor in the spring, continued to fall over the world and on this city, drifting its dust into the pavement cracks, lodging in plants and mosses and in our hair and bones. I know from my work diary for that day I was seeing patients, so that Rachel was likely not in my thoughts except when I drove by her street, as I did every working day as I went down the boulevard and past the Paradise Stores.

I have sometimes thought I could remember my journey home that day in the rain, quite late in the afternoon, passing that secure world containing Rachel for the last time, although in truth it could have been one of a hundred journeys like that. I lived not three miles away from her in the suburbs of this Midlands city; my life continuing its course, not sensing anything unusual, nor having any inkling of that taking place which was to change everything.

Rachel had invited a teaching colleague to dinner at her home. She was a new member of staff, needy and garrulous and going through a difficult divorce. Rachel attracted people like that. Her guest came at nine and pressed the bell but received no answer. Rachel had a ground-floor flat, and the visitor could see the lights behind the curtains. She rapped on the window and called out her name but could not raise a response. Eventually she went away assuming she had been forgotten. On the following day Rachel had not turned up to work at her secondary school in a dormitory suburb. She usually travelled by bus to cross the great sandstone bridge over the river loop that separated this part of the city.

Although by nature Rachel was a little absent-minded she was a steady, reliable member of staff and usually came in early to prepare lessons. She rarely took sick leave. Assembly came and went and lessons began, and still Rachel had not fetched up, nor had there been any call. Her planned guest of the previous night told the others in the staffroom about her failed dinner appointment, and the first ripple of apprehension spread. There was no reply when her telephone was rung save her recorded voice saying "Leave a message."

Rachel's personnel file was eventually opened, and other calls were made. Her next-of-kin was contacted. This was her younger sister, Catherine, who lived fifty miles away. She had not heard from Rachel for some weeks. Mid morning two of her friends from the school staff paid a visit to her building. Still the everyday world continued to run, postmen completed their rounds and retired people walked their dogs down her quiet street with its old high-gabled houses. The two teachers, initially self-conscious and hesitant about disturbing Rachel, became more concerned when they saw her mail still hanging in the slot and her windows curtained. They rang the doorbell insistently until a sleepy Iranian postgraduate student let them in to the building. They asked him if he had seen Rachel and rapped loudly on her door. The only sound from within was the steady monotone signal of an inert TV station. The student had noticed nothing untoward and scarcely knew of Rachel's existence. Later in the afternoon, after Catherine had arrived, another neighbour in the shared block was found who sometimes watered Rachel's plants when she was away and retained a spare key. Rachel's two friends from school and her sister persuaded this neighbour to give up the key; they unlocked her flat and entered it, thus signalling Rachel's first displacement from everyday life.

Within, her household objects lay scattered about just as they were when she left the evening before. Her work clothes lay jumbled across her bed, onions waited on a chopping board in the kitchen and a light on her telephone answering-machine signalled that it had messages.

Rachel's colleagues and her sister disagreed about her clothing, her eye colour, her height and her weight when hesitantly describing her to the desk sergeant at the local station as he filled in a missing-person form with painful slowness. No one at that time knew what she had been wearing on the previous night or when exactly she had returned home from work. The police usually liked to wait twenty-four hours before listing someone as missing, but something in the frantic tone of her sister's concern made them take this one more seriously, and checks had already been made to see if Rachel had been admitted to any local hospital. The police asked for a photograph which the three of them had not thought to bring, so they had to hurry back to her flat where they found and opened a pack of holiday photographs taking one away with them. It was of Rachel sitting at a café table in Barcelona, in the summer sunshine of that year, one hand holding a cocktail glass, smiling at the camera.

The photos also featured a snub-featured man with tinted glasses, smiling in that lost world of all holiday snaps, pictured arm in arm with Rachel and singly in front of an ornate building where flags were flying. Rachel rarely spoke of him, but he was the steady man in her life. He was a technical translator, and they had been together for years. His name was Layton; he accompanied Rachel to some of the school social events. Catherine had met him occasionally when visiting her sister. He travelled a good deal and came to her flat for a few days at a time to stay with her before moving on to another job. They also went on holidays abroad together. Staring at the holiday pictures, it occurred to the three of them that this was the explanation: Layton had visited unexpectedly. He had swept Rachel away on a mystery date, a surprise weekend, and this had all been an embarrassing mistake, a sudden, sinister forking in the path; but now everything could be set back on its accustomed track.

This hope evaporated within the hour. As Rachel's school colleagues were leaving the flat, resolving to tell the police about the possibility that she had gone away unexpectedly with Layton, the phone rang loudly. It was Layton calling from Hanover. He had been intending to leave a message, and at first he thought that he was speaking to Rachel, surprised that she was back from work. He sounded shocked to hear of Rachel's disappearance, not having heard from her for several days despite trying to ring her the previous night. He agreed to fly back immediately.

The uniformed police went through the flat early on Friday evening as it became clear that she had not been admitted to any hospital, nor had she been arrested, nor shown up in any refuge or hostel in the city. Rachel's private spaces were quickly invaded in the process of her becoming a missing person. The police checked for signs of a break-in, they took her bank details, listened to her phone messages and made a list of her main contacts. I was not one of them.

Layton turned up on the early-evening flight from Germany and checked into a hotel although he had his own key to the flat, not wanting to stay there without Rachel's permission. They stuck a letter on her door explaining that everyone was concerned about her, just in case she turned up and was surprised at all the fuss. But she didn't appear; there was no call and as each hour passed she moved further and further from our world. The hospitals were checked and rechecked in case she had presented in an amnesiac or fugue state. Layton toured the casualty departments of both large hospitals in the city, talking to staff and showing her photograph to reception and nursing attendants. On police advice, the local press were contacted and the lunchtime Saturday edition of the *Evening Post* carried a front page headlined "City Woman Missing" with a studio photo of Rachel showing her in a formal pose with an unfamiliar, wavy hairstyle. That picture was to be used by the police and the press agencies as Rachel's official picture. Later, so much later, it appeared on a web site featuring people who were missing.

I noticed none of these first indications of events as I pursued my weekend, even though I had leaned over the counter of the off-licence buying cigarettes, with copies of the local paper heaped in a stack by the till with her picture on the front page. Nor did I watch the local news on TV, and I missed seeing her sister on the Saturday evening news slot with her frightened eyes, standing outside Rachel's flat with Layton and other members of the family in front of the cameras.

★

Jayney Kirkman was a fifteen-year-old from one of the villages on the outskirts of the city which had become a commuter estate. She was blonde and slight, and her pinched, elfin face became a familiar sight for a while on hoardings and in press announcements after she disappeared on her pre-school paper round one rainy autumn morning the previous year. The only trace was her little trolley, still stacked with papers with the house numbers ringed in pencil, found tipped on its side in a nearby lane, thick with seeding grasses and nettle. There was no forensic evidence, no leads and no arrests, only reports of a light-coloured van which was never traced. Jayney had not been found, although there were vague sightings and hopes were raised in the first few months before she quietly joined the lists of those missing with no clue to their fate.

The police at that time had been criticized after the Sutcliffe case in West Yorkshire because of their uncoordinated approach and their failure to understand the mind of the man doing those things. I, too, had listened to the taped voice of the hoaxer with his menacing Wearside drawl who had led them so astray and who had introducing himself with "I'm Jack." A rising number of women and girls had gone missing; some were found dead, others simply disappearing in other parts of the country. The year before Rachel had gone there was the case of Suzy Lamplugh. She was an estate agent who disappeared following an appointment in a run-down house in London's Fulham with a mysterious Mr. Kipper. Although I had little interest at the time in crime or the disappeared, I recall watching the first television interviews with her quietly-spoken parents in their ordered sitting-room, plates gleaming on a sideboard behind them, her mother holding Suzy's wide-brimmed straw hat with its pearl scallop ornament, found on the back window-shelf of her car, a last emblem of their daughter's existence.

A new breed of offender seemed to be on the loose, showing distinctive patterns of behaviour. Police began to speak of "crime signatures" and a repeating series of crimes, although the profiler Robert Ressler's newly coined description "serial killer" had yet to make its imprint. A number of forces had begun to pool their inquiries after three little girls went missing in the North of England and the Scottish Borders. The bodies were found in the Midlands within a triangle of interconnecting roads. One girl had been found floating in the river a mile from the school where Rachel taught. A dog walker out along the flood defenses by Wilford Church, next to the wide river, had found something floating and, thinking it was a bag of clothes, had pulled it in with a stick until he saw the fair hair fanning in the brown water. Her abductor had not yet been found and would not be until the end of the decade. In view of the local disappearances and the suspicion that there were men out there systematically taking women and girls, the county force had formed Operation Beekeeper, a standing inquiry centre using the new Holmes computer system which was to be activated early on in inquiries for missing females. Once district police had screened out the drunks, the domestics, the mad and the impulsive, any missing woman was to be a Beekeeper case and went to CID at Central.

By the early hours of that Saturday Rachel's disappearance went to Beekeeper. CID held offices at all the sector stations, but their base was at Central in the heart of the city, a four-storey limestone 1930s' building. Its piers, pocked with wartime bomb damage, seemed a breakwater or buttress elbowing out at right-angles to the inner-city slums of Radford. It was always hot in the building, and the open first-floor windows spilled light on to the straggling tea roses that bloomed late in the season in the raised beds by the street below. The Beekeeper room was active that night with a team of detectives and uniformed staff putting data into the Holmes computer system, sitting in front of a row of screens with Rachel's photo pinned up next to the dry wipe boards showing the division of detective tasks. Some were assigned to interview all known serious

15

sex offenders in the area, looking for access to a vehicle and their movements on Thursday night; others coordinated searches with uniformed police and the divers wallowing in the black water of the canal behind the boulevard. Some checked with traffic division for suspicious vehicle movement; yet others interviewed neighbours and made inquiries on the street. Rachel's doctor and dentist were contacted. They discovered Rachel's early-evening visit to the Paradise General Stores and recovered the images on the security camera. They went through Rachel's rooms so thoroughly that it brought Catherine to tears to see them prying at her floorboards and probing under her bed. Lights flickered in her rooms as scenes-of-crime officers took photographs, fixing an image of her rooms as Rachel had left them.

They found a little black business diary with motivational sayings for each day and showed interest in a succession of inked crosses until Catherine pointed out that they were probably the days of her period. They also found a brown manila envelope under her jumpers in a clothes cupboard. The envelope contained my letters and cards written over the years and a few photographs of me. They matched this with a battered red-leather address book decorated with gold fleurs-de-lis. I had bought it for Rachel in Italy years ago, and in among all the other names was mine recorded in her strong, looping, generous hand under J for Jack, the addresses crossed out over time as I had moved, leaving only my work number and just the letter J scrawled next to it. CID showed the address-book entry and the contents of the envelope to Catherine on the Monday. It took a while for her to place me, for we had met only a few times over a decade before but she eventually came up with my name. Thus our secrets were displaced by events.

★

I imagined Rachel again and again over time; seeming to come closer and closer, letting the door to the Paradise Stores clatter behind her, her flats going *slip-slap* on the pavement, her jeans making a lisping sound as they rubbed. I would see her pausing for a moment. What had distracted her? I would make out the gleaming tarmac, shadows of vehicles moving. Something was up ahead of her, something moving, straining at the leash. I would try to make it out as again she came closer, scuffling under the glare of the street lights, passing the parked cars, the hooded bus stop. The image would then jerk back. I would rerun it again like an old film: Rachel always walking towards me, yet ever receding as if on an escalator. *Slip-slap*, her footsteps kept coming. I would shift my focus, try to get ahead of her, try to make out what was there moving under the shadows of the plane trees. Then the image would readjust and I would be back at the beginning with Hedgepeth and Canter leaning near my desk, those first emissaries to my world, announcing that everything was going to be different from now on.

They came to see me where I held a training psychotherapy post in a Victorian building which had once been an annexe to the city asylum. The asylum had been built on a ridge line, so you could see the huddled city below. It was a Tuesday morning, and the September weather had flared up warmly; the cries of schoolchildren newly returned to school echoed around the car park. The police were waiting for me in reception and a secretary handed me a message sheet with their names written on it: DCs Hedgepeth and Canter.

"What is it about?" I asked, but the secretary could not say, shrugging and glancing at the pair of them standing in the patients' waiting area. They asked to speak to me in private, and we walked in silence down the corridor past the therapy suites. I brought them into my office which also served as a consulting-room. One of them was a square-faced blonde woman in her twenties, wearing a twin set with padded shoulders, with a Princess Diana sweep-over fringe and fading holiday tan. She had pushed up the sleeves of her dark jacket to show strong-looking forearms. She sat in an easy chair while her male colleague remained standing, and I drew up the chair behind my desk where I swivelled uncertainly facing them. I noticed for a moment the transparent hairs on her forearm outlined by the light from the window and a slim gold chain on her wrist. The male officer was a little older, jowly, with sleek black hair. He remained silent with a bored expression throughout. All I remember of him was the shuffling sound of his gleaming chestnut brogues as he roamed over my office, peered at my books and pictures and lightly tapped the buttons of the therapy-session tape recorder. They seemed in no hurry, so I asked, "How can I help you?"

The woman detective did not immediately answer. She looked up and asked, "Do you know Rachel Hauser?"

Both of them stared at me to measure my response, I suppose, and I looked back at them, unable to say anything.

The female DC drew out a shiny black-and-white photograph from her bag and added, "This is the person we are talking about."

I looked down at it. Yes, it was Rachel, my Rachel, and yet a remote image, not like her at all. I knew something dreadful had happened. I held on to the picture and looked out of my office window at the blank sky for a moment and then back at the photo. My desk phone began to ring as if the normal world was trying to reassert itself then as suddenly it stopped.

"Yes, I know Rachel," I eventually replied.

They had more questions.

When did I last see her? What was the nature of our relationship? Did I know why she might go missing? And, lastly, "What were you doing last Thursday night?"

I found a form of words. I had last seen Rachel two months previously. We had taken lunch together. We were friends from university days. All this was true in its own way. My words blew about the room and a brief silence followed.

"And on Thursday night?" repeated Canter.

On that night, I thought, I came home, showered and slicked my hair back with gel, put on a silver Ciro Cetterio suit and waited for Louie to come in from work with her things in a bag. We stood in the kitchen under a bright light like children at a feast and sniffed amphetamine sulphate from a neat paper wrap. Louie licked all the edges of the wrap then fluffed out her golden hair with a blow-dryer and applied her makeup, squinting a little in the smoke from the cigarette burning in the ashtray by the mirror. Then we went out as we did most nights; alert and bright-eyed, enjoying the clash of sounds, running on sulphate in those whirling hours, accompanied by the stuttering tempo of New Wave in the city clubs, or reggae at the Hippo Club, or the blues dives in Radford and then tumbling home, drunk, wired and forgetful, screwing on the living-room carpet by the light of my fish tank.

No, I could not tell them that. What I said was that I stayed home alone that night, not wanting Louie to be mixed up with this. They asked me if anyone could verify that I remained at home all evening. I could not, and Canter said that they might have to make checks, speak to neighbours. They asked again if I could think why Rachel would disappear. Did she have enemies? I could not think why Rachel would go. The thought was ridiculous. Perhaps she went because we could not love her enough, we were not fit for her, dear, sweet Rachel who could not think ill of anyone.

The police seemed satisfied by my subdued responses. Canter wrote the inquiry telephone number down on a blank sheet of session notes on my desk. They took down my date of birth so they could make checks on me. Before leaving, Canter leaned forward over my desk and tugged Rachel's picture from my hand where I had continued to grip it. I stumbled along behind them back to reception with the late September sunshine falling on to my face through the plate windows, my heart filled with panic at the thought of living in a world without Rachel.

★

I often think of her waiting for me in the night, sitting there on my empty bed. It happened in France three years after we had first met. I had wandered back through the streets of Alençon after a drinking party. It was lucky that I was on my own. My footsteps resounded on the cobbles of the narrow winding streets and the town hall clock was striking 2 a.m. I turned the corner under the Ricard sign by the bar across from my rooms and was surprised to see a light on in the windows. Rachel had arrived unannounced earlier that evening, having decided to see me one weekend on impulse, travelling all that way to see me from England for just a night. I had not seen her since Christmas. She had taken the rattling country bus from St Malo and had charmed the concierge into letting her in and had waited for me for hours, sitting on my bed in the lamplight. There was relief that I had come home alone and wonder at her naïve, loving gesture of travelling all that way. I will never forget her face in the lamplight, waiting for me like that. I could not resist taking her photo with my little Instamatic. Later in

19

the faint, blue dawn light, unbelieving of her sudden presence, I had reached out from under the bedclothes to touch the heap of clothes that she had left on my bedside chair as she negotiated the unlit stairs in the chill air of the old house, making her way by torchlight up to the bathroom on the next floor.

She had to return to England next morning to catch a ferry home in time for work. After we had awoken I watched her sitting on the same rickety bedside chair, pinning up her long hair, still talking, mumbling about inconsequential things. The pins in her mouth moved as she spoke, as I gazed at her and listened to her harmless chatter. She sprayed a little Opium atomiser on to her neck from a yellow flask. That intense, spicy scent remained on my pillow for days. Next she came over to the bed and laid the side of her cool face on my hot naked belly, and I placed my hands on her head, feeling the coils of hair and the little pins catching at my fingers. "Your tummy — it's rumbling. Time for breakfast," she said, and we scrambled up and went across the road in the clamour of Saturday-morning market traffic to the zinc-topped tables of the corner bar. We sat as the coffee swirled in front of us, and I watched her fingers with their bitten nails tearing at sachets of sugar. My eyes were on her face, searching its expression lines, noticing the faint pits on her forehead from the measles she had caught when we were students and I had nursed her back to health a year before. Her clear grey-blue eyes with their large black pupils returned my gaze, and then she leaned forward and put up her hand to touch my face as if to remember it better.

We walked back through a street market and stopped by the stalls. I bought her a silver bracelet with amethysts — her birth stone, with the clasp in the shape of two hearts joined together. The street seller had offered it to us as we paused by her stall saying, "*L'améthyste, celle est une pierre sacrée, pour la protection.*"

Then we went back to my rooms, an hour left before she had to go. She quietly pulled up her red cotton shirt, one button pinging off to settle under my bed, lying back, giving herself to me as I pressed myself to her one last time. Before she left she clipped the bracelet on to her left wrist, turning it in the light from the window saying, "I'll always wear it to remember this moment", then we rushed down to the bus station, her hand burningly hot in mine. I felt a prickle of childish tears, yet I also felt a strange relief to see her go as I watched her make her way with her duffel bag slung over her shoulder, awkwardly climbing up the steps on to the bus, squeezing through the bustle of farmers' wives and children in town for market. And when the bus left with a rattle and a cloud of diesel fumes I could just see her hand fluttering, waving goodbye to me out of one of the narrow side windows before the vehicle turned away on the road north.

We had first met as students three years before on a December afternoon in England as we ran to lectures in a rattling, icy shower. We had both happened to pause for shelter under a laurel shrub by a path as she struggled to open her umbrella. I offered to help her and she had allowed it. That's how I first remember her — a tall girl laughing with flakes of sleet clinging to her long hair. She had laughed as I also had difficulty opening the stumpy little brolly, and she had shared its shelter with me in her impulsive, informal way as we walked on awkwardly together with the flakes of ice rustling on the fabric. We spoke a little to each other, and I remember wind-driven strands of her hair flicking me lightly across the face as we went along. We rushed inside the lecture halls, and that afternoon we saw each other again as we came out and waved shyly to each other. We were both studying languages, both nineteen and in our first term at the university and new to the city. I could not stop thinking of her after our brief meeting, and I waited for her outside the lecture halls over the next few days and looked for her among the knots of long-haired students. I saw her walking with her girl friends a week later and joined her on the path, her companions falling discreetly back as we crossed the grass of the campus to the halls of residence. We talked as we strolled, clutching our folders, and by the end of that walk we had come to an unspoken understanding. I never really asked her out; we simply became attached.

We were together for five years and were bound by our initial fierce attraction and by our painful immaturity. When I think of those days, I again see the line of her pants under a cotton floral dress as she walked in front of me to lectures. I remember the lingering musk smell of her on my fingers and the glowing image of her face in profile and the delicate scroll of her neck illuminated by candlelight in my student rooms. I can still hear her breathy voice and slightly odd English, for her first language was German. I remember men looking at her as she walked by my side, seemingly unconscious of her effect on them. I also think now of her tearfulness, her trustful nature, her serious eyes searching mine; her puzzlement at my evasions and her bouts of doubt and insecurity which soon blew over.

Once, walking together in our early days, we came across a small sapling in grassland by the side of a road, loaded with dozens of young swallows which, for some reason, had chosen to cluster on the little tree, clinging to the branches in moving knots and bunches. We stopped to watch as more and more swallows arrived on the tree, bending and overpowering it until it went right over and the topmost branches touched the ground. As we stood there I noticed tears coursing down her cheeks and when I asked why she was crying she replied, "I know it's silly, and I don't know why, but that little tree just reminded me of us ... what will happen to us."

I could not tell what this scene meant to Rachel. Perhaps she sensed that we would overwhelm each other in the end and that we needed separation. We never lived together, nor do I recall us ever discussing the likelihood of it. We were both solitary in our own way, and maybe our separation was prefigured in all that passed between us.

Three years passed with us together in a self-contained sort of way. I am sure at the time that we assumed that it would always be like that but I had to spend a further year in France as part of my degree. I was sent to Alençon in Basse-Normandie teaching English to bored teenagers in the last year of the *baccalaureat*, living in rented rooms high up in an old house in the Rue du Temple near the corn exchange. Meanwhile she had begun the first year of teacher training, staying on in the city that we had shared.

We had parted in a matter-of-fact way as if leaving each other for a weekend. At first it was a sweet pain to be apart, and I half enjoyed the first lonely nights in Alençon with the drunks howling in the empty streets after the Toussaint's holiday festival, listening to the rattly sound that Citröens used to make accelerating over the cobbles in the early hours; watching from the dirty windows of my flat on weekends as the rain drifted over the limes outside. I looked forward to her letters which arrived faithfully, saving them as I walked to the school to read them in the staffroom with a coffee and Disque Bleu before classes. They were sunny, chatty, hopeful letters that spoke of ordinary life at home. I arranged for occasional phone calls between us from a cubicle in the Bureau de Poste. It was strange and moving to hear her faint voice against the babble and noise of the reception area outside.

I cured my restlessness by long walks in the surrounding maize and sorghum fields and with bicycle rides to the beech-covered uplands. But gradually I grew used to being apart from her, little by little I turned to other distractions and fell in with a new set of friends — mainly young teachers, some of them former *soixante-huithards* hiding out in the provinces. They were radical and passionate, and nights were spent drinking, debating and flirting. I think they were flattered to have a young foreigner with them, and I, in turn, was pleased to be in their company. I returned home at Christmas, and our separation seemed only to have sharpened our ardour. All seemed well between us, although I returned to France readily enough, and, as the months rolled round, although Rachel's letters continued to arrive, my replies to them grew more delayed.

Despite everything that she could do to keep our link alive that year in France, this was really the end of this phase of our being together. I had showed that I could live without her. I had become more wordly; looking at others, yearning for others, sleeping with others, and after that knowledge there could be no going back. When I returned to England her simple gifts seemed not enough and her embrace a constriction. I felt there was something unserious, childish even about our love, and I took our world apart piece by piece. She tolerated my growing absences, although it grieved her, and I could not conceal my unresponsiveness and the fading of my belief in us. We still sometimes went away together; we took trips riding on my motorcycle and spent a holiday in Italy — once staying in rainy, autumnal Pisa for a few weeks. Eventually, however, there were longer periods apart and rows sometimes engineered by me. How ashamed I am about them now. And in the end I passed the virus of loneliness on to her.

Within three years of my return from France I informed her one early winter that there was someone else in my life and that we should end our relationship. I told her this while we were on an old double-decker green corporation bus as it shuddered along the boulevards, and yet it was I who wept for what I had done as the bus rattled along and she who did the comforting with an arm around me while I sobbed in a selfish paroxysm of guilt and loss on that narrow, hard bus seat.

Later Rachel sent my letters and photographs back to me in a gesture of hurt. I eventually returned them to her once the shock of parting had healed (they were to be found by the police searchers), for although this was a painful ending, a severing of the safe bonds of first love, we had merely passed to another stage of our relationship. In truth we never really left each other or gave each other up, although we both took lovers and allowed others to believe that they were special also. After a pause of a year or so there was an exchange of letters and a resumption of seeing each other. There was something arousing in the familiar prod of her belly against mine as we embraced again, and so began a slower rhythm of meeting, a process of not letting each other go. We began to meet, coming together especially on significant days of the year linked to our previous life together which Rachel commemorated and which I viewed with amused tolerance at the time, yet which later were to become secret anniversaries of the heart that I would celebrate when we were apart and she was quite gone from me.

Our meetings were at first hesitant, and one lover or another would hold us for a while, but we settled over the years to usually meeting in school term times. We developed a cryptic way of contacting each other. She would send me a postcard from abroad, usually Bonn or Stuttgart where her father's family lived or even from places that she must have visited with Layton. It would carry a cheerful, laconic message which was a signal for me to ring her at work a week or so later.

24

I grew to love those assignations, something in me enjoying the clandestine and the forbidden. We would meet like spies, almost always at her place, usually agreeing to meet at lunchtime or early afternoon. My feeling of expectancy would mount through the morning and I would enjoy the contrast of my erotic tension with the office routines that trudged on around me. I would invent external appointments, sometimes even a mythical research committee, taking the bleeper if I was on call, and would leave the office, feigning nonchalance, then drive the short journey from the psychiatric unit to the street in a nearby residential quarter where she continued to live until the day she disappeared. I would park a little way down from her address, continuing an instinctively discreet way of being, and would arrive at her door just bringing myself like a business call with no presents or flowers.

I would press the bell push bearing her name, hearing it trill inside her flat and would pause, shifting my weight, glancing around sometimes to take in her quiet street with the parked cars waiting for their owners, perhaps noticing beads of moisture on the grooved lilac leaves by her door. Then her steps would sound, *click, clack* in her hallway then *clonk* as she stepped down on to a wooden step to the door. Then there she was, opening the door to me with an amused expression on her face, offering a cheek to kiss. It was sometimes a shock to see her after a while, for I carried a template image of her in my head as she was when we first met. She would seem unfamiliar for a moment, my eye confused by a new hairdo, by different clothing or an unfamiliar angle to her face as she grew older, then the image would readjust. She also felt this, I guess, and sometimes on first meeting after three months or so we would be cautious, barely touching each other at first. She would usually hand me a glass of white wine when I arrived, her amethyst bracelet still there on her wrist and she would say, "Look, I've poured you one already."

We would often sit and talk for a while politely, even formally. My eyes would rove over her flat, tuning in to her life again, noticing the same waxy-leaved monstera plant that got slowly bigger each year, the large blue-spined German dictionary always there somewhere on her bookshelves; my gaze running over the modest curve of the oak table leg below the heavy white lace table cover, which she spread in a continental fashion over her dining table. As the wine warmed us she would pull me unspeaking towards the bedroom. And so we would lie embracing, sometimes with the sunlight falling across us from the uncurtained windows. Sometimes she would fall asleep in my arms for a while, breathing softly, and I would lie there, my gaze moving over the Schiele print on her wall, and the view of red rooftops and the upper plumes of a large poplar seen through her open window. In time she would rouse herself and pad away in bare feet to return ceremoniously bringing food to the bedroom on a tray: crusty white bread and dark rye, cream cheese and pink ham and more chilled wine. We would clink glasses and I liked to watch her supple pale back as she leaned over the edge of the bed to fetch out the bottle to fill our glasses again. We would spill wine and breadcrumbs, and I remember her spluttering an unladylike "Oh shit!" then laughing when she bit into a tomato sending a jet of juice and pips to spatter the bedding.

There was a photo portrait of a man by her bed about whom I never asked — perhaps it was Layton or a predecessor — and she never bothered to turn the picture aside. Sometimes the phone would ring, and she would take the call naked, caressing me with a smile, for we both knew that we would betray others each for each. Sometimes she would tell me of other lovers and erotic films she had seen or fantasies that she had indulged. I would lie there silently, listening, feeling privileged and at peace. We would rarely reminisce. It was as if our lives concentrated on that vivid, present moment. Then, it would be time to go, signalled by the afternoon light failing outside or by a change of mood or an unbidden sigh, and it would be time to re-enter our external lives. We would gaze at each other for a moment, and then I would gather my things, she handing me my tie, my bleeper, my jacket, and I would leave a little drunk, dishevelled, with no words or expressed sentiment. She, closing the door, not following me out, just giving a smile, a look, and there was the ending as it was the last time I saw her. I used to say to myself as I brushed back past her lilac shrub on the front path, "Until the next time", yet there was to be no next time. Thus we had lived in our strange alliance, not together, liking it that way, holding to a pact which had been set to last.

★

My psychiatric textbooks spoke of the urge to search for a departed one as the first stage of grief. Back home from work, I drove slowly down the boulevard looking down her road, although I did not then know about her last visit to the Paradise Stores, and, as darkness fell that first night, I began to search, haunting the road outside her flat, walking her neighbourhood and trying to listen to what the place told me. I even stepped into the small garden at her front door, pressing up past the lilac to listen at her darkened windows. Once there I heard the faint warbling of her trimphone above the sound of evening traffic and a distant train shunting in the goods yards. Perhaps it was another lover ringing just to hear her voice saying "Leave a message", as I also rang many times until three weeks later her phone line was cut off. "Leave a message" — how I longed to do that, and what message would I have given her? I would have told her how much I loved her, although I never said so when she was with me. After listening at her window I stepped up her path to lay my hand on her front door, the image of my hand remaining for a moment, displacing the thin condensate of early autumn chill, then gradually vanishing although her name continued to glow, illuminated by the bell push button, "R. HAUSER" in her familiar handwritten capitals.

I had to be careful, as the neighbours were alert and, once, all the lights were on in her flat with people moving about. Later, in that first week, someone must have reported me, for a patrol car came cruising down her road shining a light into the shadows. I spent the first days at work hoping that she would ring or leave me a message. As the nights progressed I would give excuses to Louie then wander the city looking in all the places that I could think of — clubs, doorways, lonely bus stations of the sparkling city, driving out to the river to an assignation place where we used to meet once long ago when we sat watching the lights on the cooling towers of the great upstream power station. The following nights I would stumble home late to my flat. Inside, the TV would still be throbbing. Sometimes I would crouch down and stare into the fish tank where the blue tetras continued to dart unconcernedly, and the TV news spoke of the world getting on with things, a fire in Puerto Rico, a bomb in a synagogue in Istanbul, people tumbling, choking, dying, but most of us here secure, watching it all on the screen, and I would lie sleepless in bed thinking: Where are you?

"What's the matter, babe?" asked Louie eventually, stroking my sweat-soaked hair one night, aware that I had fallen away from our nightly clubbing, making excuses and showing no appetite for our previous sensual nights. She had begun to go out on her own after a week or so, and sometimes she would ring late at night to ask if she could come over and after a while a taxi would deposit her. I would be roused by the clump of car door closing, or a burst of radio traffic and the clattering sound of a diesel engine, then she would stumble in, illuminated for a moment in the doorway, her hair outlined like a golden halo in the headlamps as the taxi reversed down my drive. She would always be drunk, smelling of smoke and alcohol, her eyes blurry.

Sometimes she would put on a little girl's voice, lolling pouting on my sofa, her handbag open, its contents spilling, calling me to screw her. "Come on, come on. Fuck me now," her voice slurring, subsiding into sleep, then she would open her eyes again when I covered her with a coat and she would murmur, "Jack, you're weird. What you doin'? Don't you want me?" Her voice would trail off, and I would tuck her into bed like a grim and sober parent, and she would be asleep, sometimes allowing me to unbutton her clothes and slip them off. I would roll her chastely under the covers and she would turn on her side, still murmuring, while I sat up in the night smoking, looking into the gas fire in my front room as it burned blue and orange.

She would often wake again an hour or two later, quite sober and lucid. It was on one of those nights that she uncharacteristically called to me as I lay beside her, my eyes open in the dark, and she asked what was troubling me. I told her what had happened or a version of it, spoke of an old friend, an old girl friend who had gone missing. I could not tell her more, although I felt ashamed for it, sitting up in my cold room. I could just see her outline in the dark and her glowing cigarette end and heard the intake hiss when she took a drag. She was sympathetic, more sympathetic than I thought she would be, although she preferred to live in the present. Louie understood suffering instinctively, yet there was a cooling afterwards, and as I declined her offers to accompany her clubbing she began to go out more often without me. Sometimes she would ring me to say, "Tonight I'll stay at mine"; at other times I heard nothing. Once or twice the phone would ring a few times and I guessed it was Louie signalling in some call box in the night. More often she would ring from inside a club. I would hear music thudding and voices.

"What are you doing?" she would say.

There would be a long pause with music hammering in the background, then I would ask, "Where are you?" But she would not answer or perhaps did not hear me.

"Do you love me?" she would ask, and I would say "Yes I do," and then sometimes I would hear other voices, men's voices, her speaking to someone else, then "Staying with friends tonight, darlin'. OK?" Rachel's going had somehow collapsed my world. I could not hold together that which once had seemed comprehensible, although despite wallowing in the pain of not knowing about Rachel I could not give Louie up entirely, for we had a strangely obstinate love.

★

As the time passed I would wake in the mornings with a groan, thinking immediately about Rachel in an unknown dungeon of the lost. I continued to drive slowly past her neighbourhood. At work I would park up in the Fiat, and gaze out on the old cans, the discarded plastic bags and other debris in the brambly scrub of the old asylum grounds. A person could be lying in there for months, even years I thought. I continued to see my patients, watching their hurt mouths and their bruised eyes in the therapy room, yet with my mind turned to my own losses. I avoided my concerned colleagues as best I could, for I knew their gaze. They had noticed the changes in me and tried to draw me out, as when in the staff coffee room my softly spoken supervisor said, "You look preoccupied, Jack," but I could not accept their help; made excuses and sped away. It was as if Rachel and I preserved our secret life to the last, which I could not admit to anyone else. Each day I followed the progress of the investigation; the national papers had got hold of it and there were articles about Rachel's pupils and colleagues. Once, Catherine made another appeal on a local TV news programme.

I could not think of her dead; no, it somehow could not be. I thought of her as a prisoner or as having somehow taken a wrong turning. I visualised her face more intensely than I ever had when we were together and thought how often when we had sex in the early days she would weep. I would gaze down at her, perplexed, not understanding. How those tears would well, washing down her cheeks, wetting her temples and tasting salty on her lips. She would sit up saying, "I'm sorry," wiping her reddened nose upwards with her hand, laughing unconvincingly, saying, "Drippy Piscean." She was a tall girl, oval-faced, with a long nose tipping up slightly at the end, a smiling wide mouth with monkeyish expression lines. Her teeth were slightly uneven with a faint, calcareous lightening on the central and lateral incisors. She was smooth-skinned with pale, almost boneless hands and bitten nails which flew to her mouth when she was unsure of anything; there was a mole on her left shoulder which was always pressed down by her bra strap. A tall, narrow-hipped, stumbly young woman who sometimes seemed absent-minded with an other-worldly air, yet at other times showing a surprising sensuality.

Once, on a raw autumn day, she stood with me at a bus stop wearing her thick black fur coat. I complained of the cold and she opened her coat, wearing just a red cotton mini dress beneath and pulled me to her, wrapping me around with the heavy folds. The heat of her body was so intense that day. Whatever images I conjured up to remind me though, I still felt that Rachel escaped my vision of her. She was always somehow moving ahead of me.

★

Three weeks passed, the national papers continued to circulate the story speculating and linking Rachel's disappearance with that of Jayney Kirkman and other girls going missing in the West Country. Each visit to the newsagent became an ordeal. Then there was a sighting, mentioned on local news radio which I heard driving back from work. Rachel had been noticed the weekend after she had disappeared by a woman who had seen the photographs and who had reported that she was certain that she had spotted Rachel walking, deep in conversation with a man on Lincoln railway station, forty miles away, the day after her disappearance. There was a moment of brief hope and an overwhelming desire to drive there at once. The police switched their inquiries, searches went on, and there was a flurry of activity. Then the story died and nothing further came of it.

She had gone as if by some sleight of hand. Her face confronted me on posters pinned up in her neighbourhood, in bus-station waiting areas and in police-station foyers. There were new searches in nearby gardens and in a public park that she had skirted on the way to work. Police teams combed the nearby railway yards, with their pallet piles, burnt-out wagons and scrubland of buddleia. The canal was again gone over by divers, and boats were checked. I searched too, walking the city, looking everywhere, seeing her in a shop queue, among a gaggle of laughing girls, or huddled in a door-way with a man. Once I chased a bus, running after it, thinking that I had glimpsed her profile among the passengers.

The local paper reported that the police were seeking a white van seen on the night of Thursday the 4th swerving about on the boule-vard near Rachel's home. A man walking home in the drizzle from the chip shop two hundred yards up from the Paradise Stores had seen a male figure in a white T-shirt, yelling, snarling at someone or something in the back of the vehicle. This piece of news filled me with fear, and with it came anger, forming from my guilt that I had not been there to protect Rachel from the unknown and the terri-ble. I began to think that in a way I had made her walk alone that September night.

I joined Louie again after that — seeking distraction — visiting pubs and clubs in the city, drinking, glaring at the men who fringed the bars and bristling in the urinals as I stood there shoulder to shoulder with them. Louie would greet the bouncers flirtatiously, and they would in turn look knowingly at me over her shoulder. She often disappeared into the heaving throng; sometimes I would glimpse her in conversations, doing her deals with her club associ-ates. They could be from any of the many tribes of the time: stocky bouncers in short leather jackets, other men with wedge haircuts and Big Country lumberjack shirts, or punks with studded jackets.

Later she would return, gesturing to me to come with her to a shadowy booth beyond the lights of the dance floor, unfolding the paper wrap, swiping off the wet slick of lager from the table top with a drinks mat, snorting up the grey-white powder with a crisp rolled note and feeling the bitter rime trickling into the sinus cavities. Fear would vanish to be replaced by bone-hard will, a chill intent and energy. I would stand on the crowded edges of the dance floors as the music pulsed, watching Louie dancing on her own, frenetic and absorbed, while I swayed in the shadowy margins ringing the dance floors, looking at the faces of the men.

We would come out eventually, clattering down the stairs on to the street when the club closed; Louie coming home with me, as the revellers streamed out, rolling against me when the taxi pulled away and we sped to the suburbs, the radio calling in rides across the city. She would always be drunk, exhausted by her dancing, the sulphate ebbing from her bloodstream, and sometimes I would drag her into my house, either straight to bed or to loll on my sofa while I watched TV with the lights off. Once, inexplicably and savagely, I took some kitchen scissors and as she lay, seemingly passed out on the sofa and lit by the flickering light of the TV. I cut the buttons off her blouse until her breasts popped out in their soft purple bra cups and then cut the bra straps and sides, releasing her breasts entirely. Still she slept on, face hidden in a tumble of fair hair. I pulled at her black slacks and tugged them down to look at her mounded belly then slid them right off, guiding her bare feet through them. She stirred and sighed, and I paused. I waited until she settled again, cut at her silky dark pants on the narrow part at each side as it stretched around the hip bone and pulled them away, then sat staring at her sex as she lay splayed and still. Later that night I guiltily hid her shredded undergarments, and in the morning she had risen and gone to work before I woke from a dreamless sleep, never mentioning what had happened to her clothes, perhaps lying awake all that time, allowing me to enact that thing.

A month on I decided to take a risk. I looked up Catherine's married name in the phone directory of the town where she lived. I rang from a phone box, out of an instinct to hide, and was disconcerted when a child's voice answered.

"Hello... Who are you?"

"I'm a friend."

"A friend of Daddy's?"

"No, just a friend."

The phone clattered down, and there was the sound of footsteps and the child's voice further away. "There's a man on the phone, Mummy."

I fed more coins in the box, then heard a woman's voice, very like Rachel's, with a familiar pitch and hesitance; it took my breath away for a moment. I told her it was Jack.

"Jack?"

"Jack Keyse."

"Oh, yes, Jack ... How did you get this number?" she sighed. "Never mind ... What do you want, Jack?"

There was fear in her voice, fear and guarded hostility. I told I needed to talk to her, to see her and talk about Rachel.

"Why don't you talk to the police?"

"I need to talk to you, Catherine. It's important for me. Please."

The pips went, and after I fumbled for more change and fed it in she said that she would ring me back. Minutes later, when I was on the point of walking away, the phone rang and she told me resignedly that she was coming to the city that weekend and we could meet then.

We met two days later on a Saturday in the foyer bar of a new city hotel chosen by Catherine. A faint reek of tar drifted into the foyer from the weekend road gangs outside, burning off road markings with an orange flame. I perched on a sofa seat and waited. Catherine was four years younger than Rachel. I remembered her as a plainer, perhaps cleverer sister. Once, at university, I had to entertain her with lunch while Rachel attended a tutorial. I remember her light eyes behind the round specs, her faint resemblance to her sister, her evident boredom, her discomfort at my attempt at polite chatter and my gratefulness when Rachel returned. She had matured to be as sensible and pragmatic as her elder sister was dreamy and forgetful. She had married a businessman in the new technologies, and when Rachel mentioned her to me we would both smile, as if we knew something superior and amusing and found something funny about her skiing holidays, her two spoilt children and her succession of new BMWs, of which she was so proud.

I made her out threading her way through the scatter of guests and drinkers. She looked well groomed and sleek; the glasses had gone, and I could now see her sisterhood to Rachel in her tall narrow figure, in her slightly flat-footed walk, and the way the eyes were set in their sheltering brow. She asked for a coffee and kept her coat on, sitting a distance away. I went to the bar to order and glancing back could see her sitting hunched, looking down at my tumbler of scotch.

"You look well, Jack," she remarked. When I returned with her coffee and set it down she added, "Why have you got me here?"

I stumbled over an account that I had prepared; it sounded stilted, but I kept on speaking. I told her that I found it unbearable to wait like this, wondered if she could tell me what the police were doing, asked if she knew anything that was being withheld by the police. I also told her that I had kept in touch with Rachel and felt awful about what had happened.

After a while she waved her hand stopping my flow. "I'm not sure why you are telling me this. Ray and I have been supporting Layton. He is devastated and stayed with us in the first week — that's why we have come up today."

Her eyes were cold and her expression severe. I begged her to tell me what happened.

She softened a little and told me of those first days, the searches, what Rachel was probably wearing, the last sightings, the police searches, the sequence of events. How the police were still treating her disappearance as a missing-persons inquiry and how the television wanted another interview as there was going to be a new appeal on a crime programme. Her business-like tone faltered and her gaze slipped away from me, she spoke of the frustration, the pain, as time passed and hope ebbed. She asked, "Do you know anything, Jack? Is there anything you're hiding?"

I spoke of my sadness, my wish to help search or do anything. Catherine regarded me for a moment, then pulling her coat round her said, "I am going to tell you something. You hurt her, Jack. You hurt my sister badly. You broke her heart. I remember her staying with us after you left her. We listened to her crying at night, many nights. I will never forget it, and you would not let her go afterwards. Her hanging on, living here for years, not leaving this city because of you, her chances in life slipping away, on her own, waiting and you not letting her live her life. It's hard to forgive that, Jack — your carelessness."

As I sat staring back at her, she turned and gestured. There was a movement behind her, and her husband Ray emerged through the drinkers by the bar to stand next to her. A thickset, balding man, he nodded to me warily, two little girls twisted in the grip of each hand where he held them tightly. He had probably been there all along. Catherine buttoned her coat and pulled on little black fur-trimmed gloves: I handed her a slip of paper with my number on it. She hesitated, then, taking one glove off, placed the piece of paper in her coat pocket and said, "Goodbye, Jack. We'll find her. When she's home safe that's all that I want. Don't call me again, will you?"

I nodded, watching her go as the bar staff moved in, swiftly rubbing the glass surface of the table with a cloth and taking away her untasted coffee.

The CID took a renewed interest in me after I had contacted Catherine. I guess she informed them, and maybe some of her anger at me was displaced hope that I could provide something to resolve the mystery.

During the next week as I was driving into the work car park, with the leaves spinning to the gravel from the fading limes in the asylum grounds I noticed a biscuit-coloured Ford Sierra that came nosing down the car park and now came to a halt across the front of my car. I stepped out with a file of clinical papers under my arm. The driver's window came down and I could see it was Hedgepeth, the detective who had come to my office.

"Dr Keyse, we would like to see to you." He spoke to me from the car. There was a studied hostility in his eyes. I felt flustered and stammered that, yes, I could make an appointment.

"We want to see you today," he insisted, with no change in his expression, and I did not argue. I wanted to be there among people who knew about Rachel and I made my way to Central station within the hour. I waited by the high wooden reception desks, among sullen youths reporting on police bail, and a middle-aged woman who sat alone dabbing at her eyes with a tissue. Hedgepeth emerged from the stairway passage and conducted me through a heavy door past the custody cells on the ground floor. I caught glimpses of faces looking back at me through grilled vents in grey plated doors, of a stained metal lavatory in a recess, and of narrow passages leading away under the station. There was no natural light here and the sound of keys clinking and of prisoners calling to the custody staff were accentuated. I wondered if he had taken me here deliberately to unsettle me.

We entered a small interview room. There was a mirror high on one wall. Hedgepeth bade me sit on a narrow plastic chair drawn up at a battered wooden table. He left the room and I concentrated on the black tape machine in front of me with piles of new cassettes heaped on top of it. I noticed that some past offender had managed to etch a furtive graffito on the table top with a cartoon sorrow face and the inscription "Gaz was 'ere". It felt unreal, yet somehow I was comforted that in an odd way I was playing a part in Rachel's life here. Hedgepeth came back with the blonde DC Canter. They carried notebooks, entered the cramped interviewing room, and sat around the deal table as if it was a séance. They reintroduced themselves with set expressions. This was to be an informal interview, entered into with my consent. "Do you have any questions?" I had many, but none I could articulate.

Hedgepeth interviewed me. I noticed his shave line, the stippled rash on his neck, and the dusting of white flakes on his shoulders under the harsh overhead lighting and felt an obscure tenderness for him. After a while he took off his jacket revealing humid patches on his shirt. He took me through the day and evening of 4th September and I listened to his voice with its flat Midlands inflexion. He asked me again what I had been doing that night. I sensed that he was leading up to a trap and admired his technique. I became vague and hesitant as he pressed me.

"Dr Keyse, you told us that you stayed in that night, but that is not true, is it? We have a witness who says that you went out that night, you had a visitor at your house and went out, not returning until late."

I knew of course that it was my neighbour, Mrs Mullender. Louie and I used to giggle in bed sometimes as we listened to her standing in her driveway next door, calling her cat, in shrill tones. She lived alone, fearful, resentful and alert, her TV flickering spectrally through her net curtains at night. She disapproved of my irregular hours and complained of the nettles and willow herb which crept across into her garden from my neglected patch, although I softened to her one night when I heard the sound of muted sobbing coming from her bedroom window and recognised that we both had grief in common.

"I put it to you, Dr Keyse, that you have not told us the truth about the night of 4th September and about the nature of your relationship with Rachel Hauser."

I kept my voice steady and spoke in terms of apology and informed them that I was not a doctor but a therapist. I also told them that I had made a mistake. That night I was with a friend and did go out. I gave them Louie's name.

Canter carefully wrote her name down and it felt like a betrayal. The heat went out of it once I had mentioned Louie. I told them she was my girlfriend. They switched to questioning me about my relationship with Rachel and I conceded that we had once gone out together. I realised then that they had my letters. I told them that it had long blown over and that we had remained just friends. They asked me about my job and with whom I worked. They listened without expression.

The interview slowed. The detectives looked at each other and there appeared to be an unspoken ending. I asked them about the course of the investigation, then Hedgepeth turned to me.

"Mr Keyse, we want you to know that we are taking an interest in you. We do not appreciate wasting time. We cannot afford anything but complete honesty in this inquiry. We may wish to speak to you again."

I stared back at him and wondered what it was that angered him about me.

As we emerged from the interview room we were met by a thickset older man in a crumpled grey suit, with wiry grey hair, and an air of authority. He did not introduce himself but said, in a Scottish accent, "I'd like to thank you for your cooperation. This is a difficult inquiry." I sensed he was sizing me up and had watched the interview through the mirrored window.

I nodded in response, saying "OK," wondering what message he was giving me.

I tried ringing Louie soon after getting out of Central, rushing to a phone box to warn her. She was not on her shift and the one phone in the nurse's residence rang unanswered. I thought perhaps she was sleeping after a binge and a late night. I called at the residence and left a message with an irritable nurse who eventually answered the door. I asked her to slip the message under Louie's door. It read: *"Regret police may interview you about night in September. Sorry. Love Jack."*

I felt too unsettled to return to work and drove out near Rachel's old school to walk the river bank, thinking of Louie among those who have loved me. I looked out at the water where rowers from the university were pulling against the current. We had met in a bar a year before. She was a staff nurse in casualty at the local general hospital. There was a pub across from the nurse's home. The nurses would come over after late shifts, hastily changing out of uniform in time for last orders. Louie was there one night; I had not noticed her before. She had blonde hair and hazel eyes that seemed to hold a mocking glint. She was well made, upright, and had a mannered way of holding herself, like a mannequin, her arms curved away from body. She had a clown's face with a narrow tippy nose and brows which rose in a circumflex arch. Her lips seemed always slightly parted, puckered in an O of surprise and showing a *diastema;* a little gap between her front teeth. She proffered a brittle glamour and on that first night I was attracted to her pale skin against the one-piece black dress with thin straps and the silver neck chain carrying a tiny jet heart, but what I most appreciated about her was her direct, uncomplicated presence. She had introduced herself coolly and I enjoyed her candid gaze, and her sympathetic, easy company.

She casually said at the close of the evening, "Are you coming back with me?" and I followed her to her rooms along with some of the other nurses. Her rooms were spread with disarray; there were dolls in national costumes ranked on all the ledges and on the floors, a litter of gold cigarette packs, Pils bottles, filled ash trays, horror video cassettes, tights, clothes, towels and makeup containers. She played her favourite song at the time, *"Come On Eileen"*, very loudly, over and over, not caring about neighbouring rooms. The others came and went. We drank bottled lager and shared cigarettes; the chorus spun around the room, Louie crooned along "Ah, come on, come on," then took my hand and we swayed unsteadily together, then she pulled away and looked at me solemnly as her last guests left and said, slurring her words as she spoke, "Well, are you staying?" and I said, yes, of course I would stay.

She was good to me, and, although she had other lovers she showed me a tender attachment, almost believing that somehow we could make something permanent. Six months into our relationship she gave me an engraved silver-plated Zippo lighter with filigree chasing. On one side it had the inscription: "*J and L Forever*". I used to play with the lighter, my fingers turning it over and over in my hands; it was heavy and satisfying to hold and had a solidity that our fragile link did not possess. I appreciated the life that Louie brought me, her amatory competence, her lack of curiosity about my inner world and her accepting presence. She offered me a continuum, a way of rubbing along and a distraction from the voices of my patients, hungering to be told how to live. Both Louie and I were on the run from memory. We both fled from pain and, as we went to the pub, speeded by a shot of sulphate, she would sometimes tell me of what she had encountered on her shifts in casualty. The man quite flat from the waist down after the great wheels of a crane had passed over him but living and speaking; the leg that came away when lifting someone out of the ambulance; people with objects in them, hammers, bolts, blades and parts of cars. The selfish, bawling drunks who demanded all her time and the quietly hopeful parents waiting to be told that their boys were dead; their motor-cycle helmets like cracked eggs under the resuscitation-room trolleys.

How she could transform herself! She would come in to my place from her shift in her work clothes carrying a bag, or I would sit there watching her in her nurses' rooms. She would seem then quite plain-looking, even austere and stocky in her dark-blue uniform, caught at the waist by a black elastic belt with its old-fashioned silver buckle, her hair pinned back, dark under the white frilled cap. She would disappear into the bathroom and would emerge in her towel in a cloud of steam, shaking out her clothes on their hangers before crouching in front of a mirror usually propped against a stool or sometimes looking down at it on her knees, hair in a towel wrapped like a turban; doing her face, a cigarette burning next to her, the TV on — perhaps a soap opera — or music pulsing from the sound system, sometimes everything on at the same time. I'd watch her shedding towels, walking around pulling at her panties where they caught in the fold of her buttocks. Then on would go the club gear and her hair would be released from the turban, at first crimped, then springing out teased and fluffed with the hair-dryer, Louie pulling at it and brushing it until it stood out in a gold curling mass. She would take a final look in the mirror at her makeup with a down-turn of her mouth of critical displeasure, a few more adjustments would be made, and then, when she was satisfied, she would snap on her bangles and rummage for another wrap of speed in her bag.

Arm in arm we would go out into the night, she walking at a cracking pace, heels down, toes forward, like a guardsman, her gold ankle bracelet swinging. In our nights there would be movement, lights, a sense of exaltation as she spun on the dance floor with the men around her, then nemesis would come in her quiet times when she would hide away, slumped, inert, not speaking. She would drift, in a sluggish state with the TV always squawking in the background, just sitting, smoking, coiling a tendril of hair or tugging at her long eyelashes. She also loved to sleep, cocooned, reluctant to get up. She would murmur in the mornings, "I look like a bag of shit," peering into the mirror with her hair standing on end, or just lying there, a shape in the bed, inanimate and grey-skinned. Then, shamefully, I could not stop resenting her and, itchy with disgust, sour and unhappy, I would recoil from her in an unloving way and despise myself for it, and after the distractions of the night I would return to pining for Rachel.

Louie rang me late that same night, very angry in a way I had never heard from her before.

"What's going on? Why are you lying?" she had complained. Apparently CID had caught her at the end of her shift, asking her to verify that she was with me on 4th September. Like the professional she was, she had assured them that she was with me and that we had been out clubbing, and had robustly dealt with their questions about our relationship. She had loyally stuck by me but felt angry and wounded, sensing that there was more happening than she could understand. I coaxed her into going out for a drink that night. She refused at first but came in the end, barely speaking, picking the labels off her Pils bottles with her long nails. As we left the bar her need for forgetfulness overcame her, she took my arm and she tottered home with me on her clacking high heels. As she pulled off her dress that night to show a one-piece satin body suit, all the rage then, with just two poppers at the crotch, I saw her eyes gleaming, watching me. I could not read their expression as I reached down and undid the poppers with a tug in a hot tangle of hair.

★

November came and still there had been no word, no clue and nothing found. Not her, not her keys, not her little umbrella, not her triangular clutch purse in green leather, not the plastic bag with her rice and cooking foil. I was left waiting and wondering, and sometimes I would dream of Rachel even when sleeping with Louie; I would dream of her coming to me in my rooms, naked and frowning and pointing to something that I could not see, then fading, going away with a rueful smile, although I tried to flounder after her.

In my waking hours, faced with such a complete evaporation of a person, what could I think? Although I conjured her reality desperately, it was as if the world had swallowed her, absorbed her on that night-time street like those fabulist books we used to read in the 1970s which described people lost in other dimensions. Yet, Rachel herself had little time for the fantastical. She preferred love stories; her favourite was *Dr Zhivago*. She sensed that we were man-made, that our agencies were of this world and, after all, although men may disappear mysteriously, in the main, there were usually all too evident reasons why women disappeared.

Winter tightened in the suburbs; my neighbours brought out blue bottles of antifreeze to their cars. The geese from the city ponds flew in circles at night, prompted to migrate but with nowhere to go. Louie's calls to me diminished.

I lived with pain, a selfish pain, and went to work to hear the groaning distress of my patients, talking out their lives to which I listened in silence until the session tape ran to a stop. I would tell them, "Your session is finished. See you next week." *Ego te absolvo,*

41

I might well have added. I had entered the work for the worst of motives: curiosity, vanity, the search for power, the search for otherness; a wounded physician seeking healing, and now it had become my punishment to endure each alloted therapeutic hour.

Then came the TV programme, the strange unreal *Crimewatch*. I had previously barely seen it, but now it was very relevant, for a trailer announced that Rachel's case was to be featured. I waited in alone that night, watching the opening credits accompanied by the pounding, whirling music and the opening images of a blue flashing light, a panda car circling a roundabout, and a policeman with his cap tipped forward speaking on a radio phone. The squirrel-faced male presenter, with his coiffed blond hair and checked suit, took us briskly through the evening's enactments. He was assisted by his female sidekick, more serious than he, the studio lights glinting on her hoop earrings as he inquired, "And now, Sue, what are our updates on last month's appeals?"

I watched the armed robbery, the rape in Bradford, the stilted dramas turning tragedy to entertainment, then Rachel's case, the shock of hearing her name in public, the actress, the ersatz Rachel, stiffly walking in her clothes. She was shown in the classroom, standing at the bus stop on her way back from work and walking to the Paradise Stores. The few clues were mentioned: the white van, the details about timing of when she was last seen, and what clothes she wore. DCI Bain, the officer in charge of the case, gave an awkward interview in the studio standing self-consciously under the TV lights. I recognized him as the older policeman who had spoken to me after my interview at Central. "This is still a missing-persons inquiry," he said, "although there are serious concerns."

Catherine made a dignified and steady-voiced appearance, and the three grey ghostly images from Mr Dhaliwal's security camera were shown. The programme ended with an appeal for wanted men, and their faces were shown in a series of mug shots.

"Remember that crime like this is really quite rare, so good night, everyone, and don't have nightmares," concluded the presenter. I could almost see him smirking.

The next day work carried me along, pushing thoughts away. I had clinical review and supervision, which I kept rescheduling as I avoided the scrutiny of others, and an assessment of a patient with a phobia about blood. She felt sickening horror at trails and speck-les of blood on pavements, or blood sudden and vivid in a lavatory bowl. I envied her this phobia, for at least it condensed her terror into one recognisable form.

At lunchtime I sat in the Fiat listening to the radio news. There was a dull thudding and popping outside as children set off fireworks. There was no news after the programme and hopes of a breakthrough dwindled; there had been so little to go on. I drove home in the dark. Entering the house I saw a flashing light indicat-ing a message on the answer phone. Of all people, it was Catherine's voice on the machine.

"Thought I'd tell you Jack, we have been told by the police there has been an arrest."

★

His name was George Adam Kress. He had walked into the police station at Radford announcing in his hoarse loud voice to the civil-ian reception staff, "I've killed that girl on telly."

There was a flurry among those producing their documents for driving offences and lads on police bail checking in. They all moved away from Kress who continued to lean nonchalantly against the counter. A duty sergeant was fetched who ushered him to the inter-view rooms. They sat him down and took a look at him, a lean man in a worn black leather jacket and soiled jeans, his tanned scalp showing through his thin hair. He had a weatherworn face, his nose like a broken blade leaned to one side where someone had cracked it. He had slightly asymmetrical eyes, which never quite looked at you straight. Most noticeable was his hoarse bass voice and his large knobbed hands, held in his lap like two brown crabs. He had a spider-web tattoo enveloping his right elbow and an image of a cherub with a halo on his left forearm.

The sergeant asked if he wanted to make a statement.

He replied, "I'm saying nothing else. I'll only talk to the bossman on telly about killing that bird. What's his name? Bain. Inspector Bain; that's it."

Beekeeper team had been kept busy by the *Crimewatch* pro-gramme; there had been thirty or so calls to the studio and to

43

Beekeeper base. There were sightings of Rachel, information on white vans, her belongings had possibly been found, and some callers offered theories about her disappearance. All attention switched then to Kress. He was whisked to Central and taken to a secure interview room. Here he seemed to be enjoying himself, walking with a cocky swagger, demanding drinks, chatting to custody staff, asking for a brief — a duty solicitor — and demanding cigarettes. When these arrived he tore the filters off, smoking them cupped in his large hands with the thumb locked round, guarding the glowing end. When he was placed in the exercise yard he turned to another prisoner, who stood with his back to the wall while Kress pinned him into a corner as he talked excitedly.

"I'm a soldier; I have "soldier's heart". That's what they calls it — "soldier's heart". I've heard about it. It's from my war experience. Falklands me. Parachute regiment. Aden and Ireland. Yes, I've served in the republic of Northern Ireland, me, that's why I done things. Things I regret."

His brief arrived in the afternoon, a woman in her thirties in a black trouser suit with glossy straight hair and designer glasses. She was from a large city firm who supplied green-scheme legal aid to hundreds of impoverished detainees each year. She wore a slightly pained expression as if disgusted by her surroundings. She and the custody staff politely playing out their antagonism. A custody sergeant opined that Kress was crazy, not the full ticket. She ignored him and asked to speak to her client in a side room.

"I'll go with you anywhere, darling," he rumbled. She winced but ushered him to the interview room and he stalked in after her, walking in an exaggerated way with his arms bunched by his side. They spent a long time closeted together while the detectives fidgeted outside. You could hear Kress's deep voice although the door was closed. Meanwhile his convictions had been obtained from the Criminal Records Bureau. They came on a print-out six pages long with his appearances listed by courts, starting with Juvenile and ending in Crown Court. He had been transferred to a Special Hospital at the age of seventeen following a conviction for wounding and theft. There were many further offences, including attempted robbery, burglary, theft and assaults. He had served seventeen years in prison in total and was on conditional release after serving a sentence for armed robbery. He had been released seven months previously from Wandsworth. Kress could not have served in the army, as he never had more than nine months out of prison since his adolescence.

Once his brief had declared herself ready the interview could begin. Bain and a detective sergeant conducted it. They enacted the usual ritual of opening new cassettes then introducing themselves for the benefit of the tape. They went round the room in order, with Kress last solemnly pronouncing his full name. Bain started with a few soft questions about where Kress was now living. Kress looked at his brief, she nodded, and he answered. Bain then asked about what he had been doing after release from Wandsworth.

Kress drew himself up. "No comment. I do not want to make a comment on that."

Bain said wearily, "Mr Kress, it is you who came to us wanting to confess to something."

There was a pause. Kress sat straight in his chair, eyes focused ahead of him as if reading from something prepared, and said, "All I will say is that I have done that girl, that teacher, and I expects to be punished for it. I took her that night and buried her where she can't be found. I feel very sorry about it, but that can't be helped now."

He sat back and folded his arms. Little else could be got from the interview with Kress answering "No comment" to everything else. The interview was ended by Bain who extracted the tape and signed the seal on it. In the custody offices opinion was divided, some saying that he was an attention-seeking inadequate, others that this was the real thing.

They asked old Doctor Barry, the police surgeon, to take a look at him to determine whether they should continue to interview him. Barry spent his working life shuttling around courts and police stations, sewing up drunks who had injured themselves in bar fights, or who had slammed their heads against cell walls, taking blood samples from drunk drivers, and arranging for the suicidal to be committed. He was a heavy man with tufted, thick, greying hair. He wore an old mackintosh which gave off a smell of sweat as it swung open to reveal a garish tie depicting a version of Munch's *The Scream*.

He saw Kress for a quarter of an hour in the tiny doctor's cubicle by the cells. His laconic opinion was duly delivered.

"Not mad but strange, not psychotic and none too bright. I would say he is fit to interview."

There were a few more interviews, but little else could be got from Kress. It was decided to charge him for breaching his licence by not living at a supervised address and to get him remanded for further inquiries. Beekeeper was in a quandary. Kress had a long criminal history but no apparent offences against women. They had tracked him to lodgings on Emmanuel Street, a squalid building used by road gangs and knockers. He probably had access to a van. He was the only lead and they could not let him go.

Central police stood back to back with the old city courts on Burton Street and prisoners could be transferred from the Central custody area straight through to the court holding cells under the court rooms. The large soot-stained colonnades with their plaques to the founding worthies of 1887, surged and echoed with life, especially on the weekday morning hearings when plaintiffs pressed up to the notice boards at the top of the steps by the doors to see where their cases were being heard. Recriminating families harangued their delinquent sons. There was a corresponding babble from the toms trawled in the previous night by the vice squad, and through the thronging mass the briefs weaved like professional sportsmen with bundles of case files bound in red tape clamped under their arms. The press men from the evening paper also came, circulating from court to court, hoping for a story, while set-faced policemen, helmets under their arms, stood apart from the throng, waiting to give evidence.

I too made my way there, up the steps and through the crowds that following morning to Court 10, where I knew the stipendiary magistrate dealt with the more serious cases. It was an oak-panelled courtroom with red leather seating, the royal crest above the bench, and an old-fashioned wooden dock in the centre of the court. The court usher in a long, black gown was already directing more than the usual attendants, as the press had got wind of a break in the Hauser case. Their headlines itched to announce a *Crimewatch* triumph. I saw a group of CID lounging near the prosecution lawyers' seats, Canter caught my eye and nodded unsmiling at me. I saw her lean over to speak to Hedgepeth, who turned around to stare briefly at me. We sat through two other cases at first, then Kress was brought up. He sat in the shadowed courtroom, staring around him, hair sticking up a little at the crown, his head hunched between the shiny shoulders of his leather jacket. The crisply spoken stipendiary asked him to state his name.

"George Adam Kress, yes, your honour," he announced in his deep voice. He then sat back with a little smile as if satisfied with himself. The prosecution summarised that inquiries were ongoing on a serious matter and that the defendant was already in breach of his probation discharge licence. Remand for reports and inquiries was requested. Kress's brief feebly requested bail, but this was crushed by the crown prosecution who pointed to his long history of convictions, and the serious nature of the inquiries. He was remanded to city prison, and, standing with two custody officers before being taken down to the cells, he suddenly twisted around to look at the courtroom behind him, his mouth agape. His eyes briefly focused on me, then passed vaguely on over the rest of the courtroom. The officers with him tugged his arms and he was gone.

That afternoon I walked back down across the city centre through the almost empty square, past the castle and down to the boulevard to Rachel's street in the gathering dusk of the winter-shortened day. I crossed to the Paradise Stores and on an impulse went into the shop, the doorbell ringing and clattering as it closed behind me. There was a smell of polish and plastic and an undertone of curry from the living quarters somewhere; the proprietor in his brown shop coat waiting by the till. The camera, on a bracket high up, tracked my progress. I walked slowly through the shop, my eyes running over the products, the brown humps of unwrapped Hovis loaves on a shelf, magazines hanging by clips from a line, some lime-coloured gloves in cellophane, a plate of samosas sitting under a humid plastic dome. I was thinking that Rachel must have seen all this, that this had been part of her world and my being there was somehow consoling. I turned and left the shop followed by the gaze of the proprietor and closed the door with a firm tug and an accompanying jingle, letting my fingers slip away from the worn brass handle.

I went back out into the street wondering: Where did he acquire her? In one of the dark entries on the boulevard, yanking her into a van, or tricking her as she, good-naturedly, tried to give directions; or later in her narrow street, at her door, shielded from her neighbours by the bushy lilac, pulling her into darkness, into limbo. I knew then clearly and utterly that Rachel was not coming back. Seeing the incarnate Kress turning and gaping in the dock that morning had sealed my remaining hope with a sense of finality, which I now accepted. I stood outside Rachel's flat in the rain, watching the gutters run with water, then I walked away as the Paradise Stores flicked on its lights in the gathering dusk.

Chapter Two
A Heart of Glass, a Heart of Stone

Once taken down from the city court at his first appearance, Kress was marched away downstairs between two officers to the holding cells. They stopped for a moment for Kress' solicitor to speak to him. She had come down from the court, moving through the throng of remanded prisoners with a look of distaste. She again explained to Kress that he had been remanded for reports, and standing tall and slope-shouldered between his escorts, he nodded and said he understood but his eyes seemed faraway and glazed. He was taken down the tunnel passage-way under the great square buildings of Central to the old cells of the police station with their metal doors that slammed shut with a dull boom. There he waited again, placidly sipping tea from a plastic cup until the transport arrived. The white, slab-sided van with recessed square windows took on six other prisoners, each sitting in their own cubicle. It backed cautiously out of the Central yard where a few onlookers had gathered, and a TV camera team followed them down Burton Street until the van picked up speed, travelling west to Sherwood along grey winter streets.

I wondered if Kress glimpsed the bare tracery of lime twigs through the high windows of the van, or the tops of corporation buses, or the sudden flight of pigeons startled by the labouring engine on the up-slope as it reached Sherwood and the suburbs. Perhaps, as they neared the prison, he made out those first fenced compounds with rags of wind-blown plastic hanging on the wire, the stumpy, pollarded trees, the wall of the prison topped by a rounded, high parapet or the campanile clock tower with its peeling façade. The van scraped slowly through the narrow nineteenth century gate, which closed quickly behind it, and Kress and the others were disgorged into the reception tank.

Shortly after, I was there too, standing outside the prison entrance imagining Kress' shadow sliding through the gate and being taken to the remand wing. I came back to the prison from time to time that winter, to gaze over at the blank façades of the wings with their white lintels and bars, thinking that Kress was there somewhere holding his secrets about my Rachel. I looked speculatively over the perimeter thinking about how a man could get in there. I observed the prisoners' families on visits as they surged out from a side door in their bright clothing. These visitors, mainly women, chattered like starlings and argued among themselves. They complained of the searches and of their men folk, their voices carried to me on the wind as I stood watching the walls and gates, as I was in turn watched by the security cameras swivelling on poles. And I would take pictures of the place myself with my old Leica hidden under my heavy coat. Pictures that I would develop later at home and study in the long nights.

It had been five months since Rachel had gone. The reality of her disappearance had begun to settle on me as I walked away from the

prison gates at weekends. Driving away from the place I would be thinking: how to get close to Kress? How to gain access? The season kept turning, indifferent, the plane tree leaves grounded, dead and swept from the pavements next to the Paradise Stores. I drove past there, listening and watching, my feelings of hatred and revenge growing in the vacuum of Rachel's loss.

I tracked Kress in that first year, trying to tune in to the processes that were carrying him along. He had been absorbed in the criminal justice system; he was put on remand, and he made occasional bail appearances. His lodgings were gone over again by CID and his van, a works Ford with rust-dimpled sides, was taken apart. Forensic Serology had examined it, looking for blood staining and had found none. It was vacuumed out and the cement and brick dust lodging in all the cracks was filtered and checked for fibres, but there was no recovered clothing from Rachel to check these finds against. Kress made no further admissions to the police, although he continued to toy with his questioners, hinting at his involvement with Rachel, and with others.

I had not heard further from Catherine but kept by our agreement of not contacting her, confident that she would let me know if something developed. The press continued to speculate and ran stories linking the missing little girls in the Midlands triangle and others that had disappeared in the West Country. I clipped out the cuttings of other disappearances, cases from newspapers and magazines, and kept them in a scrapbook, but could not bear to add Rachel's press cuttings to the grainy images of that sisterhood of the lost.

★

The Spiritualist church was located near Pugin's Catholic cathedral and the Canning Circus cemetery. There was a plaque outside on the white wall of the church informing that it was founded in 1860. I had gone there instinctively, seeking answers but not really believing that I would find any. The church was quite close to Rachel's old flat and we had passed it many times together. Although brought up a Catholic, Rachel used to say if she would belong to any church it would be the Spiritualist one, although I do not know if she ever attended services. I remember, reading a book about spirit photography at the time, about Mumler and his spirit photographs of the nineteenth century and of mediumship in general. I recall huddling up to the little gas fire in her flat when we were students, with her drying washing hung around me steaming gently while I showed her the photos of ectoplasm emerging from the mouths of mediums. I also spoke about the legions of First World War dead, Raymond among them and Frederick Myers, President of the Society of Psychical Research, who left tantalising, abstruse messages with many mediums in the 1920s. Such was my enthusiasm for the subject that I encouraged Rachel and a few of her friends to dabble in an amateur séance one night. We lit candles and placed the letters of

51

the alphabet on scraps of paper onto a circular, glass-topped, coffee table, then joined hands with each pressing a finger onto an upended glass tumbler. After a few false starts and giggles, we were all surprised when the glass began to move about, sliding from letter to letter, dragging our hands with it. We tried to spell out what it was pointing to, but we struggled to agree on any comprehensible word. At last, as if in a fit of pique the whole table appeared to be moving and bumping up and down under our hands. All at once the candles flickered and one of Rachel's friends fell backwards, screaming in histrionic fright. She threshed about on the floor so much that her plump little breasts popped right out of her low cut blouse. This brought a halt to the proceedings as we calmed the frightened girl and Rachel never allowed me to repeat the experiment.

I entered the church one rainy February night. The congregation came in, mainly in pairs, shaking out their umbrellas. They commented on the weather as elderly, smiling attendants handed out hymnals. I took my place at the back of a large room with polished pine benches facing a lectern. Strangely, the walls of the room were covered in chintz wallpaper, giving the impression that this was someone's commandeered, old-fashioned sitting room. Behind the lectern on the wall was a large plaque showing an emblem of a sunburst over a blue sea. Against the sea was an image of an open book. The words *LIGHT* appeared against the sun image, *TRUTH* was shown outlined against the watery element and *NATURE* appeared in capitals on the open pages of the book. A woman sat in a wooden chair next to the lectern watching the sparse congregation enter and adjust themselves on the plain seating. She was in her middle years, with a strong jaw line and greying hair swept back from her fore-head. I fancied that she regarded us with amused, shrewd, compassionate eyes. I recognised her at once from the flyer I had been given advertising private sittings from a medium called Mrs Durrand, clipped from a local paper which I found left in the therapy waiting rooms at work. The flyer text ran:

52

Sad? Confused? Grieving?

**Private Sittings with Gifted
Experienced Local Medium.**

The Spiritualist National Union

**A Chance to Consult the Spirit World
for Guidance and Healing.**

Returnable Fee

I impulsively rang the number on the leaflet, thinking irrationally that there must be some purpose to my discovering it. I asked for an appointment and a crisp, voice told me,

"You will want to attend our service beforehand. We find it is helpful for communication."

I found myself here a week later, as the congregation trickled in, watching five or six elderly ladies with grey curls under wool berets, their heads turning to peep round curiously at the congregation, ignored by a Caribbean man sitting alone and erect in a double-breasted suit and by two loaf-haired women with large, gold hoop earrings who looked alike and who sat chewing and staring stolidly ahead. At length Mrs Durrand rose accompanied by soothing opening chords from a Hammond organ. She stepped forward and greeted us:

"Especially those who have come for the first time tonight."

Clear, bell-voiced Mrs Durrand, in a smart twin set and a Hermès scarf, spoke about "our church", made reference to the Fox sisters, those New England rappers, and about comforting messages she hoped that would be here for us to night. We sang *Jerusalem* in a shaky chorus with the rich contralto of Mrs Durrand sounding above all the others. I mouthed the words, angry with myself, embarrassed for being there yet also oddly soothed by the artless simplicity of the place and these people. A prayer for departed pets was then made for they also have a spirit life. "Thoughts of the sick for healing" and "visualisation of healing" followed, announcements for study nights on the history of "our noble movement", and then a homily from the medium as she paced on the raised wooden dais before us, tall, elegant hands clasped before her. Her court shoes sounded rhythmically on the floorboards as she paced she spoke about the creative force of the universe, this power that we know as God creating life in all we see around and also the life beyond death. I followed her words and her command of us with some admiration despite my discomfort. At the close of her address she said: "Science has revealed … as we know, matter cannot be destroyed, it is merely energy and it can change its form. That is why tonight, tonight, dear friends, we invite communion with the spirits, from those who now live in the Spirit World, who, I am sure, will reveal themselves to us, to bring comfort and help to those they love."

We were then invited to sing a hymn. The organ swelled and, led by the medium, we sang to the tune of a TV advert of the time, "*I'd like to help the world to sing*". I also murmured out the last stanza while glancing sidelong at my humble companions singing lustily beside me between the narrow benches:

Drawing nigh with clouds so tender
To the gates of paradise
Then my soul with pure devotion
Spreads her fondest grateful wing.

The plodding organ died away. There was a pause that preceded the demonstration of mediumship. I could not help feeling a prickle of apprehension. Mrs Durrand stood in front of us, head bowed, her navy and white scarf heaving as she breathed deeply. The small congregation shuffled and coughed then fell silent. I tried to push thoughts of Rachel out of my mind. I watched with premonitionary fear as the medium stalked around the front of the room going *clunk, clunk* in her court shoes, her head sunk on her chest, chin buried in her scarf. Suddenly she raised her head, her eyes smiling and serene.

"I have here a young man sitting with companions, they are very gay, laughing, I think I have the name Norton, no Newton."

There was a nervous rustle from us sitting there before a middle-aged man whom I had not noticed before, replied calmly, "Yes I think I can take it."

Mrs Durrand went on, eyes closed again, speaking in an odd, forced intonation.

"This young man, oh he is laughing, joking, sense of humour is what I get, yes joking with his friends, all those other young men sitting waiting somewhere."

"Yes that's right," said the respondent, "That's my uncle; he was a pilot officer, killed in the war. Newton. That's the name of his aerodrome. He was in a Fairey Battle squadron, most of them were lost."

"He says that there is someone else here, someone who passed over later, they are arm in arm."

"Yes I understand," said the man, "That's my father."

"He is saying he was ill but has recuperated in the spirit world, he is rubbing his chest."

"Yes, he had cancer," said the man.

"Well, he is better now you understand; he wants you to understand that. Fading now…" said the medium as she began to pace again, she stopped and her hand suddenly stretched out and pointed at us.

"I have a lady here, grey hair, with a little dog." She fixed on me for a moment and I shrunk down on my bench.

"No, the lines are not getting through." She said impatiently her finger moving over the congregation.

"I think we can take it," said one of the sisters with big hair.

The medium continued, "She is showing me her feet. I can see feet. They look a bit swollen."

"No that's not Gran," said the woman looking at her sister beside her who was also shaking her head, her large earrings waggling. "'Er feet weren't swollen, no."

"Yes, I see special shoes, slippers, dear, she is showing them to me. No, I'm not getting through." The medium moved on continuing to proffer the message until a thin, red-haired woman with anxious eyes and bony shoulders near the front spoke up.

"Yes. It's for me I think. It's my old neighbour, she were good to me. She had bad feet."

"She is looking concerned," continued the medium. 'She is saying you need to take care of your health, not leave things, not put things off, has there been a concern about your health dear?"

"Yes," says the cadaverous woman.

So the messages flowed, vague entities sending ethereal concerns to our humdrum lives. My fear of the occult gave way to discomfort. I began covertly to look at my watch and wondered how to creep away. Then the medium closed the demonstration. There was a prayer of peace and one last bumbling hymn. The congregation shuffled out with a thudding of benches. Tea was served from a large urn in an adjoining room and a lottery draw commenced. I moved to the door, coat in hand.

"Mr Keyse, I presume?"

My flight was arrested by Mrs Durrand. I turned to see her cleaving the bowed shoulders of the throng. She put out her hand.

"Mr Keyse, I am pleased to meet you. Not going, I hope; have we disappointed you?"

She looked at me shrewdly.

"Come, I will do your reading now. That is what you have come here for after all."

I followed her, still holding my coat, as she walked ahead of me down a dark, narrow corridor and into a lamp lit, smaller room. I became aware that we were followed by the bustling form of an apple-cheeked woman with the twinkling confident gaze of an adept.

"Rene, my assistant," announced Mrs Durrand with a brief sweep of her arm.

We had entered a room with two easy chairs facing each other and a side table upon which stood a vase holding flowering stems of witch hazel. The room was pervaded by a sweet cloying smell. There was also a smaller chair in one corner under a print of Durer's praying hands. Here Rene took her place after asking me for the modest fee which she tucked into a small metal cash box balanced on her knee.

"It helps us to continue our work," she murmured.

The medium sat facing me smiling; her hair in the lamp light shone gold through the grey. I felt disgusted at myself for being weak-minded enough to be there, yet compelled to go through with it. I took my place in front of her. She had loosened her scarf and I could see a pendant on a chain around her neck in the shape of a heart.

"Please be at ease, Mr Keyse. You have never consulted a medium?"

I shook my head.

"No, I thought not. Simply respond if you understand but if you do not understand the message then please tell me. The spirits sometimes find it hard to communicate."

She sat for a moment, her head lowered, breathing deeply. I remained sitting, controlling my urge to run out of the room, to soil myself no longer with this farce. Mrs Durrand suddenly brought up her head. I could not see her eyes, they seemed to have half-rolled in their sockets giving her face a creepy, vacant expression. There was long pause. Silence seemed to press on me in the room.

At last she said, "I have entities who want to speak to you. Who is there? They are there but I cannot make them out. They are as forms seen through frosted glass. There is a man, he is saying very faintly, how can I say it. Yes, slowly now. Bless you, yes, I translate it, "grief is love, grief is prayer", he is showing me something, two people standing on a street, a man and a woman, a dog scuffling about, lamplight, darkness, and another woman leaning, stooping low to the dog. Yes I have it. There is someone else there, also wanting to communicate. It is her…"

Mrs Durrand's eyes popped open and refocused on me.

"Has there been a recent passing?" she asked.

I shrugged, my throat constricted, I felt unable to speak. Her eyes half-closed again.

"I will ask again, … she is there, on the threshold, a young woman, yes, standing upright now, I can see her hair… I sense pain, a sudden passing."

Her face convulsed and she clutched at her brow but kept on speaking, "Water, trees, a brow of trees, an impression of stillness and she is saying, a haven … no I can't catch it."

She gave another grimace and a shudder then jumped in her seat, moaning and humming. Her chair made a cracking noise. I felt startled and my skin crawled with a shameful fear. I also started forward and put my hand out as if to steady her as she swayed quite close to me.

"Do not disturb her love, let her work, it might harm her if you touch her," murmured Rene behind me.

After a long pause Mrs Durrand spoke again.

"I have seen something, something bad, a presence of it, something not rubbed out, you cannot rub out, and also I see a loving spirit. I sense love and pain, a soul finding its way like those stairs at night, laughing now, says she can't always see, needs a light to show where she is going. Keeps saying one word like an echo, I can't catch it — art heaven? Alf heaven? No, it's not English, I don't know if I have got it."

She made another jerking grimace.

"I'm losing them now."

She rolled back in her chair with another cracking sound making me jump again, and then she sat erect breathing heavily. She opened her eyes and took out a hankie from her sleeve and pressed it to her mouth. I again smelt the cloying lilac scent. Her eyes opened again looking at me as if out of a long tunnel.

"They have gone dear."

Mrs Durrand continued staring at me for a moment then her gaze rolled over the room in an unsteady way as if she was disorientated. Her companion moved forward to give her a glass of water. She said, "I'm sorry that I could not get much, I hope you could take something from it dear, we cannot tell what the spirits bring. That one took a lot from me. Show him out Rene please."

I left the church having declined their offer of a cup of tea, feeling shaken. The wind tore at me outside and I slipped into a nearby phone booth. I opened the door with a creak and confronted the smell of piss and musty damp. The stink in there was a relief after the cloying atmosphere of the church. I stood for a moment in silence, my forehead resting against the chill glass of the booth. Then I rang Louie, selfishly looking for flesh and companionship, wanting to dispel that feeling of murmurous loss that the medium had engendered. The phone rang at Louie's nurses' residence, an abrupt female voice answered and there was the sound of feet in the corridor as Louie was roused. She sounded tired, telling me she was on early shifts. We had not spoken for several days. I asked if we could meet that night although it was already getting late.

"Ok, we'll go for a drink," she agreed reluctantly.

I chose the Lions as a place to meet; large Victorian sculptures that crouched facing each other in front of the Council House on the main square; a favoured meeting place for lovers. An hour later I could make out her blonde hair bobbing through the crowds of late week revellers. She wore a full, billowy, print dress with a leaf pattern coming down to the calf, over which she wore an Alexon coat swinging open as she strode across the square towards me, a ciggie already in one hand.

The gold chain gleamed on her ankle as she perched next to me on a bar stool, one red-nailed hand resting proprietorially on my knee as she scanned the smoky bar for her cronies. I was so glad to see her. So many things about her made me grateful to be with her, her acceptance, her intuitive sense of my need for companionship and her robust presence that cleaved away ghosts.

Louie had the effect of making the memory of that little room in Canning Circus recede. I felt so grateful for that but somehow could not express that feeling to her. After the alcohol had dispelled my initial caution, I mentioned going to a spiritualist church and she instantly detected betrayal, her antennae were sharp like that. Her mouth twisted scornfully and she blew out a puff of smoke, "You want to tell me about it?" I shook my head, more bottles of Pils were ranked in front of us and we gazed out at the bar in our alliance, listening to the roar of a hundred shouted conversations, looking out at the drinking throngs, gangs of lads in shirtsleeves despite the chill weather, girls larking about rubbing crisps into each others' hair and laughing. A song on the sound system playing the anthem of the time again and again, the languid voice of the singer sneering above the tumult, "You've got a heart of glass, a heart of stone, just you wait until I get you home."

Some of the rooms were grubbed out of the sandstone bedrock of the city and we crouched in one snug corner where we sniffed white powder from a wrap that Louie had produced. It left a bitter taste at the back of the throat. At first this gave a numbness and a feeling that it had no effect, yet gradually I noticed that Louie's eyes had seemingly grown larger and deeper in their gaze, and were somehow full of life and sparkling. I tried to speak to her, conscious of my lips moving, finding it hard to get the words out, my thoughts whizzing and the words stumbling slowly after them. I felt terrifically better as if the ice had left my heart and I experienced a burst of love, gratitude and closeness to Louie. I took in the air in the room. It was laden with sweet tobacco and drink fumes. It smelt glorious. I thought I could sample each individual swirling

59

molecule in that air. I concentrated so much on breathing that suddenly, when moving, I found that my leg muscles were stiff and cramped as if I had forgotten how to use them. Louie and I gazed at each other with a look of infinite understanding and confidence in each other and, for a moment, I felt a wonderful sense of protective grace. I was suddenly struck by a momentous idea that we are all thought, not body at all, that we are shadows moving in a dreamscape of ideas and that we could do anything that we chose and we had only to imagine something in order to create it. These ideas quickly evaporated to be eclipsed by the forgetfulness of the body. We then concentrated on dancing together for hours it seemed, hemmed in by a tranced swaying mass of people at a late night disco, held in a cavern at the back of the pub, facing the DJ who was nodding and crouching at the turntables above us until, at last, the music ended and we headed back home.

We hailed a passing cab for the last mile and rode in silence. Louie lolled against me, one hand kneading my thighs and we tumbled out, close to the hospital staff residence. There, in the car park out by the dew-shrouded parked cars, she backed onto a car bonnet and pulled me to her, her breath sharp with booze in the night air. She hooked her legs around my hips and I put out a hand to steady myself on the chill metal of the car.

"Come on, let's do it here," she whispered, tongue waggling, rustling, in my ear, fingers pulling at my belt. But I was fearful and reluctant as the drug oozed out of me, somewhere nearby a door opened, there were voices and footfalls and I jerked away from her. She pushed past me with a sigh and we clattered into the light and warmth of the nurses' block, her coat swinging as she stomped ahead of me down the hushed corridors.

Once in her room Louie slumped sulkily in an easy chair amid the usual clutter. She was evidently angry with me and my refusal and put on deliberately loud music. I stood in the yellow light of her bathroom splashing my face with water, I felt flushed and unsteady, something still pounding, making the sound of the sea in my ears. I found a yellow plastic razor on the edge of her bath and came into her room clowning, pretending to shave her legs as she sat smoking, legs over the arm of the chair, ankle chain glittering. She shifted her legs apart a little.

"You can shave me all over if you want," she said and looked at me challengingly with her eyes still drug-darkened, like black pools rimmed with silver. And so, I fetched a little bowl of warm water and some soap. I knelt before her as she slipped off her pants and I pushed a towel under her as she continued to sit with each leg hooked over the arms of the chair. I soaped her there, the water droplets hanging on each hair then began cautiously to strip away with the blade, at first safely high on her mound, then circling inward. I was lost in ferocious concentration, the music had stopped, there was just the sound of faint rasping and the occasional twirl of the razor in the bowl. One of my hands resting on the cradle of her pelvic bone, the other cramped around the slippery stem of the razor. As I shaved her, I looked intensely at the stipple and whorl of hair, the secret fissures emerging while she lay back smoking, gazing at the ceiling, sometimes speaking to me, her belly pulsing as she spoke. As her genitals emerged, she shifted and some-times my wet hand pulled at the skin of her inner thighs to reveal the tender slope of the underside of her buttocks, the towel clung to the damp skin. I worked on like a penitent until the job was done, I dabbed at the faintly reddened areas and at last stood back from my handiwork. Louie yawned and looked down. She seemed bored now and the effect of the sulphate was ebbing. I felt exhausted too, my jaws aching from the speed-induced clench of the facial muscles. Louie picked up a make up mirror and angled it to examine herself and said, "That looks like a good job. Well, do you want to try it out now?"

She spread the towel onto the carpet after sliding away the litter of other damp towels, clothing, overflowing ash trays and make-up bags with the flick of one bare foot, pulled her print dress over her head, lay back on the towel and yanked me onto her.

Later that night, lying cramped on her narrow single bed in the overheated room, with the background thrum of the pipes some-where, I woke to find Louie deeply asleep on her back, one leg lying heavily across me. I had been woken by a dream of Rachel rising, shimmering from the sea. I lay awake until dawn, Louie's head on the pillow beside me, thinking of Mrs Durrand's room and the message *Aufheben*, remembering Rachel once proffering me a crocus flower after a spring shower and saying "look — *Aufheben*".

61

★

The pale fire of the low winter sun just cleared the walls of the remand block and sent wheeling shadows across his cell as he hunched there through January and into February. After his return from yet another court hearing, Kress threw scalding water over another prisoner on the landings and was sent to the "seg" — segregation on a lower level of cells with no prisoner association. Once there he began to deteriorate further. The whole wing knew he was unravelling, his hoarse voice sounding loudly from his cell calling to the screws, throwing food trays against the cell wall, shouting to the pigeons as they fluttered near the window ledges despite the sharp wires to prevent them landing. He lay all day on blue rubber matting on the floor, his room lit by a bare bulb guarded by a mesh screen, only occasionally getting up to look at himself and bare his brown root teeth at his reflection in a metal mirror screwed to the wall. As the weeks passed he shed his clothes, preferring to huddle naked under a blanket. He smeared shit streaks on his wall, into which he would read grimacing faces while he muttered a mantra, which would occasionally explode into a scream:

"I hate all slags … I hate all slags … I HATE ALL SLAGS!"

On and on he went for hours until the other prisoners battered on their walls and doors, yelling at him to shut it.

Spring moved, clouds drifted past his high window, rain fell, feeding the wired gutters burbling out to the courtyards far below. He continued to shout to himself and to huddle in his blanket and he was moved to the hospital block, a thronging narrow space with cells down each side of an inner courtyard, occupied by the sick prisoners who moved about the central area during the day: a few amputees, some on detox from heroin, and the "ravers" like Kress, "nutted off" in prison parlance. Kress was seen by the red-faced prison doctor who referred him to a forensic consultant who didn't think he was dangerous enough for High Secure. Kress helped things along when a routine cell search revealed regurgitated chlorpromazine tabs in a window crevice and a biro stem, ground down to a point with a tape handle, hidden in his bedding. His notes on toilet paper in a childish, rounded hand detailed his plans to grab a depot nurse on her regular morning round to treat the psychotic patients; notes about holding her hostage, making her pay. He was again referred to high secure hospital under Section 48 of the 1983 Mental Health Act. Transfer of a remanded prisoner. This time he was accepted and he was soon decanted into the prison transport, this time moving forty miles north.

Thus, Kress came to be caught up in the hospital, the secure psychiatric system from which he could never leave, guilty or innocent, unless pronounced sane. I knew this because I had cultivated a secretary who had an access password to the computer records for prison psychiatric reports and records of court appearances. I had plied the secretary with chocolates, listened to her worries about her children's difficulties at school and passed flirty jokes with her. After prompting her to boot up the system I would urge her to take a break and would sit in her swivel chair, among the kitsch clutter of her desk, looking at the screen which listed clinical activity: who had been asked to assess whom, what was the outcome. Some of this was recorded in basic numeric codes which I read from a code book also held by the obliging secretary who did not question my glib explanations for wanting this information. I would flick through the diagnostic shorthand notes and the details of places and dates. This allowed me to track where Kress was in the system and what his likely future movements were. When logging off, the green characters would gradually fade then disappear with a pop, the trace evaporating as information on Kress also stopped once he entered the hospital. They had their own systems, and there were no insecure links for other eyes.

The Beekeeper enquiry had begun to lose interest in Kress at this time, as a new lead had emerged. During a case review, held in an attempt to find new progress, someone had again looked through the video tracks from the Paradise Stores and noticed pictures of a lone male on the two successive nights prior to the Thursday night that Rachel disappeared. They linked these pictures to the description of the driver in a van who also wore a white top, according to the witness who saw him when he was walking home from a local chip shop on the night. The image quality was poor but the CID agreed that the man pictured could not be Kress. He had a thickset build, he seemed younger, had a distinctive heavy face and cropped head, whereas Kress's hair appeared longer even allowing for the three month elapse between the September picture and his arrest. So confident were they that this was a significant lead, the police released the image to the local press and it appeared in the city's *Evening Post*.

I stared at the image when I first noticed it and clipped it out to  study. I was disappointed because I had at first seen Kress as the certain agent involved in Rachel's disappearance and my vengeance had fixed on him. Now it seemed to me that she could have fallen victim to any from an unknown male tribe out there that inhabited the shadows of the city. There were so many like Kress. This was one more of them with his stocky build and bull neck striding in the fuzzy Betamax frame. I studied the image carefully noting the left forearm where there was the shadow of a tattoo with some lettering above it. This was the last and most distinct image taken forty minutes before Rachel's picture was captured for the final time on Mr Dhaliwal's camera. I studied it, remembered it and put it aside, still wanting to follow the trail of Kress into the hospital.

My colleagues definitely thought I was crazy to be interested in forensic High Secure for it was a blighted, discredited branch of the system. My puzzled clinical director commented, "Are you sure about this Jack?" as he signed off my secondment request to be transferred. I had driven out there in late summer, nine months after beginning my search for Rachel, following Kress's track, wanting to take a first look at where I was heading.

Louie came along as she was happy to do something different on the weekend. The wind ruffled her hair through the open car window in the late spring warmth. She placed her bare feet up on the car dashboard, the fine blonde hairs on her legs transparent in the sunshine. We drove north on the Roman road to Newark then swung off into a nest of country roads. The hospital was shown on no map. We finally stumbled on the place among the sloping fields of uncut wind-rippled young barley. It was a shadow, a masked line, settled in a knap in the wolds and folded away from the prying world. We stopped by the gates with their pineapple-topped finials above high brick columns.

I cut the engine and got out. There was the sound of hot metal ticking, a wood pigeon calling somewhere, and the soughing of the wind through avenues of Lombardy poplars. In front of me was a line of dark fencing, some neo-Georgian blocks with coppery-green roofs and further off, a huddle of red buildings which I guessed must be the five-stepped entrance lodge that discharged patients had mentioned to me. Two men cycled past, bulky figures in long blue coats despite the warm day. They wore chains hanging from their belts by a loop at their sides. They nodded cautiously in greeting while looking carefully at me and at Louie in the car. She had swung her door open, stretching her legs out into the sun. I could see her looking at herself in the driving mirror then rustling in her bag for a cig. I stood for a while by the car, thinking of Kress and trying to sense him there somewhere behind the blur of dark fencing. The place was not as I expected, not a portentous place like Broadmoor — the other great High Secure asylum — with its great walls and towers. No, this was hushed and discreet, like a provincial agricultural college, half-forgotten out in the fields. Afterwards, all I could remember about the hospital was a sense of isolation and of absence, a place where time passes slowly and where the wind sighs in the restless poplars.

This glimpse of the hospital posed a challenge to our relationship. Louie drifted in the continuum of her social life in the bars and clubs and I was tied to the city for different reasons, forever searching, registering the pulse of the city and scanning for some clue to what happened on that September night. It seemed strange to consider working long hours far away in this rural place. Perhaps I already sensed that I was losing Louie anyway. We always had a cool alliance. And in a way I had chosen her for her matter of fact ways, her hostility to introspection and for her instinctive recognition of the deeps and losses in life. But recently I had begun to sense that Louie had begun to slip further away from me. There was something too smooth in her explanations about nights out with friends. Her diminishing phone calls to me spoke of other interests. A few weeks later she rang me after work asking me to drop round and see her. There was something unusual in her tone which I somehow connected to other small recent signs of distraction and worry: the way I sometimes caught her looking away, lips pursed and lost in her thoughts, or turning from me in the night when I reached for her, saying oddly and passively, "May I sleep now?"

The TV news that night showed the same footage repeatedly. A mob clawing at a desperate man at bay on a car roof in Northern Ireland, soon to be overwhelmed and killed. The scene playing again and again of the victim, his handsome face and well-cut floppy hair still intact for a moment before the hands of his destroyers pulled him down. This image kept running in my head as I went round to Louie's that evening. She met me without an embrace and sat in an oddly formal manner then handed me a little folded card. The card was headed "*Department of Genito-Urinary Medicine*" and contained instructions to report to the unit because of being in contact with a venereal disease. I stared at her while she looked back at me with an expression that I couldn't quite catch; some fear yes, but also a strangely triumphant, even excited air.

"You are going to kill me aren't you?" she said evenly.

I shrugged; in truth I felt little right then. It is always some relief to a betrayer to find he has been betrayed in turn. I pocketed the card and quietly asked her what it was about and she spoke of meeting someone else, telling me in a matter of fact tone as if it was an illness she had contracted, something beyond her control. Her new mate was apparently called Neville, a gangster, a bouncer. She even showed me a Polaroid picture in washed-out colours of a large, pin-eyed man in a black coat with stiff, thick hair and a big lop-sided jaw line. Louie told me that it had ended, although I didn't believe her. He had gone down with VD and had been told to inform her and she in turn was telling me. The GU clinic apparently called it "the chain of contact".

I returned home and lay awake imagining his bacilli running through my system and took myself next day to the clinic in the annexe of the old city general hospital. There I sat in a high-walled waiting room among other gloomy males desultorily looking at motoring magazines. I heard one man shouting in a complaining manner to reception staff in the background, "I have been coming here for ten years…," and I shared thin smiles with my fellow sufferers. There was a brief interview with a medic, his shadowed eyes made no expression as he listened to my sorry tale. He read me a list of prepared questions from a sheet :

"Mucal discharge?

Pain in the urethra?

Pain on peeing?

Proctal pain?"

No, I had no pain, just numbness as I sat in a curtained cubicle and peed into a tube. A male nurse swept into the cubicle, grasped my cock in a plastic-gloved hand and briskly shook it and squeezed it to gain a further sample then dismissed me.

"There you go matey … we will let you know."

I went back out into the streets to confront a chill breeze and the sound of insensate traffic.

I received a small blue card from the clinic a few days later letting me know that I was clear of infection. Louie and I continued to go out and even sleep together although she would often turn away from me at night and I would look down at her while she slept, my hand brushing the cool skin on her back and finding myself wanting her more than ever. As we walked between bars, she still sought my arm and rested her hand on my knee, although now she seemed jumpy and distracted and we avoided some parts of the city. She told me she was "sorting it all out" and we avoided overt discussion about it. She did evening shifts and sometimes we would not see each other for a few days. Once, when I called for her at the nurses' residence, I saw her speaking on a pay phone. Her eyes briefly meet mine through the glass of the phone booth, not really engaging, her face looking frozen and shuttered in some way.

"Just talking to my friend Annie," she said a little too quickly as she let me in.

There were evenings after that and lovemaking too, but there were too many spaces between us. Although our bodies moved together we had somehow lost our touch.

★

Pinsent reappeared, like a portent of what was to come, just as I was working out my last months before transfer to the hospital. I had seen him about a year before: a gangly youth with lost, blue eyes. He had soft, white hands and a whispery voice; his forehead and cheeks were pocked with acne scars. He was well known to psychiatric teams in the city because he suffered from an unnameable anxiety that drove him to turn up in hospital casualty at inconvenient hours, usually in distress in the middle of the night. He would be tearful, demanding help but unable to explain what was bothering him. Sometimes he would drink in order to rid himself of his dread, and his troubles were written off as being alcohol-induced by some clinicians. There was something uncannily determined about him, despite his quiet, cringing manner, and he would stand in reception rooms unspeaking yet irreducibly there until staff saw him and reassured him enough for him to melt away back to his lonely city flat. I remember him in the summer of that year standing by a water dispenser, meek but incredibly stubborn, in a busy outpatient's reception. The other patients moved around him. His hands hung by his side and his pale eyes calmly passed over the people around him. He kept asking the receptionist the same question every few minutes speaking quietly with a passive, lowered head.

"Am I going to be seen now miss?" and again, "When will I be seen miss?"

The harassed receptionist tried to placate him, rolling her eyes to her colleagues when she thought Pinsent wasn't looking.

The duty registrar that day was a friendly career doctor heading for a comfortable consultancy. We had often passed each other in the nurses' home and in local bars (for we both dated nurses). He

68

treated me as a fellow roué and would generally greet me with genial bonhomie. This time I saw him in the clinic and he beckoned me into the consulting room. We tipped back the moulded plastic chairs and shared a cigarette despite the hospital rules about smoking. We bitched about work and about the autocratic consultants. After flicking his spent butt expertly through the air vents into the car park below, he turned to a heap of clinic notes on his desk for the afternoon patient list and showed me Pinsent's thick file.

"What are we going to do with him then? A real heart-sink patient."

I looked briefly through the heavy notes with mild curiosity as the registrar told me about his demanding stubborn presence, opening the door a crack to point out Pinsent standing at the end of the corridor. The file held numerous duplicate sheets of accident and emergency contacts, follow-up letters and reports from liaison psychiatrists. Pinsent complained of a fear of something horrible happening, he sought reassurance that this wasn't going to happen but could not name what it was that frightened him. He lived alone in the city, his parents were separated, his father an alcoholic. His mother was disappointed with his lack of purpose, but she was also wary of him. She had reduced contact, insisting he leave home and live independently and was reluctant to be involved in his care. She was sometimes rung up by casualty staff asking if he could stay with her to help him through his numerous crises and sometimes she would reluctantly allow that for a few days. Diagnostically he was mostly written off as having a personality disorder, or as having an idiopathic anxiety syndrome with alcohol dependence. He was a difficult man to help and rarely responded to follow up appointments. Most doctors pacified him with a two week course of benzodiazepines and a chat to ventilate his fears. My friend the registrar announced, "I often think that when men come to see me complaining of anxiety they are actually depressed. I tend to prescribe a course of antidepressants. You can rarely go wrong with that."

I shrugged and slid the notes back on his table.

"Oh well," he yawned and stretched in his plastic bucket chair, "I suppose I had better see the chappie or else he'll drive our receptionist bonkers."

As I left I remember seeing Pinsent looking down the corridor towards the consulting room, waiting to be freed from his terror.

I next saw him in the autumn of the following year on one of my last jobs before I transferred to the hospital. I had been called to see him at Central police after he had killed his mother. It was the same Pinsent, sitting, eyes closed, in a glass-fronted cell in blue paper overalls after his clothes had been removed for forensics because they were entirely blood-soaked. His face was blue-tinged in the overhead light, his acne pits grey. I was shown in to the cell and his eyes flicked open, pale gooseberry in the light. I moved quietly towards him, feet sinking into the soft, rubber flooring of the restraint cell. We sat facing each other on a low bench. There was a smell of cleaning fluid and soap from him. The police had allowed him to shower after his arrest. He answered my questions with no change in expression, speaking in a well-educated, low voice. He denied psychotic symptoms or mood disorder. I could elicit no gross symptoms of illness although there was a strange impression of absence and emptiness from him. He did not want to talk about the killing.

"I don't know what happened. It just happened," he said.

He shrugged, moving his hands slightly. I could see a tattoo of a crab on his forearm. Pinsent turned his gaze on me for a moment, saw where I was looking then said, "That's my star sign, cancer, the crab."

He was willing to be interviewed and didn't want a solicitor. The police asked me to attend as an appropriate adult in the interview, as they thought he might be mad. The Police and Criminal Evidence Act required an appropriate professional to be present and I was always happy to be contacted and to trawl the police stations in the night.

We entered one of the interview rooms. Perhaps it was the same one where I was questioned soon after Rachel disappeared the previous year. I ran my eye over the blank walls, the bare deal table, the ranks of recording machines and lists of instructions to staff from the custody sergeant. There was a single mirror high on the wall. Two CID entered, well groomed, smelling of expensive aftershave and dressed in identical suits. They were superficially friendly and solicitous towards their prisoner, yet making it perfectly clear in their formal manner that this was a man already separated from his fellows. Pinsent sat through the ritual introductions at the start of the taped interview, calmly sitting close to me, his thin fingers interlaced.

He was at first cautioned, "You do not have to say anything but it may harm your defence if you do not mention when questioned something you later rely on in court … Do you understand?"

Pinsent looked perplexed. "No," he said, "I don't understand."

The detective repeated the caution very slowly. Pinsent again looked puzzled and shrugged, "No. I don't get it."

The detective then recapitulated in a different way: "If you do not tell us something, then if you mention it in court later, it may be viewed as harmful to your defence."

It was clear that Pinsent could not grasp this obscure warning at all. He hesitated, looking to me to throw him a lifeline but I averted my gaze.

With a sigh he said, "Yes I understand," and the interview proceeded.

The police described the events of that afternoon as they knew it. Pinsent had been drinking wine with his mother at lunchtime at her home in the Meadows area, a riverside estate in the city. It was his mother's birthday. The two had had a problematic relationship but things were getting better. At some point he had taken a kitchen knife and stabbed his mother forty times, then phoned the emergency services to report what he had done. Then he had run out into the quiet suburban street shrieking, kicking cars and waving the bloodied and bent knife at passers-by. He had been arrested by an armed response team after a tense standoff in the street. The CID asked Pinsent for an explanation of events, but he shrugged listlessly, "I can't really remember … I don't know."

One of the dapper, smooth-faced CID officers said, "Perhaps this will help you remember Mr Pinsent? We are now going to play a tape of a recording of your 999 call to emergency services earlier today."

He leaned forwards and inserted a cassette into another tape machine I noticed that Pinsent had tightened his hands into tangled bunches in his lap. The tape began.

There was the sound of indistinct knocking, static, then a sudden low voice, indisputably that of Pinsent saying, "I have killed my mother," then the female operator saying "What service do you require?" then an unearthly roar rising to a shriek, "I haaaave killed my MAAATHER!" Then the *clack, donkety donk* sound as the phone was dropped and dangled on its wire, and a low distant booming sound, probably the noise of Pinsent slamming his mother's front door as he ran out onto the street.

"Are you there, caller?" the operator's voice sounded again then the end of the tape clicked shut. One of the detectives switched off the tape machine.

Pinsent closed his eyes for a moment and rocked a little. He was asked if he wanted a glass of water. He shook his head.

"I want to go to my cell now, take me back please." He kept on repeating that calmly and stubbornly as the police attempted to ask him if that was his voice on the tape. As the questions went on he began to scratch at his hair and scalp. I noticed my table notes and sleeve darkening and saw that a thick drizzle of dried blood flakes, which must have lodged in his hair despite being washed, were dropping as he scratched, speckling everything around him. I shifted away from the contamination. He did not appear to notice. The questions went on but little more could be got from him. He had retreated to an inner world. His terror, having at last come to pass, had now left him a hollow man.

He was photographed and finger printed and cooperatively gave a DNA mouth swab, a new procedure in that year, opening obediently as one detective dabbed at his gums with a spatula. He stood meekly, listening with lowered head as the custody sergeant read out the charge.

"That you, at number 23 Meadow Lane, the Meadows, on the 25th day in November this year in the jurisdiction of the Crown Court did murder Alice Elisabeth Pinsent contrary to Common Law."

Pinsent nodding and saying "Yes, yes, I understand."

Pinsent was later assessed by successive forensic consultants and was pronounced schizophrenic. He came before the courts and was transferred to the High Secure hospital under the Criminal Procedure Insanity Act. So not tried by reason of mental incompetence. One way to look at him was to see that it was a disease process by which the whispery, occult voices nagged at him, tormented and commanded him to destroy, and it was these that he had fled from over all the years beforehand.

I was less disposed to see Pinsent's crime in that way for I was following a different trail, studying at night during Louie's increasing absences, reading up on forensic history, thinking about Kress and about how to follow the trail of the deviant male. I fed my ideas by reading how Francis Galton discovered fingerprints, and recognised in the loops, arches and whorls, the signature of heredity and of race and predetermined paths. I read about Alphonse Bertillon's anthropometry in *Histoire Naturellement de L'Homme* and his threefold measuring system of the portions of the body of the criminal. And, of course, towering Lombroso who identified the stigmata of the atavistic essence of the criminal while doing autopsies in the 1870s in Italian asylums and prisons. I read how he noted asymmetries, peculiarities and anomalies, the marks by which the stigmatic can be recognised. I delved into the indexicality of the photograph, lingering over copies of early Bertillon register photos of the New York police, kept in the reference sections of the hospital library. These registers showed rank upon rank of images of criminal men depicting a thousand expressions, except those of joy. Often the photographs showed lowered faces and distorted features as the men attempted to prevent the camera from recording their likenesses. To me these faded photos were the phantom spoor of the nature of evil. I used to stare at the rows of them, flicking through the pages of the photographic registers again and again as if trying to locate something precious there.

I looked at the Tattoo Index of Scotland Yard from the 1880s by which they logged criminals by the marks on their bodies, because Galton, Lombroso and Lacassagne had all identified the tattoo as the mark of the criminal. Tattoo, *tatu* in Polynesian, meaning an indelible mark or as some have said, the word itself representing the tapping of a little wooden hammer driving the ink-primed bone needle into the skin. How I loved the passage from Lombroso's work on the savage origins of tattooing, when he comments that on the left arm of a prisoner there was found the words, commemorating a vanished lover, "*Quand la neige tombera noire/B... sortira de ma memoire.*" I delved into more modern work, reading Kretschmer's *Physique and Character*, or the American psychologist Sheldon's work on criminalogenic body shapes, and later still on XYY chromosomes, the genetic markers for violence and sociopathy.

Thus I prepared for my entry to the hospital in pursuit of Kress and his kind. Sometimes I would set aside the medical library volumes at home, in my chair, next to the hissing gas fire and I would conjure up both those faces: Kress in the court, Pinsent under the cell light. Then sometimes, I would stand up and go to look at my own face in the old, art deco mirror above the fireplace. I would look at my reflection which stared back at me while I traced with one finger, the curve of my cheek, the domed forehead, my skin still young then, elastic, as my finger prodded, finding the bone beneath the mask of flesh, murmuring to myself, *"quand la neige tombera noire…"*

★

Louie hadn't been ringing me much and so my nights were long and solitary. Somehow it had begun to matter more to me and I would lie in bed imagining what she was doing with her gangster lover. One night she made my heart race by ringing late, sounding distressed from a pay phone saying, "I'm in such shit, I can't tell you," then rang off abruptly. The following evening I called round unexpectedly to find her getting ready to go out. She dismissed the upsetting call on the previous night.

"Just going out with the girls tonight, alright love?" She said as I watched her open a pack of Bruce Oldfield sheer black stockings, pulling them up one after the other and clipping them to the suspenders against her white thigh. As she was doing this, one of her friends, another nurse in curlers with a face pack, lingered at the doorway saying,

"Someone's in for a treat tonight." She giggled then saw me and said, "Oops sorry."

I drove Louie into town for her assignation and after she'd jumped out of the car with her purse to buy cigs from a newsagent, I rummaged in her handbag as I waited with the engine running. I found mascara sticks, Kleenex, a pack of condoms in a gold and white pack marked *"fetherlite with sensitol"*, an atomiser and a key ring which I did not recognise with a tiny teddy bear and an attached label reading *"love is forever"*. Louie clattered back in the car. There was a flash of her gold anklet chain as she folded herself into her seat. She was chatty and breezy, giving me a quick peck on cheek before leaving to merge with the thronging clubbers on the street.

I felt sick after she had gone, thinking of how I had taken her to see her pin-eyed lover. I wanted to displace these feelings and find something for myself so I forsook my studious nights and returned to a bar near the hospital where I had first met Louie. There, in the clamour and the blue-ringed smoke I encountered Lisa, another nurse. We had chatted and flirted a few months before and I had spent an evening listening to her pour her heart out about being ill-treated by a neglectful lover. Afterwards she sent me a garish card with a cartoon of a piglet on it bearing the message "To my Special Friend". She was a sweet, plump, Geordie girl with an ash-blonde bob and conspicuous black roots. I had felt a passing erotic curiosity in her but had been wary of her submissive neediness. This time I was pleased to see her and she was happy to join me.

She gamely tried matching me drink for drink. We raced away in a taxi to the blues clubs of Radford and ended up at The TomTom; a Caribbean den where ranks of black women in long dresses and headscarves gyrated slowly to the reggae beat while their men lounged by the walls in a haze of ganja smoke. I bought some grass from two snickering Rastas, and got them to roll up spliffs for me then smoked them ostentatiously with Lisa puffing away inexpertly. We swayed groggily to the music, my arms wrapped around her solid waist. Back in a taxi home she clung to me with hot little hands whispering in her slurred Geordie accent: "Maybes we can get hitched, have a life." She accompanied me to my place following me blindly, obviously drunk and ill, a sweaty sheen on her face yet still stubbornly clinging to me. I felt a hostile curiosity and uneasy squeamishness about her and asked her, "Are you staying?"

"Aye, I will," she said softly blinking, almost in tears. Perching on my narrow bed she asked me for a shirt as a nightie. I gave her one of my white work shirts which later I pulled up to her shoulders in the darkness, heaving myself onto her, her head turned away as if in pain as I drove at her. Poor Lisa, in the morning tugging her tights on over her thighs, her calves red and mottled and puffy from the drinking, sliding her feet into shabby wide pumps and combing her hair in my austere bedroom. She humbly asked for a lift back.

"Well, I doan know if we will be seein each oother again?" she said. I gave a non-committal reply and dropped her off at the nurses' home, looking up at Louie's curtained windows as I stopped the car. I knew that gossip ran like a bush fire in that place.

I got some angry calls from Louie at work later that day, saying she wanted to talk to me. I made excuses, wanting to avoid a confrontation, then as she raged on at me over the phone, I attacked her back, snarling about her infidelity. She slammed the phone down. I returned home late, still feeling angry, having stopped off at another bar that evening, not wanting to go home. I knew at once that someone had been in my place. Louie had evidently come to the house that night. On the mirror above the fireplace was scrawled a message in carmine lipstick: "*FUCK OFF YOU TWAT!*"

My diaries were lying open and scattered across the floor, polaroids of Rachel were thrown about and crumpled with other photos. Louie had also scrawled on some of the diary pages with eyeliner pencil in slanting, savage strokes: "*Fuck off … suffer … sick bastard.*" I had underestimated her passion, her jealous rage, her desolation and was astonished and shamed by it, standing there in the ravaged flat with photos scattered at my feet, the phone began to ring again and the fish moved in their tank expecting food.

Chapter Three
Cutting the Worm

Hunter entered the water at night having cut a wake through the nettle stalks along the river bank. There was no water in his lungs, the autopsy was quite clear — it was the cold that had killed him, stopping his heart, weakened as it was by decades of inactivity and by smoking all those roll-ups during the long hospital years. The late autumn weather had been mild, but the chilled water had taken him, killed him and sent him floating back to the hospital.

He had lasted two years out, one of the few to be discharged from maximum security, a burned-out schizophrenic, whose offences were lost in time. He had been housed in a council maisonette on a large estate in the city. Too old, lonely and disconnected to start a new life, he had become frightened by the malevolent local children who had sensed his strangeness and scratched at his front door at night, shouting after him on the street. The weak thread of connection between him and care workers could not sustain him. And so he rolled with the river down Clifton Reach, southerly through the deep flood prevention channels and past the glittering, night-time city. Dawn found him bumping over misty Shelford Weir, then the river swept him seaward through the water meadows where cattle grazed, past the raw, new estates and disused bomber bases to tumble under Newark Bridge by the beet factory where the high-sided, white vans rumbled overhead, taking men to Ranby Prison, Lincoln and the hospital.

He went with the river as it looped, slowed and began to meander, as it reached the fenny, flat lands where the wide bean fields opened out. Here Hunter, or what had been him, nudged the muddy banks and lodged in the intake grill of a power station on the west bank of the river, the hospital side. Nearby stood a country parish church, where could be found the graves for the hospital dead. Forty or fifty of them, each with similar grey headstones bearing a name and a date, sinking slowly into the thatch of rarely-mown grass. After autopsy and inquest and enquiry reports, Hunter joined them.

We stood together for a moment by the graveside looking down

at the pale wood of the coffin and the thick clods of red earth heaped up on a tarpaulin nearby. Bartram removed one black leather glove, stooped and tossed a fistful of earth to clump down on the lid with a thud. Bill Ponds did likewise. The committal over, we remained awkwardly together as the chaplain hurried away, her parka jacket flapping over her robes. Bartram said, "Well, it was difficult to get the Directorate committee to allow poor old Hunter here but it was the right thing. Well, hadn't he floated his way back to us after all?"

He paused, looked up at the sky and hitched up his cashmere scarf to the biting wind. "Blow, blow thou winter wind ... Thy sting is not so sharp as friends remembered not ... Eh Jack?"

I smiled and nodded, well used to Bartram's playful allusions although I knew that he hid a sharp dislike of the patients beneath that avuncular manner. We walked away from the grave, down the lines of head stones, back towards the flat-topped church tower as behind us two workmen began to fill in the grave. Bill Ponds followed, picking his way over the uneven path between the frozen mole hills. He was a tall, thickset Barbadian, popular among the patients, a calm, compassionate man. He had nursed Hunter for years and they had both served out their time in the villas. Flecks of snow began to fall, eddying around the dusty windows and the eroded, sandstone pillars of the old church. Faraway, against the wind, could be heard the growl of tractors working the land and the distant clamour of the rooks that inhabited the hospital poplars.

Bartram offered Bill Ponds a lift but he gravely declined, "I likes to walk when I can," he said in his deep voice.

We passed him as we drove away, marching steadily down the hedged lane to the hospital, his pork pie hat tilted against the snow flurries. Bartram hunched over the wheel of his battered Volvo. My feet crackled on a heap of debris in the passenger foot well where I could see piles of old sandwich containers, promotional material from drug companies and oddly, a green plastic watering can sitting there among the litter.

"It's strange when we bury them like this," said Bartram as we ground along slowly down the slippery road. "It's as if their lives have been completely taken by the hospital and their ends only have the meaning that we give them."

"And hospital accounts pay the ferryman," I said and Bartram laughed, glancing at me as I stared out onto the whitening fields.

I had come on the early shift that morning, as I needed to complete some paperwork before attending the funeral as the departmental representative even though I had never met Hunter. I had walked through the empty, early morning car park that day, a little stiff after the hour-long drive from the city. A few rooks sidled across the tarmac, there was a frost shrouding the windows of the night staff cars and the hospital flag pole began to clank in the chilly breeze. A grey light showed through the corridor vents as dawn broke. I passed the block wards on the way to my office compound. I could hear the chinking of key belts and chains and the crack of doors unlocking as the handover took place after the night shift and night security reports were exchanged. I could hear medication trolleys on the move down the corridors and the squeaking, clatter of breakfast containers going down to the blocks from the kitchens. There was a low murmuring as the first patients assembled to be shaved by staff, as the fire lists were made up and the radio man on each shift made his voice check to security control.

I went out into the cold air of another wired court and drew back the metal gate latch. Above me, in the misty light, a heron silently glided overhead. I entered my office building and paused on the second floor to look out of the barred window toward the red brick hulk of the assessment block. I imagined Kress stirring there, not far away. Perhaps he was rolling a cig, or queuing for hot water and the medicine round. I paused on the landing to look out at the triple barrier of the hospital, wall, ditch and wire, thinking how small the place seemed from this vantage even though, turning and turning upon themselves, the inner corridors unwound for miles. The early morning light gleamed on the pale coping of the rounded wall parapets and mist curled in the hollows of the ditch. In the field beyond the wire the rooks clambered steadily in twos and threes over the furrowed soil. In my mind I was determined, after this funeral was done, to start to close in on Kress.

Having returned to the hospital with Bartram, I could see his junior doctors already waiting for him on the path by the staff entrance, he hurried on ahead of me. I watched him forge on past the lodge house, his staff grade medical juniors following him, briefing him before the mid-morning ward rounds. He was already undergoing the security searches at the staff carousel and metal detector as I entered. I showed the security reception my key chain, key card and ID. Although I had undergone this process many times since starting at the hospital two months previously, it continued to be a tense affair. Staff queued to enter past the signs reminding employees of what was forbidden and moved into the reception area one by one through a sliding transparent door. The place echoed to the sounds of rattling metal stiles, as if at a football ground's entrance. At every tenth entry a buzzer sounded and a special search ensued for both incoming and outgoing staff. There was also the archway of a metal detector where a body search always took place, for the hospital was a place where not only the patients were invigilated. In the old days, staff were not searched but after a spate of enquiries, escapes and scandals, security had been tightened.

Now all were searched for contraband: weapons, cameras, phones, chewing gum, newspapers, medication, cameras, items of glass, unauthorised keys of any sort, food — the list was long.

Everyone knew the procedure. We had been trained to administer it ourselves. I remember studying the searching procedures manual with its flow chart on how to rub down a male subject. I had to repeat it time after time under the dyspeptic eye of a senior security nurse who would sigh heavily as he observed my hesitant practice attempts on another member of the training course.

"No, Mr Keyse," he would bark, "you are not asking him for a dance. Approach the subject, stand facing him, give him clear instructions, ask him if he has anything he is not authorised to have, then start on the procedure, pockets, headgear, collar, tie. And so on, carry on, Mr Keyse." I would fumble over my colleague once more and all the time that I was practising to be a jailer I would be thinking my own unauthorised thoughts and plans for which no guard could find evidence.

On re-entering the place on this day, a member of security approached me with the usual ironic courtesy of "Do you mind, sir?" I remember his hands running lightly down my torso and my legs as he worked his way methodically over me. Pockets — emptying them, headgear — none, asking me to run my fingers through my hair; fingers moving down my tie, turning my collar out and feeling round it; working his way down; his hands touching me like a brisk, no-nonsense lover. There was little dignity in being searched; sometimes there was banter between the parties but more usually uneasy silence. I stood still with my hands raised and could faintly smell his sweat underneath the aftershave.

"Twist, please," he instructed and I twisted my belt buckle for him to inspect behind it. Looking over his stooping back, I could see Poynton, the chief ferret, staring back at me from an observation hatch by the glass fronted booths that held the key racks. The security man worked his way down, patting as he went, crouching to slide his hands down the back and sides of each leg, all the way to the ankles. As ever, the genitals remained unprobed, the only unregulated area for staff, although a hand-held lollipop metal detector was waved over that area. I recalled Bartram once laughing about it: "Heaven knows what squalid little room you would be taken to, with boxes of rubber gloves, if that thing went off when it was waved at you down there!"

Once screened and searched, I advanced to the key cupboards. There were four keys needed: two heavy new magnetic ones with slab-sided shanks for the main doors and two older ones of polished brass for side rooms and offices. The key men waited impassively to receive you, giving out keys from large swivelling carousels in return for a key card with your name and department, which was then hooked up in place of your key. I received the heavy bunch through a slot in the screen, clipped them to my key loop and waited by a gridded gate to be allowed through into the body of the hospital. I imagined Poynton still watching me but I did not look round.

The gate slid back and I entered the first corridor. Outgoing staff congregated here; there was the sound of banter and the constant jingling of keys as staff adjusted and unhooked their belts. On and through the first heavy main door, the lock going *riprap* as the magnets engaged, and then out into the first wired yards between the buildings, empty apart from a few starlings on the frozen grass. I entered the Edwardian blocks, the old heart of the hospital with its worn red brick and narrow windows masked by heavy, rust-pocked, white painted bars. Here I passed through long, muffled corridors where the daylight filtered in through overhead, barred circular openings.

Here, away from the vigilance of security staff, I could feel secure in my purpose and my step would quicken, my keys jingling in their pouch. Here, too, I would first encounter groups of patients. They would come, sometimes singly, corralled by staff, or six or seven at a time, herded, moving in single file on their way to gym sessions, workshops or the psychological therapies unit. When I had first walked these corridors they had seemed shadow-men, these inhabitants of the place, muffled; slow-paced figures beside the confident escorts, with their crackling two way radios and stentorian shouts of, "Keep to the right lads." These patients would murmur to each other or sometimes call, "Hello, boss," to staff they knew. My gaze would pass eagerly over their faces as they shuffled past but I did not see Kress among them.

On this morning I had hurried to Eaton Ward, a treatment ward on the lower blocks. Patients passed through the hospital from admission wards to treatment wards, then out of the blocks to the villas which stood further off in the hospital compound. Sometimes a patient would become snagged on a ward for years and others would flow backwards and, at worst, they could be sent to the feared D3 or Dove intensive care ward. This was for the especially fractious or dangerous where time passed slowly in perspex-fronted cells. Each ward had its own regime and its own folklore. Eaton Ward was a ground floor ward which had held men for years since the hospital's inception. I often imagined their accumulated pain, their loneliness and sweat settling like sediment in the shadowy, echoing corridors. Eaton was known as a dumping ground, a Sargasso for patients who were too intransigent or damaged to respond to the latest therapies. The staff were, in the main, good hearted time servers who ran a regime of benign neglect. Patients often lived there for years, serving out the years along with the staff.

I turned off the main corridor, then entered the dark, fusty air lock — a sealed access chamber designed to prevent a sudden patient breakout from the ward. I pressed a buzzer and peered through the vision slot to check that no patient was lurking by the doors. We had been trained to look through these slots, through the fingers of an upraised, protective hand in case anyone on the other side poked an object back through at us. A buzzer sounded signalling that staff were aware of my presence on the other side and were observing the entry corridor. I opened the ward door using both hands, *click* as the key went home and *clack* as the turning handle shot the magnetic bolts.

Lazaro usually haunted the entrance corridor to the ward, a paedophile with a whining, scouse accent and a doughy, half-formed face as if he had never fully matured. He would scurry beside incoming staff asking over-solicitously "How are you this fine morning, sir?" He was frightened of his fellow patients who hated him as a nonce and he was careful to stay next to staff at all times. He would often hold a rolled newspaper, pretending to do the crosswords while secretly tearing out pictures of children to carry off to his room. He would stick close to staff where they lounged to chat and watch the patients playing snooker, and he would invariably follow me down the ward, engaging me in ritual conversation.

This morning I was surprised to see that his chair was empty and there was no sign of him. There was just one nursing auxiliary standing in the ward corridor, key belt dangling, watching my entry. As I entered he gave me an unfriendly nod and returned to the pages of the *Mirror*. The smell of cooking, of cigarette smoke and of polish reached me — the scent of dead time, dead hopes, the odour of futility on this forgotten ward.

I went quickly down the central axis, greeting the staff and patients in the association area. I looked along the west room corridor to see a uniformed cleaner washing the floors and the murderer Heinrich Grau slumped in a worn leather chair. I raised my hand in greeting and Heinrich turned his sharp face like an old bird to give me a jerky gesture in return.

Padraig was also there, leaning in a corner, in a worn grey suit, his bony skull gleaming under a clipped fuzz of hair. He beckoned me over, hissing out the words "What news fer me?" as he always did, his hands rubbing at the sores about his sharky, thin mouth with its wrecked teeth.

"No news Padraig, I'm sorry," I replied. He was always waiting for notification of a transfer back to Ireland which would never come. Scurrying after me down the corridor he whispered, "Hey mistorr, mistorr, it's de blacks and de English dey arr poisoning me, help me please…"

I kept walking towards the staff office, shrugging off Padraig and the other importuning patients. There was often a feeling of tension when specialist staff entered the nursing station offices. The nurses lived with the patients, served out their time with them and rubbed shoulders with them. They lived on terms of familiarity with men who were once feared, loathed and now were largely forgotten by the outside world. They often regarded specialist staff as dilettantes and tourists who did not really understand the dangerousness or the humanity of their charges.

Eaton Ward office this morning brimmed with special tension. I realised it at once and as if to signal this, the office phone rang constantly, the external bells echoing down the corridor outside. A staff nurse, whom I did not recognise, cradled a phone with a lit cigarette jutting from his fist in defiance of the regulations. He blew out a tusk of smoke and stared at me while continuing to bark instructions down the phone. Two auxiliary staff leaned over the patient movement board, making adjustments in red felt tip according to the day's activities. I could see that Lazaro's name had already been rubbed off the board. A security team member was also standing by the barred window, leafing through the patient files.

More nursing staff arrived with a clatter of keys and the rustling hiss and static from their radios. The staff nurse banged his phone down and began to brief them about patients. Glancing at me suspiciously for a moment, as if in doubt whether to speak in front of me, he then went on to tell them that Lazaro had unexpectedly gone berserk at breakfast, jumped on patient Hobman and tried to stab him in the neck with a shiv made from a honed-down tooth brush stem melted onto a nail. Lazaro had been hauled off by staff, secluded and was now transferred to Dove ICU. This was to be my first conscious memory of the existence of Hobman.

There was a sudden banging on the reinforced glass of an observation window next to my chair. I saw that I was being regarded by a patient called Andre. He was a fairly harmless, damaged man who had set fire to another patient's trousers during a psychiatric ward squabble many years before and had got transferred to High Secure. He wore an old yachtsman's cap at an angle, like Humphrey Bogart in *The African Queen* and he wagged his large forefinger at me in remonstrance. Above the battered brim of his cap he had stuck a yellow post-it label with HEAD OF SECURITY written on it in wobbly capitals. Andre continued to gesticulate, his eyes rolling behind thick glasses, and then he mouthed and bellowed through the reinforced glass, "Devil eyes! You have devil eyes, Dr Keyse!"

Bored by his antics, I looked past him into the smoke room. In one corner a patient they called Dancing Tony jigged alone, headphones clamped to his head under a pulled down baseball cap. He moved with a graceful, restless motion. His eyes remained closed and his lashes were long, feminine and very dark against his greeny-white pallor. I did not know his offence and hence had not shaped my hatred for him. I stood up and leaned nearer the meshed glass, looking beyond the dancing figure, and beyond Andre who continued to mouth and point, to make out the figure of Hobman, hunched in a chair, seen in profile, outlined against the smoky light of the window vents. All I really knew of Hobman, at the time, was that he ruled the patients on the ward. He was feared among them and one glare from his tattooed face was enough to clear a room. He largely spent his days in the smoke room having refused therapeutic groups. He tolerated huge, bumbling, histrionic Andre whom he treated as a clown, court attendant and errand boy and he seemed rooted now in his preferred place. There was no outward sign of the attack on him by Lazaro.

Dr Bartram bustled into the office followed at a distance by his junior staff grade Dr Rahnem and the other clinicians behind.

"Good morrow dear colleagues, are you joining us? Chop, chop. Jack and I have already been busy this morning seeing poor Hunter off, haven't we Jack?"

He smiled at me and made sweeping gestures in an effort to chivvy the nursing staff into the review room; his starched white shirt front, topped by a magenta bow tie, gleamed in the yellow light of the ward room.

The review room was usually locked, but now stood ajar as clinicians trooped in followed by the sullen group of ward staff who disliked Dr Bartram's autocratic ways. It was a small room with high, unadorned walls and a window which appeared to be permanently open, summer and winter. I saw that a tendril of ivy had crept over the lintel from the outside wall and had begun to coil around one of the thick window bars. There were ten high backed chairs in a semi circle. Two months previously it had been discovered that some enterprising patients had slit the backs of the chairs and installed a hidden still made from plastic bottles in each chair with the intention of making alcohol from a concoction of dried fruit and yeast made from Marmite. The sulphurous bubbling from within the chairs had not been noticed in the weekly ward reviews but a cleaner had eventually discovered the workings. This room had been locked ever since and Bartram still joked about it, pretending to reach round the back of the chairs saying "Fancy a gin and tonic anyone?"

Bartram took centre stage and gestured to incoming staff where they should sit. I watched his hands moving and his quick eyes measuring the responses to his eccentric, controlling behaviour.

Junior medics sat closest to him, then psychologists and social workers, lastly ward staff and students. As a therapeutic specialist I occupied a middle ranking position in the hospital pecking order and I was pointed to a seat next to Irina Starsha, the ward psychologist. She had turned her sleek head as I entered, switching off her attention from poor Dr Rahnem the registrar, who continued to stammer out one of his halting anecdotes without an audience. Irina rarely contributed to clinical meetings, apart from occasional terse, peppery comments in her slightly accented voice. She sometimes mimicked Bartram to amused ward staff in the office after meetings. She caught my eye with an ironic lift of her arched brow and a flicker of amusement in her eyes. Her musky perfume reached me as I squeezed through the circle of chairs to take the seat next to her.

The room was nearly full and the air was already close. A young student nurse leaned back in her chair yawning unselfconsciously and revealing a tanned abdomen adorned with a single silver stud in the belly button.

"Thy belly is like a heap of wheat set about with lilies," declaimed Bartram looking challengingly at her, tugging at his greying side whiskers.

"Do you know the Song of Solomon my dear?" The fair-haired student giggled, blushed and looked blank and I could see a folded anger in the tough features of the grizzled charge nurse. Bartram fed his vanity by scoring off low-ranking staff.

The staff nurse requested that the meeting should firstly attend to patient Grimpen who had become disturbed after the incident on the ward and who needed attention.

"If we must see him then wheel him in, but we really should try and focus on Hobman and make an effort to get to the bottom of this Lazaro business," Bartram replied testily.

"Take me to D3 doctor, take me up the blocks, take me to Dove, anywhere but here, I've had it here, can't stand it no more!"

Eddie Grimpen addressed Dr Bartram, ignoring the rest of the assembled professionals. A large man in his forties with a pear-shaped body, greasy blond hair and a fleshy, sallow face, he stood in the doorway, swaying slightly.

"Come in, do," said Bartram, indicating a chair set by the door.

Grimpen reluctantly sat on the edge of the chair as if about to flee. Sweat beaded his forehead and he continued to speak jerkily through gritted teeth. His nicotine-stained hands twitched constantly over his face.

"I have been here twenty years and this ward is the worst. Arsonists, rapists, child molesterers, not me. I didn't even manage to kill anyone and I'm stuck here. And now there's that nonce. Someone's going to be knocked off, I'm telling you. I can't stand it. Someone will get me next, and I've done nothing."

"Do calm yourself, Eddie, and tell us what you mean by 'knocked off,'" said Bartram.

A sly look crossed Grimpen's face and he reached for a rollup from the pocket of his shirt and began to roll and squeeze and play with it in his fat fingers. All eyes in the room seemed to be on Grimpen's hands as they palpated and manoeuvred the bulgy spill of tobacco. I noticed the sinews working on the white forearm with the prison tattoos, naively drawn, an anchor and an eagle with outstretched wings and his name "*eddie*" in faded lower case on a scroll. He had been in for twenty years, having tried to kidnap two teenage girls on a Cumbrian farm using a home-made firearm. His purpose had been to rape and kill them.

"I'm saying nothing. Just get me out of here. Things happen here which aren't meant to happen," Grimpen said. His eyes darted around the room then seemed to fall on me for a moment.

At this moment Poynton slipped into the meeting and moved behind us, keys chinking softly, to perch on a metal cabinet which stood in one corner. Grimpen's eyes followed him and his voice trailed off. Patients feared security, and Poynton in particular. They called him "the ferret". Grimpen would not respond to further questions from Dr Bartram and simply threw his arms up in jerky motions saying, "I've told yer, I've told yer, I've said it all." There was a silence then Bartram said, "Alright Eddie, we will consider what you have to say and in the meantime you might be helped by a change in your medication."

"No more tablets doctor, just get me out," Grimpen called from the doorway as the charge nurse ushered him away. As the door opened the noise of the corridors rolled in to the review room: insistent phone bells, slamming doors, keys rattling in locks and the distant shouting of a patient.

"I think we could do with increasing his depot and his lithium dosage," said Bartram once the door had closed. Dr Rahnem bent over the thick file scribbling notes and instructions for blood tests and medication changes. No one else in the room was asked for their opinion until Bartram turned to the slight figure of Poynton.

"Eddie was talking about people being knocked off on the ward, Mr Poynton. Can you give us the benefit of your wisdom as to what is going on?"

Poynton paused and swept the room with his pale gaze. A pack of Royals edged out of the chest pocket of his uniform white shirt.

"Well let's see what we have," replied Poynton. "Hobman says he doesn't know what it is all about. Lazaro was not popular. We have a security report from a month ago in which he reported a threat from an unknown patient." Poynton handed round a single sheet photocopy of a drawing of a stick man suspended from a gallows. The initials TL were written below the hanging figure and a speech balloon drawn by the head with the words "*HELP!*" written there.

The paper shuffled from hand to hand in the room and I looked at it carefully before handing it to Irina. Poynton commented, "This looks like a joke, but is in fact an implied threat that Tony Lazaro is due for the chop. We also found this in Lazaro's room this morning," continued Poynton waving a tape cassette. "We found a written transcript of the contents of this tape made by Lazaro — we think. It contains a description of some of his offences against children either for the purpose of masturbatory gratification or for selling as porn to other patients. There were also pictures of children torn out of newspapers." Poynton passed round another document. When I received it I just glanced at the first lines which read:

"that nichole she was a real slut you knoe. I pulled her down. tony I love you shagging me she said. Ah and that little blue clip in her hair and her smooth thin licle legs and her mate in the doorway waiting her turn…"

I gave the photocopy to Irina who made a slight *moue* of distaste when she received it. Poynton continued, "Lazaro himself is saying nothing. He is still presenting in a histrionic state on Dove. The odd thing is the ligature mark on his neck. There is no noose in his room and we know that it is unlikely to be an item of clothing as the skin is abraded and raw, as if it has been compressed by something thin and tight."

"Food for thought; perhaps we should do further snap searches on the ward looking for a ligature," said Dr Bartram and the discussion eddied back and forth in the review room to which I only half-listened.

"Well, let's wheel Hobman in, see what he has to say," I heard Bartram saying.

"I'll fetch him," I offered, standing up. This surprised the meeting as the nurses usually went back and forth fetching patients. On a conscious level I wanted to show as a newcomer that I was comfortable and unafraid on the wards but now I think that I was also obeying some instinct, perhaps I was summoning up Hobman to begin to play his part in my story and that of my quarry: Kress.

I went out of the review room into the ward corridor where patients milled, unsettled by the activity from security.

I looked into the smoke room but could not see Hobman in his previous position and I went down the west corridor where the room cells were located. I passed the battered metal doors each with an observation shutter and identifying names written on erasable plates:

Kirk ... Razaq ... Field ... Grau ... Hobman.

A hooded figure sat nodding and rocking in a chair at the quiet end of the corridor. It was JJ, a head-injured man with abnormal aggression, whom staff found easier to handle if his head was covered by a light towel during the daylight hours of patient movement. I ignored JJ and peered into Hobman's neat cell. There were no pictures on the wall and just a line of paperback books carefully arrayed along one shelf. There was a chill breeze from an open vent and I could see snow falling past the window bars in the block yards outside.

"Yes, doctor. Are you looking for me?" A quiet, pleasant voice sounded behind me, I jumped a little and turned to see Hobman calmly standing behind me. I thought that he must have moved very silently and swiftly. Up close, I could see that he had regular, aquiline features although the eyes were drawn to the markings on his face, its form and expression cancelled out by the images imprinted on it. The eyes were unreadable.

My gaze skated over Hobman. I told him that he was required for review.

"If I am called then who am I to refuse?" he said, still standing close to me.

Suddenly a grating voice roared out, "I can see yer. I can see yer fuckin' laughing!"

The noise emitted from a dark, round, feral face with brown, stump teeth under a knobbed and welted shaven skull. It was JJ. His towel had slipped off his face and his squinty eyes had focused on us. He began to make convulsive jerks in his chair as if about to leap up and Hobman took my arm and pulled me back down the corridor with him. An auxiliary nurse deftly slipped behind JJ crooning to him, "Alright boyo, it's alright, everything is fine now," and adjusting the towel to fall over his face again, patting and rubbing the coiled arms until JJ subsided and slumped back like a toy with a dead battery.

The auxiliary looked indignantly at us for disturbing his charge. I thanked Hobman for moving me away from JJ. His lips twitched into a slight smile as he walked beside me to the review room.

Hobman sat for the review in the chair that Eddie had vacated. He looked calm and composed and thoughtful as if considering something. He seemed oblivious to our concerted gaze. I found something strangely compelling about him. I know now that he was probably listening to a woman's voice in his head. She had accompanied him for many years, fading sometimes when he was loaded with medication, but since he had been started on an oral antipsychotic he would hold the white bitter tablet at the top of his throat, wriggle his tongue to show the staff it had gone, then spit the pill out later in his room.

Sitting in that review room her voice was probably clear and strong again.

"*You will lobotomise them, scopolomise them, drag them to hell with ten mighty midgets,*" she would say. He called her the White Lady or the White Sister of Utopia. She also told him to write to his estranged, older sister whom he had not seen for ten years since the murders.

He wrote her long letters, elegiac and touching, calling her his lover, his butterfly, his mother, *"I bless you, I bless you with my body, and I am soft for you but hard for others."* Postal security always found the letters and they were returned to him in ward review by Dr Bartram. The White Lady told him that his sister received them in spirit.

The White Lady had been there from the beginning, or perhaps from when his mother left the family when Hobman was an infant. He believed that she moved the strings of his favourite toy — a puppet Pinocchio — and made it dance. She had whispered her calm instructions to him when his father had alternately cuddled then beaten him and called him "his little mate'; when he could hear his two older sisters whimpering in their rooms after their father returned from the pub at night. Sour-breathed and spit-laden he would rant to the children, "Let me tell you about your mother, that cow, that crow, that cunt!" After his mother had finally abandoned the family, just disappearing in the night, the child Hobman took to painting his face and sitting in an Indian tipi that his sisters had helped him make. He called himself Big Chief and spent all his time there where all would be well. Once his father played along, even painting his face as part of the game and they could be seen together in photos he had kept, now lodged in the hospital files. Perhaps it was in the tipi, decorated by sun and moon symbols, a masked face and a phoenix-like bird when the White Lady first started speaking to him.

She had also guided him through his school absences and his removal to the learning disabilities classes. Her cool voice had comforted him when he saw his mother on market day in the small Norfolk town they shared as she walked past with a new family. The

White Lady had also instructed him to take back from the world, to take what was due to him. And so he truanted and stole from local shops and the White Lady's voice was ecstatic and singing when he

hid under the old timbers of the staithe down by the silted harbour, watching the moonlight on the curving estuary out to the Wash, drinking cider and taking deep breaths from glue tins. The White Lady also told him he could walk on water, he could do many things but first there were tests, first he must go on a journey. So, as a teenager, Hobman travelled from home, drifting, stealing, holing up in bed and breakfasts and hostels, always pursued by the tinkling, insistent voice that said, "*They are laughing at you, they are shining their lights on you.*"

When stealing would not provide him with enough keep, for he was an incompetent criminal — he tried to work. In the East Anglian market town where he had found himself, the labour exchange sent him to do day work in a chicken factory where he slammed the heads of birds with a stun gun before they were hoisted and had their throats cut. He spent some of his first week's wages on a haircut which sheared off his long, straight, auburn hair and he stared at his newly angled, ascetic features in the dim mirror of his lodgings.

That night the voice said, "*This haircut is no good, it is shit, your life is shit, they have done it to you, they have taken you from your true lover. You must kill this time. You must kill a priest to make it right.*"

Hobman went to a local church that night. A comely, Anglican church set around with thick-boled limes. St Barnabus, meaning "son of encouragement". Hobman came to the church carrying two sheath knives and a wooden club as instructed by the White Sister. The church was unlocked, this was a quiet place with no thought then of men like him who come in the night and he waited through the hours of darkness thinking and preparing and chanting to himself as if in the sweat lodge rituals of the American Indians that he had read about.

In the morning an elderly churchwarden came to ready the church for the day's services and was surprised by the thin, tall, young man who had been hiding, watching him for some time and who had ordered him to, "get on the floor, on the fucking floor." Hobman raised the club intending to stun the old man before cutting him, as had been done to the chickens, but the churchwarden had seen a murderous anger in his eyes and determined to escape. He parried the first blow with his dustpan and, though Hobman rained blows on his back and head, the plucky man staggered out of the vestry door crying for help. Hobman remained at the main doors of the church, club in hand, as if reluctant to move out into the daylight and the churchwarden crawled on all fours to a nearby road.

The White Sister's voice grew faint for a while after that as Hobman was arrested, assessed as mentally ill and medicated. The courts decided that he did not realise the nature and quality of his act and he was processed through the secure system until such a time as he was fit to be let out. Six years passed, and he moved to a day release unit not far from his childhood home. The years had blunted the severity of the crime, the attack became "common assault" in the clinicians' reports, the presence of two knives was forgotten and no one ever spoke to the victim of the crime, the elderly churchwarden who had died a year after the attack. Hobman was not even a model patient. He was surly and uncooperative and downplayed the events that had led him to his detention. His consultant could see no evidence of schizophrenia and came to believe that Hobman's crime was the result of drug-induced psychosis. His medication was withdrawn and no one noticed any evident ill effects although the White Sister of Utopia came back full force into his head. She told him to prepare again and he spent his benefit money on long-planned facial tattoos, his war paint: writhing serpents on each cheek, a skull on one temple and a sun cradled in a crescent moon on the other temple. These symbolised death and transformation and were a statement of intent that he was about to emerge into the world in a changed state.

Hobman's new face caused some unease to the nursing staff at the unit, as did his angry moods and threats to other patients. Observations were increased. He once even spoke about his voices and his anger, his longing for his sister and about his wish to kill, to kill a priest and by killing to transform himself. He told it to a junior occupational therapist, an older woman who had taken the trouble to befriend Hobman and listen to his rambling concerns. A good-hearted person who wanted to help, she gave Hobman a book that was found on him after the killings. It was Winnicott's *The Child, the Family and the Outside World*. The OT was worried about his fantasies and wrote them down in a report which was naïve but detailed. No one read it or paid much attention to it on the clinical team because she was not respected and her voice carried no weight.

Hobman remained free during the daytime to roam and the White Lady said to him in her cool insistent voice, "*killeristic, serialistic, feed the serpent now.*" It was two weeks before Christmas; Hobman helped put up the ward decorations then he was given day leave to wander the outside world. He was never to return.

The Maitlands were a retired couple living in a bungalow half a mile from Hobman's father's cottage. They lived next door to the church and Mr Maitland spent the day moving jumble items from his garage to the church in preparation for a Christmas bring-and-buy. Hobman must have been there watching with his illuminated face on that day. He had connected the Maitlands to the church and marked them out as his prey according to the delusional correspondences of his internal world. He had slipped into the house when Mr Maitland left the back door open. Hobman carried a Bowie knife with a compass in the handle. He went upstairs and lay on their bed and drew the covers over him and waited as the Maitlands went about their day, unknowing of his presence in their home. Mr Maitland washed the car and ran errands until evening came on. Hobman threw back the covers and watched the full moon rise from the bedroom windows before descending the stairs to find them. He surprised them making tea in the kitchen and he had to subdue Mr Maitland by hitting him on the head with the knife handle. He tied them both with scarves and tights taken from upstairs and led the elderly, trembling woman upstairs to her bedroom and left the husband bound on the kitchen floor. He strangled Mrs Maitland first with a scarf and then went to the kitchen and ate some of their food where it lay set out. He smoked a Red Band cigarette while looking down at Mr Maitland on the floor. He then strangled him. Before each one died, Hobman told them their spouse would die also and now it was their turn, leaning over them with his painted face, wanting them to know.

Hobman had still not finished, he took a little money and food and went out in the early morning to his father's house. Later, the police logged sightings of him in the locality. He was easy to remember with that face. The Maitlands' bodies were found by their son later that day and Hobman was reported missing by ward staff when he did not return. News of the killings spread quickly but Hobman was not immediately linked to the event. His father may

95

have sensed something however because Hobman later reported that he seemed afraid of him. The police called at his father's Victorian cottage in a leafy village cul-de-sac in the afternoon looking for Hobman, because of his absconding from hospital. He stood upstairs watching them from behind the curtains, as his father denied seeing him to the police, who stood in the doorway but did not enter the property.

Hobman strangled his father later that night with a tie. He must have surprised his father as he was still quite a powerful man and was likely to have put up a struggle. A radio was playing a quiz program at the time and afterwards Hobman told investigators that after strangling his father, he had yelled out, "Answer the question! You can't answer, why not Dad?"

Two days passed until forensics produced Hobman's prints on a plate in the Maitland house and they found a Red Band stubbed out in a plant pot. They broke in to his father's house to find Hobman watching TV. His father's head was discovered in a kitchen cupboard and the torso on the bed. Hobman seemed confused and disorientated. He had stopped hearing the White Sister's voice from the time he entered the Maitlands' house.

That had all happened ten years ago. Hobman had then entered hospital time and had been shaped by the limbo of assessment wards, by dialectical behaviour therapy and by great quantities of antipsychotic medication. His case had been presented to conferences under the heading "*Mad or Bad? An Atypical Presentation*". No one visited Hobman from the outside world. He had spent two long years on Dove after he attacked a nonce with some batteries wrapped in a sock, because he hated those who hurt children. Now he had fetched up on Eaton, seemingly burned-out but still possessing a residual menace to staff and patients. His long hair was prematurely streaked with grey, although he was not yet forty. He was now a little stooped due to scoliosis and the face was lined below the vivid tattoos, but he was still very strong in his upper body. Staff had reported seeing him doing press ups in his cell at night.

He now sat before us in the review, Bartram trying to engage him, asking about Lazaro and the incident at breakfast and about why that might have happened. But Hobman politely denied any difficulties and parried any attempt to acknowledge that he might have played an active part in provoking Lazaro, "What can I say? These things happen here, people get ill," he said blandly with a ghost of a smile, and he made a cupped hands gesture to signify a displacement of any sense of responsibility while catching my eye with an ironic glint in his stare, which could almost have been a wink. Eventually Bartram dismissed him and wound up the review with the agreement that Hobman should be put on close observations.

Snow fell more thickly through the day. I peered through the bars from my second floor office window, watching it cling to the black wire, layering the rounded parapet on the wall and capping the camera hoods on their poles. It drifted round the blocks, covering the litter of paper, excreta, soiled underwear and old shoes flung out of the windows by patients. The snow muted the constant cawing of the rooks and the clanging of the lodge flagpole in the wind. Even the air raid howl of the hospital escape siren, which cranked up every first Wednesday of the month as a test, sounded muffled and distant that afternoon. I watched as the snowplough rolled out and made a sweep of the drive to ensure access, for the hospital planned for all eventualities. The great boiler house thrummed maximum power, heating the long corridors, the workshops, the smoky day rooms and the shuttered seclusion cells where naked men writhed beneath rip-proof canvas sheets.

The advent of snow meant that I would stay over in hospital accommodation, as I often did now, preferring this place, and being close to Kress. Here I felt unreachable, far from phone calls from Louie and from direct reminders of Rachel and the past. In one sense I had been preparing for years to exist in this place, this vacuum with no love. I remember in particular that night, lying in bed, fingering the ridged, fresh scars on my chest and belly, listening to reports on the radio in my little hospital room that at first were confused, telling of a fire, a crash, a plane down in the border town of Lockerbie, the enormity of it being grasped slowly through the night. When I eventually slept I dreamt of falling into a limitless abyss.

★

Kress had been in the blocks eight months by the time I got near him. He came into the assessment unit, on the B block wards that were called Brunel, Beatty and Burton. Kress came into Brunel or B3, an admission ward situated on the third floor top of the block for higher security. The ward looked like a long corridor with a projecting nursing station at the centre. Here a close eye was kept on the new admissions, who were encouraged to keep to their cells until staff got to know their propensities.

Kress was happy enough in his narrow room where he could touch each wall with his outstretched arms. He had few possessions: some cheap clothes, a few food items from the hospital shop and a picture he had torn out of a magazine that he had found on the day unit. It showed a photograph of a sailing ship at sea under full rig. His transient psychosis had settled with chlorpromazine. The tablets had also made him lethargic and his body had begun to grow heavy. In association time he sat smoking in the day room. Other patients gathered near the wall-mounted cigarette lighters; personal lighters were forbidden. They clustered together there like pigeons at a feeding tray. Lying through the endless days and nights on his bed, listening to the constant tread and key-chink of the warders outside, he began to croon to himself. The medication made him dribble, stiffened his arms and made them jerk involuntarily, yet he was content on his own, with only his body to explore. His belly burned hot from the hospital fare, his farts delighted him and he revelled in his homely, personal stench. He would spend hours gazing at the crawling shadows on his ceiling, his tongue flicking around his palate, exploring the mossed relics of his crumbling dentition, sniffing his armpits, or picking at his toe nails that grew with incredible vigour and independence, curling and digging into the skin of his toes. Yet Kress himself remaining immured, static, barely moving.

He had been subjected to all the filtration processes of entry into High Secure, being first gone over by security in a holding cell with hand-held detectors and his few possessions screened. All his clothes were taken away, scanned, laundered and returned. Having made sure that he had not ingested anything metallic, he was led down the corridors to Brunel, in a paper boiler suit with a posse of staff on each side of him. He was told his rights, had a visit from the chaplain, received a talk from security and had his photo taken by a large format camera. His tattoos and scars were also recorded. They found and noted an image of an infant with a halo and underneath the name *"Annie"* on his left arm and the spider web inked onto his right elbow. He was no stranger to institutional regimes and he settled to the numbing hospital routine, morning tea, med rounds, breakfast, staff utensil count, dead time, the sun moving beyond dusty barred windows, the TV in a puddle of blue colour high on a wall, sound turned down low, bleached faces staring up at it from worn chairs in the day room.

Kress would gaze at the other patients to pass the time. He would watch as patients roared and kicked at staff who would swiftly overpower them, sometimes using the 444 security emergency squad with shields and helmets who would drag the patient to the muffled seclusion rooms where they would exist for hours or days, then cautiously be let out again on four man unlock, moving unsteadily back down the corridors. Kress had few diversions, only the weekly ward quiz, run by a female OT, her rump rippling under a blue nylon trouser suit, while twenty-four pairs of sex-hungry eyes burned her up with their combined gaze. There was also the weekly ward outing down the corridor block to the shop where he could buy small necessities with an allowance token. Here there were remembered bright colours and familiar names from the outside world to be seen in the front covers of the magazines, and the familiar packaging of Wills Gold Flake, Park Drive, Maltesers and red and white tubes of Colgate toothpaste.

My remit did not include Brunel, yet I had to see him and in my first month in the hospital I invented a research project where I proposed to screen assessment patients for suitability for psychological work. Lax, burned out Dr Colt, my supervisor, turned over my memorandum proposal and growled, "Alright laddie, if you haven't got enough work to do already, go ahead."

My first step was to obtain access to his files. This was easy, for copies of all current documents went to Medical Records. Hospital files at that time usually contained a rich haul of depositions, evidential letters, trial reports, prosecution correspondence, details of next-of-kin as well as the usual clinical reports of my colleagues. I experienced an expectant thrill as an indifferent secretary handed me Kress's already heavy file, which I carried up to a reading cubicle. It contained the expected array of information and a few laconic notes from Dr Virdee, the consultant on Burnet.

It seems that Kress was born in Canvey Island in 1949. There was a family history of poverty, alcoholism and subnormality. *"Heavy genetic loading,"* commented Dr Virdee in slanting, green ink on the margin of a psychology report. Kress was one of two siblings living with his parents in a council bungalow on the low-lying island. Their cluster of council houses looked on to an earth sea wall, then the estuary mudflats, and beyond that the North Sea. His father was a seasonal worker in the fairgrounds, who also helped run the Punch and Judy stall and deckchair concession along the front. Just after midnight on the 1st February 1953, a tidal surge, driven by a high wind, topped and breached the sea wall and torrented down Anderson Crescent, flooding the Kress home and killing sixty of their neighbours. His father got the family out onto the roof where they huddled together in their night clothes. The army came in three ton Bedfords through the brown wash at dawn to rescue them, but Kress's sister Annie was by then dead in her pyjamas, killed by the cold. Kress had little memory of it all. The family were rehoused on the mainland, then settled back home six months later when the sea wall had been raised. Back in the repaired house, his mother sunk into a depression and his father took to drink. She eventually killed herself by putting her head in the gas oven after wrapping up his school sandwiches for the following day.

Nine year old Kress and father lived on together in the house. Kress became difficult at school, lagging in his lessons and some-times being sent home for punching the other children. He developed a morbid fascination with the memory of his dead sister, confiding in her guiding spirit which followed him protectively. He was a dim boy who could barely read, doing well only at the Canvey Island Boys and Amateur Boxing Club. Eventually the authorities noticed his failure to thrive and he was taken into care for a year in Rochford. He enjoyed the ordered regime there, but deteriorated again when he was returned home at the age of fifteen. The follow-ing year, he set the entrance arcade of the island's miniature cinema alight with a milk bottle of petrol siphoned from his father's car. Kress had been taunted by some other boys there because he would not dare ask a girl to hold his hand in the back row. His revenge was to set the place alight, dancing with sexual glee as the island's firemen struggled to put out the flames with their antiquated appliances.

He was caught and sent to High Secure, which was then called "Special Hospital", at Ashworth Adolescent Unit near Liverpool. He was discharged at the age of twenty-two, angry and drifting, and soon committed other offences: assaults, drunkenness and an attack on a woman whom he apparently just picked up in the street in a sort of bear hug. Perhaps this was a half-hearted attempt to abduct her — something that Beekeeper enquiry had not managed to discover. Later he was sacked as a labourer on a building site because he had been found to have constructed a niche, which he had filled with bones and skulls grubbed out from a run-down Victorian cemetery nearby. He had punched the building site foreman when he tried to remove the bones, and was sent to prison again. His disastrous career continued with more prison time, assaults on others and from others, release, then prison again for a lengthy sentence for armed robbery, which was actually a pathetic attempt to hold up a betting shop with a plastic toy Uzi in a paper bag. When released he drifted for six months up to the time of Rachel's disappearance.

He had said nothing about Rachel to the clinical team. He had retracted his admissions to the city CID, saying that it was all a cry for help and he didn't know anything about disappeared women. Disappointed, I waded on through pages of reports. His transient psychosis had been resolved with medication. He had undertaken the Personality Diagnostic Questionnaire, the Hare Psycopathy scale, the Wechler Adult Intelligence Test and other measuring devices. What was revealed, in the flat reductive language of psychiatry and psychology, was that he fell into an abnormal personality syndrome congruent with antisocial personality disorder. His WAIT score indicated that his overall IQ was a shade above learning disability. His psychosis was considered likely to be a transient phenomenon, a decompensation in response to the stress of imprisonment.

The recommendation was of therapy, time, containment, further assessment, and that he be maintained on antipsychotics in case he had a schizophrenic illness. He was detained in the hospital, not due to offences but, because of his mental state and potential for harm.

He was rated a risk to women with an abnormal interest in children and in particular little girls. There was some evidence that he had hung about schools in the past and had tried to speak to children, but he resisted any exploration of this. The notes revealed that CID, from the Beekeeper enquiry, had interviewed him and I was thankful that I had not run into detectives Canter or Hedgepeth in one of the hospital corridors for they might have asked awkward questions as to why I was in this place.

I felt disappointed after so much anticipation of what could have been in the notes. There was no acknowledgement here of how this man's malign presence could have come up against Rachel's track through life, nothing about his thoughts and desires as he bumbled and blundered his dangerous way through the city at night. There had been plenty of serial murderers who were more incompetent than he. And if he had not taken Rachel then why did he claim a hand in her disappearance? I wanted to know all about him before I finally dealt with him. I had a powerful sense of wanting retribution for the distress that he had caused. There was no alternative; I had to see him myself.

I was able to see him some weeks later with the early spring sun burning brightly outside. I walked slowly up the B blocks, preparing myself for the encounter. When I reached Brunel and pressed the air lock buzzer there was no response and I cautiously let myself in using my own keys. No-one was there, none of the 24 patients and no staff. On the empty ward, phones were ringing and cell doors were left ajar. I stood for a moment, dazed by the unexpected emptiness of the place, until I realised that they must have left on the weekly shop visit. I wandered in and out of offices and rooms, noting the mug-strewn staff desks, the jokey messages left on staff lockers, the blue caps hanging in the staff room. The seclusion room was empty, the wadded flooring still bearing the impression of the last occupant. I moved along the corridors until I found Kress's room. There was a stale smell in there, a tumble of bedding, biscuit wrappers, a pair of old stained jeans, and a grey jersey with maroon hoops. I also found a creased picture of a sailing ship sellotaped to the wall. I wondered why it had caught his eye, perhaps a childhood memory of the yachts and barges on Benfleet estuary. As I poked around his room there came to mind a favourite song which Rachel and I used to croon along to —*I wish that I'd sail the darkened seas on a great big clipper ship sailing from this land here to that,* — and I hummed the song once more as I ran my fingers over his things.

A succession of thuds and the clank of magnetic locks heralded the return of the ward and I could hear the patients chattering and laughing, excited by their purchases as they waited for the rub-down search in the air lock. I did not immediately see Kress in the throng but sought out a charge nurse who was surprised to see me on the ward. I told him I needed to interview Kress. He did not question me; he just flicked a look at my ID badge and yelled for Kress up the corridor.

Kress materialised beside me. He appeared taller than I remembered and formed a large dark shape in the corridor. "What's up boss?" he asked in his hoarse voice.

"Doctor wants to see you now." Turning to me, the nurse asked, "Do you want any of us in with you?"

I shook my head. I could handle Kress on my own. The charge nurse unlocked a side room and gestured to Kress to enter by jerking his thumb. He slouched in reluctantly while I took the seat nearest the door.

Kress sat facing me, rubbing his eyes and looking resentfully at his brown paper grocery parcel that he had brought into the room and left on the floor. His hair seemed longer and was now quite bushy. His face had filled out compared to the gaunt, feral features that I had first seen in the courtroom the previous autumn.

It was as if the hospital regime had somehow neutered him and smoothed him out. He looked at me with blank eyes, saying in a deep voice, "What's it about?"

He seemed uneasy under my stare, moving restlessly in his chair. I shuffled the file, kept my eyes on him, registering everything: the blue shell suit with a crew neck, the food stains down the front of it, his canvas shoes with no laces or socks, the hairs that sprouted on his ankles. I noticed his blunt, thick fingers and wide, grooved nails and wondered what those hands had done. All that I was really aware of was an intense, all-consuming hatred for him. He remained sitting in front of me, a bemused, vague figure, his back to the light. He squirmed in his seat, putting one knee down then lifting it up again in a dystonic movement probably caused by his medication. We went through a charade of questioning and I asked him about his offending.

"Look first for the *eschaton*, the known thing," as Dr Colt used to intone in forensic psychotherapy lectures. I asked Kress about his behaviour with women, what he had actually done in detail in his various admitted offences, his attitudes to children and the nature of his contact with them. He answered me guardedly, monosyllabically, with the stock patient responses.

"Don't know boss, what are these questions for?"

"Can't remember, it's me tablets, everything's fuzzy."

"You tell me, it's all there, written dahn already."

I plodded on calmly, asking the same questions over and over, although I could not bear to utter Rachel's name in his presence and referred to her as the "missing teacher".

Suddenly he could not disguise his resentment any longer, "Look... I've done nothing," he interrupted, "made stupid confessions. Don't know why I'm here. I've gone over this already, dozens of times, what do you people expect of me? I don't know anything about the fucking teacher. Never did do. I made it up after I saw the case on telly. It was all so stupid; I just wanted someone to notice me. That's it. Can't you people see that? I can't talk about it any longer."

He snatched up his bag of groceries and half-rose then thought better of it and sat down again.

"I need help, I can't stay here, it's doing me head in, I've done nothing, them CID banged me up." He paused, panting slightly, his divergent gaze encompassing me.

"What are you going to do for me, doctor? You have got to help me. I've done nothing wrong."

I gazed back at him in silence for a moment as I came to my own internal decision, then said, "Oh, I will make recommendations to the hospital that you need help. A move on, I think."

"Thank you, I would be very grateful, doctor. Can I go now?"

"Yes, I have finished with you. You can go," I said, for in truth I did want to be rid of him, after wanting to get up close to him for so long I now felt disgusted with this pitiful man. He began to rush away, grabbing his food parcel, then he hesitated and turned and put out his hand. I pretended to collect my notes and nodded coolly to him for I had no intention of touching him. He retracted his hand and scurried down the corridor. Before leaving the ward, I left a note in the ward notes: *Patient reviewed. Recommend transfer to Eaton Ward for therapeutic regime.*

So began my campaign to transfer Kress to Eaton Ward where I had some control of the territory. I knew that patients could wait years on assessment wards but I thought I knew how to exploit the rivalries and the tender, touchy egos of the medics there. At first I wrote cautious reports recommending transfer, then I lobbied psychology and the ward managers before turning my attention to the committee that met weekly to decide on the movement of the hospital's patients.

We usually met in a small room dominated by a large oak table, where panel members had to squeeze in with their looped key belts tangling on the high-backed chairs. On one white painted wall there hung a print of the elder Breughel's *Ship of Fools*. The table was heaped with plates bearing sandwiches, canapés and fruit supplied by the canteen. The meeting was chaired by Dr Davidson, the clinical lead for the directorate and an expert on the organic psychoses. An acerbic Scot, he allowed no trace of humour to colour the proceedings and he would turn sharply if Dr Bartram yielded any jovial comments. Bartram was usually there, lounging back in his chair, unselfconsciously grabbing at the sandwiches, dropping crumbs down his bow-tied shirt front, or tugging at his sideburns in a gesture of frustration when the discussion irritated him.

Other consultants came to this meeting, one or two like Bartram with some commitment to the smooth running of the hospital, some absorbed in parochial concerns, yet others on the edge of their competence, struggling to survive. Tina Reed was there as ever, dressed entirely in black, with her kohl-rimmed eyes blinking nervously behind fashion glasses. Loud, opinionated, elegant Virdee, perching alertly at the end of the table, also contended with the others. Psychology was usually represented by Irina Starsha but her chair was empty because clinical matters came first for her and she was often late or absent for these meetings. Cobb, the head nurse, occupied a corner chair, always uncomfortable among the doctors. He would come to the meeting already armed with the occult power of the nursing view of how things should be arranged, hatched in the smoky review rooms with other ward managers. Lastly there was me representing day services and psychological therapies. I had worked my way onto this committee over the months despite my comparatively low level of seniority. I qualified for my place there by my apparent enthusiasm for the job, for my colleagues thought that theirs was only a nominal presence as they considered that most decisions had been carved up already between the medics and the nurses.

Davidson called the meeting to order and the scatter of conversation hushed. He worked through the previous minutes with pedantic thoroughness and distributed the papers containing the current bed state. I sought out Kress' name on the Brunel Ward list; an assessment and high dependency ward which decanted patients into my own clinical area of Eaton Ward. Patients moved between wards like a game of snakes and ladders played by the clinicians, and this committee confirmed those promoted up to rehab or going down to high dependency and assessment. Ward movement was slow as usually only death or transfer would allow the movement of patients within the log-jammed wards and barely ten patients a year trickled out as discharges to medium secure facilities in other parts of the country.

Bartram commented, waving a sandwich in one hand, "Well at last we have a little movement in our area. We transferred one patient to Dove last week because of concerns about security after one patient attacked another. Odd business, we may have to transfer Hobman too if he proves to be the source of the trouble."

Davidson rustled his documents and reminded the meeting that the first item on the agenda was ward transfers. The names on the page seemed to shimmer under my gaze as I stared down at them. I ringed that of Kress with my pen, circling it darker and darker until it was obliterated. I knew that at least one patient was in front of him; some of them had waited longer than Kress. I knew how long exactly.

Tina favoured Ghedi, a knife killer, a round-faced young Eritrean, usually clad in a white dishdash whom she considered half-cured, and Bartram spoke up for Demetrius Jones, a stately, tall, completely deaf black man who had run amok on a north London street dragging his dying landlady after him by a washing line noose around her neck. Bartram saw his illness as tempered and his patient now ready for a rehabilitation stream, even if it was the dead stream of Eaton Ward. Dr Virdee favoured Kress, it was hard to say why although I had lobbied him and made arguments. Perhaps he wanted me to owe him a favour; or then again, maybe he had simply tired of this inert patient.

Virdee added, "He is compliant with meds, we have stabilised his psychotic symptoms. He will begin to regress if he remains any further on our, let's say, turbulent ward."

I was reluctant to show my hand too readily but as Bartram began to launch into a further appeal for the committee to consider Demetrius Jones I leaned forward and added, "and this man Kress is most suitable for the therapeutic pathways on Eaton Ward in particular." I spoke clearly, forcefully even. Bartram looked surprised.

"Pathways?" said Bartram "Is this the road less travelled?" he boomed.

"We should fit patients to the therapies that we have available for them rather than shifting them to wherever it is expedient to house them," I responded and indicated the offending behaviour groups that I ran with a psychology assistant on Eaton Ward. There was a brief silence in the meeting since overt conflict tended to be avoided. Bartram seemed to divine that he had been outmanoeuvred in some way and cast a puzzled look in my direction.

Dr Davidson said, "It looks like Kress has several votes," and Bartram responded with a shrug of resignation.

"Well it seems that you have taken the interests of this patient to your heart, Jack," he said, "however it is I who will have to take responsibility for him on Eaton."

Bartram looked round the room, then said, "Alright, I will take the recommendation. Kress will be the next to transfer to Eaton." He glanced across at me with a tight little smile as we broke up and squeezed out from around the large meeting table.

It was hard to resist doing a fierce little jig of victory in my office later; a war dance, for yes, Kress was coming, at some time, once the hospital had slowly ground out its processes. He was coming to my ground on Eaton Ward.

Heinie was given me as a case during my first weeks in the hospital; or rather he seemed to pick me out, in a way. He was Heinrich Grau, the longest-term patient on Eaton Ward. A man in his forties but looking older, with the appearance of a hunched, ruffled, elderly vulture. He had a bobbing Adam's apple and pale eyes that sometimes flickered with menace and which, at other times, were filled with a crushed pathos. He would shuffle up to women visitors and follow them, repeating the same things in a high reedy voice: "I am not a sex man. I am not a sex case here. Demons, demons approach me. *Mein* Uncle Heinrich he says '*der ist*'."

Tough-minded staff would brush him off but Heinie had a talent for finding the polite or the soft-hearted and he would batten on them, jabbering a repetitive refrain of German words pronounced with a Wearside inflection. The cynical regular staff would be amused to see him attach himself to the hospital chaplain, or a lady from the patient befriending service. Sometimes when the female visitor would attempt to move away, a timid hand would hold her sleeve, then would grip more and more tightly as she tried to detach herself from him.

I first saw him in a ward review meeting on Eaton in the late spring while waiting for Kress to come over to the E blocks. I did not know it then, but my dealings with him were to be prophetic of much that was to take place in the hospital. This particular meeting was chaired by a relief consultant covering for Dr Bartram who was on leave. Once perhaps, she had been a bright-eyed young star of the profession. It was rumoured among the nurses, who usually knew these things, that she had been a Child and Adolescent psychiatrist but had been retrained as Forensic after a clinical disaster. She treated staff and patients alike, with a condescending tone, which I thought probably masked an immense professional disappointment. She took centre stage in the ward review with a pile of notes propped on her lap. A jewelled crucifix on a chain plopped out of her ample décolletage and dangled as she leaned over the notes, and studied the case summaries as each patient rolled in. She did not know the patients at all well and her function was to review medication and deal with crises. However, she could not resist demonstrating her sense of her own forensic acuity and clinical skills with each patient that presented themselves.

Heinie was called down the corridor when his turn for review came. He sidled in, bobbed and curtseyed in a jerky motion to the gathered ring of seated staff. The well-spoken, modulated voice of the consultant bid Heinie to sit and he did so, glancing around the room with his ears turning this way and that. I thought that he must have attended many hundreds of such reviews down the long reach of his admission here.

The consultant leaned forward and said in an encouraging voice, "Tell us how you are. Tell us how you are feeling Heinrich."

Heinie looked at her with calculating eyes, then he yawned widely showing two blackened tusks. He shut his mouth again with a snap and put a shaky nicotine-stained finger to his lips to signal that he would not speak. A staff nurse in the meeting sighed impatiently and began to interject but the consultant signalled him not to interrupt.

"I am told that you speak German, Heinrich," she continued, tapping at the thick file on her lap, "That's very clever. I speak German too. Would you be more comfortable if we spoke in German?"

Heinie regarded her then nodded his head in a quick dipping motion.

"*Jetzt mein lieber Herr, sollen wir uns unterhalten?*" She said invitingly, pronouncing the words in a slow anglicized way.

Heinie stared at her face, then he dropped his gaze to run slowly and frankly over her breasts and thighs. She stirred uncomfortably and visibly attempted to control herself, reaching up a hand to smooth her white collar where it folded over the cardigan.

Heinie made hissing and spluttering noises while his eyes remained steady on the doctor. He then said very clearly and slowly, "*Meine Augen tauschen mich nich. Du bist eine Kartoffel!*"

"She looks like a potato!" whispered one charge nurse to the other and they both snickered. The consultant flushed and banged her notes down onto the table beside her.

"Well, we don't seem to be getting anywhere with this patient. Does the ward have any concerns?" She turned for the first time to the two ward nurses who had been trying not to look at each other. Yes, they said. Heinie had been asking to attend Sunday service again. He had been banned for improper conduct at the service some months previously when he had dropped his trousers as the female chaplain was about to address the congregation. The medic rallied and turned once more to Heinie with a fixed smile on her rubicund lips.

"You have a right to attend church, Heinrich, because spiritual matters are important. They are important to you, aren't they?"

Heinie stared fixedly at the dangling crucifix on her shelf-like bust then, lifted his head to shriek out very loudly and suddenly: "You'd betta fookin believe it miss! I'm a fookin believa I am!" Heinie laughed and laughed to himself until he nearly choked. Then became still and grave again, while the clinical staff tittered behind their upraised notebooks. Heinie the enigma, folded in menace, a man from the kingdom of death, who, in other times, would have been put to death. My quest to grasp the nature of evil began with Heinie, my first charge in the hospital.

I approached him in the ward corridor after the review with the relief consultant.

"Are you a priest? A priest man?" Heinie asked.

"No, a therapist, come to help you, work with you." In that moment I found the man's being intense and overwhelming and I gazed over Heinie's head, as if unwilling to look into the fire.

"Are you shy of me?" came the reedy voice. "Are you shy of me, Father? If you have come to help me then hold my hand." He stretched out his hand, I looked down at it, that thin, trembly hand and for some reason I held his dry claw, then pulled away and agreed to see him weekly. "Yes, I will be seeing you, Father," said Heinie, smiling and backing away, making saluting gestures as he retreated.

As the ensuing weeks passed Heinie stayed with me, clung to me. I grew used to seeing his ruffled hair and stooped shape bobbing down the corridors after me, hearing that insistent shuffling and the high voice calling, "Father, Father!"

The ward staff saw Heinie as a comic figure with his flapping, baggy trousers, always at half mast; his coming to the nurse station door on every hour — wheedling until a staff member would roll a cigarette for him from his allowance — he was not trusted to possess tobacco himself in case he smoked it all at one go, or was bullied out of it by a personality disorder patient. His dependence on staff brought forth scorn, as did his terror of other patients.

"Plankton," one nurse described Heinie to me, alluding to the idea that the hospital was a place where creatures fed on each other. Staff were amused when Heinie was once found in the latrine naked, standing with arms spread out as if crucified while Padraig's stubbly head moved over his chest and loins. What pact had been made between them? None could tell, the intensely paranoid Padraig spitting venom and unease and Heinie, that puppet man, a ventriloquist's dummy with a heart of menace. In the notes the staff nurse on duty carefully wrote : "*21.19 hrs. Patient Field found sucking on Patient Grau's nips in main corridor latrine. Both patients advised against such activity.*"

Heinie drank vast amounts of water as many of the long term ones did. They crouched at the taps, in wash rooms and latrines, gulping down load upon load of water, until the salts began to leach from the body, and brain, and the mind spiralled more crazily than ever. The clinical term was polydipsia and it sent the mad ones madder till they had to be banned from going to the wash rooms unattended, but they always got at water somehow as even the hospital could not deny them that. They could be recognised as water drinkers from the way that they reeled, wheezing and gasping with fused eyes, spinning down the ward corridors in a delirium.

It was chiefly in the treatment rooms, away from the ward, that I saw Heinie as that year passed into summer. He would be taken down with two escorts, turning right down the great central corridor of the blocks, past the workshops. Then pausing at each unlock at the large wooden doors that guarded the corridor, illuminated by the light falling from ceiling port holes. Heinie would stand during the unlock procedure, a slight figure, murmuring to himself or pressing his face to the small barred windows to look into the neatly grassed enclosures, which occasionally sprang to view along the corridor. On they would go, with the escorts' keys clinking in their pouches, on and past the giant kitchens where the rattling trolleys were being loaded for lunch. I would imagine Heinie and the escorts progressing nearer and nearer as I sat waiting in the treatment room. The perspex entrance door was partially covered by a blind but was clear at the bottom so that one could see the boots of the escort arriving with Heinie's shuffling feet between them, wearing trainers without laces. The escorts would sit in the waiting room on easy chairs, their radios squawking from time to time. The walls were covered by patients' art work taken from occupational therapy classes. One picture would often engage Heinie's attention and he would gaze up at it as he sat waiting. It was a poster-sized naïve painting, unsigned, in water colours, representing Christ's face in outline, crowned with thorns, looking up to a dove shape in the sky, with sketched puffball clouds and the wobbly words "*the abode of the heavenly spirit*" written at the top. Christ's face was covered with blue fingerprinted blobs representing tears streaming down and gathering into a blue puddle at the bottom of the picture.

Heinie would drag his eyes from it when I emerged from the treatment room announcing, "It's time for your session," then he would meekly shuffle in and the escorts would reach for the magazines heaped on the low table in front of them.

Those sessions! Initially Heinie would face me alertly and would greet me, "Hello, Father," or sometimes "Hello, Father O'Shaunessey," perhaps after some long forgotten hospital padre.

Sometimes I would insist on Heinie calling me by my correct name. He would repeat it slowly and thickly like a foreign word but it would usually slip from him. I had become ineluctably, "Father", *vater*, priest and confessor who came robed in darkness with unknown purpose to Heinie. What had he to offer his therapist in return? Only his pathos, his body, his antics, or his silence. What in turn did I want of him? The hospital wanted a psychological program for even the most institutionalised. I recalled Dr Colt, on the podium in the forensic psychotherapy lectures, speaking of, "the pathogenic secret". Its power to hold the patient in its thrall. The secret that must be worked through, brought to consciousness and by that means draw the sting and dangerousness of the aggression that has arisen in defence of that secret. At that early time in the hospital I had not entirely brought to mind what I wanted from Heinie. Perhaps I was practising for my encounters with Kress. It was enough to be there with him in front of me and, initially, I was strangely thrilled to have my first patient there. A man who had preyed on women and tried to take them. I wanted to follow the secret route that had led Heinie to abduct, hurt and kill, to understand his phantasy, the unconscious idea that led him to atrocity.

Week by week Heinie sat there, often turning and twisting his head, his ears translucent in the light through the barred window, turning to examine a paint blob on the wall by his chair, wordlessly pointing at it or looking at me with a grotesque flirtatiousness. I plodded on the surface of speech. It was hard to determine what Heinie was conveying to me. He had found his own language, sometimes speaking in the dialect of his County Durham childhood, sometimes in mangled German, or in neologisms of his own devising.

"*Mein* uncle Heinrich," he would repeat, "says '*der ist*'."

When asked, "what do you mean by '*der ist*'?" Heinie would look perplexed, shaking his head and repeating "*der ist*", "the is", again and again to himself in a scratchy murmur. Sometimes when pressed by me to explain something he would stiffen in his chair and wave a shaky finger at me saying, "*Der Man den ich gesehen habe*", "that man that I saw", as if pointing out to me that I was committing the sin of trying to be objective. For in Heinie's world there was no objectivity, only process, a perception of the world through the medium of his sadistic consciousness. Heinie was also comfortable in the long silences, where we would sit, unmoving, unspeaking. His gaze would be turned inwards, veiled, while the sounds of hospital mowers reached us, distant calls, booming doors from the upper blocks or a collared dove chirring its song from outside. It used to sound to me as if it was insistently calling "*Who? Who are you?*"

Hours and weeks passed, the sessions dragged and began to turn on a spindle of pain where Heinie unwound his slow, stumbling syntax of halting, barbed words interspersed by long silences. During these interminable sessions, unbidden images of my past life, of Rachel and of Louie, and all my losses flared and beckoned in my head.

Heinie seemed to enjoy the weekly trip through the blocks to the therapy sessions until the fifth week, when young swifts went shrieking around the blocks, and, in the July heat, patients dangled their arms through the window bars of the upper blocks. Heinie might have felt comfortable coming along to see me, but I had begun to stoke a rage against him. In one summer session, feeling a little vengeful at sitting there so painfully with this man, I pressed Heinie, preventing him from lapsing into silence. I made overt interpretations about his silence — suggesting that Heinie was angry with me and still angry with women after he had begun to whine that he was "not a sex case, not a sex man." In therapeutic terms it could be seen as a helpful challenge, prompting an arousal in the patient so that he could enact his central conflicts, but in reality it was prompted by a desire to provoke and punish him. I think now Heinie realised this at some level. He started to sigh to himself, great gusty sighs and I said, "I think you are sighing because you want me to feel sorry for you." Heinie looked at me for a moment, then pointed to a distinct scar on his temple. I asked him what that was and he replied speaking clearly for once, "Staff in Dove washrooms years ago, they held me head with wet towels squeezing it by twisting them towels then rammed me head agin the door handle." His face squirmed with self pity, his fingers rubbing at the star-shaped scar and tears glinted on his lined cheek. I felt unmoved by the pathos. It made me feel even angrier with him and I continued to press him, "You have been treated badly, but you have also wanted to hurt others to make yourself feel better. That is why you killed Margaret Maywood isn't it?"

Heinie looked shocked and uncharacteristically intent. His eyes flickered briefly with menace, but they clouded over again. He whimpered again, "*Mir ist kald,*" "I'm cold", while rocking in his chair his arms crossed over his thin chest.

"That is correct, isn't it Heinrich? You have wanted to hurt and kill to get your own back for all the bad feelings that you have had, that is why you killed Margaret and attacked those others. And you still feel like that, don't you?" Heinie did not answer, but sat looking down, breathing heavily. After a long pause his breathing stilled and the pathos dropped away. He stood up and said, "Why did I kill that Margaret? Ask me ma." He then turned and rapped on the door for the escorts to take him down the blocks.

In July sunshine, I drove a hundred miles north east on roads not built when Heinie had come to the hospital, to County Durham and the valley of the Wear. Moon daisies flared on the banks of the motorway and kestrels hovered above the seeding grasses of the verges as I drove mechanically, turning over Heinie's story and thinking of the live past coiling below the surface of the present. I came to the place mid morning in hazy sunshine. The traffic bunched on the broad motorway behind a white prison van, probably a transport going to Durham gaol. I cruised behind it before taking the turn-off.

The Wear glittered in its stony bed as I approached the town through a litter of estates built around the modest Victorian core. I thought of Heinie's victim, Margaret Maywood, aged twenty-three, returning home in 1973, back from the West Country where she had kicked over the traces with a man, back home but heavily pregnant and alone. I stopped the car and got out. It was a quiet place with half-empty, rain-washed car parks waiting for market day. I walked up the high street past the red-liveried frontage of a pub called *The Lambton Worm* towards my place of rendezvous.

The flat-toned clock of St Mary Cuthbert tolled out midday as I sat in the Washington Tea Rooms, looking out on the high street, hemmed in by stripped pine tables with their paper doilies and folded paper napkins. I had looked distractedly at brochures, articles on folklore and flyers about local walks and activities of interest while waiting for Mrs Grau, who had consented to meet me here not wanting to see me at home for fear of neighbours and of the elders at Kingdom Hall.

She came exactly on time and gravely shook my hand. She was slightly bowed, but still a stately woman with newly permed, grey hair. Seventy-eight years old, in a tan pleated skirt and cashmere cardigan. She wore a large pearl-bordered intaglio broach and a wedding ring held on a gold chain around her neck. I looked into her bewildered English face, seeing Heinie's domed forehead and prominent eyes there as she stared back at me. She had spoken to me on the phone a week before, following receipt of a delicately worded letter requesting information. She had not had contact with the hospital for many years. She had tried to see Heinrich ten years previously but he had said such terrible things to her when she had tried to visit, so upsetting. Her voice wavered on the phone and she spoke of that scar on his temple and the humiliation of the searches. She had consented to see me, to talk about the past and I had felt guilty, not wanting to open wounds. But she had sounded grateful to talk to someone about it all.

115

Thus, Mrs Grau sat down with me at the tearooms and I rose to buy her a hot drink, clumsily moving among the clutter of chairs. We then huddled over the small table, as if conspiratorial, our drinks untasted. Mrs Grau told her story simply and steadily with few interjections from me. At the end she departed with a cool hand-shake. I watched her through the café window as she threaded her way through the straggle of shoppers.

Walking back to my car as the day darkened, I retraced Heinie's story. First, as in every human story there were the parents: Ada

Hinchcliffe as she once was, from Houghton a few miles upstream on the Wear. She became a land army girl in 1945, very pretty in brown britches and a wide-brimmed felt hat, working on local farms while the men were away. Then the denazified Germans began to appear. One was a personable, handsome former Oberleutnant Grau of the Luftwaffe, a co-pilot on a Heinkel bomber shot down over England early in the war: Oskar Grau, his last name meaning "grey", but with a root word tokening "dread" in German, *sich grauen vor*, to have a horror of. She fell in love with him, the clever, quiet German, an engineer and good at mending the old Massey Ferguson tractor that pulled the harrow and the trailer. Heinie had few possessions on arrival

at the hospital apart from two worn photos which were kept in a side docket of his ward file. I removed them as I thought that no-one else would appreciate them. The pictures were of his parents in wartime showing his mother smiling, unaware of the future, and of his father in uniform reminding me of Heinie in the neurotic sideways tilt of his body and the thin, clenched hands by his sides.

Mrs Grau showed great independence of mind when faced with the collective disapproval of her family and community. The couple got engaged, married in 1947, and settled locally while his former comrades were repatriated. Oskar was happy to build a new life since his Rhineland hometown was bombed out. He found work in a garage as a motor engineer, retaining his accent although with a Wearside inflection in the vowels. Mrs Grau spoke of his love of good manners and of correct conduct.

"Yes we were happy," she said in response to my questioning. "Well," she hesitated, "we were happy at first."

Heinrich was born in 1950, an only son, with a German name in a close-knit town with the men just back from the war and everyone still plunged in austerity. They lived in a newly built terrace house in the town and at first all was well. "He was a quiet boy," commented Mrs Grau, and devoted to his father, conscientiously trying to learn German from him early on and asking to go with him to work at the garage. I could see on the reverse of his father's photo that Heinie had proudly written *"Mein Papa"* in childish script. Mrs Grau then described a gradual darkening in their lives: the first difficulties at school, the bullying, the taunting by other pupils about his German father and the war, how one night someone daubed "Heil Hitler" in white letters on their garden shed. Mr Grau was strict at home and insisted on Heinie speaking German but Heinie was a poor pupil, there were tears and punishments and a growing sense of separateness in the boy.

His parents became increasingly involved with the Jehovah's Witnesses when Heinie entered his teenage years. I was not sure how they were recruited, only that Oskar was the first to join. I asked Mrs Grau, but she was uncomfortable with the questions as it was against the rules of the church to discuss its business with non-Witnesses. Oskar Grau the outsider, the foreigner, had sought the fellowship of the Witnesses in the early 1960s. The first duty of those joining is to the church and not to his non-Witness spouse and so Ada soon joined her husband in the windowless Kingdom Hall not far from the High Road where I now walked.

The Witnesses were a community of perhaps sixty souls in the local area and the Graus worshipped with them, socialised with them, and were regulated by them. They joined a world where feast days and holidays and birthdays were not celebrated, a world toiling in the "time of the end", where Satan is the invisible ruler and where God is not omnipresent but served by his faithful and discreet servants, the Witnesses.

Oskar Grau grew troubled by his gawky, friendless son and when Heinie finally slipped away from school without qualifications, he arranged for him to work at his garage sweeping up, washing cars and making tea for the mechanics. Heinie proved inattentive and unreliable at work. His mother would beg him to get up in the mornings as his father fumed in the car outside. The apprentices at the garage attempted to chaff with him and play their accustomed pranks, but Heinie would not be drawn.

The garage had to let him go in the end because of his poor work performance. His father did not oppose it, relieved perhaps that his son would no longer contradict his own meticulous approach to work. Thereafter Heinie drifted, taking on odd jobs, the occasional decorating or gardening work for other Witness families, or just spending his days absent from home. "Just walkin' aboot toon," he would tell his parents when they inquired about his disappearances. Despite this failure and in spite of the social revolution of the early 1970s that swept the community around him, Heinie remained externally dutiful and attended Kingdom Hall, especially the Theocratic Ministry School where members practised witnessing to each other. His mother recalled him speaking in particular to the text *Ecclesiastes* xii 1, dressed in a new suit bought for the occasion; "*Remember now thy creator in the days of thy youth while the evil days come not.*"

At some stage Heinie's wandering about the small country town took on a sinister pattern of staring at and stalking girls and young women. We do not know when he began to think obsessively about girls, or how often he rehearsed fantasies of abduction and possession. There were three offences in the year before the killing; they seem to occur suddenly, out of the blue and in close succession. The police at the time could find no preceding evidence of any stalking or Peeping Tom behaviour. I was sure though that Heinie had hunted and wandered and struggled with his rage and desire throughout his miserable adolescence. It is as if, in the early summer of 1973, Heinie suddenly exploded into acting out his desires. What happened in detail is described in the yellowing witness statements and probation reports appended to one of Heinie's bulky hospital files. The first victim was a schoolgirl of sixteen, coming home from school on the bus. She reported a stranger with flap ears who suddenly emerged out of thick shrubbery close to the bus stop. A shiny-faced man who yanked at her arm and tried to drag her into the bushes while the other hand clawed at her pleated school skirt. She screamed and struggled and, as suddenly he was gone, leaving her shocked and flustered.

It happened again two weeks later when another schoolgirl was seized at a bus stop and again an attempt was made to drag her into bushes, but a passer-by shouted a warning and the attacker ran off. More seriously, a few days later an older woman, returning home from the Green Shield shop in town, was grabbed again at a bus stop, her shopping bags dropping and spilling in the path as she was suddenly pulled with a fierce grip on her wrist. A thudding punch to the ribs left her winded and unable to call out. Off-balance and gasping, she tumbled into the lilacs of a civic shrubbery as the attacker, a dark shadow against the sun, crouched above her, clawing at her breasts and under her skirt with sharp-nailed hands. For a while she parried and pushed away his lunging grabs and he would shake her grip off with a twist of his wrist. She rolled out onto a path that went through the shrubby lilacs and he tried to pull her back. She turned onto her belly and reached out, seized a bundle of low branches and hung on as he pulled at her ankles to drag her back in the shadows. She found the voice at last to start screaming. He knelt on her back for a moment then she felt the weight go off and he was away, running, feet slapping in panic flight.

He was caught, of course, so distinctive and alien in this small town. Perhaps one of his schoolmates had responded to his description or neighbours became alarmed by his stare. Anyway, someone called the police after an account of the offences and a photofit, a wraith of Heinie's image, appeared in the local gazette.

He was arrested and his father went with him to the station. Heinie quickly confessed and was charged with indecent assault and went before the magistracy. He received probation in those liberal, oddly innocent times and no one recognised the malevolent potential of the young man. Ada spoke of her shock and alluded covertly

119

to the resulting pressure from the Witnessing society. Heinie was brought to the elders after his court appearance to be reproved by the judicial committee. Ada also spoke of the shame and her incomprehension of his behaviour. Heinie had few explanations; he began to blame being led on by lads, being shown dirty magazines by the garage apprentices. Oskar Grau's suffering was great as he felt the disgrace keenly and perhaps he feared persecution in the community. Heinie was contrite and made promises. He was driven once a week by his father to see Mr Singleton, the probation officer in his Durham office. Singleton's reports survive in the files, in the fading violet typescript of flimsy letter copies, *fundamentally a young man with maturational problems … some strange ideas … a supportive family.* Mr Singleton arranged for Heinie to start a gardening job in the council-run pleasure grounds that skirted The Castle, a Victorian hulk of a building on the outskirts of town. Heinie went to work there, raking leaves, clearing moss, going through a simulacrum of working as a park keeper but alive and alone with the thoughts in his head.

Heinie worked there through the winter and into the spring of 1974, dropped off each day by his father who called for him again in the evening. His supervisor also kept an eye on him and his hours were strictly regulated, although as spring swelled so did Heinie's appetite and rage. Margaret Maywood had returned to the town the previous year having been reproved for her unchastity in running away with a young man, but she had been accepted back into the Witnessing community. She had given birth to baby Elisabeth and had stayed with her parents for a while. Showing a streak of independence, she had newly set herself up in a ground floor flat in a rented house at 19 Poulson Street. Heinie had gone to the same school as her and sometimes saw her in the evenings at Ministry School when texts were discussed and there were readings. She sometimes took baby Elisabeth with her and the congregation were helping her settle into her new flat. The Witnesses were good with things like that.

And so, one day Heinie pestered Margaret to let him help her with moving furniture to her new place and bringing down household items stored in the annexe to Kingdom Hall. Apparently Margaret reluctantly agreed saying, "Yes, tomorrow night after Book Study at the Hall." Heinie waited through that next day, a Tuesday, filled with blindingly simple desire then in the early evening he loitered in the street outside her place. I also stood at No 19, a few hundred yards from Kingdom Hall and behind the backyard of *The Lambton Worm* pub, from where I could hear bottle crates being stacked. I imagined Heinie there waiting, perhaps shrinking from the footsteps of passers-by and hearing the music and voices and clatter from the pub. Now, as I looked at Margaret's house in the blank daylight, it seemed much as it would have been in 1974, with its worn, red brick frontage, sparrows rustling in the gutters and a single path leading to the front door. Heinie had walked up this path for his appointment, a knife tucked in his waistband, his hand reaching for the brass, crescent-shaped door knocker.

As to what happened then, we can surmise some things and we know the basic facts. Margaret let him in, babe in arms. He had brought the knife to subdue, not wanting another struggle as with the woman in the shrubbery. Perhaps a deluded part of him believed that he could possess this fallen woman, this unchaste one and that she would gladly give herself to him. What we do know is at one stage she got on her knees to pray because Heinie told the police that she did. But I wondered if when confronted by the raging, desperate Heinie, she had attempted to get him to pray with her to ask for help for himself. Heinie began to slash at her as she knelt, filled with anger and disappointment that he could not penetrate her any other way, not even Margaret the fallen one, tainted by Babylon. Seven wounds were recorded, at least one entering the chest and into the lung. Baby Elisabeth slipped from her mother's arms and fell to the floor receiving minor injuries. Somehow Margaret got away, opened the front door and fell onto the path in the front garden. Neighbours found her crawling about on the narrow grass lawn.

Heinie remained inside the house for a minute as Margaret was pulled away. She could still speak and warned the neighbours about Heinie. As an ambulance was called, he fled by the back door, leaving baby Elisabeth crying on the blood-spattered hallway floor. He ran away towards the Castle. He crossed the bridge over the Wear, cast the knife into the dark water curling over the stones below, then hid in the undergrowth that surrounded the large building. At some stage he must have heard the ambulance siren wailing down the valley, taking Margaret to Dryburn Hospital in Durham.

In Casualty it was found that Margaret had acute blood loss of fifty per cent, and her haemoglobin levels were critical. Staff set up a plasma rig and they approached her for blood typing. She had remained conscious and firmly told staff that she was a Witness and would receive no blood and no plasma. At that time, faced with acute sudden blood loss, there was little else you could do apart from use a saline drip. It was then not possible to haemodilute or use gelatine solution to increase volume or inspired oxygen concentrations to raise haemoglobin. They hooked her up on saline but it was not enough, as she continued to leak blood from internal injuries. The nurses pleaded with her but in study class the text Genesis IX.3 was well known to her, "*Only ye shall not eat flesh with its life that is, its blood. For your lifeblood I will surely require a reckoning; of every beast I will require it and of man.*"

The Senior House Officer argued with her and rang the Registrar asking if he could treat her under Common Law but no, although pale, sweaty and fading Margaret knew her own mind. It is recorded that she was clearly told that she was going to die unless she accepted blood and she understood that but she held fast to the last. Despite her sins the Witnesses had taken her back and she clung to that loyalty. Margaret, alone in Casualty on that May night, stood by the promise in *Acts of the Apostles* so often gone over in Book Study evenings, Chapter XV.Verse 28 where St Paul instructed, "*that you abstain from that which is sacrificed to idols and from blood and from what is strangled and from unchastity. If you keep yourself from these, you will do well, farewell.*"

Farewell indeed Margaret. She died within the hour.

News reached the Graus quickly that night. Heinie had been seen talking to Margaret and she had named him while waiting for the ambulance. Their world crumbling, they waited with a police car outside their door until acting on a hunch, at midnight Oskar went with the police to the Castle grounds on Lumley Hill and they cruised the sweeping park roads until they saw Heinie huddled under some lime trees. Heinie listlessly allowed himself to be delivered to the brightly-lit interrogation rooms in the police station where suddenly eager to please, he confessed readily saying that he wanted sex from Margaret but not to harm her, saying that he had struck out at her in a panic. He was charged with murder, later emended to manslaughter, and remanded to Durham prison.

The Witnesses reeled under the publicity but comforted each other as best they could. Margaret was buried and baby Elisabeth cared for by her grandparents. Heinie was not thought mad by the court. His father attended the trial but Ada could not bear to see her son in the dock. He wore the same Sunday suit that he had put on for delivering a talk at Kingdom Hall five months previously. The defence plea was not guilty in that there was a new intervening act, *novus actus interveniones*, between the wounding and the death, namely Margaret's refusal to take blood, hence bringing about her own death. The plea brought forth a judgement that would stand in criminal law, Regina versus Grau. It has been taught to generations of lawyers ever since. The judgement holds to the principle that you take your victim as you find them. This meant that in making Margaret his victim Heinie took on not just the physical woman but her religious beliefs also. This principle in law is also called the "thin skull rule", whereby a light blow administered to the head which kills a thin-skulled victim still results in a death accountable in law. Heinie's action led to a chain of causation and that made him guilty of the killing. Heinie was found guilty and sentenced to life. He went to prison and quickly deteriorated. He heard voices, felt persecuted by demons and was transferred to the hospital. The Witnesses closed ranks. The Graus continued to worship alongside Margaret's parents. Heinie was formally disfellowshipped from the Witnesses, irrevocably cast out from the company of the saved. Oskar's health deteriorated with cardiac problems, aggravated by stress and worry and he was dead within ten years. Heinie retreated into madness and remained sealed in the hospital. Baby Elisabeth grew up in the Witnessing tradition, married and eventually moved away.

On my way out of town, I stood on Lumley Hill below the Castle that had now been turned into a hotel with a sign saying "*Private Road — Residents Only*". I walked under the limes thinking of Heinie's last night there, whispering to himself, "*der ist, der ist*" and I looked out over to the huddled town to the east, circled by the glinting river.

That night, driving back, following the stream of tail lights on the motorway, I turned over all the reasons that could be given for what had happened. It was not just the schizophrenia burning in Heinie's brain, nor the family's alienation from the community, nor yet the obduracy of the Witnesses conflicting with the turbulent *zeitgeist*. Nor could it be only Heinie's shock at realising his own ugliness as the world saw it, and which made women shun him. His malignant, dazed, sadistic personality seems to have just sprung into obdurate being without explanation. I had a feeling that, although Heinie may have been immersed in his dream of evil and moving alone in the world on his lethal purposes, somehow we were also all there, implicated, sharing and involved in it all. It was if he had filled a void — that place that we flinch from in all but our most unconscious thoughts and we have a strange responsibility for that state of affairs.

It seemed to me then that my journey could bring no explanation, only the husk of truth. For some reason I thought of the pamphlet I picked up in the Washington Tea Rooms, an account of the legend of the Lambton Worm, a ballad and Tyneside myth. "Whisht lads haad yer gobs An aa'll tell yer boot the worm," runs the ballad and the story goes thus: the young knight John Lambton, fished in the Wear one day while escaping from church attendance. He found an ugly, worm-like, writhing creature caught on his hook and thought he saw a reflection of himself in its glaring, goggling eyes. He threw the thing away down a well and tried to forget about it but, filled with obscure regret, he went on a long penance to the Holy Land. While he was away the worm grew and grew to form a giant creature that terrorised the neighbourhood, eating cattle and consuming children. It slept on Lumley Hill and its tail grew so large that it lapped the crest of Penshawe Hill. News reached the knight about the depredations of the great serpent-like creature that he had unwittingly unleashed and he returned home to consult a sibyl on how to defeat it. She told him that he must stand in the Wear in armour covered with blades of steel and wait for the "worm" to seek him out and destroy itself. Afterwards he was to kill the first living thing he saw otherwise a curse would fall on him and his family. Accordingly, the knight constructed a suit of armour covered in blades and stood waist deep in the river, warning his family to stay away. He also arranged for his most faithful dog to be unleashed. The worm sniffed him out, struck and writhed around him. There was an almighty struggle, but in the end it mortally slashed itself on the armoured blades until it weakened and dissolved, piece by piece and was carried off in the current away to the sea. Exhausted but victorious, the knight climbed out of the river to see his jubilant father coming to greet him. His father had forgotten to unleash the dog in his excitement. He flinched from striking at his father and instead severed the head of his faithful dog when he got home. Thus, although the worm had been destroyed, the Lambtons lived on to carry a terrible curse to nine generations for disobeying the sibyl's instructions.

On the following day I returned to the hospital making my way through the bustle of Eaton Ward at the beginning of the morning shift. I was eager to see Heinie, to somehow communicate with him, feeling that in some way I now shared something with him. I saw him standing at the ward office door, holding a red plastic mug in his shaky hand. Heinie saw me and pulled at his fringe, giving a mock tug of his forelock. I gestured for him to stand in the ward review room, which had been left unlocked ready for the morning reviews. I told him that I had seen his mother the day before and that she sent her love and greetings. I saw a hardness creep over Heinie's face. He swayed on his feet, gave an inward whistle of breath then exhaled, puffing a stale blast of tobacco-sour breath into my face.

"So you have been to see my Ma," he said looking at me as if I was a betrayer. He swayed again very close to me then went on, "I am brave, me. I have the feet and hooves of an antelope, I am a beast me. Ma she wants to know me as I once was, *verstehen*? Not as I am." He stared at me with his pebbly, grey eyes, then flicked out a hand and brushed it palm downwards over the hairs on my forearm where I had rolled up my sleeve. I recoiled from the intimate gesture and took a step back. Heinie continued to stare at me, "I'm not going to see you no more mister. I'm not goin' down the block corridor to see you no more, not fer all Christ's tears," he said and turned and moved away as the nursing auxiliary shouted, "Hot water up!" Heinie shuffled after him waving his mug, calling out, "Coming boss." He declined to attend that week's therapy session and thereafter all appointments with me, and when he encountered

125

me in the corridors or review rooms he would back away from me, placing a forefinger to his lips to signify muteness.

"What have you done to Heinrich, Jack?" asked Dr Bartram after observing one such episode. I shook my head, not answering, thinking of the Lambton Worm beating itself out on the cursed knight, writhing, severing and erasing itself on the current and being swept away.

★

The ambulance had come from the county hospital at Redford, crossing the seven miles of autumnal countryside on a dim, rain-swept, late afternoon. Its blue light flickered along the bare ploughed land and the two-tone siren raised a few lapwing and rooks to flutter up from the field margins. They turned the siren off when they reached the hospital and just rolled over the speed bumps, the blue light flickering silently over the lodge house frontage. There was no need for hurry and bustle. They had been called automatically by security response but Kress was long dead, hanging on a knotted lace in his room on Eaton Ward.

It had been JJ of all people who had found him, hooded, muffled JJ, who had sensed something as staff busied themselves with clearing away ward tea and preparing the meds trolley. It was shift handover, the most popular time for suicides in the hospital, when there was plenty of movement and distractions on the ward. JJ had taken off the towel that usually was draped over his head and stumped down the corridor and peered through the half-open door of the cell; he had blundered to the nursing station, mouthing and pointing, until staff followed him and began to run. JJ had then slumped back in his chair at the end of the corridor as staff rushed in and out of Kress' cell and called 444. He gave up waiting to be attended to by staff and flopped his towel over his own face, grumbling and growling to himself as the ward teemed around him like an upended hive.

When staff had got to Kress's cell they found the metal door ajar, and the room seemingly empty with a thin, late afternoon light falling from the barred window onto an unmade bed and the crumpled picture of a clipper ship taped to the wall. A red and white football shirt was thrown over the end of the bed, and there was a

126

sealed meal tray with its plastic cover on the low bedside table. Kress was a shape in the corner, out of the line of sight of the door. The toes flexed downwards, one sock half off revealing a darkened sole. A pool of piss formed on the red floor tiles and a baggy leg of the tracksuit was soaked. The head was a tousled balloon jammed hard against a cupboard door, the face partly visible, plum-coloured with a noticeable swelling around the mouth.

They grasped him awkwardly by the hips, feet slipping in the mess and lifted him up. A staff nurse found the ligature buried deeply in the neck and slid it up and away. It was a knotted boot lace, slipped through the narrow crack by the door hinge. The knot held the weight despite the design of the cupboard which was aimed at reducing ligation points. Poynton came and a security team crawled over the room, the ambulance was summoned then sent away. Photos were taken and the Redford police informed. LeGryce, the hospital police liaison officer, came and looked the scene over and talked to Poynton. The ward notes were examined. Patients were interviewed but did not report anything significant. Nothing further could be got from JJ who became abusive when they pressed him, and gestured them away. There was suspicion on Hobman, but Andre said they were playing cards together all of the late afternoon. The other patients were jumpy, Grimpen saying "I told yer. I told yer". That night an autopsy was held in the hospital mortuary with Bartram standing uneasily by the table, for hospital rules insisted that the consultant should attend their own patient's post mortem, an old rule designed to ensure that prompt action was taken within the wards should a homicide be detected.

This I learned on the following day at the ward debrief where we all had gathered. Poynton was there, documents in front of him, watching us as we came in. He chaired the meeting as it was seen that clinical matters gave way to security business.

"Let's see what we have," said Poynton, waving the papers and looking round the room. "The PM indicates vagal inhibition as the cause of death. The greater horns of the hyoid bone were fractured by squeezing from the ligature. There were fine scratches on the palms of both hands and excoriations on the dorsal aspect of the left forearm. There was a graze on the left, fifth knuckle and evidence of a broken nail of the third digit of the left hand. These injuries are not really commensurate with defence injuries, and are more likely to be involuntary movements during strangulation by the ligature."

He looked up then announced, "The PM seems to indicate suicide."

"I can attest to that," said Bartram, "I must protest however to the medical committee about this old fashioned rule that consultant attend the post mortem, it's really too much to see one's own patients flayed before one's eyes."

Poynton went on as if Bartram had not spoken, "There was no suicide note and no evidence of a recent deterioration in mental state. No history of deliberate self harm. He had been on the ward only four days and staff here had not got to know him. The only unusual element was his insistence, that afternoon, on taking his dinner in his room. He had not done that before, as far as we are aware, so why then? We can only presume he wanted to be alone or wanted to avoid someone. LeGryce in liaison is satisfied that this is a suicide. I would like to look more closely at the patients to see if someone had a grudge against Kress or if a patient had put pressure on him. It's hard to see why they would hold something against a newcomer. Of course we had the Lazaro incident earlier in the year, Hobman, however, says he knows nothing and has a witness to support him."

"Any thoughts?" said Bartram.

"Is it sexual?" asked Irina the psychologist, looking down, her face hidden by her hair. "Is it auto-asphyxia of some sort?"

"Could be, but there is no history of self-ligation, is there, Mr Keyse?" said Poynton, looking at me. I shook my head.

"I sometimes think we know so little about our patients. 'The heart that lives alone, housed in a dream', eh?" mused Bartram. "I really hope this will not be a case of *hic occultus, occulto occisus est?*" The ward review staff stared back at him warily then after a pause he said with a hint of a smile, "It's a well known epitaph, it means — 'here lies an unknown, killed by an unknown'."

And that was it; the hospital would hold its enquiry, although suicides were quite common, numbering maybe eight a year out of six hundred patients. Hospital social work located Kress's father who was still living on the island. There had been no contact with his son for twenty years. They took him back home to be buried at Canvey cemetery on the higher ground overlooking the Pitsea Marshes and the estuary out to the sea.

And CID and Beekeeper were informed that their former suspect could no longer be interviewed.

A week or so later, I was sitting in my office, writing up notes, when I heard a quick pacing tread on the stairs and the chinking of a key holder. It was Poynton who entered quickly after knocking, his eyes flickering over the things in my office.

"Mr Keyse, do you have a moment?" It was not a request. He perched on the edge of a file cabinet, slightly above me, and folded his thin arms over his starched, white uniform shirt and fixed me with his watery, pale eyes.

"There had been developments with the Kress thing."

"Oh yes?" I replied, keeping my voice low.

Poynton took out a small plastic bag and flopped it onto the desk in front of me. Inside there appeared to be a brown paste-like substance that looked like dried yeast. "We found this in Kress's door lock. It's some sort of home-made glue made of animal fat or suet scraped from dinner plates. Someone poured it in the lock, the key turned a bit but the tongue did not go home. Old Kress was locking himself in but the door was not secure."

Poynton was referring to the patient's own room keys on the treatment wards. Unlike on the assessment wards they could lock themselves in to their own cells for privacy on Eaton. This protected them from the other patients but the staff held master keys that overrode the patient's own cell lock when they required to enter.

Poynton continued, "Kress was new, he probably didn't realise that the lock was not working properly."

"That is interesting. What is the significance of this?" I gestured at the plastic bag.

"And another odd thing," he said, ignoring my question, "the door hinge on the cupboard looks like it's been forced or pried open a little to increase the gap so that a ligature could be inserted. Although, it could have been Kress' weight pulling it out I suppose. Now the PM said suicide, but just supposing there was a very strong man, he could get the noose around the neck, tighten, elicit unconsciousness, then haul him up."

He paused for effect and stared at me. I remained silent. "I'm thinking of Hobman. Nothing happens on that ward which doesn't involve him. I have kept my eye on him since the Lazaro thing. Even though Lazaro is long transferred to the C blocks he is still frightened of returning to Eaton for some reason. You saw Hobman, I believe, just before Kress transferred, did he say anything of interest in that session?"

"No, just routine," I replied. "he expressed his usual delusional ideas about the White Lady and wanted his letters to his sister released by Dr Bartram, the usual stuff."

Poynton leaned forward to pick up the sealed bag on my desk and stood looking at me and then said, "That's all, just thought I'd ask. Can you write it up? Exactly what Hobman said to you that day, and forward the details to me? We are going to transfer him anyway as a security precaution. LeGryce and Redford CID are satisfied, but just thought I'd ask."

He turned as if to go then asked, "Are you settling in alright here? Where was it you came from before us?"

I gave a few anodyne answers and wondered if somehow the Beekeeper team had spoken to Poynton, then I sighed with relief as his footsteps sounded on the stairs as he departed, and I waited for the dull boom and clank of the outer office door closing.

After he had gone I paced my office thinking of the afternoon in the clinical review room ten days before. I had spoken to Hobman as he sat facing me in one of the worn-out easy chairs. He had hunched himself forward, his face in shadow.

I had said to him, "Hobman, can I tell you how you recognise a nonce?"

And I remember him looking at me in a surprised way, with a hint of a smile, his eyes fixed on mine, "How boss? Suppose you tell me."

"By his tattoo, Hobman, his tattoo on his arm, of a little girl dead, with a halo, her name was Annie."

"Is that so?" he said, "And when will I see that tattoo, boss?"

"Soon, very soon, Hobman," I had answered.

PART TWO

2001

Chapter Four
When Black Snow Falls

It had begun with the mundane tasks of a September day, or as mundane as anything could be in that strange place. I had walked with an escort team to the chapel to pick up a patient who was going to a review. I recall looking at my dim reflection in the perspex of the chapel notice board as I leaned against the opposite wall in the corridor. I could just make out my purse-lipped expression, the jaw line melting into middle age. I remember the escorts murmuring to each other, the sound of keys chinking, the hiss and sputter of their radios and the muffled calling and hooting of patients in the nearby hospital swimming pool. Inside, the imam's reedy voice could be heard, calling noonday prayer to bear witness to Mohammed, the messenger of Allah. *"Ash'hadu anna Muhammadar — rasulullaah,"* his voice rising and then falling to a dying cadence. Inside could be heard the rumbling chorus of the worshippers in reply. *Allahu Akbar.*

The escorts made wry faces to each other and looked at their watches as the chanting went on. A smell of chlorine drifted through the bars of the gate that led to the swimming pool area. A group of learning disability patients emerged with their guards from the pool changing rooms. They passed us in silence then started whooping and screaming at each other as they moved away down the blocks. At last the sound of chanting ended in the chapel, the door opened and there was a shuffle of slippers as the Muslim patients emerged. There was Razaq the Somali, a few Mirpuri Pakistanis — mainly honour killers — and some Caribbean converts with small *kufi* prayer caps on the backs of their heads. All were marched off to their wards and the robed imam was taken back to the lodge gate. At the last came Yunus for whom we were waiting.

Yunus was a Turk from Ismir, a pudgy man in shirt sleeves. He was thirty-five years old. His name meant "dolphin" in Turkish. He grinned obsequiously at me with his head tilted to one side.

"They have all arrive-ed, sir?" He asked, anxiously checking that his solicitor and translator had turned up for his annual review.

"Yes, Yunus — all are ready for you," I replied.

His solicitor and translator had indeed arrived, and also representatives from advocacy, security, day services, psychology and Dr Bartram himself. They sat waiting for us, ranked in a circle, in one of the new review rooms off the blocks' corridor. This was the usual style of the hospital now. Patients were given a large forum for reviews although, in reality, the key decisions always fell into the same hands. Bartram chaired the meeting, older now, a little more plump and grey but still with the sartorial flourish of a maroon-coloured bow tie, still making his dry, precise little gestures, adjusting his sleeves fussily and pulling at his grey, lamb chop whiskers. I remembered as I looked at his soft features that he had once told me that he was a vegetarian, "because there is enough blood in my world."

Yunus's dark eyes moved anxiously as he surveyed the assembled clinicians. He held his head slightly to one side for he had developed a torticollis, a wry neck, due to the neck muscles being twisted by the dystonic side effects of medication. He was requesting transfer to a Medium Secure facility in London and believed that he would be granted this despite being advised to the contrary by staff. He also continued to deny his offence in a naïve, dogged, continued protestation.

He had killed a young, sick prostitute in the rooms that he rented with some other migrant workers in Kentish Town five years before. He had picked her up and allowed her to sleep on his bed after using her, and then smothered her as she lay. He carried her to his bathroom, put her in his bath and stabbed her with a kitchen knife. We had no idea why he killed her. He revealed a mass of paranoid beliefs when he was first admitted. His victim had been found in the bath by another lodger. I visualised her floating there in the dark water like Ophelia as I listened to the debate going on around the review room.

"No sir, I did not do that thing," he continued to protest his innocence even during the review.

His solicitor, a sweaty, pale Englishman, tried to intervene and speak for him.

"Under Article Eight of the Human Rights Act, my client has the right to home and family life and we can argue that he should be transferred to the London area so that he can be nearer to friends and family."

As the solicitor continued to plead for his client, Bartram leaned over and whispered to me, "Can't we deport him? Hardly a cockney sparrow is he?"

I smiled grimly, for Bartram had come to recognise that we shared something unspoken between us, a retributive stance towards patients. We listened to the solicitor's presentation, then Yunus gave a long peroration in Turkish about a miscarriage of justice which was translated back by the young interpreter while Yunus continued to interrupt him in English, "You must understand, me, I am a sick man! An innocent man!"

The other representatives of the hospital delivered their reports of progress, some added anodyne comments like a school report that does not want to offend the pupil. Others were more damming. The solicitor fenced and quibbled when clinicians mentioned his client's poor motivation, his denials and his reluctance to engage with therapy. He was going nowhere.

At the close, Bartram addressed the meeting. "I think the clinical team are in agreement." He paused and looked at me, "I think this patient needs to remain on a treatment ward for a further year, he needs to do offence-focused work and to do so in the sustained treatment context of the high secure setting."

I nodded and said, "I must concur."

As this was translated back to him, Yunus began to scream and point at us with his eyes bulging in his contorted, lop-sided face. He shouted in English, "You are oppressing me! You are oppressing me! I should be cared for by men of my faith! It is you who will be punish-ed."

Bartram signalled to the escorts to lead him out, two nurses stepped forward and held him by the wrists ready to arm-lock him but he shuffled out between them, still shouting, "Listen to me, you must listen … this is a wrong … this is a wrong thing!"

I walked back to the office compound after the review along with one of the junior medics, a new registrar, a tall, handsome, woman in her late twenties. She had all the confidence of her training, but she was an innocent in the secure world in which she found herself. I could see that she kept a pack of Silk Cut cigs in her key pouch. I never ceased to wonder at the stress and exposure a woman could feel under the daily stare of the sex offenders although some female staff perhaps enjoyed that *frisson*. Ahead of us, I could see Bartram walking alone with a sheaf of documents under one arm. She asked me about the black prisoners and the growing industry of equality and rights workers, translators and advocates. I told her that nearly thirty per cent of the prisoners could now be identified as being different in ethnicity or culture. My voice betrayed no sense of what I felt about that, for I was a spy in this house and I thought of Bartram saying to me once "You know, Jack, few of us transcend the simple need to belong and to be with our own kind and our prisons and mad houses hold the casualties of our society's wilful dismissal of that fact."

Orange and yellow hawkbit flowers blazed on the lawns in the compounds as we walked, a lone plane droned high in the blue above and flecks of straw from the recently harvested fields clung to the fencing wire. The patients may have changed with the world outside but the staff here had remained much the same. Local men and women made up the bulk of the nursing auxiliaries, Midlands white working folk, fathers and sons, and daughters now also coming to work here. The few foreign nurses never lasted very long here, although Bill Ponds still remained on Eaton. We passed lines of escorted day unit patients returning for their lunches. The canteen now provided vegetarian, halal, kosher and diabetic meals. We went by a group of patients who had been allowed out to sit in the sun next to one of the villas. They had thrown some bread on the grass for the sparrows and were now encouraging the ward cat to catch the birds. This cat was one of the few sanctioned animals in the hospital, apart from the sniffer dogs which were sometimes taken out to check visitors and staff for drugs. The patients fell silent as we passed and the cat crouched with flattened ears and lashing tail. I sensed the patients' eyes probing the outline of the young registrar and they moved their faces in the sunshine as if scenting her sex as she walked along beside me. The sunlight shone through her skirt and her hair gleamed in the sunlight. I imagined them weighing her up as a sexual being and for a moment I too was aware of her legs swishing under the long skirt. Her conversation faltered under the combined impact of their stare and we walked on in silence.

A single leaf fell from the beech tree by the path, spinning down ahead of us. The leaf had come from a tree that had been a sapling when I first came to the hospital, now it stood thirty feet high, its lower branches lopped at the insistence of security.

We arrived at the canteen gate and caught up with Bartram as he fiddled with his keys. "Are you joining us, Jack?" he asked.

I declined his invitation, although we sometimes sat together for meals at work. We had developed a mutual, wary familiarity, a respect for each other that had grown over time. When we ate together we would often talk of forensic history and famous cases but we never mentioned personal matters. Both of us chose to be prisoners here for our own private purposes. Much of the arrogance had gone out of Dr Bartram these last five years after his son's death from meningitis in his first term at university medical school. He came straight back to work after the funeral, seeing patients and chairing clinical meetings as he always did. His bowed shoulders spoke of his grief but few dared ask him about it. When I offered my condolences, I remember him pausing in the corridor and his grey eyes flickering up to meet mine.

"Thank you. There is only the work now, you understand," he had said before tramping away down the corridor, holding his usual bundle of case files.

Bartram went into the staff canteen with his junior. I turned back to the annexe to my second floor offices. I felt restless. Something about Yunus had stirred at feelings that rose like black mud within me. It had been his self-centred rage, his denial of what he had done and his wish to have rights when he had taken everything that was important from someone else. Perhaps it was easier to hate someone so alien and so obdurate. Such feelings were usually dormant in this place now, occasionally flaring up like today, although at some level I was always searching for someone who was responsible.

My fear of discovery had diminished over the years as I had justified to myself that what had happened to Kress had somehow been necessary, a cleansing. I also respected those nobler, caring spirits who worked around me; but I was sure there were other men who worked here for their own reasons and there were some who hid their dislike for the patients more imperfectly than I did.

A light breeze moved through the bars of my office window, stirring the desk papers and front sheets of the case notes lying there. Those clinical notes and legal depositions were often a walk into hell where the victims crowded to me. I still did not know what exactly had happened to Rachel and I did not realise then that it was all soon going to blow wide open. The investigation was no further on and birthday dates and anniversary days came and went, still with nothing known. September days especially reminded me of Rachel and fifteen years had elapsed without news. I kept a folder in my rooms at home about serial predators that had been caught, bodies found, forensic discoveries made and articles about the advent of offender profiling. Rachel was quite gone. She had been declared dead after the required seven years by her sister and a death certificate had been issued.

The original details of the investigation now gathered dust in a folder somewhere in Central Police Station, the reports and the photos by SOCO of her room still preserved. The man with cropped hair in the white tee shirt had never been found, Kress had been ruled out as a suspect, and Jayney Kirkman remained missing. Inspector Bain had retired and new priorities pressed in, controlling Yardie gangs in the city, keeping alert to terrorism and pursuing affirmative action in police recruiting.

My restlessness that day made reading files impossible and I decided to walk the perimeter of the hospital. I went out and through the new gates. Hospital security had been revamped and there were glass sliding doors and sophisticated scanners in the reception area although the same wooden carousels still rotated, bearing bunches of keys that were watched over by leathery old guardians. There had been an expensive complete relock by the Home Office after a set of keys had been taken from an unwary student nurse at a patient dance and not recovered. The new keys gleamed in their serried ranks. New double mesh perimeter wire with concrete aprons and deeper ditches had been sited all around the hospital and smooth round coping topped the walls. Pressure sensors were now placed under the grass margins next to the wire. Cameras swivelled at every corridor and were angled densely above the main entrance. Leaving my keys and relieved to be free of their weight, I went down the lodge house steps, counting them as I went. I struck out west along the staff sports ground where the corner flags tugged in a warm breeze. The old, overgrown staff cricket ground and bowls courts were disused now and adjacent the new, gleaming Personality Disorder Unit loomed over them. I walked briskly around the perimeter of this unit and headed off towards the fields through stands of rustling poplars that I had first seen at the hospital years ago on that September day with Louie.

I cut through a salvage dump for the maintenance gangs, and passed heaps of discarded hospital fittings. Then I was out onto the fields with their margins of red soil framing the wheat stubble. After a while I became conscious of my breathing after the surprising exertion of picking my way down the rutted track. I paused and looked around. Far off on a ridge, a tractor toiled over a field carving a dark brown plough line in the pale stubble. A white spume of gulls writhed in its wake. The path where I was walking was littered with wheat chaff and harvest debris. I resumed my stumbly walk and turned over thoughts of the morning as Meadow Brown butterflies flickered up from the dusty grasses. I remember thinking that I had read somewhere that country folk used to say that butterflies were the spirits of the dead, coming back, signalling, and reminding the living of their presence.

My momentum slowed and I stopped and looked back at the hospital, not really far off but seeming quite distant, the boiler house chimney like a silver pencil, the perimeter wire invisible, and the brown-roofed villas looking like little knots of suburban houses. The silence seemed profound, exaggerated by the discordant song of tree sparrows feeding off the harvest chaff.

I would often think of the victims on walks like this. A host of them unshriven, restless, reproachful, their lives cut short, tainted by those contained over there in that clump of buildings. My life had little else to counter those thoughts. I had some professional satisfactions in a job well done, sometimes just relief at getting through a day. I still dreamt of finding Rachel and of discovering what happened to her; but mostly that urge had ebbed to a dormant ache. Those other victims stood in for Rachel in my mind. She occupied a separate place where I would not allow thoughts of the cruelty and torment she may have suffered to develop. No, those other victims represented that. I found it hard to forget all the details I had gleaned from the files and the confessions of the perpetrators themselves.

They came to me like ghosts, those old ladies found dead with semen in their mouths, the little girl hanging all night in a wood from the bending sycamore branch; the ligature deeply incising the neck, naked apart from one remaining sock and sandal, leaking blood from her cleft. Her killer was caged over there and I passed him every working day. Partners and wives also killed by those close to them, stunned, stabbed, battered, slashed at, often with samurai swords; a weapon for the righteous and the deluded. Whole households burned by arsonists, known and unknown to the victims. Children killed by their parents, like the little girl strangled with flex by her mother who announced in therapy "I didn't want her to be raped like me." Victims in droves. The wounded also, the little boy with his penis severed by his father's cleaver, "because Elijah demands a sacrifice". The child stabbed in the vulva with a biro by the school bus driver, "Mr Billy has gone and poked me," she cried to her teachers. Rape victims, so many, their accounts covering pages of witness statements and their shaky signatures at the foot of every page. The statements often ended with a pitiful inventory of clothing taken from them in evidence: skirts, bras, tights, and shredded knickers, referred to as police exhibits numbers one to infinity. So much taken from them and no note as to how they had fared subsequently, for the rights of the perpetrator had primacy in these times. The children of those victims, their wives and husbands, bereaved lovers and their families living on in the knowledge of what had happened. They also haunted me.

Standing there in the heat of that fine day, the September dust blowing over my office shoes, I felt lost, unsure of what I was doing, unconsciously following this path in a place that I hated and needed. I surveyed the reeling vista of the empty fields with the distant shadowy stain of the hospital, then plodded back down the track.

I came back through the hospital grounds on the lawns leading to the lodge house steps and joined a column of staff coming in for the next shift. They went in to work quietly with their heads down, flicking away cig stubs, not noticing the glossy-backed, young starlings, scrambling and pecking at the fallen apples under the fruit trees outside the lodge. I recalled one grizzled, old charge-hand explaining to me the feeling of imprisonment among the warders themselves, "You see, Jack; there is a walking-in walk and a walking-out walk."

I joined the line of men going in, those quiet somnambulists who shuffled in line through the sliding doors of reinforced plexi-glass and submitted to a body search. I watched on the scanner screen as my leather jacket passed through it, showing a ghostly image, an orange shadow with the zip, black and distinct, curling within, like the skeletal backbone of a snake. I was processed on from one check to another, received my keys, clipped them to the key belt and followed the early afternoon tide of staff flooding the block corridors. I passed through the Eaton airlock and walked down the familiar central corridor with its unchanging smell of floor polish, of cooking and stale, imprisoned bodies. Most of the patients had gone from my first years at the hospital. Grau had left for medium secure. JJ went to a specialist head injuries unit, Grimpen was long dead. He had died of a heart attack on the ward. Unwanted by his family, he had been buried under one of the lop-sided gravestones in the village hospital graveyard alongside Hunter and the rest. Most had been transferred in the endless hospital shuffle from ward to villa and back again.

I stood with a group of staff who were waiting for afternoon review rounds. We gathered near the door to the patients' smoke room. A few of them were sitting there with a TV flickering high up on a wall. I noticed Yunus lounging in a chair among the others. As soon as he spotted me he leaped up and approached me.

"You sir! You! You! You are not a bad man. Help me! You can help me! Talk to Dr Bartram please!"

"Stand back Yunus. The decision has been made," I replied.

Yunus began to wail and slap his head. One of his flailing arms brushed against me. I called to the Team Leader, "This man is assaultative!" Three burly staff appeared and began to drag Yunus to the seclusion room. He twisted in their grasp and began calling to me, "*Allahu Akbar! Allahu Akbar!*"

★

Hospital security was on the alert at the Millennium and they had more work to do after the world terror events. The Muslim patients were carefully noted and some were segregated because the other patients had begun to attack them. Security was stepped up. The paranoiacs breathed new life and fed off the malign energies that had been released. I remember Halliday particularly, a young man who had killed his girlfriend in a seaside town four years before. He had attempted to mummify her body according to ancient Egyptian practices, the techniques of which he had gleaned and adapted from history books. His girlfriend's body had been found wrapped tightly with bandages and tape in his bed-sit rooms with biro tubes inserted in her nostrils to drain the fluids from the brain.

Halliday entered the ward review rooms and distributed a neatly presented manifesto to us. He had created it during his day activities in occupational therapy and the opening paragraph read:

Exposure of world plot to implant humans with dragon fly mouth-parts, electronic chips and metallic implants under surgery, at the dentist or the doctors. Radio wave activated. You are then controlled. Those involved in this: CIA, IRA, the Iraqis, the Illuminati, John deLorean, the Matrix, Al Qu'aeda.

"And you and you," he also said, pointing at us clinicians sitting there, "Doctors especially."

He swept back his long hair to reveal a handsome face with intense dark eyes. He frowned as he spoke about the conspiracies raging about him and sometimes he laughed a little to himself, showing his stained, sharp teeth. Our attempts to reason with him seemed to amuse him greatly, as if he had caught us out in some way.

Something about Halliday's terrible certainties seemed to infect me with fear and there were days when I could not help from trying to make sure that Irina was safe. I would submit to the urge to drive to her home in a suburban road a few miles from my place in the city. Her house was an elegant, two storey building faced with white stucco. The suburbs had crept round the old place and were kept at bay by a sagging brick wall. I often sat in my car, discreetly parked across the street, and was relieved to see activity in the house beyond the wall. As I sat there, I remembered those times when I stayed there myself, nine years before, when her husband was away, sometimes cradling her infant son, or sitting down to meals or us lying together in the marital bed. I had waited outside in the street like this so often, out in the cold, after she had sent me away at the end of our relationship, but had kept away these last few years. But now I would return for a while, staying on until I was satisfied that all was well and thinking about our brief, intense affair.

We had met in the first weeks after my entry to the hospital. She also worked the Eaton Ward like me. I sensed something untoward about her from the other staff, something apparent in the way they looked at each other when her name was mentioned. At first I thought it was some sordid scandal or gossip about her but later I heard that there had been a security alert when a notorious psychopathic patient had fallen in love with her during therapy and had planned to take her hostage, but had been thwarted. This incident seemed to have given her a certain glamour among the nursing staff. I think that this was somehow an acknowledgement of her seductive power.

I first saw her in ward clinical meetings and remember noticing her incredibly lustrous hair, which often fell forward across her face and watching her small-boned feet in trim, white socks and sandals as they tapped impatiently during the meetings. I also remember her slipping into a seat beside me at the directorate referral panel, with a fleeting whiff of some heady scent. I saw a crescentic scar on the smooth skin near her wrist bone on her right hand. There was something exciting about that scar and I found that my eyes fixed on her restless, long-fingered hands. I recall too, standing behind her in the line for security search, that first autumn in the hospital, as she irritably turned out her pockets at the staff security gate and seeing a little bottle of Chanel's *Cuir de Russie* rolling out onto the examination tray. The security staff searcher held up the flask of amber liquid and announced in a triumphant, and an accusatory tone, that this was a forbidden substance and she replied in her accented English, "Really, this is ridiculous," turning to me for support with arched eyebrows.

I had walked quickly after her in the corridors, trying to keep up with her fast, swaying pace, noticing how she occasionally gave a nervous head toss, flicking back her hair from her face. I found myself wanting to know more about her. I manoeuvred to get close to her, rationalising that she would be a useful ally in my campaign to transfer Kress to Eaton. In reality I began to enjoy being near her, smiling as she sniped at the doctors in meetings, or defended the departmental position in a feisty exchange with hospital managers. She was a serious and sharp presence, yet mysterious and also vulnerable in some way. I found myself marking out her place at meetings and looking for her in the long, block corridors. I might have waited months, years, like this, admiring her, mildly intrigued by her, sometimes my attention waning, swept up in my losses, still raw with the loss of Rachel. Then one winter's day, a year since I had come to the hospital, and two months after the extinction of Kress, I was called to the medical offices by Dr Colt who thumped down a bundle of reports on the desk in front of me and growled, "Now this is a case for a bright spark, Hosannah Njie, the sleeping beauty of Burnet Ward, who has got them all stumped. Why don't you team up with Irina and take a look, a second opinion to help the clinicians there? That would earn us brownie points with the Directorate."

And thus I was drawn in, to become a fly that shakes in the web.

Hosannah Njie slept day and night on a wheeled bed on Calder Ward, one of the block admission wards three stories up. Hosannah had been sleeping like this for two months. It had started in the autumn, staff had begun to find him huddled in a chair in the smoke room or slumped in the latrines. He was locked out of his room in the day time in an effort to keep him on his feet, but eventually he lodged in his bed, first of all sleeping right through a few days and nights, and afterwards wandering the ward with blank, dead eyes; then spending longer and longer periods in his bed and now permanently slumbering. He laid full stretch on his back, his dreadlocks hanging down the sides of the bed almost to the floor. A bottle of saline had lately been attached to one of his arms out of concern that he was dehydrating. When staff came into his room, with food or drink, he would allow them to sit him up and he would silently take nourishment from them, spooned into his mouth, his arms remaining slackly by his sides. Once his attendants had gone he would lapse back, only his chest faintly rising and falling with an even breath. Sometimes his bed would be wheeled out to catch some winter sunshine in the day room, where the other patients regarding him warily, or down the corridor to a treatment room for physiotherapy and for neurological tests.

He would lie unresponsively wherever he was taken, his eyes closed, a huge dark shape covered by a sheet, his once powerful legs stretched out straight, his feet overhanging the end rail. A specialist hairdresser would come every two weeks to dress his locks and rub oil into his skin. His mother would arrive from time to time and sweep through the ward with her flowing bright robes and toque-like head scarf wailing, "Hosannah, Hosannah, what have they done to you, my innocent boy!"

Hosannah slept on through everything, except sometimes in the deep watches of the night shift he would suddenly jerk upright. In a sideways swinging motion he would slide out of the bed with incredible speed, his catheter and drip swaying and rattling, to void a heap of faeces onto the floor, then as quickly he would be lying back in his usual prone position by the time the night staff had put their heads round the door to his cell.

I was delighted with Colt's suggestion, read the copy reports and rang Irina about our proposed joint work. Her initial response was cool and guarded.

"I don't see why we should do Burnet's work for them," she told me, but I explained what a strange case this was, a challenge and a curiosity.

She said, "In my country we have a saying, 'Beauty does not season soup.' You understand? I do not have time to chase after clinical wonders like this." But I persisted in my arguments and eventually she sighed and acceded. I enjoyed listening to her voice on the phone, noticing the way she dropped the definite article sometimes, and how she stressed the final syllables of words.

We met in her office a few days later. I had felt anticipation in the days leading up to it. February daylight fell through the barred windows into her office with its neat piles of clinical journals, and a large framed poster on the wall showing a montane landscape.

"That is Tatras mountains," she said shortly when I asked where that was. A blue vase containing early, pale narcissi stood on her desk

145

together with a postcard image of a virgin and child propped against the in-tray with *Matka Boska Chestochovsksa* written beneath it. I thought that the image looked like Irina.

"Black Madonna of Czestochowa," said Irina in response to my query. There was also a framed picture of a fair-haired infant in a romper suit being held up by the hands of an unseen person.

"My son," she answered tersely in a tone that did not encourage further exploration when I asked who the handsome little fellow was. She stood defensively behind her desk, a slim figure in a black Jaeger trouser suit, with a peach-coloured silk blouse and a single string of pearls just visible. I remember thinking that she wasn't that attractive, and trying to pick flaws in her beauty, noticing the frieze of tiny moles on her throat above the gleaming pearls, the blue shadows under her eyes. Her hands fiddled with the reports on Hosannah that I had brought, her eyes were cast down, fixed on the papers on her desk, signalling that she wanted to get on with business. We sat down and talked over the case and about how the current clinical team had struggled over it.

There had been much debate. First of all Hosannah had been seen as a case of schizophrenic catalepsy, an unusual but well-documented phenomenon in psychiatry, a state of lack of response in the patient with an element of muscular rigidity whereby the limbs stay in the position that they are placed in by a second person. Old texts books, in the medical library, showed white-coated doctors moving the limbs of inert patients, demonstrating the condition called "wavy flexibility" whereby the arms and legs move according to the shaping desire of the manipulator. Yet Hosannah did not improve with antipsychotic medication and one Registrar then claimed that this was really a neurological and movement disorder caused by the medication — a Parkinsonian rigidity induced by the doctors themselves. There was a switch round and Hosannah's meds were tapered off and he was even tried on Ritalin, an amphetamine-like substance in an effort to reverse the effects of the antipsychotics. Yet still he slept on week by week, with little evidence of change.

More ideas followed. Was this a willed mutism or some form of depressive stupor?

Staff tried to creep up on him in the night hoping to catch him awake and once a video camera was set up and trained upon him for

146

twenty-four hours yet it revealed no extraneous movement or clue that he was faking. He slept on, although it was true that there seemed to be an awareness somewhere there for he appeared to recognise familiar staff and allowed them to sponge him down and fix the catheters, yet his muscles grew more rigid when the doctors handled him. Concern and a sort of embarrassment grew. The hospital had to wake Hosannah up. ECT began to be mentioned as a radical treatment but the consultant in charge shrank from that option.

And so, Irina and I agreed to go up to Calder the following week. We met in the corridor by the canteen where she stood waiting for me at the intersection, a thin, slight figure outlined against the barred window grating, with her arms folded and her hands inside the baggy sleeves of a loose, mauve cardigan. We proceeded to the C blocks and Calder Ward on the third floor. Outside it was a bitter February day, the hospital gardens were frost-crabbed and thickly bundled staff in long coats stamped along the paths in the wired compounds. Our footsteps sounded loudly on the block stairs, her keys jingled and I admired the deft, practiced flip of her keys into their pouch as she did the unlocking ahead of me. I hardly spoke, aware that I tended to chatter inanely in her company. I wondered what she thought of me, glimpsing her serious face in profile through the veil of hair, as she leaned forward to insert her keys in the ward door, thinking that she looked preoccupied, even a little sad. We entered the ward offices on Calder with its bleak, sea-green walls, the tea rota lists drooping on the walls and the patient movement boards gleaming under the neon strip lights. The bored staff sat around, unfurled tabloid papers scattered on the desks and cigs burning, against regulations, in aluminium ashtrays.

"Come to see Hosannah, have you?" said the charge nurse. He seemed pleased that his ward was holding the hospital's curiosity. He enjoyed airing his views to us about this odd ward pet that was drawing visitors and relieving the tedium of the long shifts.

"Well the docs think it is this syndrome or that, but we think he is having us on in some way," he said as he led us through the ward corridors. We followed him warily for it always paid to be careful on unfamiliar wards.

We were ushered into Hosannah's room. It was hard to make out anything at first as the window was curtained but we could just make out a dark shape. The nurse snapped on a side light to reveal a wheeled bed, laying on it was Hosannah with his felted, thick dreads hanging almost to the floor. Irina and I looked at each other unsure how to behave. It was oddly intimate, crammed in there with this sleeping man. He wore light, cotton pyjamas buttoned tightly over his chest and his neck jutted thickly from the neatly pressed collar. There were few decorations in the room, just heaps of neatly folded, bright clothing, a garish greetings card with a picture of a lion on it, and a few cassettes on a shelf, one of which showed Bob Marley's *African Herbsman* showing a picture of the singer with a halo of afro-styled hair. A single battered photo with scrawled writing on it was also propped up there. I touched it with one finger.

"That's his older brother, also a con. Taken during his first prison

stretch. He's doing a ten year sentence now," said the nurse. "Hosannah still hero-worships him. You can see the resemblance."

The nurse brought in two chairs and then left us with Hosannah. I gazed down on the handsome, calm face with that mass of stiff, tumbling hair, his hands lying there with their pale palms downward. I was aware of Irina as she sat on the edge of her chair, leaning right over Hosannah. Her cardigan rode up revealing pale skin against the top line of her cotton panties which had a daisy motif. I shifted my gaze guiltily as she looked back up at me, she then leaned forward again and pulled up Hosannah's pyjama sleeve, exposing the silky brown skin. I could see that she held a pin and was jabbing it into Hosannah's arm. He moved his hand away in a flexuous movement. She looked over at me and I grimaced. She then pricked the skin again, the skin seemed to flicker and something registered passing over that shadowed face and again the hand moved away restlessly, seeking to avoid the goad. I was struck by the sight of her pale, long-fingered hands resting on the patient's forearm and by the oddly intent look in her eye. A rising wind moaned round the blocks. Irina looked at me again as we crouched together over Hosannah.

148

"Strange isn't it? I feel he is aware of us," she said, almost whispering. I felt her breath on my cheek and I nodded, while looking at her, at the hollow of her ear, the corner of her mouth. She again moved forward, this time with her hands on his face, then she moved one of his eyelids upwards, exposing the glaring, fixed orbit, then let the lid fall closed again. She sat back on her chair and remained there, hand propped on chin, looking across at Hosannah. I remained standing a little behind her, also staring perplexedly down at him, when suddenly Hosannah gave out a low groan, a very deep and loud and terribly unexpected sound in that close room. He jerked into movement, bringing an arm up for a moment to touch his face. As he did that Irina jumped up, grabbing my arm in an instinctive movement and we both leaped in fright at this unwonted sign of life in the patient.

"You have gone and woken him up now," I said. We both exploded into giggles and came out of the cell laughing like children, the ward staff looked suspiciously at us. I enjoyed our little scare for it was first time that she had touched me and also the first time I had seen her smile.

"Well, what do you think?" I asked her as we traipsed back down the block steps.

"I don't know…," she said, "I think it is hard to be scientific about it when it is almost emotional to see him lying like that. I will check and consult, read up in my neuropsych books — and there is his history to check." We agreed to meet up at the end of the following week to discuss the case further. We bade each other farewell, and she gave me a warm smile as if we had shared something intimate. I watched her walk swiftly away down the block corridor until the first doors closed behind her.

Like Irina, I also wanted to find out more about this enigma. I wanted to impress her with my clinical acumen I am sure, but for my own purposes I was always searching for the key to predators, even though I had now seen dozens of them.

He had come to hospital by prison transfer after being convicted of his second rape at the age of twenty-six. Prison staff had become concerned about him quite soon into his sentence in Cat C prison. He did not socialise with the other prisoners, preferring to keep to his cell even in association time. At night, voices in his cell could be heard. These turned out to be him speaking to himself in different tones and even arguing with himself. When staff slid his viewing hatch back he would turn to the slit with froth-flecked lips saying, "No, nuttin' is wrong." Then later the voices would be heard starting up again. He became unpredictably aggressive, sometimes swinging at staff trying to bring him meals. He was segged off, then moved to the hospital wing where he began to laugh to himself booming laughter that echoed around the small block. Staff noted that there was always something willed and implacable about him. He would keep on exercising far into the night, under the glare of single bulb in its wired cage, loping round and round his cell, his dreads bouncing on his shoulders. When he was taken to see the prison doctor, he stubbornly blocked out the session by closing his eyes and counting down, "Five, four, three, two, one … Five, four, three, two, one." in a deep voice, repeating this every time the harassed doc attempted a new approach. After months of this behaviour he was transferred to the hospital for assessment.

Hosannah had been born in coastal Nigeria and came to this country with his mother. The family had settled in Harlesden in the 1970s. He was seven years old. His elder brother had preceded him to live in London with an aunt, and had already become a violent offender. Hosannah looked set to follow his example. He was sent back to Nigeria to stay with family for a while, but he returned more obdurate, more evidently alien and now filled with a sexual anger. He was convicted of rape on a woman at the age of nineteen, sentenced to six years but did three and a half. Then he was back, drifting in the London streets. He failed vocational college, he smoked weed and grew his dreads under a Caribbean influence and began to see Babylon as oppressing him. His mother retained an unshakable belief in him and continued to push him to stay on in college, get qualified and be somebody.

A year passed since his return from the first sentence and he had begun to hang around Kensal Green cemetery while he was supposed to be in college. What was he searching for among the monuments to Victorian notables, the catacombs and the laurels? A victim I guess. Eventually he spotted her, a teenage French *au pair*, newly arrived in the country, incautiously taking a short cut to her lodgings. Like so many predators, he had sensed that she was not

150

tuned in to her surroundings and had marked her out and hunted her down. In the still light of a late summer afternoon, he had slipped from the dense evergreens and seized her, battered her, stripped her, cracked her head against a gravestone until she was unconscious, then raped her.

When she came to and began to stir about, he tried to throttle her with her handbag strap, dragging her around the gravestones. Perhaps he didn't want a witness like the girl in his first offence. The *au pair* passed out again, and at some point he stuffed dirt and twigs into her mouth and throat and up her other body passages. Then he left her. Surprisingly, she survived, got to her feet, half-choked, and staggered for help. Her assailant had been tall and black with dreads. With his history it didn't take long for Hosannah to be picked up by the police and the victim identified him. His mother put up a barrage of defence; she said he was at home all the time, she could not believe he was capable of such a thing and she drummed up a campaign with the local black residents association. She also under-played his first offence saying it was all to do with a vindictive ex-girlfriend. But no one else was very enthusiastic about his inno-cence and the heart went out of her public campaign. The courts had little doubt and convicted him without fuss. Undaunted, the doughty Mrs Njie still believed in her son's innocence and cam-paigned for him when he was in prison and now harried the hospital, seeing her son fortnightly on a long trek up from London.

She came in traditional Nigerian dress, treading majestically up the empty hospital drive heading for the lodge house steps the folowing Saturday afternoon after I had seen her son with Irina. She had come up on the London train, alighting at Redford and travel-ling on to the midday bus service to the hospital. She sat very upright in the half-empty bus with a few incoming staff as the other passengers. Security staff saw her substantial, swathed figure march-ing up towards them, the great head dress nodding like an Amazon's plume, and they prepared themselves for trouble. Time hung heav-ily for staff on the quiet weekends but this they could do without. Just as on previous visits, she carried bulging carrier bags filled with blackened bushmeat delicacies, yellow mangos, sweet potatoes, and other vegetables. All of these were confiscated once she had arrived at reception in line with standing security regulations, while she protested loudly. Female staff who had drawn the short straw also had to pat her down over her wraps and they made her loosen everything down to her blue flowing *buba* under-dress, and then they made her unpin her headscarf. All the while she railed at them with abuse, curses and complaints. There were further ructions when all her gold jewellery set off the scanners and she refused to take her bangles off.

Then came the long tramp down the corridors with the escorts, she was grimly silent now, rearranging her wrappings as she plodded between the key-jingling escorts. The ward staff had been warned by gatehouse security that she was on the way and were preparing for the storm.

Mrs Njie wept to see Hosannah utterly unresponsive as usual — her kiss once more not awakening him despite her fervent prayers. One seamed old charge hand offered her a placatory cup of tea out of politeness but this was refused.

"What you put in it? God knows, same as has poisoned my boy," she said.

I waited for her, in a side room out of sight, listened to her ranting on. I had come in on the weekend to see her and waited for the tide of upset to subside before introducing myself.

Eventually she consented to see me. She was initially suspicious and wanted to see an ID badge.

"Doctor? Not a doctor? What are you? I have not met you, what you want of me?"

"No, not a doctor, a weary hunter, looking for the truth, Mrs Njie," I should have said as I sat down to face her in the bleak, cramped, interviewing room.

Surprisingly she was quite likeable. She kept a wary gaze fixed on me. Her magnificent, imposing, head scarf wagged at an angle as she went through her initial litany of complaints. She slowly warmed to her theme when invited to tell her side of things. She told me of coming from Ijebu in Nigeria. Her husband — shiftless, untrustworthy swine that he was, had worked for an oil company, sent money at first but that had dwindled to nothing after a while. She spoke of her older son, in prison, giving out a gusty sigh, "and my Hosannah, that's not his given name you know, that is his second name. Yoruba name our children on the eighth day and I called him

Hehinde, 'the one who lagged behind', for he was the second of twins. The first I named Taiwo meaning 'he who pretasted the world' but Taiwo died at seven years. Got meningitis. He was always stronger, brighter and Hehinde struggled and was weaker, needing special love. I send my older son ahead to relatives in London, to Englan', this islan'."

She sighed again heavily, looking up at the vents to the harsh, percolating light, then continued, "Hosannah, is his second name, it means, *Glory to the Lord*. We jus' used it in the family and it stuck. He went to school in London but did not do well, not helped much by the teachas. They used to complain to me that they find him sleepin' unda benches in the school dining room, and then I could not get him to school, jus' wanted to stay in bed and I had lot of trouble with the eldest also. We are not understood in this country, it is all so hard for us."

Her small, sharp eyes regarded me and I nodded sympathetically.

"I tried to straighten Hosannah, sent him back to Ijebu, looked after by my sista, she was strict, too strict mebbe. Beat him, shut him in hut, work him and he came back worse but there was no harm in him. The harm comes from dis place."

She leaned forward and rummaged in her bag and took out a creased photo.

"This is Hosannah at a birthday party, first birthday in Englan', I keep it to remin' me how things were when we first came here. You see sir, to us Yoruba, head is the essence of personality, in the head is character, it is from God, the quality of that head shows the quality of the life. We say amongst us, *Iwa l'Ewa,* truth is beauty," she said tapping the old photo.

"This little boy Hosannah — my boy, he cannot have done what they say, I brought him up and I know that."

She drew herself up and pressed the photo to her large, swathed bosom, then sighed again.

"I can only be patient, patience shows respect for life, for we have a saying, *the river it never rests*; it is from looking at the Niger at home. All will change, it will come right, we shall see. The love that we put in cannot be wasted."

In the end I got away from her even though she followed me down the ward corridor, still calling out, "You will help us sah, you have kind face." She managed to get through the hospital switchboard a week later and harangued me on my office phone, asking for help with an appeal against the injustice of his imprisonment and help getting proper treatment for him. I gave anodyne replies but could not somehow bring myself to hurt the feelings of that woman, even though she had played such a large part in creating her son. I would not help her for in truth I hated her son, feared him and woke once sweating in the night after dreaming that I was holding a pillow over his face, and his hands came to life and thrashed blindly at me as I pressed the pillow down over him.

I stayed late in the medical library looking in the anthropological sections, trying to find a model for Hosannah's suspended animation. I found something of it in the *hauka* movement in West Africa, which flourished in the 1950s and 1960s. The *hauka* men expressed their hatred for their colonial masters, and for their own demeaned lives, by wild dance ceremonies where, through a process of possession, spirits visited them in a trance state, moving and shaking the possessed to caper in a parodic satire of their masters then to fall into a deep trance and sleep for hours and even days. The *hauka* dancers woke after their trance, strengthened to deal with the degradation of their lives. I wondered if Hosannah had peered out from his Auntie's hut watching the *hauka* men dancing and then collapsing and had somehow learnt from that experience that you can eclipse any reality, deny anything, even from yourself. In that sense, I mused in the library that there were always *hauka* men in every culture. Hosannah, in that way, was likely to be a brother to the one who took my Rachel. And, at that time, I did not see that I was a *hauka* man too.

Time seemed to pass slowly until I could next meet Irina. I found myself thinking about her, lying in bed at night wondering what she was doing, not wanting to imagine her other life, married and with a child, though I still lurched with feeling over Rachel and Louie also, who still rang me sometimes on raw, lonely nights, leaving slurred messages on the answer phone, "Where are you? We should be together …" Messages that I never returned.

I rang Irina on the arranged day. She greeted me cheerfully, as if this was an everyday thing, and unexpectedly suggested that we

154

meet outside the hospital car park, under the vigilant cameras. She drove quickly and I watched her hands on the wheel with that crescent scar near the wrist bone and felt a quiet joy, as well as a fear, as we raced out, driving fast past the power station where it sucked at the river, past the old church burying ground and out east to the wide bean fields by the glistening river.

We found a little village called Little Raneham which had a raftered, low-ceilinged pub where a sycamore log fire sputtered. We ordered food that I was too excited to eat. I toyed with a salad, as I listened to her talk about Hosannah, looking at her face, the high cheekbones, finding something achingly familiar about her presence yet also feeling that I was there with a person so utterly other and unknown. There was something electric and active about Irina. Once she had focused on you, her wilful driving energy pulled you in.

"God knows what it could be, a sleep disorder, possibly a form of narcolepsy? I have looked in neuropsychology books but nothing quite matches his current state." She chattered on about our clinical work and then listened patiently to me talk of the willed trance states of Yoruba culture and the *hauka* men.

"Yes, but where is the spell that will wake him?" she said, smiling a little mockingly at me as I earnestly described my anthropological angle on things.

"Perhaps only freedom will wake him, the chance to find new victims," I suggested.

"That is very pessimistic of you," she said.

I looked into Irina's eyes as she spoke, those dark eyes with their slanting, folded lids, signs of her Tartar ancestry. A constant animation seemed to light up her face as she spoke to me and I remember trying to pull back away from that current of energy. Irina continued talking to me however, sometimes tapping me lightly on the forearm to emphasise a point. We eventually walked out into the sunshine, scuffling side by side, through the blunt, late winter grasses in a lane behind the village. We talked in vivid bursts as we walked along, of cases, hospital business, yet all the while I was wondering what she was feeling and thinking about me. Was she also experiencing excitement and discomfort in my presence? I kept my eyes fixed on her face, trying to sense what was happening, watching as she turned at one point with a sigh and the return of a look that I had seen on her features before. She turned to gaze out at the wide, empty fields then said, "Well, Jack, we should go back now, our work is waiting ..."

Hosannah slept on through February and into March yet something had awoken between Irina and I. We met more frequently for lunch, or chatted in corridors and lingered together in the car park before setting off for home at the end of the working day. She seemed pleased to see me and I looked forward to going to work and encountering her. I also looked out for her car on the road as I pelted along towards the hospital each morning. In early spring I had been asked to attend a final review of a patient, in a low secure unit, who had been transferred from the hospital and we needed to sign him off. I suggested to Irina that we could go together. I had dropped this into our conversation as we were walking to ward reviews one morning. She stopped in the corridor with her arms folded over her narrow chest, meeting my gaze for a moment, then agreed, "OK, yes, why not?"

Dr Colt noticed our travel request.

"Two seniors going out for a review?" he rasped to me but I stood firm, gave him a line about how much we had worked on the case and he laxly acceded as I knew he would.

We went to see Monty. He had a diagnosis of organic personality disorder, a tall man in his fifties, whose thin body was bent like a paper clip. Irina and I faced him in the plush review rooms of the private secure facility three hours drive away on the moorlands near Stockport.

"What are they doing here?" he demanded, pointing at us with a bony finger, for he had recognised us as hospital personnel at once.

"You don't own me no longer, do you get ma drift? Do you understand?"

The low secure clinical staff, his new minders in this more benign regime, tried to soothe him and told him that the meeting was about closure, a formal handing over after a probationary period, however he remained suspicious and angry, sitting on the edge of his chair as if about to charge at us. We were unmoved by Monty's hostility. We remembered him lurching aggressively around the villa for invalid patients with a cycle helmet jammed on his head to protect him from his frequent falls, maliciously jabbing his elbow into the more infirm patients as he passed. Severe epilepsy, and other health problems, had eventually quelled his malignancy after twenty-eight years in the hospital.

He had stabbed another patient in an epileptic colony in the sixties. Now his energies were doused, he had become muddled by medication, by his frequent fits and by renal failure. The extraordinary thing about him was that he had completed a circle in his life without knowing it. I experienced a strange moment when casting through his notes, looking at old letterheads when I realised that this expensive place built on a Victorian core was the same institution where he had started as an inpatient before his index offence nearly thirty years before. Now the "epileptics colony" was called "Ravens View Mental Health Facility" and the old Victorian blocks of the original place had undergone a corporate remodelling. Yet it was the very institution where he had stabbed another patient all that time ago. This transmigration was unrealised by Monty and by the new hospital, which had reabsorbed him. I did not point it out to Monty or the new staff, although Irina and I smiled at the irony of it afterwards as we walked back to the car. We both knew as therapists that line about how the end of all our exploring will be to come back to the place where you had started.

Our smiles faded, however, when we looked through the perimeter fencing to see a lit window of some uncurtained slop room shining out in the dusk of late afternoon. We could see a large, completely naked man with shiny, marbled skin and two staff standing on each side of him in plastic aprons and rubber gloves hosing him down and scraping matter off his hind parts while the naked man howled and bellowed like a beast. Irina turned to me with a shudder, "You never get used to it though we are supposed to treat them as if they are the same as us. But they are different aren't they? When I see things like that I feel so lucky that we have minds, that we have control, yet we can so easily lose it all."

We travelled back in silence for the most part. Irina sitting next to me, looking thoughtful, staring out at the landscape as I drove through the bleak Pennine towns in the late afternoon light, past the stone walls coming down like black ribbons off the hills and the derelict, industrial chimneys signposting our way. Irina, absently smoothed back her hair sometimes as she gazed out, passing me sweets occasionally with her fingers just touching mine, at other times just smiling across at me, her face glowing in the instrument lights as evening came on. Once, we slowed in stalled traffic for a while, outside last season's blackened teasel heads were illuminated in the headlamp's glare. She turned to me then and said, "It's good to have a home to go to in this world, no?"

"Well, it depends what you have waiting for you there," I replied.

We arrived back late at her house. Would I have done anything differently knowing what was to happen? I guess I would not. She invited me in. I followed her as she walked up the path to her house, ducking my head under the leaning cherry. Her younger half-sister Gosia has been baby sitting and rose sleepily from the sitting room couch as our footsteps resounded on the polished parquet flooring. It was a feminine room with naïve paintings of rural life on the walls, a vase of early tulips on a polished coffee table and a lamp shade with Slavonic embroidered scrolls around the rims.

There was a swift exchange in Polish between the sisters. I caught the words "*Mój kollega jest,*" and Gosia repeating the words, "*Dlaczego? Dlaczego, Irina?*" then she shrugged and went to fetch her coat. She seemed so unlike her sister with a lush figure that contrasted with Irina's nervy slenderness, a fleeting similarity perhaps in the slanting, eyelids and something about the curve of the brow line. Anton, Irina's child, sat in a high chair drumming with a spoon on the plastic tray in front of him. He was a yearling in a blue romper suit with a cat motif. Irina's sister stood by the door putting on her coat giving me a nod and a studied look and saying simply "Good evening," to me in an accented voice.

"*Proshe,* Anton, give it to me, *dzhenkooye,*" said Irina tugging the spoon away from the child's hand.

"Gosia spoils him with sweet drinks and forbidden food," she whispered to me while ushering her sister out.

"Your husband, he isn't here?" I asked when we were alone and her child squirmed and cooed in his chair.

"No, he is away a lot," she said and shrugged in a resigned, dismissive way.

"He bought me these," she said, pointing to two, iridescent, green love birds sitting silently in a cage in the corner. "I think they are both males, anyway they fight."

She gave a tight little smile. I noticed a picture postcard lying on the kitchen top of The Little Mermaid of Copenhagen, showing the bronze mermaid, in repose and passive with her apple breasts. She gestured towards the card and told me that that her husband was in Denmark on an academic conference. She made me coffee. We stood in her kitchen; our movements seemed uncertain; our fragile intimacy evaporating under this exposure in the marital home. We sat in silence drinking our coffee, sitting apart in large armchairs with the little boy positioned between us, battering on the resounding plastic of his tray with his fists.

"Ba, Ba, Ba,... Da, Da Da," he called.

I felt foolish and uncertain as if I had built up a connection with Irina which had no substance.

"Well, really I must be going," I said, finishing my cup and standing up as if to leave, Irina got up, and standing close to me she held out her hand, clasping mine briefly.

"No, stay will you Jack? I don't want you to go. Come on … stay. I will cook something for us both." So I stayed on until much later that night, and at the candlelit dining table with Anton bathed and put to bed by both of us, she had raised a glass to me over our meal, looking at me and saying, "Well, what shall we drink to?" and I gazed back at her.

"To us of course," I replied eventually and we looked at each other for a moment and she also raised her glass saying, "Yes, to our friendship."

Later, I wandered in to her kitchen to fetch more wine and noticed once more that postcard from her husband and turned it over to read the neat male writing on the reverse. The message ran *"This reminds me of you in the bath. All my love, Aidan."* and I felt a thrill of pleasure as I stood there reading it.

★

There was a deserted building, a roofless, ruined place, standing in the barley fields within sight of the hospital perimeter. I had no idea when it was deserted. It could have been fifty or even a hundred years ago. It just stood, inexplicable and alone, in the middle of a

159

field by the embankment carrying the rail line. Security had been on the alert and had reported movement by the old building. Someone had been seen there, a female figure, perhaps signalling to the hospital. Poynton set up watchers with binoculars and  sure enough the next morning they saw a distant figure toiling across the thick soil of the field. She stood for a while near the shell of the building, then could be seen determinedly waving towards the hospital, before she slipped away back through the hedgerows. She returned on the next day just at the time when the villa patients were coming back from their day workshops. Again, you could make out a small figure waving and sheltering from the November drizzle in the crumbling doorway.

Who was she? And why was she waving? Attention focused on the west side of the perimeter, particularly the two story Maple villa whose patients required to be kept in conditions of reduced security, and which stood close to the wire on that side. Perimeter cameras revealed the figure of a patient signalling back through the bars from a second story villa window. A squad was dispatched and the villa staff alerted. They found the patient to be Pinsent, the same Pinsent I had seen fourteen years previously soaked in his mother's blood in city Central police station. They also caught the woman on the field margins as she clambered through a gap in the haw hedge to reclaim her bicycle.

It turned out that she had passed through the staff entrance each working day for the previous five years, until she was sacked by the hospital some weeks before. She had been part of a cleaning team that serviced the villas and had got on quietly with her humble job until she attracted the attention of security staff. She had begun to linger overlong on Maple and nursing staff had reported that she had been seen whispering to Pinsent, spending periods in his bedroom. A snap search found that she was carrying letters from him and a booklet of love poems, signed by Pinsent and composed by him. She was a local, a divorcee, a plump, shy, middle-aged woman.

160

She said that she and Pinsent had fallen in love and she had stuck by him, obviously communicating and by-passing security.

This was not the same blood-scaled mother-killing Pinsent that I had seen in a paper boiler suit all that time ago. No, this was Pinsent *redivivus*, seemingly unbothered by the fuss about the cleaning lady, composed, calmly indignant about his privacy rights, his hair now neatly cropped, his skin smoothed by hospital antibiotics and improved nutrition. He had been rinsed of his psychosis by medication, his crab tattoo had been lasered off at health service expense but he had retained his stubbornness, his will and his endurance. He had concentrated on improving himself, taken secondary academic qualifications by mail, and then an Open University degree in psychology. He had edited the hospital journal *Open Door*, in which he also wrote execrable verse on themes of love and spirituality. He had joined the panel of the users committee which processed complaints about staff and agitated for better treatment. A handsome, confident, authoritative Pinsent who had cultivated the cleaner with small attentions. He had divined her need, and "love" had grown in that unlikely setting.

We are not sure how long it had all been going on, maybe for months. Poynton had been very concerned about a breach in security but not concerned enough as future events were to bear out. Her visits to the empty building were stopped after pressure from the local police and her contact with Pinsent seemed to dry up. Hospital management were relieved that the press had not got wind of it and were simply pleased that it had all seemed to blow over. There was a review about what she might have told him about locks and keys, the layout of the walls and fence, about the ID tags and the procedures that kept the place safe. She had sat tearfully in an interview room in Redford police station indignantly denying any indiscretions, "Our love was not like that ... you don't understand."

And it was plain that Poynton did not understand their love. He had made her go over and over what exactly she had told Pinsent and what he had wanted from her. I imagined him later, in his office, in a haze of smoke, going through the lists of the other patients on Maple, looking for significance: Mattie Dread, Jim Popple, Heinrich Grau, Nelson Bamangwato, Martin Hobman, and his finger stopping at Hobman. Yes, he also was there, a friend or let's say a confidant of Pinsent, quiescent, waiting, watchful Hobman, who had not caused further problems since the Kress incident years before. Poynton took no action after the furore had died down. Perhaps he was losing his touch and, like most others, he was just grateful that the inappropriate relationship had been snuffed out.

I did not at first see Hobman's link with all this, and I did not know if Poynton had also noticed that Hobman managed to get himself placed in a west facing window looking over the fencing to the winter fields. Nor did I look too closely as to how Hobman managed to get the reduced security of the villa setting in the first place since his care had been taken over by other clinical teams over the years. I simply marvelled at this woman's dogged love, coming each day to wave to her imprisoned lover. I did not begrudge love finding its way. Who knows, maybe Pinsent actually cared for her.

I found it strangely hard to remember now what it was like to be with a lover myself, so wrapped up in loss and revenge. It was nearly ten years after Irina had gone and middle age was overtaking me. Bartram once watched me rushing to reviews at this time, with a wedge of files under my arm, ignoring a lissom female student nurse who was passing me in the corridor. He wagged his finger and said, "*Qui finem quaeris amoris*, Jack." And when I did not catch his allusion, he translated, "As Ovid has it, 'You who seek an end of love … be busy and you will be safe'."

Bartram had the knack of striking to the heart of things and I nodded back to him in acknowledgement. I had indeed kept myself alone, sleeping with women sometimes, yes, but even this less frequently, for it had all begun to leave me feeling too exposed. It was somehow too shocking to encounter another being for I remained locked in encounters with those that were lost to me. Sometimes I would try and remember what it was like to make love to Irina but the memory became like a drawing on a steamy window, with the finger moving again and again over the image, making it more smudged and blurred with each new marking. But I did remember Burgh-Next-The-Sea, the first place where Irina and I had become lovers.

As the security flap died down about Pinsent's waving cleaning woman I couldn't help but be distracted by Lynch, a new patient, whom I had been asked to check out. I had seen in his file the name of his hometown, Burgh-Next-The-Sea and that name alone drew me to the case and back to the past.

It was Irina who had suggested the place. She invited me to her home one Saturday afternoon a few days after our trip to see Monty. It had been wonderful to hear her voice over my telephone at home inviting me to come over right then and there. She needed my help with something and I was the only person she knew who would be able to help. I arrived cautiously, not wanting to encounter the husband. She proved to be alone and Gosia had apparently taken Anton away for the weekend. Irina was waiting for me in her hallway. Her face looked grey with strain and she held her hands close to her chest, knotting and kneading them anxiously. There was a broken pane in one of the antique glass panels of her front door and an implication that it might have been broken in some domestic squabble. I imagined a heavy, male hand slamming the door. It pleased me to go out to the building supplies shop to buy those items for the task of repairing the door: tack hammer, glazing pins, the gleaming replacement pane handed to me wrapped in newspaper like a slice of fish.

Irina made me cups of tea and hovered about as I worked and she expressed surprise at my practical ability — although I well knew that the dissembler must be able turn his hand to many things. I remember the linseed tang of the putty, rolling little beads of it on the balls of my fingers, seeing my whorled thumbprint on the new glass, finding satisfaction at leaving my *imprimatur* there. Irina looked back at me, through the glass of the new pane as I stood outside fixing the beading. "Job done," I called eventually, swinging the door jocularly and gathering my tools.

"I don't know how to thank you enough," she said, and came towards me with a quick movement. She hesitated then stood up on her toes holding me by my shoulders and pecked me on the cheek. She lowered herself still holding my shoulders. We both came together again with a spontaneous movement that turned into a battering, awkward kiss that was so hard our teeth clicked against each other. Then we stepped back while I still clutched my tools. "I'll call you," she said as she closed the door behind me.

I heard nothing further for several days and she did not turn up to work. I found myself at directorate meetings, looking at her empty chair and wondering what was happening but knowing I could not ring her. Five days after our kiss, there was a knock at the departmental door and the secretaries were handed a padded envelope addressed to me. Inside, I found a small, glass, ornamental box wrapped in tissue, decorated with blue cornflower motifs stained onto the glass. Inside the box was a small, folded card with an image of a Polish salt miner from Wieliczka with a shako-like cap, depicted holding up a lantern and on the card in Irina's slanting hand was the message *Thank you for being my friend*. The box sat there on my desk, glinting in the light all week and then the weekend came and went and still no news of Irina.

A few days later I saw her slim back in the hospital canteen queue. I saw her talking animatedly to two young male psychology assistants and felt absurdly jealous. I saw her notice me, acknowledge me with a quick nod, then turn her head away and continue talking to her colleagues. I felt childishly crushed and stumbled to my table with my food, sat numbly there for a while then stood up to go, but was suddenly surprised to see her near me. Her hand lightly touched my arm, drawing me away from the crowded canteen tables.

"Can we talk?" We moved away from the groups of key-chinking staff, their ID badges flapping as they leaned to look into the food cabinets.

When we were out of earshot of the others, she whispered so quietly that I could hardly hear her, "I want to get away, things are difficult at home." Her face had a mournful look and she went on, "Gosia can look after Anton."

I did not say anything, not sure what she wanted of me, thinking perhaps that she wanted me to feed the lovebirds.

Then, astonishingly and miraculously she asked me, "Will you come away with me somewhere … for a few days?"

I hesitated out of disbelief and surprise at what I was hearing and she said fiercely, "What's the matter, don't you want to be with me?" Then, at last, I stammered out my agreement.

I do not know why she picked Burgh-Next-The-Sea. Perhaps it was a chance choice or maybe she had been there on some past family holiday. I did not even know where we were heading until the next week. It was a working day, both of us giving hasty excuses to the secretaries at work. Irina slung a road map across to me, when she pulled up outside my flat in her little Micra.

"We are heading for a place called Burgh-Next-The-Sea, you can tell me how to get there," she said, and I leafed through the map until I found the place on the southern shoulder of the Wash as it empties into the North Sea. I remember looking down at the map as the car jiggled about, tracing our eastward route with my finger on the page. Irina drove intently, hunching forward at the wheel. Torrential rain fell through the early part of our journey as if the elements were trying to prevent our progress. The windscreen wipers battered wildly as we plunged down country roads. We drove on without stopping until we neared the coast. I covertly glanced across at Irina trying to sense what she was feeling. She looked serious and tense, as if angry at herself. Sometimes she gave me a fragile smile in an attempt to reassure, and then her face would fall back into that intent look once more as she strained the little engine of her car.

At midday we glimpsed red, sea-eroded cliffs with broken woodland along the skylines. We splashed through swelling culverts as they overflowed the road. We plunged into more deeply rural places, rattling down lanes with shingled walls where wind-shaped trees leaned over the road until at last we came across our first glimpses of the sea on our left.

We paused near Brancaster, a coastal hamlet on the road. The weather began to clear and a fitful sun came out as we bumped down a ribbon of tide-washed tarmac between stands of last season's high, tawny reeds. We stopped in a gravelled car park and switched the engine off. The sound of the wind reached us, young herring gulls watching us from bleached posts. On the dunes beyond, the coarse-bladed marram grass rippled. I asked Irina if she was alright. She nodded, rubbing her face with her hands then touched my hand with hers. "Just feeling strange," she said, "not sure why we are here, I feel that really I don't know you, though I want to be with you."

"Let's walk, find where we are," I said and we went out on Brancaster Sands, the tide on the ebb. Far out, the broken-backed, black shape of a sunken ship wedged on the sands could just be seen against the dark edge of the sea. Dunlin flew past, skirling on like smoke along the shoreline in front of us. The air was full of their calling as we walked across the wet sand. We wandered the expanse of the empty beach, all the way to where an area of creeks and muddy gullies stopped us from going further. There we crouched in the lea of a dune to lie on the dry sand in a hollow between the grasses. We clasped each other and she put her head on my shoulder and we remained there like lost children, looking up at the sky, listening to the salt hay whisper and the song of the birds. Later, walking back barefoot on the ribbed wet sand I turned back several times to see her behind me laughing, lifting her cotton dress to reveal her slim legs, running awkwardly and fitting her footprints into mine as a chill tide rose behind us, welling up and erasing our tracks.

We drove into Burgh, and found the hotel where Irina had booked ahead. We signed in as Mr and Mrs Starsha, using Irina's maiden name, then bumped our bags up the narrow stairs and into our room. Inside, there was a faint smell of damp; faded prints of boats on the Broads lined the walls and a bunch of limp forget-me-nots sat in a vase on a side table. There was a thick quilted counterpane on the bed and Irina plucked at it disapprovingly then prowled the room with a look of unease. I sat on the edge of the bed and took her hand. It burned hotly and she moved about uneasily but did not pull away. Then she said, "Lets go to bed ... we don't have to do anything," and we lay at first fully dressed under the bedclothes moving our hands awkwardly over our bundled shapes, then more ardently as we warmed until something loosened and we fell upon each other completely. We remained like that together as darkness came on and the other guests shuffled past our door to dinner and we paused, shocked perhaps by having done something from which there could be no going back.

She was a revelation to me, the heat and silkiness of her skin, and when we slept I had a brief, vivid dream that I was a little boy again at a 1960s dinner party, spying on the adults in their chatter and smoke and stealing up to a coat stand where the fur stoles hung, moving my face over them, scenting their perfume and savouring the delicious pleasure of sliding my hand again and again into the silky pocket of a woman's heavy coat.

As evening came on we talked a little and she ran her fingers over my chest and belly, feeling the welted, lateral scars that ran across there.

"What are your secrets, Jack? What are these scars? Tell me your secrets," she urged, "and they will be both of ours." Well, I had secrets enough. I told her something about those scars on my chest and belly and wanted to tell her everything, but I knew even then that Irina was only free enough to give me a part of herself. I kissed her own scar on the right wrist bone which I had watched all those preceding months. She told me that she had received it from a childhood dog bite in Poland and had remained always a little afraid of dogs ever since. We reluctantly detached ourselves from each other for a while in the early evening and wandered the wet streets of the out-of-season resort. I asked her if she was OK. She said, "Oh yes, wonderful. You are my first real lover though my husband has screwed dozens of women. As far as he is concerned I am visiting my mother."

I made no reply, her other life was never far away when we were together. We walked down to the slippery wooden piers where a spring tide of glistening water swirled below and the shrimp boats chugged out for the night's fishing, their lights swaying into the darkness. We passed a child on a quay, pulling up a large crab on a hand line. The crab was red and dripping and feebly moving its legs and the boy brandished it at his parents with a scream of triumph. Irina said, "I hope Anton is alright," and I murmured reassurance.

We walked down to the edge of the town and stood under a creaking pub sign, near a white stone monument showing a wreathed anchor, commemorating a maritime disaster. The pale stone gleamed in the lights from a fish dock and we stood there arm in arm for a while facing the sea, then turned back to our hotel room.

The wet leaves of the holm oaks rustled in the main street outside the hotel as a gale began to blow up. We listened to the wind later that night as we coiled and coiled around each other, sometimes pausing to hear the restless, lonely coughing of some salesman in a neighbouring room. In the morning, Irina threw the bedroom window open and leaned out into the cool air to look outside with only a bathroom towel wrapped around her. I lay in bed watching her and thinking of that image of the Copenhagen Mermaid. We stayed two days. On the second day we went to the nearby pilgrimage site of Walsingham and watched pilgrims walking bare foot to the shrine in the spring rain. Inside the church Irina offered me a candle, her face glowing in the light from the flame. "Go on, Jack, light one for someone whom you have loved and who is no longer here," she said.

Burgh remained sharp in the memory. Though we went to other places and other hotels, somehow our track was later erased by sadness and the bitterness of rejection. And so it seemed strange and fateful, to see the place named in a new set of case files that were plumped down on my desk nine years later. Reading and pronouncing the name Burgh-Next-The-Sea on Lynch's home address made me think of Irina and brought back the memory of us quoting the lines from *Little Gidding;* "coming back to where we started and knowing that place for the first time". The appearance of that place name would have been enough to draw me to the case yet also it had its own clinical interest.

I had been asked to risk-assess Lynch as there was something not quite right about the case. He was on Burnet, Kress's old ward; four months into a prison transfer for assessment. He had come from Lincoln Prison after an incident in his cell. He had taken his cell mate hostage, bound him tightly to a hot radiator with electrical flex peeled from his cell lighting system, stuffed a biro into his hostage's ear and threatened to ram it into his brain if his demands were not met. He wanted a prison transfer and for his complaints to be heard. Lynch seemed to be psychotic, stumbling about his cell, muttering to himself, his captive quivering and moaning and Lynch yelling threats to the prison security staff who had begun to mass on the landing. After a few hours' standoff, he began to set fire to the cell with shreds of lavatory paper. He was rushed by the riot squad with their shields and helmets. He was overpowered and his hostage released — shaken, but relatively unharmed. Lynch was sent to us at High Secure for psychiatric assessment for six months. Once he arrived at the hospital, however, he appeared to be cheerful, helpful and cooperative and with no sign of psychotic illness. He seemed to enjoy the hospital regime, praising the food and the level of care, offering to help the staff with minor tasks and zealously reporting to staff on the other patients' behaviour.

Lynch's index offence did not seem to be that serious compared to his peers. He had stolen pewter ware from the Anglican church in Burgh-Next-The-Sea, part of a long list of property offences which had earned him a cumulative sentence.

The nursing staff had theories that the hostage had been a staged event with his cell mate's connivance to allow Lynch to serve out the rest of his sentence with soft hospital time. Perhaps he had sadistically enjoyed binding his hostage, or then again maybe it had all been a transient psychotic episode prompted by smoking skunk, readily available in the prison, or some sort of confusional state brought on by taking pilfered tablets from the hospital wing. The conventional psychological tests on him gave anodyne or contradictory results. He seemed proof against the usual filtering and assessing methods and I had been asked to see him to give a final view on his dangerousness.

I walked through the area where the patients exercised and noticed Burnet ward out on their allotted weekly session in one of the fenced grassy compounds in the brisk air of a late November day. The rooks rose and fell in clouds on the bare fields beyond the wire. The staff heard me coming by the clank of the gates and watched me approach over the rough grass. They lounged in a group still wearing their long blue coats, although uniforms had been officially abolished some years before. Most of the patients crouched in the lee of the wind in an old concrete shelter. They wore baseball caps and knitted hats, some were crouching glumly smoking nub ends cupped in their hands, a few kicked a ball about on the thick wet grass. I asked which one was Lynch and a staff nurse pointed to a man in his forties pacing restlessly away from the others by the fence, he occasionally stooped from time to time to pick the last of the yellow hawkweed flowers from the turf, crushing the flower petals in his hand and gazing out to the fields through the wire. He was a powerful figure in an unbuttoned denim jacket. As I chatted to the staff he came striding confidently past us with an assertive, rolling gait giving me a flickering, appraising glance, trying to identify me and place me in the hospital hierarchy.

169

I went on ahead of them and sat reading Lynch's file in the nursing station as they came trooping back from the courts. He was forty-seven years old, born in Birmingham, one of seven children. His Irish father was a labourer in the building trade who had married a local woman. She had developed a wasting disease when young, and faded out of their lives. At first she had been glimpsed by the kids in her wheelchair manoeuvring to avoid her husband's flailing fists and drunken rages, slipping them food in compensation for some beating or other, still producing children despite her increasing disability. Then they were brought to see her in a hospital bed; then at last she disappeared, fleeing to be looked after by family, then eventually quite gone from their lives. The children, some of them very young, were left in the care of Lynch *père*. He took to locking them in a cellar while he went out to work. He painted the image of a skeleton on the wall of this chamber in phosphorescent paint and left them in the dark to scare them into obedience. Johnny Lynch, this patient, the eldest boy, began to escape through a coal chute to steal food from neighbouring properties to feed his hungry siblings. When the father came back, the children, both boys and girls were often taken out of the cellar to be abused. "Oh, he was always fucking us kids," Lynch told the clinicians carelessly later.

It was the 1960s; care agencies eventually noticed the family after neighbours saw the hungry, filthy children creeping in the yard. They were split up into care, and placed in council run homes which were run by paedophiles according to Lynch. They took him to houses in the leafy suburbs, Edgbaston and Selly Oak, to be buggered by more men. Then he was moved again, this time to a Catholic care home in the countryside, run by priests where again sex-hungry hands mauled at him. Eventually he was released into the world at sixteen, with no idea where his siblings were, back in his home city, fending for himself by stealing and scamming, already building to be a career criminal. He had also been in and out of prison and had been known by many names. Then in the late 1980s about when Rachel had disappeared, he had fled from Birmingham and washed up in coastal Norfolk settling in sleepy, seaside Burgh. He had survived by cheating the benefit system, by conning tourists and by house burglaries committed in all the little hamlets along the coast. He had probably been in Burgh while Irina and I had spent our first nights there.

"More sinned against than sinning then, is he?" asked Bartram when we discussed Lynch in directorate review a week later. I was unsure about that, for when I interviewed him after reading his file he was pleasant and plausible enough. I was always looking for that lone shark who might have encountered Rachel outside the Paradise Stores and I needed to know more about his story. I had been shown to his cell where he was sitting on his bed after a ward meal with headphones on attached to a cassette player. He was nodding and crooning along to the music with his back to us. He sensed that we were there and whipped around, then pushed the headphones off his head and regarded us with alert, brown eyes.

"Sure we can talk," he had said pleasantly enough with a slight Brummie inflection in his speech. He paused for some reason and went to his basin and washed his hands carefully, almost overelaborately, rinsing each finger like a surgeon ready for an operation. Then he accompanied me to an interview room, the same one where Kress and I had once sat. I took him through his story, checking for inconsistencies, wanting to get a feel for the man. He rattled through an account of his painful childhood, the relentless cruelty and the later betrayals, talking about it all glibly, easily, although there was a hesitation when I tried taking him off the path to clarify this or that fact or write down a name. He had recently reported his childhood abuse while in prison and belatedly, the system, which had been sensitised by other abuse scandals, had begun to arrest his previous tormentors, the police questioning retired people who had once worked in the care system. There had already been one suicide in custody of one of the accused; Lynch looked almost disappointed when he had heard about it.

He asked about possible compensation for his childhood abuse and I felt that I could not begrudge him that. He spoke about his adult years quickly, plausibly. I noticed that he made discreet little sallies at getting information from me, asking about my "nice watch", my accent, other things — "not a married man then are you?" Innocent-seeming questions, but I realised later that I had been almost imperceptibly tipped off course when asking my questions. He had a charm and a force to his personality, despite his rough exterior, and I

171

felt that I had to work hard to hold my balance. I had to bring him back over his account to address the more obvious gaps in his story. He spoke of an early marriage in Birmingham and tried to skip over the narrative, but eventually acknowledged that he had married a woman who already had two daughters.

He spoke more readily about Norfolk however, extolling the beauty of it, the peace of the sea and the long beaches, and of Burgh in particular, saying, "Do you know Burgh, Dr Keyse? Have you been there?" I nodded and he went on: "My favourite place there, where I sat out with friends is outside the Lord Nelson pub under the monument to Eliza Adams, to those drowned in the lifeboat way back when. That's what I look forward to be doing, sitting again soon with a pint in my hand at the end of my sentence in the spring next year. You will write for me to probation? Won't you? Can't you move it along for me? You see, I want to go back to the loves of my life…" He responded to my interrogative glance with a playful smile.

"Oh yes, Bella and Shauna. Who are they? My babies of course." He fished around in his denim jacket and took out two tattered photos from a leather foldover. The pictures showed two large Alsatian dogs.

"These are my babies in the back yard at Burgh. They are looking

forward to me getting out. My wife is looking after them, but she doesn't walk them properly."

"She's the other love of my life, of course," he added, quickly laughing.

Afterwards, I sat in my office turning the case over. I felt uneasy about the gaps in his story, that thread of truth that he had somehow hidden by his clever, swift answers. I was also sus-

picious of his plausibility and his charm. I decided that I would go to Burgh-Next-The-Sea and sniff around there a little, also unable to resist returning on the eroded track to the past. I rang his wife's number that was recorded in the file under next of kin. A low hesitant voice answered with a murmurous Norfolk accent.

"From the horspital? What you want me for?"

"We like to involve family, in helping our patients, helping with rehabilitation." There was a pause, an indrawn breath.

"Getting out then, is he?" Her voice tailed off. I gave her an account of not being sure yet when he would be released, of needing to understand him, and about how everything discussed would be protected by confidentiality.

"I suppose it's alright you coming to see me, so does John know? Is he alroight about it then?"

I had pressed Lynch about going to Burgh and wanting to interview his wife and for the first time I saw his easy confidence slip. Initially a fearful look sprang up in his eyes and he became defensive.

"I don't think that is necessary, what you want to do that for?" he had said at first. But I had lulled him with talk of probation, of rehabilitation and preparing for a return to the community and he had eventually said, "Well I suppose so, but don't let that Josie chatter too much, talks the hind leg off a donkey, that girl," and he laughed uneasily.

I drove east from the hospital and quickly crossed the flat alluvial lands speeding down the quiet roads. I clipped the papery red rags of road-kill as I swept into Norfolk. Gulls flickered across the road as I ran down that same coastal road from Hunstanton, watching the sea wind fitfully clearing the mist and briefly sighting the grey-brown Wash to my left in the winter sun. I passed a road sign for Walsingham and also thought, for a moment, of Irina bending over a candle saying, "Light one for someone you love who is no longer here."

At last I came to the edge of the Wash, the staithes where Hobman also had once brooded in his childhood, past Brancaster, the beach where Irina and I had walked and held each other, then on up the winding road to the shingled walls of Burgh. I found and followed the road where Lynch had lived called Eel Gill Close, it straggled through cheap housing then petered out in allotment lands that led on to the salt marshes. I parked and sat in the car

173

looking over my notes. At a bend in the road behind me stood the Chandlery, an eighteenth century building with thick flint walls which had not kept Lynch from breaking in. In the car mirror, I could also see the slope-shouldered bulk of St Nicholas's Church — the scene of his last robbery. He had kept his thievery brazenly close at hand, as if despising any attempt by his neighbours to stop him. In one of the files that I had brought were documents from the local police mainly relating to that final burglary. A police note read, *this is a one man crime wave.* I also noticed several reports of domestic incidents involving Josie and Lynch.

I left the car and walked downhill through the estate towards the house. Bleached summer deck chairs sagged askew in one front garden. In another stood a Datsun Cherry with a sprung bonnet, its tyres melding into the tarmac. Lynch's low two-storey council house had a patch of lawn and a large pampas grass blowing in the wind. Josie Lynch greeted me at the door. A slight, doll-like woman with a puff ball of auburn hair, she was tremulous and frail-looking but once quite pretty, her blue eyes had the slightly yellow sclera of a drinker. There was a tremendous barking from the back yard as I shuffled into the house past bags of dog food and piles of old newspapers. Josie sat slumped and small, protected by the wings of a large tattered armchair with an over-flowing ashtray perched on one arm. A TV flickered in the background with the sound turned down. I sat talking to Josie for several hours as the day darkened outside, and at some time, she got up to make tea in stained mugs, starting the dogs barking again. I saw large shaggy shapes jumping up at the back window.

She described meeting Lynch at a night club in nearby Fakenham in the 1980s. She was a young, thin teenager, really quite childlike in those days. She took out a picture taken of her that first year they had met when they lived in a caravan by the salt marshes. I looked at it while she spoke to me and I found it later still tucked into my clinical notes. It showed young Josie sitting smoking in a sweat shirt surrounded by the same clutter in which they still lived. "I had to take proof that I was eighteen in them days so I could get in pubs and bars. I was so young-looking then. John was from Birmingham, he was much older than me and very confident with it. He always had cash and he swept me orf my feet I suppose."

174

She paused to light another cig and I noticed her hand slightly trembling.

"I first had doubts a year in," she continued, "my sister complained about him pestering her, she was only thirteen then. I didn't believe it, didn't want to believe it. He was really furious when I mentioned something about it and denied it and we soon moved from the caravan to a house, but we didn't last long there either because it burned down. I now think he burned it himself  for the insurance or because people were pressuring him to move on. We moved and moved after that, all the villages we lived in. I think sooner or later the villagers at each place realised he was robbing them week after week and doing other bad stuff and they would drive us out eventually."

I was struck how oddly trusting she was to talk to me like this.

"What could I do? You see I loved him." She looked at me hesitatingly and then fear surfaced, "What I say, you're not going to put down are you? You're not going to tell 'im I said these things?" I assured her about confidentiality, about how her information would be protected but it sounded hollow to my ears.

She spoke of the beatings she had received from Lynch, at first reluctantly, then out it came in a flood. She held her face up to the light from her dusty windows to show me the thickened bridge of her once pretty nose.

"He broke me nose," she said, then held her nose and waggled it loosely. "The bone is gone. It's just cartilage 'olding it on now, the doctors said."

"Once I made him go, made him leave. It was after he started teaching martial arts to the girl next door, four year ago. She were fourteen. He kept goin' round there everyday. This place has thin walls. I could hear him sexing her. I told him, 'I won't stand for it.' He cracked me in the face and left, didn't see him for some months after that but I knew he was there somewhere watching me. A police sergeant once told me that John was the best burglar that they ever come across. I think he came in at night in this house and took things, stared at me while I slept. I just felt that he had and sometimes I woke up scared in the night, as if something had moved in the room but I couldn't see anything. Once when we were first together, I woke to find him under the bed clothes at night with a torch staring at my privates. He is strange my John. Well, after the girl next door thing I threw him out but I began to sense that he was around. I got scared and called the police, but they were fed up on me and did nothing. One night I thought I heard something and got up and came downstairs."

She paused to light a cig.

"It was dark. I called out his name then something went smash on the back of my head. I was spark out for hours then went round to the neighbours dripping blood and half-senseless. I got taken to horspital. It was him there that night who hit me. God knows why. I know of course it was him, though he later visited me in on the ward, acting all concerned like, with flowers."

And so it went on, her frightening story, how he came back, made promises that things would be better, and settled for a while. Then the unexplained cash would appear in big rolls in his pockets, the mysterious phone calls and his long absences at all times of the day or night. Then the complaints about him came to Josie's ears, from whispers and rumours or from confrontations with angry neighbours. How Lynch had been seen hanging around little girls and teenagers. How he had struck up an alliance with the deck chair attendant on the summer beach, giving out ice creams and treats to holidaying children. How he was often seen around Abraham's Bosom, a sandy hollow behind the pine knolls near the shoreline, approaching children, handing out presents that he funded by his burglary forays in the neighbourhood. He whiled away the hot summer afternoons, lounging on a bench outside Burgh toilets, near the hotel where Irina and I stayed. Offering rum and coke, ready mixed in a bottle, to giggling teenage girls; offering it to the young girls "in return for a feel in the toilets, like".

She reeled on with her story, spoke of more savage beatings and his long absences. Then his nemesis came in the shape of a pewter jug used for filling the font at St Nicholas's church, and a few household items stolen from the nearby Chandlery on the same night. A holiday maker found his haul stashed in a sandy pit near

Abraham's Bosom on the beach and his fingerprints were identified on them. A search of the house revealed more incriminating items. It was a third offence and with three strikes against him he was given a longer sentence than usual.

"Are you relieved he is away inside?" I asked and she shrugged in a resigned way then looked fearfully towards the front door.

"He will be back. It wouldn't surprise me to see him now at any time, on any day. He always gets his own way my John," and I found myself glancing nervously towards the door as well for a moment imagining Lynch's shadow at the mottled glass.

The afternoon darkened outside and in the room I could hardly make Josie out as she huddled in her chair. Her story had slackened and petered out. I had coaxed out of her as many names and dates as I could, but now she had fallen silent as if exhausted and empty. I told her I must be heading back.

"Wait, afore you go, I want to show you something," she said. She got up and opened the back door and called out, "Shauna … Bella!"

I felt a stab of fear as the two large dogs ran in and circled stiffly around me with rumbling growls and the hair ruffed up on their necks. I rose from my chair in alarm but Josie shouted at the dogs, the growling subsided and they began to turn and turn around me, barging against me and sniffing at my legs.

"Give me your hand. I want to show you something," she said. Her cold hands grasped mine and she pressed my fingers into the stiff, thick fur of one dog's neck.

"Run your hand over. Can you feel it?" I couldn't feel anything at first as I nervously prodded at the harsh thick fur of the dog which stood stiff and tense, its head averted. Again, she pressed my fingers deeper under the fur, onto the dog's skin and then I felt a running lattice of distinct welts and nubs and scars right along its neck and flanks.

"What is it?" I said squeamishly, removing my hand.

"He says he dotes on them, but he would take them out night after night on the Buttlands, the dunes out there. Would take his air pistol and shoot at them as they ran about. Plugging them again and again. They'd come back whimpering and bleeding most nights. He would never admit to it but I knew he done it. That's my Johnny, he hurts the things he loves."

177

The dogs milled near me as I rose to leave and I could hear their barking as I walked away. I made my way down to the harbour end of town, stopped by Dogger Lane and walked to the harbour wall. The Lord Nelson pub sign creaked in the sea breeze as I stood by the sea wall, built after the 1953 floods, the same tide that had killed Kress' sister. I walked a little further and passed the rocket station for the maritime distress maroons and watched a late fishing boat unload a few dripping boxes of mussels, whelks and crabs. The sheds and rope makers' yards were vacant now and one local, in a hooded jacket, stood with a fishing rod and seemed to be watching me as gulls flitted above me in the murk. As I walked, I wondered, why did Lynch like the monument so much and that view from the Lord Nelson pub? And then I looked landward to see the public toilets and behind them a children's playground with swings and parallel bars, deserted now in the dull misty light.

Ah yes, of course, I realised then. It was a place for holiday meat and I imagined the summer scene, the crowded playing fields, the little girls on the swings and Lynch sitting there watching with his pint from the Lord Nelson. I walked back to the car now shrouded with droplets of sea mist, accompanied by the *clanga clank* sound of wind-slapped rigging in the harbour.

I drove back west on the coastal road past Brancaster beach and past those long erased footsteps of Irina and I. As I drove I had the feeling that Lynch's reality had now almost eclipsed my own tender memories of that first night in Burgh. It was so hard to hold on to what was good, and perhaps it was somehow easier to deal with a present evil than dwell on the hurtfulness of lost love. So, I turned over the problem of Lynch as I drove on the darkening road back to the hospital, and began to plan what to do about him.

I fixed him soon after. I did it for all victims that I had encountered, for Josie and for the purposes of my own revenge of course. I made checks, found that in his first marriage in the 1980s he had been suspected of abusing his step daughters in Birmingham but had flitted away to Norfolk and escaped investigation. I collected his aliases told to me by Josie, listed those victims she could name, circulated the details and found out new information about him from other police forces. I informed Probation and Child Protection Police Liaison about his activities and wrote a damning report. I recommended transfer to the new sex offenders unit whose high, corrugated walls had just been built as an annexe to the hospital, where there was no prospect of removal unless he could show that he had been cured of his dangerous desires. Lynch was thus sucked into the psychiatric system, where he thought he would have an easy time and while away his short sentence.

His transfer to the special unit was accepted in early December and a little while later I found myself walking the main block corridor on a chill day, the boiler house at full stretch with wet sleet mixed with sooty particles falling from the long silver chimney. I saw a shambling line of patients with their escorts approaching along the corridor. My usual vigilance was a little relaxed and I was surprised to see Lynch suddenly swing out of the line and lunge at me despite the yells of the escorts. His face was contorted with rage as he growled, "You fucker, fuck you, with your lies about me, I will get you, you will pay for it, that's a promise." He then spat at me before the staff hustled him away. I brushed his spittle off me and continued down the corridor where, beyond the portholed windows, I could still see the grey flakes continuing to stream down as I went into the canteen for the staff Christmas dinner. Those lines from Lombroso that I used to love came back to me: *Quand le neige tombe noir, B ... sortira de ma memoire.*

Chapter Five
Black Doll

I did not then realise all that Max would mean to me when I first saw his sweaty broad face in the review meeting. He had been recently transferred to Alder Villa and now stood his ground. His feet were planted a little apart to steady himself as he swayed about in the review room, holding onto the back of the chair keeping us at bay with his angry protestations.

Alder was a quiet annexe in the hospital, with a long balcony area attached to it surrounded by a few, straggly viburnum shrubs. In the 1920s the tubercular patients were left out in their beds there in the belief that fresh air would clear their clotted lungs. It had remained as an invalids' villa in the hospital ever since, inhabited by elderly patients and by the chronically sick. Max was newly placed there because of his diagnosis. The registrar to Dr Reed — a bluff young Irishman with a rugby club tie — walked along with me, briefing me about Max and his illness as we passed the seated patients in the day rooms. We were interrupted for a moment by a thin, elderly man who had spotted me as a newcomer, got up, took a few wavering paces towards me, and announced with quiet pride in a high, clear voice, "Good morning sir! I am the oldest patient in the hospital! I am eighty-two!"

He proffered his tremulous hand to me which I ignored. I never shook hands with the patients now, having learned the games of dominance that they so often played. The registrar commented, "That's Ernie. He is our oldest, but by no means the least dangerous. Hit a woman with a sock that he had filled with rocks. He had followed her in a public park, two days after we last let him out to a probation hostel at the age of seventy-six."

We both chuckled and shook our heads with grim professional humour as we threaded our way through the clatter and bustle of the morning shift; the sound of music from the patients' radios and the whistling of the cleaning staff as they buffed the floors.

"Now our friend Max here," continued the registrar as we manoeuvred along through the throng, "well, he was set for a career on the PD units, an out-and-out psychopath, you know but began to cough you see, and sweated and had lower back pain, hid it doggedly-like, until he couldn't hide it any more. Well now, no surprise when he came out with an abnormal radiograph and the lung section proved it, stage four, undifferentiated, large cell carcinoma of the lungs, our boyo has got three months tops. That's why we want you. We need to decide what to do with him."

We sat facing him in the review rooms as a thick February mist rubbed itself up against the barred windows. Max remained on his feet, twisting about and refusing our offers to sit and make himself comfortable. He was clad in a blue cotton shirt, his sleeves rolled up from the institutional heat of the villas, with a rose-shaped tattoo showing on his left forearm with the characters LL inked in above. He still looked so strong, so alive; there was a real vigour to him. I imagined the blood pumping the proteins that fed the abnormal cells deep in his lungs. There was also something familiar about him which I couldn't quite place, something in the deep-set hooded eyes and down-curving mouth. Not an unpleasant face when seen in repose, but as he yelled and snarled at us, I saw something that could be much more frightening. I continued gazing at him as I sat in the review rooms with Tina Reed, the registrar and nursing staff. We were also accompanied by the physician from the patient treatment centre as we tried to explain his diagnosis to him and its implications.

"Perhaps we need the chaplain," murmured Dr Reed as Max began to yell at us.

"No, doctors, you have got it wrong. There is nowt wrong with me that a bit of building up won't cure."

Eventually his rage subsided and he stumbled forward to sit in his chair, putting his head in his hands, and then looking up to glare at us from time to time, "My God! No. I do not want to hear this!" he suddenly erupted again. "I'll have my solicitor on you, torturing me like this. I have 'ad too much to cope with as it is." He muttered into his hands for a while then lapsed into an unresponsive silence.

After a while, it was clear that we had reached an impasse and we dismissed him. "OK, Max, you can go," said Dr Reed. He stomped out and went off to crouch in the lounge day room where we could still see him, through the translucent panel in the review room door, furiously rolling a cig and shaking his head to himself. We remained in discussion.

The registrar asked, "What's the prognosis?" as if he did not know, directing the question at the physician who looked after the primary care unit.

"And shouldn't we stop him smoking?" added Dr Reed.

"Well, it won't make much difference," said the young brusque physician. "He is end stage really. X rays show that it's in his lymph nodes and in his bones. It will usually show in the legs and hips next. He will get sicker quite soon and he won't be very mobile. We can start giving some chemo to slow the process but really it will be palliative care that he needs."

Dr Reed said, "The hospital is not really equipped to look after him but where could he go? We have already had to shift him with escorts back and forth from the local hospital. It's a strain on staff resources. He should really go into some sort of hospice. We will have to sort out the legalities of it, but what about the risk?"

Jack, could you look at his notes and give us an informed view about him and his risk, what we would have to think about? I guess security will have to be involved. He would also have to be conditionally discharged by a tribunal."

"Sure, I'll check on him," I agreed, and walked away from the villa into the mist. As I strode off down the path between the villas I could hear the rooks making a muted cawing somewhere in the murk beyond the perimeter wire. My mood was lowered, whatever he had done it was grim to see such a distracted and doomed man, although a thought kept nagging at me. I could not make out where it was that I had seen him before. I am sure I had passed him on the blocks corridors a few times over the last years. Max was one of many out of the hundreds penned up here with whom I had no direct dealings, although I tried to scan most of them. No, it was something more specific that nagged at me.

At the next opportunity I went to the records rooms above the blocks and waited impatiently for the gurney to come trundling along bearing his close-packed notes. The large, buff ledgers fell open to form the usual archaeological layers depicting a patient's career through the system. Max had come in to the hospital by court process in 1988; he would have been twenty-four or twenty-five then. Interestingly, he came from the city and was originally arrested there. He must have been swilling around the detention system at the same time that I was trying to track Kress. The index offence was attempted murder.

One hot August afternoon he had presented to the casualty department of the main city hospital, asking for help, saying that he had head problems, wanted a rest, and wanted to be helped because he could not control himself. He was seen and screened and then turned away by junior staff. There were the original Accident and Emergency flimsy contact sheets in fading violet ink in the notes, with the diagnosis written in: *acute situational reaction* then in larger slanting capitals in a different hand *NPD*. NPD stood for No Psychiatric Diagnosis. It meant that this man had no definable or treatable mental illness in the opinion of the junior, or his registrar. Max was just one of hundreds of the disturbed, the damaged and the angry who washed through A & E's doors.

He left a quite detailed account of what happened after that with later clinicians, which was easy to reconstruct as I turned the brittle pages in the large files. After he had been turned away from the hospital he returned to wandering in the city centre, drinking from a bottle of White Lightning. It had been a sunny Saturday afternoon during an August heat wave. He finished the bottle and walked down past the strolling crowds and the rattling fountains with empty drink cans floating in the green water. Buses full of weekend shoppers drew up and departed in a haze of diesel fumes; pigeons scurried in droves, looking for discarded scraps and shop girls swung their legs on the council house steps. A gang of punks were laughing, perhaps they were laughing at him. On the studded leather of their coats, he read emblems of his own demise. One had the message "*Why?*" picked out in stud heads. The word "*Why*" turned in his head.

He went into a sports goods store and bought a knife, a lock knife with a bone handle, quite expensive, with an engraved blade showing the image of a leaping salmon. He stepped from the store and took a taxi through the crowded streets. He asked to be dropped at the railway station — it was only a five minute journey. He paid his fare with his last £5 note and as the driver leaned forward to find change from a bag under his seat Max thumped the knife into the taxi man's back between the shoulder blades, the point of the blade wedging in the fifth lumbar vertebra. He left the knife wagging there as the driver slumped forward. Max rummaged under his victim's legs as he choked and gasped and he took the hidden money wallet from under the seat, then wandered away casually into the nearby railway station. He bought a platform ticket and sat ostentatiously eating sandwiches and drinking bottled beer at the railway buffet while speckles of blood gleamed on his shoes. He was arrested soon by transport police after he was pointed out to them by passengers also waiting on the platform, and who had sensed the menacing strangeness of the man.

It had been a pointless crime. A *decompensatory act* as the psychiatrists identified it, borrowing from cardiology the concept of *decompensation,* the temporary scrambling of the balancing systems of the body. This decompensation had engendered an act that had ensured his removal to a secure place. He was also identified as a dissocial personality disorder and by that label they incorporated all the nameless hurts, abruptions and losses that had gone to create that envelope of emptiness that was Max.

There was little in his notes to explain the development of that personality. He had been born in the northern suburbs of the city. His father was a textile worker. He had died when Max was sixteen, of lung disease caused by dust from the work fabrics. His mother developed an anxiety disorder which prevented her from venturing out of doors very much. She coped by taking the new-fangled diazepine doled out by her family doctor and by drinking sherry in the afternoons before Max got back from school. His younger sister Theresa kept the family going by her selfless care and support. Young Max was a sour, isolated adolescent with a poor concentration span and a disconnection from the feelings of others. He hurt the family cat; he attended school rarely and hung around the local woods, starting fires there, watching them blaze all day. He was no good at games. One day the school sports pavilion burned down. Max was questioned but nothing was proved. He used to steal pointless items from his friends and family. His mother eventually kicked him out and he drifted among the drinkers and the vagrants of the city.

Then we know less about him. He was convicted of the statutory rape of a thirteen year old girl when he was eighteen, did three years in young offenders' prison then was back out in the city, labouring on building sites, doing van deliveries and some cabling work for a phone company. As I mused over the case, I reflected that he was just like the older Kress; really they were brothers, *sembables*. Their mutual denials and lack of connection with people linked them. I found a comment scribbled in the margin of one of Max's reports *"this is a man without conscience"* written by a medic or forensic psychologist.

Yet, still, I did not see it. I turned to other tasks, helping the staff on Alder Villa prepare for his removal to a hospice. I even went to the women's villas at his request to explain his illness to his girl friend Maeve, who was another patient in the hospital. She was an arsonist, one from the small contingent of women detained in that male environment. They used to hold hands at the dances at the Blue K, the patients' social club. I also supervised the packing-up of his belongings from the block ward where he was kept before his diagnosis. I was approached there by Mattie Dread, a young patient who sauntered up as I watched the nursing auxiliaries heaving the heavy cardboard boxes filled with his scrap books and old newspaper clippings.

"What up wit' Maxie sah?" asked Mattie.

"Maxie is not well and will not return to this ward. That is all I can say," I replied,

The auxiliaries laughed and one said, "He is even sicker than you, Mattie, and that's saying something." Mattie made no reply, just making a clicking noise of disapproval in the Caribbean fashion.

As spring turned a month later, I had still not recognised Max until one day when I was hurrying to the review rooms on the villa, distracted and late. I rushed in, a little breathless, fidgeting with my keys and joined the review which had already started. He glared at me irritably as I entered. He had visibly begun to decline by then. He had constant pain and night sweats. Chemo had resulted in his hair dropping out in patches. It had then grown again unevenly,

185

long at the sides and thin and wispy on top. He seemed resigned, slouching there in a light-coloured shirt, his thick tattooed left forearm and the metal band of his fake Rolex gleaming in the review room lights. His belly prodded through the shirt and the light reflected on his shiny, sweaty forehead.

"How are you Max?" said Dr Reed.

"Alright miss — I mean, doctor. Thank god that chemo has stopped. It played hell with me hair."

He drew his fingers through his hair and turned to one side to show his snub-nosed profile. I connected him in that instant. That's where I had seen those deep set eyes and shiny brow. I sat through the rest of the review looking at him from one side and then another, listening to the account of the legal moves taking place to release him from the hospital on the grounds of his terminal illness. After the review I rushed back to the archives and ordered up a gurney. I carefully checked his year of admission and lifted down the original admissions file and there he was on the front sheet as expected, the image from the plate camera showing Max full face and side view in large definition. Younger, fuller-faced with down-turned mouth and his hair cropped very short to show the gleaming scalp.

I rocked back on my chair, those files heaped up close to me in that little room next to the roof rafters. I remember looking at my hand as it rested on the file, noticing the slightly puckered skin, the diamond-shaped ridges and the speckling of sun blemishes across the knuckles. So many years had passed, grasping for this moment and even then I could hardly believe it. Could it really be him, sidling up after all this time, ushered in through a back door? The man with the shaved head, caught by the camera in the Paradise Stores, and perhaps the same snarling man seen in a van a little later in his white tee shirt on the night of the 4th September so long ago? The police perhaps not finding him because he was already in their system. And, he had been in the hospital all along while I scented and sniffed around him.

I drove home quickly that afternoon with the windscreen wipers battering as fierce, spring squalls swept the countryside. Already playing in my mind was the vision of me entering my flat, dragging out the old folders with their rime of dust and unbending the stiff, yellowed newsprint to reveal that security camera image striding back from the past.

★

The yellow bars of the external vehicle-lock gates opened, accompanied by the whooping noise of a warning klaxon. An atlas grey Mercedes people carrier, with especially strengthened, smoked windows and a meshed, rear cage purred forward then halted. Security gave the exterior of the vehicle a last sweep. Inside the carrier, Hobman sat in a wired enclosure and looked out of the dark windows. He could just see the outside world through the glass and he confronted his own reflection there. His hair was thick and grey now, the nose more bony and pronounced. Images still coiled on each cheek and his temples despite offers of laser removal. His three escorts settled in as the vehicle glided away with Hobman scanning the gate, the wall, the fence, the grass between fence and wall and the swooping ditch beyond that. He had not been out these gates in fourteen years and there was an intensity in his gaze not readily apparent to the escorts who looked back at him through the mesh of the cage. He appeared to yawn and then to stretch a little, shifting in his seat in his borrowed Topshop black suit which was a little tight around the chest and shoulders. He continued to view intently the sports field, the white blur of the old score boards, the bowls court and the staff car parks.

The clinical team had deliberated a long while before making the decision to let Hobman go to the funeral. The older sister of that blighted family had died of breast cancer a week before. Hobman had often tried to contact Fiona over the years, writing her love letters full of fury and regret, which were not allowed to be sent. The delusional intensity of that obsession had seemed to ebb over time and the number of his letters had diminished in recent years. After her initial diagnosis she had several years of life and she tried to build a cautious connection with him, sending him birthday cards and a few simple gifts. Hobman remained quiescent all that time. She eventually arranged to visit him and they met briefly in a hospital review room accompanied by four escorts, her husband and the other remaining younger sister Nikki. The meeting lasted ten minutes. Fiona was already frail and

187

ill. Brother and sister sat with few words between them, they held hands for a while and Hobman gave her a gift he had made in the day workshops. It was a tiny model of a sail boat, a skiff or barque with unfurled sails.

It was hard to tell what effect this meeting had on Hobman. He seemed more withdrawn than ever. Then she died, and Hobman applied to attend her funeral. He had been a quiet patient for years now, taking his meds and keeping out of trouble. He had started a hobby of leather binding during his day workshops, and had become skilled at tooling leather — helping to bind the cover of the large bible that rested on the chapel lectern. His fingers were strong and dextrous from pushing the awl through the material as well as from hard work in the gardens and woodwork shops. He no longer actively menaced the others, although his fellow patients tended to fall back and form a space around him like an invisible barrier, as he glided down the corridors. And so, they let him attend the funeral, judging his risk to be low. He now carried a letter in his suit jacket which had been passed by security, he wanted it to be placed in the coffin with Fiona and there seemed to be no harm in that. They didn't quite see its significance at the time. It was reconstructed later by Poynton from electrostatic analysis of the writing pad.

My darling lost Sister Fiona,

It's been years since I expressed my feelings for you and now it is too late. Now all I have is our forgotten land of Utopia. I release you from our bond my darling Fiona.

My sister, my loving sister. I see us still, falling in the fresh grass, laughing together in the sunshine in that field at the back of Southey Street and you telling me not to stop.

I bless your cheek with a kiss in memory. You're the only woman that I loved. How I often think of Southey Street when I came to see you as if to seduce you. But you seduced me in the end.

I always felt open about our love and I feel that you guided me and guide me still. I am sorry that it has come to this after all these years.

Do you remember you making me a teddy and his little clothes? Dad didn't care for us tho I am sorry that I killed him. He was evil to us and you understand that I know.

*I dedicate my entire life, my entire sex to you. And I am sorry that I
have hurt you.*

*I want you to know that you are as rare and precious as a butterfly in
winter, as a peacock in the spring and you know that our love has always
been a strong shoot, a strong spring shoot.*

*I am so sorry that I left you behind once and I want you to know I will
not do that again. I promise to join you where Nikki takes you. I miss you
so much that it hurts. I have studied Indian philosophy and psychology for
many years now, and carpentry and leather craft.*

*I have made myself better. I make friends and I am an empathising
person and I know how to share pain. May we pass our lives over to God.
May we pass in peace.*

Your loving brother

Martin xxx

The letter crackled in his suit jacket pocket as the Merc turned
out the hospital gates. Hobman continued to stare out at the shorn
barley fields, at the huddled village and the cemetery for the hospital dead, as they headed east out over the river. He looked down
at the water as they crossed the bridge and fingered the stiff edge
of the envelope in his inner pocket. They drove for two hours out
to the flat, fenny lands of his childhood and stopped in a lay-by for
him to piss into a bucket, moving awkwardly in his handcuffs, and
one of the escorts let him comb his lank hair while looking at
himself in a driving mirror. They stopped at the low-roofed crematorium on the outskirts of a Norfolk market town and the
letter he had written was given to the funeral director to be placed
in Sheila's coffin. There was a swift fifteen minute service, the song
"You are the wind beneath my wings" played over the crematorium
speakers. Hobman stood quietly at the back with his escorts next
to the sprays of forsythia and daffodils. The other mourners kept
glancing uneasily back at him over their shoulders. He seemed to
sway for a moment as the coffin moved jerkily away on a conveyer
belt behind the curtains at the end of the ceremony. Nikki was not
allowed to embrace him but Hobman was permitted to talk to her
for a brief moment. He whispered something urgently into her
ear with his head close to hers before he was whisked away, back
to the carrier which had remained with its engine running in the
car park.

189

As he was escorted back to the vehicle he looked up for a moment to the wide, empty Norfolk sky and took a deep breath of fresh air before ducking back into his wired enclosure. Travelling back, his face barely changed expression, his gaze appeared inward and the escorts might have heard a dry rustling murmur and seen his lips moving as he crooned to himself: "I can fly higher than an eagle…"

Spring came to the hospital, collared doves mated in the wired-up gutters, masonry bees came probing around the concrete stanchions and pitted brick work of the perimeter wall. They were looking for nesting sites little knowing that security would gas them as soon as they were discovered. Hobman seemed to settle back readily enough on the villa, diligently working at the carpentry shops and even making himself useful, popping his head around the office door, running little errands for the staff, offering betting tips and the like. In his review medical notes the registrar observed "*I think we are beginning to turn a corner with this patient.*"

★

I had seldom forgotten Hobman's presence in the hospital over the years. We would nod as we passed each other in the corridors, but I had little direct contact with him except once in those early months of my affair with Irina. It was at the M Spot, a club for patients in one of the annexes off the blocks. It had once been a small gymnasium and then it had been done out like a 60s coffee bar where the privileged patients could go to socialise during supervised sessions. There were posters there of rural scenes and of health advice on the walls. Cups of tea and cakes could be purchased with tokens and a dummy Wurlitzer played a recurring tape of hits. One of the security staff once said to me that during the war years, when the hospital population swelled to thousands and there were few guards, this place had become the assignation rendezvous for the patients. There, inset into the walls, were two large wooden cupboards just large enough for two people to squeeze into at the same time. This was where in the old days patients went to couple, while someone distracted the guards or bribed them with a packet of fags.

I had seen Irina on the blocks shortly after we returned from our trip to Burgh-Next-The-Sea and I had drawn her down to the M Spot, wanting to plan our next meeting — thinking that the place would be clear of patients. It looked empty and there was only the sound of a water heater clicking and the far-off booming of doors. We were standing close to each other, leaning up against the old cupboards with one door just ajar, when Hobman emerged from an alcove, a tea towel over one arm, seemingly alone, looking unsurprised. His eyes flickered between us as he advanced closer and closer to us.

"Well, Mr Keyse, a pleasure, Miss Starsha also, clinical discussion is it you're having? Am I interrupting?" His eyebrows arched ironically although his painted face remained grave.

I knew he had immediately divined that there was something between Irina and me. He appeared to breathe in deeply as if scenting us, as we both shrank back by the cupboard doors.

"Pay no mind to me, I am on tea duty as you see, they also serve and all that," he said.

We must have appeared startled and guilty, and I wondered if he had been listening as we had stood murmuring to each other.

"Mr Keyse and I go way back, but unfortunately you have never offered me therapy, what a shame I must say," he said looking at Irina, "You are good at it I hear … I have received testimonials …"

"Here on your own, Martin?" I managed to ask.

"Oh no I am never alone for long, Mr Keyse, you know that." As he spoke, as if on cue there was a flurry of activity behind him and an escort came in, stubbing out a cig, casting us a suspicious look and calling out, "Haven't you finished yet Hobby?"

"Ready, boss!" Hobman answered, storing away a bucket and cleaning materials in a side room. The guard locked the slops room and Hobman turning to me, flicking his wrist in a key-locking gesture. "*Click, clack.* Hey Mr Keyse, *click, clack*, a lock should go. Don't you remember our old days on Eaton?"

I nodded saying, "Yes, I remember."

He turned to follow the guard then swung around to us and made a benediction, his illuminated face turned intently on us, his hand raised. "I bless you both," he murmured and blew us a kiss.

His whispery, soft laughter washed around the room as he was escorted away.

191

Irina and I joked about it afterwards and she asked me what his strange comments meant. I gave an anodyne reply yet inwardly I shuddered, thinking of Kress swinging on that knotted lace. Hobman's blessing was really a curse, there was something unsettling about it but we soon forgot about that as we went, hot-faced and secretive, out to our assignations that early summer, our miraculous summer.

We met in Redford sometimes, at our favoured place on Gun Square where a Crimean cannon was sited down the main street pointing to where the inhabitants milled on market days next to the long rolls of cheap carpets and the stalls for second hand tools. I would watch her coming to see me and, as she neared, she would often dip her head in a characteristic, nervous head toss, flicking the hair back from her face. We would stroll together past the market stalls, past the watch repair booths and the stalls of repro fashion clothing where Asian traders lounged by the empty fountains. We went to the old *Sun* pub where we would huddle in a back room. Sometimes we would walk along the side streets, arm in arm, while all around us this worn-out little town went about its business: graffiti shimmered on walls, the school children in blazers skulked at the back of the bus station, and the shabby goods in the shop windows faded in the intense summer light. Irina and I did not mind, wrapped in our world of brief happiness. We smiled at the glistening plastic and gilt bust of Tutankhamen in the front window of the amusement arcade, and watched benignly among the broken glass and litter of the municipal gardens where young girls with pert faces and mottled, pale legs and white socks, screamed, "Wanna shag?" and the older boys shouted back, "Slappers!"

We conformed to a degree of circumspection, yet we also took many risks. We had a scare when we once saw Poynton walking ahead of us on the main street, off duty, yet with his head weaving about alertly. We looked for other places after that and settled at a nearby tree-sheltered fishing lake. Here we would embrace in the car while outside the fishermen crouched, waiting under their green domed umbrellas. Once, Irina brought a flask of tea with her, a wifely gesture which I resented, pulling up her jersey and telling her to strip. She took her clothes off awkwardly as a child would and curled naked on the back seat, her skin making squeaking sounds on the car leather. There were red lines on her legs where the seats pressed and she began to cry, her face hidden by her hair.

"Not like this Jack, I don't want to like this."

And I relented. My hands slipped away from her for, in truth, she denied me little, coming to me in my flat whenever she could, always leaving a discreet message before she did so. I guess that the loyal, sullen Gosia covered for her or perhaps she simply managed her husband extremely well. It intrigued me how ready she was to betray the eminent professor. No sooner had she waved him off at the airport then I was arriving with my bags ready to move in to the marital home for a week. Anton used to greet me not with, "Da, Da," but with "Ja! Ja!" We both laughed about it. It is strange how such an erotic bond makes one so callous. And I performed all the duties of a husband — even tending to Anton while Irina went to her psychology department meetings and evening clinics. I would sometimes lie in bed with him in the early evenings as she worked, enjoying the strange novelty of that infant being with his heavy, lolling, downy head. And I became skilled at soothing him when he had teething pains, rubbing ointment onto his gums and carrying him around Irina's bedroom in the dark, crooning a song from my childhood, while he grizzled and then slowly settled.

Jolly boating weather,
Hay harvest breeze.

Anton began to grasp out to me in particular in the evenings, calling

"Ack! Ack!" and Irina would murmur sleepily, "Sing him that song again Jack, he loves it."

I would lean over him, cleaning him down as he babbled and wobbled his legs about, looking down at his curled, soft member, her husband's child, my enemy's child.

Irina and I maintained a strange, illusory existence during her husband's absences. We even went to the cinema together to laugh at *The Silence of the Lambs,* newly out, knowing that our killers were, in the main, much more banal. But more often, we hid in her house, away from the eyes of her husband's academic colleagues who lived nearby. Here we maintained our pretend life. We would cook up exotic meals in the evenings, then would bathe together in candle-light once Anton was asleep. Sometimes I would help with Irina's forensic research — discussing interesting cases as we lay together.

Then the weeks came when her husband returned from his conferences abroad. I imagined him moving about in his home. I scanned Irina's face at work for signs of tension, yet she seemed outwardly calm. Sometimes I would worry intensely when she did not appear at the hospital or contact me at home for a few days, imagining violent, marital quarrels. Yet she managed it all with disturbing ease. I began to think that all marriages must be in accord with deceit like this. She somehow kept him happy as well as satisfying me. Although always on that first night when he was back and I was displaced, I would feel sick imagining him lowering himself on her and I could not bring myself to ask her directly about it, though once she offered. "I don't want anything between us Jack. Ask if you must."

But in the end I preferred not to know. Though one night I crept to her house in the night to peer over her crumbling garden wall to see a lit bathroom window and her slender figure combing her hair, clearly distinguishable, then behind her I could make out the shape of her husband moving behind her, and I crept away again, ill with misery.

Irina did not want evidence of our affair. She was cautious in that. She asked me once not to send her letters and she forbade me ever to take her picture. All I had from her were a few brief notes on scraps of paper arranging assignations — and of course that little card she sent me with the picture of a miner from Wieliczka at the very beginning. She gave me other tokens over time, in particular a medallion of the Black Madonna of Czestochowa, which once belonging to her grandmother.

"Wear it always for me," she said leaning close to me, fastening it round my neck. That heart-shaped trinket was my most treasured possession. It dangled to tap secretly on my collar bones as I walked, and to clink against her silver necklace as we writhed against each other in the summer afternoons. Yet I always wanted more from her.

Once she came to see me for ten minutes on the pretext of getting a babysitter before going out to dinner with her husband, servicing me slickly, professionally, and then slipping her evening dress back on, no need for a brassiere with her tiny breasts. She rewrapped her shawl, then dabbed herself with *Cuir de Russie* and leaned forward saying, "I have bought you something special. Let this be yours. It is from myself entirely."

She handed me a little photo wrapped in tissue and as I gazed down on it, I was puzzled.

"What is it?"

"It is me as a girl with my black doll, I so loved that doll, I cried when it was taken from me. In Poland it was a rare thing. I had such a love for it. My black doll. Now, sometimes, I think in a strange way you are my black doll."

She then embraced me and said with a sigh, "*Partir c'est mourir un peu*. It's always like that with us, no?" then she flitted away back to her dinner party.

Long after she had gone, I stared at the photograph she had given me. I saw Irina as an infant, quite recognisable, with her familiar fringe and clutching her black doll. I wondered at our passion which had so dangerously carried us along, and half-remembering my own black doll, my own hopelessly loved object. In time, I reached up to place the photo with her other offerings to me, grouped on my mantelpiece to form a little shrine: the glass box with blue cornflower motif, her cards and notes to me in a bundle, a drawing that Anton made and a sheaf of seeding barley and poppy heads she had picked for me once during a country walk.

That intense year with Irina nearly displaced everything that had driven me up until then; yet as August still burned mid-way through I could already see the rowans setting on fruit and the first yellow leaves in the street limes. Irina's husband had gone to teach at a foreign campus for a few weeks earlier in the month and once more I moved in to the family home. I suggested that we stay up one night and look at the Perseids. Irina asked me what these were and I told her that they were stellar dust, filaments from the tail of comet Swift Tuttle which revisits every year from the north eastern sky. The comet could obliterate the Earth but contents itself with looping around us each summer, shedding in its wake thousands of fragments that burn up in our atmosphere.

I woke Irina at 3am at the peak of the meteor showers and we both stood barefoot under a cloudless, starry sky in her garden. The city was stilled and, in the pre-dawn night sky, there was a faint penumbra of blue on the horizon. The first ones came, faintly visible with transparent orange tails: earth-grazers, the astronomers called them. Then we could make out twinkling silver and orange showers and tumbling streamers of light weaving all along the horizon's edge. Irina turned to embrace me in her nightie, "I must fetch Anton and let him see this also."

And we took him out, cooing sleepily, staring up at the gnarled branches of the cherry and at the roof lines of the city.

"Oh darling, thank you for showing me these. What shall we wish upon these stars?" Irina asked, then went on in a rush, seizing my hand, "Oh, I wish that we will be here next year to see them together once more. Oh yes, it shall be so. It will be so."

We went back to bed as the first birds began to cautiously sound and she whispered to me then, "I feel that I am truly your woman."

And we lay there holding tightly to each other.

Although these were precious weeks together, I can now see that within them there were signs of the trouble to come. Anton became so familiar with my presence and also his speech was improving so that "...Ack, ...ack" was recognisably becoming "...Ack, ...Jack!" And although sometimes we would make love while he obliviously played with his transformer toys nearby there was a growing mindfulness and consciousness. Once getting out of bed with my hair tousled up, I caught an unexpected image of myself in their bedroom mirror as I thrust my feet into her husband's large slippers. I am not sure what I saw there: an intruder, a changeling perhaps. Shortly after that, uncharacteristically, Irina said to me, "You come in to me night after night, Jack but I feel I really don't know you."

★

Plip plop, the liquid from Max's drip fell into a glass bottle hanging by a wire on a cage frame over his legs. He moved painfully as I entered his room.

Plip plop, more droplets fell. He gestured towards his swollen calves which emerged from the pyjama legs. His feet were bound up in support socks of a bright primrose yellow colour.

"I'm no better, boss, you see, but I'm still here! They have got a drain on me legs as they're a bit puffed out like." He smiled thinly through cracked lips and drew his hands over his bald scalp. His hair sprouted thickly on the sides of his head and I noticed that his nails were also growing with strange vigour.

A plate of jam sandwiches lay on his blankets; one of the sandwiches had a single bite out of them. He motioned to them. "It's all I can keep down now, boss."

I looked down at him as he lay there, strapped into pyjamas with Velcro fastenings for the ease of his uncoordinated fingers.

Plip plop. I sat cautiously on the chair by the end of his bed. He raised his head to speak to me then began to wheeze and flounder. He reached for a ventilator mask, fumbled with a nebuliser vial then pressed the assembly to his face. He gestured apology to me, with his face occluded by the mask. A steamy smell of eucalyptus permeated the room. I could see his eyes were closed as he gasped and I looked around his room as he continued to heave inside the mask. I saw the black-painted oxygen cylinder to which he sometimes spoke, thinking that it was a little child or perhaps a woman. There was a collapsed, folding wheel-chair and a cabinet on wheels holding tablet boxes and a plastic container of orange squash. A rounded, wooden crucifix lay on the cabinet looking like a knuckle or a root, worn smooth with sweats of agony, given him by the oncology chaplain. Biros threaded onto strings in some way with distinctive knotted loops were laid out in rows, as were the spare rubber tubes of his nebuliser kit. There was a shelf of video tapes and back copies of TV papers with neat annotations all over them in his spidery writing. He had decorated the walls of his little room with a copy of a red screen print of Che Guevara. There were also photos of his sisters' children in school uniforms and a few tourist nick-knacks brought back from holidays by his sister while Max was locked up over the years.

Plip Plop. What was that yellowy liquid? I had no idea. He eventually put his mask down and steam emitted from his mouth like smoke. It was an eerie sight. I visualised him in the crematorium with the smoke emitting from his gaping mouth like that. He began to cough then he bent forward and covered his face again with the

197

mask. I shifted my gaze to look out of his ground floor window. Beyond there was an undulating lawn framed by dense shrubbery. Max took his mask away with another jet of steam.

"Still here, boss," he repeated and my gaze returned to him. He grinned faintly, stirred a little and sat forward to sip a drink from a cup with a spout. His bottle went *Plip Plop Plip* in a flurry and he grimaced and sighed.

I had spent the spring of that year looking for a place for Max to die as he faded in the hospital. Even Poynton realised there was no point in hanging on to him. He had become a burden with his endless trips to the district hospital which required additional escorts and his sweaty, wakeful nights on the villa and his groaning which disturbed the other patients. I had also begun to plan how to wring the truth out of him before it was too late. It had proved hard to find somewhere for him. Most secure residential homes took one look at his history and rejected the case. But I found a place: thirty miles away, a great square hulk of a place called Haven Court, built of blackened sandstone, set in overgrown park land. The old Georgian house housed eighty dementing elders. The doors and windows were wedged and alarmed up, and the stolid staff marched down the piss-stinking corridors, unfazed by the shrieks of the poor inmates. It lacked the sophisticated containment systems of the hospital, but it was obvious that the weak and sick Max would not even make it down the long, curving drive. Security came and looked it over and gave grudging assent. It was unusual, but everyone gave up on him as he was sinking fast.

The system worked surprisingly swiftly. A tribunal released him, the last papers were signed and the patient transport Merc rolled up through the old gates. The vehicle drummed over the weed-choked cattle grids, while he winced and groaned inside, then out at last onto the rutted drive, his first freedom in fifteen years. The staff unloaded his hospital things, cardboard boxes full of photos, scrap books of newspaper cuttings and his bunches of knotted string. His gentle sister, Theresa, visited bringing luxuries that were not allowed in hospital: lighters, cans of drinks, containers of deodorant and hair gel. He still fussed with his appearance.

My ostensible role was to monitor risk, check on his psychological wellbeing and to advise staff on how to handle him. As a senior member of staff I had no supervisor now, Dr Colt was long gone and no one would question my long absences from the hospital. I first drove up there in late May to make my initial visit to see him. Late lambs were frisking in the fields, swallows ranged through the parkland trees and the sycamore leaves were emerging like red fists. I sat in the car outside the Lodge and savoured the moment, opened my brief case to check on the contents and ran my fingers over the shiny casing of the taser. I called it my taser but it was really a home made stun gun. I had taken it off a psychotic man years before when working in the forensic community team. It had been made by a paranoid man, a skilled engineer, an academic living in a web of conspiracies. It had an anodised body with two sharp prongs projecting out of its snub, shiny body and it was wired up to an industrial capacitor. It could be plugged into the mains and charged up to deliver a massive voltage.

When I had originally taken the stun gun from the patient I had tried it out in my office. I rolled up my sleeve, not really believing that it worked, and then I just touched the prongs to the skin of my forearm. *Wham!* A terrific pain coursed down my arm and I lost all coordination and fell onto the office floor. I came to with my face pressed to the carpet. There was a smell of dust and a terrible metallic taste in my mouth. I was impressed by its power and I stored it away thinking that it might come in useful one day. I had no detailed plan as to what I would do with Max, although I was thinking that once I had extracted truth out of him, I could slam the prongs in to him. The shock in his weakened state would probably do for him and the prong marks would not be readily detectable with all his other intubations.

I had an addition to my preparations, stored in an inner pocket of my briefcase. It was a glass bottle containing GHB — Gammahydroxybutyrate, as the pharmacists called it. I had bought it for a stack of notes in a trance club in the city. I knew it would be popular in that sort of place because of its use as a date rape drug. It was colourless and odourless and broke down in the body. It was a powerful depressant, rendering those that take it at first garrulous and over-confident and then in higher doses, hapless and semi-conscious. I had armed myself with the stuff thinking that I could slip it to Max to make him talk.

I rang the bell in the doorway to Haven Court. A slattern in a stained nylon shift let me in and bade me sign the visitors' book with a biro hanging from a piece of grubby string. *Person visited?* Moribund Maxie. *Purpose of Visit?* To extract the truth out of him and send him to hell. Well, that was in my mind but I signed the book with ironic courtesy, "Oh you have come to see our Max, yes he's no problem, not like some of our others," the assistant chattered to me as she cast an exasperated, look at a bewildered, elderly lady who approached us and quavered, "Have you come to fetch me?" before being firmly ushered away, "How many times 'ave I towd yer Molly, back to yer room."

We marched along dark corridors. Lights glowed on alarm panels and each set of doors were opened by complex levers, set too high for weak and uncertain arms to reach. I was led into Max's room.

He was seated next to his bed, cheerfully shredding heaps of tobacco onto his bed cover. He nodded towards his piles of brown flakes, "I like the air to get to it before I use it."

There was a scuffling sound and a telephone linesman emerged from behind a cabinet and yanked at his tool belt, which had pulled down the back of his trousers.

"Look cable … just installed!" said Max grinning and gesturing triumphantly to a large TV screen showing a history channel with black and white pictures of hundreds of soldiers running and falling. The matron of the place entered and plumped down heavily on Max's bed as he hastily scraped his tobacco heaps into a plastic bag. She asked if he was comfortable and if there was anything that he required. She spoke to Max as if he were a hotel guest. He kept looking across to me with a sly smile.

"Not so bad eh?" he whispered loudly when her attention was distracted by another member of staff. I sat feeling bewildered. I had come to bear down on a dying man yet found myself unsettled by Max's lively comic presence. I edged my assassin's case under my chair with my foot. Max continued to chat with the matron as she perched on the inflatable mattress, built to ease bed sores, which gave under her weight and creaked whenever she shifted. A dietician bobbed in and engaged Max on his menu choices for the next day. It was obvious that the staff preferred talking to Max than dealing with the emptied-out minds of the other patients and indeed they brought out a cheery side to his personality. He joked and chaffed with them and whenever there was a lull in the conversation his eyes would be drawn back to the great TV screen which now showed ancient Egyptians in white loin cloths toiling up pyramid blocks, then a mummified foot looking like a twig, and once an image of the Haj swirling like a vast milky way around the black cube of the Kaabah at Mecca.

"I can look at history all day, I can," he said and ostentatiously sparked up a rolled cig, sucked at it with hollowed cheeks then blowing out a blast with relish. The matron got up and opened the window; the TV engineer completed his wiring, demonstrated the controls for the massive set then departed. Somewhere an alarm sounded and the matron scurried away. Then, there was a pecking and scratching sound at his door which slowly opened and a bewildered, hollow face appeared with a puff ball of hair and a mouth like a soft pit.

"This is my room — why are you here?" The elderly woman announced firmly. "My Ernie is coming to fetch me you know."

I ushered her out gently as her bunched fingers scrabbled at my arm.

"Them biddies are always coming to my room at night," said Max, "lost, I expect, poor old souls."

I thought how strange it was to see how genial and solicitous he had become once removed from the hospital. I was at last left alone with him. He seemed to be watching TV but then turned to me and his dark eyes met mine.

"So, boss, why are you coming to see me here?"

I drew breath, the toe of one shoe resting on my case as he went on, "I thought the hospital couldn't wait to get rid o' me, what do you still want from poor Maxie?"

Before I could answer and perhaps misinterpreting my silence as embarrassment he said, "Oh you don't have to say it, I see boss, you want to talk to me about death and that, see me off alright." He heaved mirthlessly.

"Yes, death and that," I echoed.

I drove to see him weekly through spring and into the burgeoning summer. June came and still Max held me off as I came in week by week, dragging my briefcase, trying to close with him yet disarmed by his odd humility and the melting of his spiky persona. Each time that I saw him I felt a relief and reassurance that he was still there, and sometimes I even began to doubt the accuracy of his diagnosis. These were happy days really, in a strange way, waiting on Max to die that summer, only spoiled by the fear that he would slip away, leaving me nothing after all those years, when all connection and purpose had waned and almost dried up. Now Max was waiting for me, my prisoner, and sometimes I could barely wait to see him as summer flared in the city and I drifted through the streets, noticing all those things that were denied to him: the creamy platelets of the elder flowers, their acrid scent mixed with the car exhaust fumes, sunlight gleaming on iridescent puddles, and the sound of sparrows quarrelling furiously in the shrubberies.

Nights were consumed walking the streets, all the time thinking of Max, about how much time he had left. Sometimes I would be panicked by the thought that he would be gone in the night and I would advance my appointment to see him. I would   pace the streets during the short summer nights, waiting for the morning appointment. I would pass girls going off into town for the night, as I did once with Louie long ago, scenting their perfume trails as they passed, listening to the clatter of their high heels as they ran for the bus, and thinking of the rattling stertor of Max's laboured breathing in the night.

I would often be there early the next morning waiting by the gates to Haven Court and looking up the curving drive into the neglected grounds. I would bump over the grids and pass through the screen of contorted old trees to confront the hulk of the place and break cover once more to enter into Max's world.

He would often greet me cheerily but with a touch of irony.

"You here already boss, is it that time again?"

Often in the early days he did not look too bad. He would always be well-groomed, with neatly pressed pyjamas, sitting up annotating his TV papers or turning the pages of a large scrapbook with the everyday world scrambling on busily around him as if there were no finitude. A radio would be on in the background as well as the TV news; there would be a smell of cooking and of floor polish. Often staff would scurry in to see him, like the dietician, saying "It's Chicken Maryland for lunch. I can recommend it."

"OK, duck I'll look forward to it," he would often respond, and then wave her out.

We faced each other, time after time, that summer, twice a week, sometimes more often. Frequently in the early days he would be alert, jaunty and scornful as I resolved to get under his skin and leech into his thoughts. My violent thoughts of ramming him with the prongs of the taser diminished. No, he was my prisoner. I had him, though he bobbed and weaved.

"Not today, boss. No talking today," he would sometimes say, feigning weakness while at other times he would turn and snarl like the old Max.

"What yer after? Can't I be left in peace? Bastard hospital, can't leave me can yer?"

At other times he was more self-pitying. I used to think then that the personality disorder that had frozen his relations with others also had a protective function for him in his extremis; it shielded him from his own reality.

Yet, little by little, over the weeks Max came to look forward to seeing me, even to depend upon me, and his eyes would light up as I entered his room. He would ask about the hospital, reminiscing about patients he had known and talking about hospital staff in a fond way as if they were old companions. Once I told him about a staff nurse, younger than he, who had suddenly died of a heart attack. Max seemed genuinely shocked and distressed to hear it.

He also begin to talk to me and to let out long-withheld things. I burrowed away at him week by week, asking him about how he was feeling, what he was dreaming about, what his fears were.

Max began to tell me a little about his family and his past. Once, replying when I asked him about the tattooed initials "LL" on his arm, "She were an old girlfriend. What a lass! I'll fetch out a picture for you to see," and he crouched stiffly to rummage in one of his cardboard boxes, hesitated, scrabbled about a little more, then drew a photograph out of one of his albums and handed it to me.

"Can't find her picture but who's this do yer think? That's me!" he announced with a sly smile.

"When I was sent to a secure unit near Manchester, 'bout '67, it was taken by my room mate who had a banned Polaroid, probably he had nicked it. I didn't see my family for a year after I was sent there for thieving and the fires. I were thin as a rail then. I shared a room, we were given barley water as a treat, never could stand the taste of the stuff again."

That picture of the lonely boy Max, already dreaming of the mayhem to come, seemed a prefiguring of his sick room now. A slim boy then, though the adult grew fat with his misdeeds. There was the same spartan order, a similar clutch of magazines over which he still liked to pore and annotate. Instead of the 1960s Grundig radio in the photo he now had  another gadget that his sister had brought in for him and which he enthusiastically showed to me.

"Look, digital! They call it the blue bullet MP3, or summat like that. Does other things too, can even record. The things they do now!"

He fell back gasping, and then smiled; he was quite euphoric that day because he had been newly given an oxygen cylinder and kept giving himself a blast from it.

He lay back on his bed; his toes curled up just like the boy Max in the photo.

"I were lovely then and I am lovely now," he murmured looking again at the photo, then whispering again, "lovely then and lovely now."

I sat watching him silently in the room. The mattress crackled as he turned to me and said, "That what I'm saying anyway boss. Heh, heh."

He confided in me bit by bit as summer deepened. It was hard to say what he thought of me, but he was happy for me to stay while he was given a routine examination by the local GP who checked on all the patients there. The doctor had whisked into the room, uttering reassurances and began the ritual of tapping at Max's bared back while listening through his stethoscope. His eyes met mine over Max's shoulder and he made a small movement, shaking his head as if to indicate that there was no hope for him, while Max continued to chatter obliviously to him.

As Max deteriorated I was able to get him to speak more freely. Sometimes I would come into his rooms and go straight to turn the sound down on his TV, leaving the images to flicker in the background as he told me about the night's pain, the aching beast of it, and his nightmares — diamorphine hallucinations.

"Do you know that stuff is the same as heroin? Who'da thought it? Me being let out of clink and given heroin!"

"What do you see when you are on it Max?" I asked.

"Sometimes faces, places, stuff that happened, mixed up like a dream," he murmured.

"I dreamt the other night or maybe I remembered. I was a kid again in the sunlit kitchen hiding under the kitchen table. Seeing me ma walkin' abaht making dinner, her white ankles moving and me thinking — that's me mum. Also, a funny thing, I remembered when I was five or so, coming in to our front room at home her friends were sitting with her, chatting, faggin' it. I remembered coming up to her and pulling at her blouse, wanting to suckle like as if I were a babby again. And she saying 'Not now, you're too old, yer daft thing,' and them all laughing and screeching. I kept on trying to suckle, 'til she hit me, making my lip bleed then I ran away, wanted to hide, wanted to hurt. I can still hear them all laughing at me."

Thus I scraped, scratched and ate into him, draining out his reluctant memories and this work made me feel so alive, so happy and condensed in a way that I had not felt since before going up the five steps. I looked forward to seeing him and often would rise at dawn, driving through the city in the light of early morning. I would park up by the iron gates of Haven Court, as the milk lorry came groaning up the road with its load for the souls caught up there, sometimes watching for a while as a mare and foal silently cropped in the waving grasses of a nearby, overgrown orchard.

To see him was a strange joy for we were both clinging to the same life raft. When he was still there after another night I would feel that we both had triumphed and he would greet me, "Bossman's here!"

He would often offer me refreshments, which I never accepted for we were here to do business, and at other times he would ask solicitously, "You look tired, boss. Hospital giving you too much work?"

I would often set to questioning him as soon as I arrived because I had found that he was most vulnerable in the mornings when he would be shattered by the night and the diamorphine nightmares. I drew him through his childhood, his adolescence and his borstal time. Often, I would start him off then sit back and let him freely associate, waiting for his unconscious to reveal his secrets.

He steadily supplied me snippets of his life and even reflected on his predicaments.

"Don't know why I am like I am, just born wi' it I reckon."

But he was still self-controlled enough to shy away from being too explicit about his offences, the fires, the things he did to girls and if I pressed him he could become taciturn and resentful.

"I've nowt for yer today," he would sometimes say. If I pushed at him about what he had done to hurt the girls he simply bowed his head and gave out racking sighs followed by explosions of coughing.

At other times there was a chilliness about him and sometimes he seemed to be fizzing with a strange energy — and the old, intent, fierce Max would reappear, ignoring me and bending over his heaps of baccy, shredding and shredding at the stuff or making little notes in a jotter, which he hid away when I arrived. Sometimes I found him plaiting string and neatly knotting it into half-hitch ends around the oxygen tubes of his apparatus. Once I asked him what he was doing with his scrapbooks, scissors and gum.

"Oh just stuff I collect," he replied, sliding his scrap book under his bed.

On days like that his eyes were obsidian chips in his broad grey face. I remember his intense interest when the nation was gripped by the mystery of two little girls going missing that high summer in Suffolk. Where were they? The nation waited in agonised suspense and Max watched keenly on his great big TV screen.

"I can tell yer," he said to me, "those little 'uns they'll be long gone now, done in. Hard to manage two of them together."

He looked interested, even fascinated, by the searches for the girls and he would peer impatiently past me to look at the screen even with the sound turned off. I couldn't get to him on those days and irritability sealed him off. Once I saw him snarl in fury as his oxygen tubes snagged on his bed frame and he spat out, "Blast yer!" to the care assistant who was rearranging them.

On days like that I sometimes had the scarcely endurable thought that I would fail to get anything from him at all.

Then, after an unbearable wait, the two girls were found dead. A school caretaker was arrested and sent up the five steps to the hospital as the nation's hate turned on him. Maxie watched it raptly on the screen and then something seemed to give in him, his health took a down turn and his belly began to bulge out, his feet and legs puffed up and oozed fluid. He was started on the nebuliser and received more diamorphine. September arrived and a gale blew up, rattling the hospital roof tiles and the gutters. I drove over to Haven Court from the hospital and found that some of the old beech trees had fallen in the grounds and were already being burned off by the landowners in a backyard *auto da fé*. This was a special day anyway, but I felt very afraid that Max was going to escape me soon and I resolved to corner him.

It was the fourth of September and he was hurting. I could see the flesh had melted off the upper body and purple patches had spread onto his neck and shoulders.

He belched and grimaced, "Sorry! The medication is hell on the digestion."

I sat down and moved my briefcase close to the chair. He kept trying to summon the staff on a buzzer but no one appeared.

"Fat lazy things, probably faggin' it," he said referring to the care assistants.

"Could yer," he said holding out his arm for me to assist him. Then he stood leaning heavily on me to pee into a receptacle. While holding his forearm I could feel the bone beneath the skin and tried not to take in the sweet rotten smell of him. He stood for a long time as I pressed closely to him and realised that this was the first time that I had touched him. The teak-brown liquid slowly filled the bottle as we swayed about and then I eased him down to collapse onto his squeaky mattress.

He lay back, his head dark on the pillow, and muttered, "Can't make sense of it boss. Can't make sense."

I moved my chair closer to him as he continued in a low voice, "Bad nights, bad thoughts. Dreams I can't stand. The TV. Them girls in what's that place? Soham." He gestures to his bed where there was a heap of tabloid papers with pieces cut out from the pages.

"The missing girls. They found them. I reckon he did them quick though. Don't think they knew much abaht it."

"How do you know that Max?"

"I should know. God knows. Interested like …. me dad liked little girls more than me though." He groaned and shifted. I thought he was trying to get comfortable and stood up to help him with his pillows but he gestured me away, leaned over and scrabbled under his bed to fetch out one of his scrapbooks.

"Look boss, I'll show yer something."

He opened the stiff, heavy pages as he leaned on the bedclothes and I saw photographs, cuttings from papers and whorls of anno-tated script going up the margins. I glimpsed some names that I knew: Jeannette Tate, the three girls in the Midlands triangle and Mr Kipper. When I leaned forward to read the annotations more closely he dragged the book away from me.

"That's enough now," he said clasping the heavy document to his heaving chest.

"What's this about Max?"

He reached for a plastic beaker and drank. His Adam's apple bobbed in his scrawny throat.

"My sickness boss. The reason I did that poor old taxi bloke to get myself sent away so I couldn't hurt others."

"So there were others? Ones we didn't know about? Stuff you did?"

He nodded and gulped.

"Yeah … Others. There was always others. Can't bear to think of it now. Things I've done. Things we have done. Seems like a stranger did it, not me, those nights when I was young when I felt I had to do stuff. Hard to understand now. A bad dream."

He lay back gasping. There then came a soft tapping at his window and we both looked up. Staff must have put out a little heap of crumbled biscuit on the window ledge. A wood pigeon was tapping at the crumbs. I turned to see Max with tears running down the lined, grey skin of his cheek.

"I'm scared boss."

The soft tapping continued as the bird fed. Max went on, "Seems like a dream — the past. Seems like it never really happened."

"It does matter Max. Real people were hurt."

He looked at me, blinking weakly. Then I leaned down and opened my brief case. I reached down and drew out a photo. "Do you know what today's date is, Max?" I asked softly.

He was a little puzzled and mildly irritated.

"Nah."

"It's the fourth of September. Do you know what you were doing fourteen years ago?"

"What are you on about?" he said, "I can't be doing wi' it."

I held up the photo.

"It's you, isn't it Maxie? September '86. Look at the tattoo there, the rose on your forearm, and the letters above it."

"Look, boss, no head games now. What is this?" His old anger flickered up then he coughed, wheezed and grimaced.

"There is little time left Max. You have to tell me the truth."

I pushed the photo towards him.

His eyes grew misty for a moment, and then they blinked clear. He snatched at the picture awkwardly with swollen fingers. Took an intake of breath and glared at me.

"Who is this? You think this is me? You're nuts!"

His tongue flickered at his lips as I went on, "I'm here to help you to tell the truth about what has happened."

"That's bullshit, boss," he rasped. "why do you want to know about this? No one has ever asked me this before."

I sat staring at him as, far off, doors thudded high up in the building and a cleaning machine whined somewhere.

Max stared back at me intently then said, "Who are you boss? What do you want from me?"

"I'll tell you something, Max," I said, "I have been looking for you for a long time. I know that you are the one. I will help you by letting you tell the truth after all these years and you will help me by telling me what you have done with her. Where she is."

"Where who is, fer gawd's sake?"

Max responded with his voice rising to a shriek, then he lapsed into a bout of coughing and lay back on his pillows looking aggrieved and a little fearful.

My chest was pounding as I went on.

"A woman went missing, a young teacher. You were seen there. That is you pictured there at that time. It is now your chance to make it right, help me and help yourself by telling me what happened and what you did with her."

Max lay very still. There was a pause then he seemed to be shaking and I could see that he was laughing soundlessly, his face wrenched up in an odd grimace.

"Oh ho, ho, that's rich," he finally choked out, "Boss, you're a sly one, coming here all this time, after something that Maxie has. I should report yer."

He stared at me then rolled away on his bed with a hissing sound from the inflatable mattress. He lay facing the window where the bobbing head of the feeding bird was still visible. Max made a rasping, rattling noise and I realised that he was crying. He turned back to me and wiped his face with the back of his hand.

"I'm whauling an' I don't know why. You are the one who is wanting help from me," he gave a choking, bubbling laugh. "Ha. Ha. Looking for Maxie to help the doc, who'd 'ave thought it."

He lay back and gasped. We sat in silence for a while. My hand moved away from my open case and I thought that we had passed the most dangerous moment. The pigeon continued stubbing at the biscuit crumbs on the windowsill outside, its iridescent back rippled gorgeously in the sunlight.

Max suddenly clapped his hands with surprising speed and force and with a shatter of wings the bird had gone.

"So, you have been trying to find this girl all these years? An' I have been running from my memories. We both live in hell then, eh boss?"

"Yea Maxie, we both do."

"I want yer to go now, boss. I'm frightened of you. I don't know who you are. I think now you are too like me with yer secrets."

At that moment a care assistant, tightly buttoned into her nylon coat, bustled in to the room and started removing an empty oxygen cylinder on a wheeled apparatus. Max croaked out to her, "Come 'ere."

I tensed to react but he just said, "Dr Keyse has to leave now, see him out Rosie, there's a duck."

I stepped out of the building feeling a strange sense of release. I was reluctant to leave the grounds and stood for a while in the empty, shattered Victorian peach house, looking down at the dried-out sandy beds where the plants used to grow and wondering at all the difficult paths that had led me to this place. I was afraid at what Max would do now that I had unmasked myself and I felt regret that our connection would be severed. He had become almost more real to me now than Rachel after all these years.

It was a frightening time after that, as autumn clenched and the young spiders threw out their webs. I did not know what Maxie would do or for how long he would last. Car alarms sounded in the night, shrilling like crickets, and I would start at the occasional thunder of a low jet as it veered off course over the city. The next days passed slowly and it was a relief when it was finally time to see him again the following week.

A young care assistant with face stud and short ginger hair slouched to the front door of Haven Court and said, "Max is not well. He told me he can't speak to you."

I brushed past the girl and headed for his room. I knew I could not afford to let him take control of the situation.

I found him huddled under a mesh of tubes. Two nurses were leaning over him, adjusting something, and I could just make out his gleaming scalp and closed eyes. Perhaps he sensed I was there because he stirred and opened his eyes. He turned his face to me without expression and made a gesture. I was not sure if it was a greeting or a dismissal. I stood watching for a while then left.

Thereafter he deteriorated more rapidly and an October phone call to the hospital informed me that he had been transferred to an oncology unit. I called there at dusk the same day.

It was a shock to see him after a gap of ten days. His face was jaundiced, his remaining hair a wiry inferno on the pillow. He lay in a crowded ward, peering up at a TV screen that hung from a bracket high on the wall. It showed a 24 hour news channel and the images flickered: a bomb in Bali, snipers on the Beltway. He looked terrible. His neck was swollen and twisted over to one side, his eyes seemed opaque. He was all hung about with wires and lines and his sister, Theresa, stepped carefully over them where they hung by his bed as she rose from a chair and came to greet me.

211

Her usually serene face was shiny as if she had been crying and she said, "He has been speaking about you doctor."

"What has he been saying?" I asked uneasily.

"He says how much he has liked seeing you these months. How you have helped him."

I made no reply and she went on, "The doctors have told me that this probably is the end."

We both looked over to him on his bed and he began to stir then moved his hand and crooked his finger, gesturing to me to come over.

I stood at the end of his bed, looking down at him, and he again motioned for me to come closer. I came forward and leaned my face close to his.

"Good to see yer, boss," he whispered. "Given up on me had yer?"

"No, Max," I replied.

He gave a little smile then said, "Listen boss, there's a joke I want to tell yer … come closer."

His wrist, with its hospital band recording his name in indelible ink, stirred and his fingers like a yellow, scaly, bird's foot plucked at my sleeve. His face came closer to me and I caught the sweet, rotten, chemical smell of his breath.

"A joke, Max?"

"Let me tell yer. You'll like it." Theresa helped him sit up a little and plumped up his pillows, "Leave us duck for a mo' would yer," he said.

"Listen, boss …" I could hear the rasp of his indrawn breath like a file dragging on burred metal. "A man was running away out of the hospital before the operation, jus' takin' his kit and leggin' it. He is stopped by the hospital porter, 'What's up mate?' asked the porter. The escaping man replied, 'I heard the nurse say "It's a very simple operation … don't worry I'm sure it will all be alright".'

'Well what's so frightening about that?' said the porter, 'She were just trying to reassure you.'

'No mate she weren't talking to me. She were talking to the surgeon!"'

Maxie convulsed on his pillows and gave out a racking cough, which turned into jerky laughter and I found myself smiling.

"Thought you would like that boss, it were me own. I made it up."

He began to cough once more but this time in retching spasms. His sister came forward and pressed a button by his bed as his face contorted.

"Jeesas it hurts T'resa," he muttered. Staff in blue and white uniforms came and one of them slid a curtain around the bed, sealing him from view. As she drew the curtain I glimpsed Max's face turned to me, just giving a nod, and then he was obscured from my sight.

Surprisingly, Max didn't die then, indeed he rallied. He confounded the doctors and although more chemo swelled and bloated him, he gained strength and began to shuffle about the oncology ward; he even smoked an illicit roll up or two in the stair well. He returned to Haven Court in November, after some weeks on the death ward, and appeared to be in a jokingly triumphant mood, clanking his drain bottles and chaffing with the residential staff as he leaned on a walking frame.

"Thought you'd seen the last of me didn't yer!"

I marvelled to see him in late November, "Still here boss!" he croaked out as I entered his room.

The TV glowed and light gleamed on heaped bags of rolling baccy. The neatly arrayed nebuliser ampoules and his drip went *Plip plop.*

"Look," said Maxie "I've outlasted the crow, it's a good day."

He stared up at the screen which showed the famous photographs of that flinty, square, chiselled face with the heap of blonde hair and the later, softer images and the pictures of those that had campaigned for her release.

"That bitch Myra, dead, gone, good riddance. I follored her over the years. That Hindley crow."

I sat with him looking at the news item reprise of the Moors Murderers, those criminal archetypes of our time. Her accomplice Brady was locked up in a sister hospital to the one in which I worked. She had died that day in prison. And I thought then of driving past Saddleworth Moor with Irina when we travelled to Raven's View to see Monty at the beginning of our affair.

"There should be a program about your stuff too Maxie," I said and he stared at me.

"Don't go there boss. Let's not fall out again," he said.

213

We watched in silence for a while, following the black and white images of the victims in their clumsy, old fashioned clothes and National Health spectacles as all the while Max's drip continued its relentless *Plip Plop*. At one stage I glanced over at him. He was not watching the screen any longer and instead he looked out to the garden where a blustery wind tossed the pale undersides of the rhododendron leaves. There was a peaceful look to him that I had not seen before.

He did not seem so bad that day, with his hair slicked back at the sides and his skin lesions covered up by buttoned pyjamas.

"All the things we might have done, eh boss?" he suddenly said to me. "The people we might have been. What would you have done if not lookin' for your girl, eh boss?"

"I find it hard to imagine that Max," I replied then prompted by a strange impulse I said, "Why don't you call me Jack?"

He smiled, "Hard to do that, the hospital drummed it in, the distance between us and staff. But mebbe we are the same. I'll tell you what, I'll help you if you help me. Help me write a letter to my sister, how I feel about her. I want to thank her, for the love and for stickin' wi' me and to say sorry for the hurt I brought into her life. I can't write too well now." He gestured with his swollen hands. "And don't have the words anyway … I'll also need you to tell me girlfriend Maeve I won't be seeing her again. An' if you do that I'll tell yer about the past, what I know, about that picture, let's see it, leave it wi' me will yer?"

I helped him write a letter that morning, sitting on his bed, using my brief case as support. He wanted to express his love to Theresa and his thanks for her selfless attention. I wrote it out as he spoke it and got him to sign it with a shaky "*x x*" for kisses. He tucked the letter under his pillow as a care assistant came in and took away his uneaten jam sandwiches. I handed him the photo from the Paradise Stores out of my case.

"Come back tomorrow, boss, and we'll talk," he said and turned back to look at Hindley's face on the screen. I stopped at his door for a moment to bid him farewell and could see him outlined against the light from the window, the cage dome over his feet, the drip bottle shining and translucent. He did not look back at me; he just raised the photo in his hand, a gesture, a good bye. It was the last time that I ever saw him.

★

Hosannah finally woke up! He who had united us in a way, had maintained his trance suspension and slept right through my nine month affair with Irina. Hosannah had slept on through our moments in the sun, but all of a sudden he began to show signs of waking up. It was announced one autumn day at a clinical meeting that he had taken up his bed and walked. He had apparently just roused himself, obeying some unknown signal, certainly not that of the clinicians who were tending to him for they had all but given up on him. He had first started stirring one evening shift by moving his arms about in an unprecedented fashion. Then staff found him sitting up at dawn, thin and weak, scratching his dreads and gazing vaguely about his room. Throughout the next day he lay on his bed and his eyes followed the staff as they moved about in his room. Later he pulled the tubes out of his arm, sat up and asked for water, then he shuffled around the ward on wobbly legs leaning on a walking aid. He ignored questions about his months of sleep and seemed as truculent and difficult as he had ever been. It was as if he had simply popped back into existence. The other patients regarded him with awe and wonder and murmured, "here comes FZ" as he slithered along the ward corridors.

"What's this FZ then?" asked one staff nurse.

"The Fuckin' Zombie that's what!" came the reply.

It was just as Hosannah awoke that Irina began to ebb away from me although I did not realise it at first. I can see it all now. There were a number of factors in it but primarily Anton was quickly getting older and more knowing.

"Ack, Ack" became "Jack, Jack". And perhaps Gosia resented looking after him as her sister slipped away to see me time after time. Had she let something out to betray us? Perhaps Aidan at last detected a rival or maybe the love just ran out in her. She still pressed me to her with a vivid current of energy when we were together, calling me, "My Jack, my darling Jack, my black doll," but the intervals lengthened between our assignations and there was something in the business-like way she buttoned up her dress after her visits to my room.

Her forensic specialism was "Dyadic Death", the killing of partners and spouses followed by the suicide of the perpetrator, and I often watched her prepare her slide shows for conferences which sometimes sent the audience gagging out of the room: vivid images of a woman dead in bed with a shattered face — shotgunned by a husband, or of a man who had beheaded himself with an elaborate, home-made guillotine after stabbing his wife. Irina was prickly and defensive about her work and although we could talk about most things she became irritable when I joked about her choice of subject. Now, little by little, she retreated from confiding in me, first about her work then about other things.

She began to give me presents instead of giving herself: a pillow stuffed with lavender, a pair of wooden Polish plates, a medallion bearing the head of Mickiewicz. One day she arrived with something stirring in a box.

"I am worried that you are lonely here and have brought you a friend," she said showing me a kitten peering out of the container.

"You can stroke her and think of me," she said as we watched the small thing gambol about on my carpet and begin to dab playfully at a house spider. "She has joy in life … *radosna kotka* … joyful kitten, yes, why don't you call her Radza?"

And Radza she became, a compact little cat with dense fur, the colour of blued gunmetal. Her eyes followed my every movement and she would mewl out a greeting to me as I returned from my long shifts at the hospital. At first I resented the creature, seeing her as an emblem of Irina's absence from me, yet I grew fond of her over time and often pressed my face to the flank of the animal for comfort.

I tried to hang on to Irina. I remember once, making love to her in a snatched moment during one of the last times in her house. We had shut Anton into his bedroom and we could hear him hammering and calling to be let out. As we lay twined together on the bed I found myself staring at our conjoined reflection in the bedroom mirror, somehow gaining comfort in seeing us objectified there. Irina turned her head as she lay and saw me looking at us like that in the mirror.

"I think you are using me," she said sulkily later. After a few days she told me, "I am getting pressure from Aidan. I don't think I can see you for a while, he is asking questions, going through my things."

Thereafter I saw less of her and she had long absences from work, and I settled to a long wait.

Then came the shock. It was a Saturday and I was pottering about the flat with Radza scampering at my feet. I had left the front door open to let the cool air sweep in and was rinsing plates in the kitchen. I heard a peremptory, loud knocking at the door and assumed it was the postman. It was Aidan. I encountered him, bulky and looming, in my hallway.

"I am Irina's husband," he boomed out. "My name is Aidan, do you have a moment? … I thought it was time that we met."

He put his hand out which I shook automatically. He had a powerfully assertive grip.

"May I come in a minute?" he announced, already advancing down my hall corridor.

I gestured acquiescence and he strode past me and I followed behind, my hand moving away from the haft of the hunting knife, hidden, taped to the underside of the hall table.

He seated himself on my threadbare sofa, adjusted his slacks and shook out the sleeves of his dark blazer as if they were in danger of contamination. I offered him a cup of tea in a reflex of politeness, which he declined, and I sat on the arm of a chair to give myself some height over him. His eyes scanned around the room, taking in my books, my poverty, my austerity. Radza scuttled at his feet and he absently reached down to stroke her back.

I was astonished at his poise and audacity.

"My wife has mentioned you; she doesn't know I'm here."

My face betrayed no expression.

"What is going on between you two? I think I have a right to know."

Again I made no response.

"We can sort this out between ourselves."

He emitted more banal phrases which fell into the space between us. I have difficulty recalling them, for I was flooded by anger and with fear and was thinking desperately how best to respond. I began to fence and to quibble with him and all the while I hated and I pitied him. I told him Irina and I were friends, colleagues.

217

I said, "You had much better speak to your wife about all this."

"And my son, you have been spending time with him?"

It was a statement that could not be denied.

"I like children," I replied.

He veered away from frontal assault and began to ask me about work. I parried his queries with vague replies.

"Secretive types you forensic ones," he said.

I replied, "We have difficult work."

And that was it.

He accepted defeat and abruptly rose from the sofa then stopped and boomed out, "You have nothing else to say?"

I shrugged in a gesture of passive negation and rose to usher him out.

"Hope you don't mind me just fetching up like this, just thought it important that we meet you understand?"

He said this as he turned again to face me in the narrow hallway, and again I was amazed at the breathtaking arrogance of the man as he checked me out and marked his territory. I sensed his incoherent pain behind the courtesy and loathed him for bringing this to me.

Then he left, and afterwards I laughed to myself at surviving an encounter with the wronged husband. I even joked about it when Irina rang me later. She apologised for his behaviour and for involving me and said that she was angry with him. Her voice sounded strained. I hoped this event had betokened a crisis and I even began to entertain thoughts that she would leave him and come to me and somehow it would all come right.

Then came Bartram's wedding.

It was the talk of the department, such a surprise. A neat, deckle-edged card was distributed to his colleagues inviting us to the civil ceremony and the reception. He was marrying Mika, a quiet, young Malaysian-Chinese pharmacist who had been a discreet presence in his hospital reviews over the previous few years. No one had noticed that they had struck up a connection. Many had not even known that he had divorced his wife some time after his son's death. The loss of the son had brought about the death of the marriage.

I went out of respect and curiosity. There were only one or two other guests at the registry office. I stood at the back and watched

Bartram's stout figure, clad in an old fashioned lobster claw coat with an ornate silk waistcoat, looming next to the trim, sleek figure of Mika in a silk quipao of midnight blue with silvered plum blossom embroidery, as they made their promises. Neither was accompanied by any member of their families and I wondered at the sacrifices they must have made to be together.

The reception was held in a community hall in the city, a place with stained glass windows depicting civic scenes of industry and leisure.

Bartram stood with Mika at the entrance welcoming the guests as we came in. Both bore expressions of triumphant wonder as if hardly believing what they had accomplished. I realised, for the first time, that beneath Mika's smooth, neat features there dwelled a determined spirit. I also sensed at once that she disliked me. Perhaps she saw my loose friendship and association with Bartram as some kind of threat. I moved past them to the main hall where buffet tables were ranked along the sides and a few couples danced in the centre. Bored and ill-at-ease, I picked up a drink and stood gazing about; waiting for a chance to leave after a decent interval.

Then I made out Irina dressed in a black cocktail dress with a little black and silver bolero jacket. Her hands rested on her husband's shoulders and he in turn clasped her around the waist as they danced together. They swirled away to the far side of the room and the music followed me as I slid away through the revellers.

There was a whooping from the sound deck as Bill Ponds capered about wearing a Caribbean straw hat, accompanying the song through a microphone, "Heard it through the grapevine," he bellowed. I walked away to a side room where the coats hung and a few guests clustered, still followed by Bill's voice, "Honey, honey I know, that you're letting me go," I heard flickers of conversation and just nodded to the familiar faces. I slumped against the coat racks in a state of shock. A few guests continued to eddy around me and the music ate away at me.

"Are you alright, old man … enjoying yourself?" It was Bartram in his splendid, baroque attire with a flushed face and champagne glass in hand.

I stammered out congratulations.

"Thank you … it's not my sort of thing, this reception, but Mika wanted an informal sort of do. Bill Ponds offered to do the music, but he's been on the rum I'm afraid." Mika now appeared in the doorway, her long, pendent earrings glinting; she smiled and gestured to Bartram to join her. "Coming darling," he called out, "just one moment."

He turned again to me and I concentrated on his excited face. It was so unlike his precise pedantic way and the surprise pulled me out of my feelings at seeing Irina embraced by her husband like that.

"I realise I might look foolish to you," he said.

I just shrugged, not really wanting to speak.

"She is so much younger… coming from so different a world."

He looked back at her admiringly as she stood in the doorway in her shiny high-collared dress, speaking to someone, shaking her piled hair and smiling at her interlocutor but with her eyes on her new husband. Thankfully there was a pause in the music.

"I've realised a truth," Bartram went on, seemingly finding it important to impart something to me, "we can love and are drawn to those that share what we are like — our kin, our siblings, our partners, and those who are similar to us. But we can only truly, intensely adore those who are not like us — those who possess an otherness. I realise this when I see Mika's little round head on the pillow. When I take her face in my hands, those slanting eyes, the alien loveliness — I have never experienced a feeling like it. We only truly love what is different to us."

I nodded, looking at his shiny, earnest face, thinking of Irina's black doll. Bartram went on, talking to me with strange, drunken urgency, "Our work takes so much wonder from the world, I just want to hold on to that extraordinary feeling I find with Mika. Hope you don't mind me talking like this. We have known each other for years, I think of you as a close colleague."

"Known and not known," I said.

Bartram smiled and said, "Ah, Jack, when I think of you there comes to mind the third Delphic maxim, not the ones everyone knows — 'know yourself' and 'nothing in excess', no, with you, I think of the other one that runs *Eggun Para B'ata* in the Greek."

"What does that mean?" I asked.

"Literally it means 'a pledge or bond alongside comes disaster'. It could also mean 'Give yourself as surety and get ruin'. I think you will know instinctively what that means for you are a driven man, although I do not know what it is that you are after."

Mika then broke in, pulling Bartram away by the hand, "Come on, dear, you really must mix."

As he was drawn away, Bartram called to me, "And you, when will you know that you have found what you are looking for?"

I followed them out of the coat room. Bartram's words had somehow given me composure and I scanned the room until I saw Irina and Aidan talking as the music thudded on, their heads close together. Then Aidan turned and left Irina and joined the crowd at the bar.

I took my opportunity and moved through the guests and appeared at her elbow. She gave a little start when she saw me and said, "I'm sorry Jack that it's like this but Aidan saw the invitation and insisted on coming … you must go now, it is very difficult at the moment … I'll call you as soon as I can."

I found myself wanting to make a declaration, "Irina I can't go on, I love you, want to be with you."

Her face looked rigid and angry in the flickering disco light and she leaned over and hissed in my ear as the music thudded on.

"Please, not you as well. I keep hearing the word 'love' and I no longer know what it means."

I walked away from her as Bill Ponds gestured to me to join him as he sung, karaoke-style, "Dock of the Bay".

I stood in the vestibule of the building telling myself to leave when I heard a loud voice yelling, "Where is he?"

Aidan pushed his way towards me, a large powerful shape cleaving through the guests. His face was twisted by a desperate rage.

"Are you fucking my wife? I just want to know."

He yelled this at close range and I could see Irina behind him trying to pull him back and crying out, "No, Aidan, please."

"I just demand an answer, are you fucking my wife?" He pushed me in the chest, "Can't you have the decency to tell me?"

"I've nothing to say to you," I replied.

He swung at me and missed as I swayed back then he tried to grab at me and succeeded in clawing a hot wheal down the side of my neck. I looked down to see the silvery fleck of my Madonna medallion and its chain fall to the parquet flooring where he had wrenched it off. Ignoring the threat from him, I leaned down to pick it up. As my hand closed on the tiny emblem he punched me in the face. Other guests seized Aidan at that point and wrestled him back. I stood and stared at him, clutching the Madonna tightly, with my mouth throbbing from where he had hit me.

I heard Bartram's voice in my ear saying, "Time to leave now I think, spring-heeled Jack."

I went out into the night, spitting out a clot of blood, checking to see if any teeth had loosened. Inside, after a pause, the music restarted.

I crept back to my flat and lay on the bed and pressed Radza to me, feeling her little bones move under the fur. I assembled a hope that Irina would ring in the night and tell me that everything would be alright. I woke with a start in the pre-dawn light and lay there moving my tongue over my swollen lips thinking of another moment four years before, a much more shocking and more dangerous event than my tangle with Aidan. This event that I carried with me as marks on my body, had burst upon me one April dawn at five a.m. I awoke in bed with Louie after we had got together again following a year's gap. We had both been asleep when a noise woke me up. I was conscious of a light shining into my eyes and I sat up in bed and made out a dark shape behind the light. A male voice then grated out, "Up you fucker … get up!"

I had begun to swing out of bed as the blows began to fall.

Louie and I had met up one night four years previously. She had rung me after a long gap, catching me on an evening when I had felt lonely and washed-out from trawling the hospital and I was happy to hear from her once more. I agreed to go for a drink. We met in town and she was nervy from the beginning, glancing about her as she talked, choosing to sit in corners of the quiet bars she picked. She looked thinner. There were finger bruises on her pale arms. Her hair was slicked back tightly with gel into a blonde *casque*. It gleamed in the light as she twisted her head this way and that, scanning the other bar guests. She talked of wanting to see me for a long time. "We should have been together — made a go of it," she said as her eyes skittered across the room.

We arrived back at my place, both of us a little drunk and she stripped as if it was expected of her. I drew my fingers over her rounded belly she told me that she was pregnant, three months gone.

"Wish it were yours," she said then fell asleep on my bed. I crawled in beside her and moved my hands over her for a while, smelling her skin as she lay there breathing softly. Her body seemed both familiar and very strange, a familiar field all ploughed over. I fell asleep without possessing her.

I awoke with the light shining on me. Neville was there standing over my bed. I knew at once that it was Neville, Louie's gangster boyfriend, although I had only seen him in that photo she had showed me long before. I also realised at once that I was in a lot of trouble. I began to sit up and found myself stammering out a weak denial, trying to make him out behind the light, seeing only a large dark shape and just the gleam of his shirt buttons and a belt buckle.

"It's not like it seems," I muttered before he hit me on the left side of the head with something very hard. I began to fight, grasping his neck with both my hands then locking my arm around him like a naked cowboy wrestling with a steer as he rampaged around the unlit room, raining blows and kicks on me and barging me against the furniture. But he was clamped too close to do severe damage. He eventually began to tire as I hung on his neck and tightened my grip. His breathing grew laboured and then he just stopped and fell to his knees with a crash. Still I hung on.

We remained like that for an age it seemed, both of us heaving for breath, with his aftershave smelling sweet and sharp. I felt no pain although I found later he had lacerated my scalp and broken some toes. Desperation brought new strength. I pulled and twisted at him and managed to fling him away from me and against one wall. He remained crouching, looking at me and I could make him out clearly for we must have torn down a curtain in our struggles. Dawn light illuminated the scene. He was bulky and dressed entirely in black with a beanie hat pulled low on his forehead.

A lull followed while he remained crouching by the wall issuing a stream of threats. I spied my trousers lying on the floor and he made no movement as I pulled them on over my bloodied and battered feet and legs. Then, once I had covered myself, he began to move and he clacked out a large lock knife, holding it low and coming toward me. I pulled off the bed sheets to catch and parry the blade. As I did so I saw Louie on the bed, curled in a foetal position with a pillow over her head. She might have been screaming throughout the fight but I have no memory of a single sound from her. He jabbed at me and I caught a few of the blows in my sheet-wrapped hands but he managed to cut me many times although I did not realise it at the time. At last I managed to grab his wrist and again we were wrestling and tumbling together with my right hand gripping his wrist. We rolled right out of the bedroom and crashed into the bathroom and I remember my feet skidding about on the blood-smeared tiles as I shook his arm. Eventually the knife went clattering away into the shower recess. Things were different after that, as I was no longer afraid of him stabbing me and perhaps he had become frightened of me in turn for he retreated into a back bedroom. I kicked, pummelled and pushed him along until we reached a window that hung open and which I assumed was where he had entered. Then I charged at him, got him by the waist and began to heave him over the sill. Then in the bizarre courtesy of our battle he said to me, "No, not the window, I came in through the door!"

I paused for a moment then shoved him once more. He fell out the window and dropped twenty feet into the shadowy flowerbeds below with a crack and a thump.

I went back into the bedroom on suddenly shaky legs and found Louie dressing. She simply nodded when I asked if she was OK. I picked up Neville's heavy torch, which he had left among the debris on the bedroom floor, and went cautiously downstairs hefting it in my bruised hand. The front door was open and the prying bar he had used to force it still lay in the entry. Thank goodness he had not hit with that. I peered out into the garden and could detect no sound or movement from him. I was leaking some blood but still not really hurting as I hobbled into my sitting room. Louie crept out and began dabbing at my cuts with wads of cotton wool. The police turned up, having been called by the long-suffering Mrs Mullender next door. Louie murmured how sorry she was and how much she regretted getting me mixed up in her troubles. The police took me to casualty to receive stitches in the scalp and chest. I declined to make a statement. Neville turned up in the same hospital a little later after being brought in by friends, having sustained a fracture to his leg in the fall from the window. I considered that we were quits. Louie rang me a few days later to ask how I was but we did not meet after that. I think she went back to Neville

Wounds and losses, and I was to gain more. Irina, who once at the beginning of our affair had run her fingers over the ridges and welts left by Neville's blade asking me how I had got them, now dealt me further wounds herself. Soon after Bartram's wedding she rang me on my departmental phone asking to see me. We met at Heaton Camp, near the hospital, a clutch of wartime temporary buildings thrown up as a temporary prisoner of war camp. We wandered around the old guard houses and prisoner blocks as an autumnal wind rattled the peeling, tar paper roofs and the shrivelled banks of nettle. She spoke of the disaster at the wedding reception, and Aidan's shame at his behaviour and the effect of all the upset on Anton. She felt confused and heart-broken and wanted to do the right thing. She and Aidan were taking sabbaticals and they were going to live in France for a while.

"I know I cannot be happy now, not after everything ... but I must do the right thing for my family. You will help me in that won't you Jack? I know I can depend on you to help me do that by letting me go."

And I acquiesced to it, somehow thinking that I could serve her by not making things difficult although it was a deathly blow to hear her say that. The wind tore at her words as she spoke, driving the leaves down the rutted old camp road as I watched her little Micra go bumping away from me.

It was strange that the reality of her departure did not immediately hit me then, even though I had clung to her like no other lover before. Perhaps I treated her leaving me like one of those waiting periods where I was put on hold until her husband went away on one of his trips and I would be summoned back once more at some time. But weeks turned to months with no news of her. Still, I clung to an idea that she would call but it was not to be until that following autumn when I saw her walking across the hospital car parks, looking thinner than ever, hurrying along with a preoccupied air. She slowed for a moment as I passed her, just

looked at me and then walked on without further acknowledgement. She had left the hospital to take up a post at another
hospital, returning only on the last Thursday of every month to
attend the regional forensic psychology meetings. Those twelve
Thursdays a year became my secret markers and I would look
forward to those afternoons when she would be near me somewhere in the hospital. I could not resist standing quietly under
the shadow of the rook-inhabited poplars to watch her drive in
and go hurrying up the lodge house steps. Sometimes, I would
draw comfort from touching the warm bonnet of her car, once I
even plucked a dandelion flower from the paving and left it on
the car door handle as a token. On one occasion, I picked up and
kept a shredded piece of tissue that she had dropped on the path-
way still retaining a trace of her scent and which I held on to for
a while until it rubbed away to dust.

Another year turned and holding Radza one day, I found a little
lump which grew into a rosy cancer in no time. The vet told me
after tests that it was an undifferentiated fibro-sarcoma, and that the
prognosis was poor. Radza was doomed and the young cat thinned
and weakened. I discovered her one November morning shudder-
ing on my sitting room floor and that was the end. I found myself
weeping over that scrap of fur as I had never done for Rachel, Irina,
or for all my losses. I built a backyard bonfire from all that summer's
clippings and sent Radza off on a funeral pyre, onto which I also
tossed Irina's notes to me, drawings by Anton, and the sheaf of dried
out grasses she had given me, keeping back only her black doll picture.

With so many scars it was hard to really want anything new and it
was easier to remove myself from all wanting entirely. Max's death
that autumn, after the long summer seeing him at Haven Lodge
seemed like another blow. I heard the news of it with a sense of
regret. He had died two days after I last saw him, expiring in his
sister's arms in Haven Lodge.

"He slipped away peaceful like," she told me later.

I drove out to the crematorium in the town where Theresa lived.
Gulls drifted on the plough lines and lines of lapwing took crooked,
hobbled flight over the salt-grey road. There was a sparse group at

the crem. Theresa tall, composed and stately came forward to greet me. There was a small knot of relatives and one long-standing staff nurse from the villas — for the hospital rarely forgets its own. I was surprised to find that Max was nominally a Catholic. The priest gave a brief eulogy discreetly acknowledging a painful journey and sins now accounted for. One hymn was sung without accompaniment. We read the words from slips of paper carefully copied out in Theresa's hand. She had chosen well, I thought. The coffin jerked away to dissolution surrounded by a few sprays of bronze and cream chrysanthemums.

As I walked away in the drizzle, Theresa called to me and said, "Just wanted to thank you for all you did for him. I know he wanted me to thank you on his behalf. He wrote me such a lovely letter. He left me instructions. He wanted you to have these. He asked if you could go see Maeve and tell her that he's gone."

"Leanne!" She called to her daughter, who came forward with a supermarket carrier bag which she handed to me. I held the heavy bag and bid farewell to Theresa, thinking how her eyes were dark like Max's. I sat in my car with the heater going and looked in the bag. Inside, I found three bulky scrapbooks with pieces of string dangling from them, full of clippings, photos and jottings in Maxie's crabbed hand and a blue and chrome MP3 player, an unfamiliar gadget which I turned over in my hands, unsure what to make of it.

★

I did not know it at the time, but Hobman was already putting his long-hatched plans into motion as I returned from Max's funeral and hurried to the women's blocks to speak to Maeve. The security men chattered among themselves as they unhurriedly issued the keys and the smell of meat and cabbage from the canteen percolated down through the blocks. The patients' artwork glowed in the wall cabinets on each side of me as I went down the block main corridor. Out on the yards, the chill gate latch stung the hand and a column of patients came tramping past under guard. One patient made mooing sounds, then another hooted like an ape and the whole column laughed and the key-twirling, muffled escorts grinned at the fun. In the women's villa nursing station cigarette smoke burned the throat, tea trays rattled and staff radios clicked and hissed. I waited as the team leader briefed her staff, then she escorted me to the review room, telling me that Maeve was due for review and it was best if I spoke to her with familiar staff present.

I rarely had reason to go to the women's blocks. I found it hard to muster the same feelings for them that I had for the male offenders. Whatever they had done they did not appear to be as dangerous as the men and it seemed wrong to see women treated like that. The women's quarters had a softer feminine feel with plastic flowers, heaps of cuddly toys and homely pictures of rustic landscapes in glassless frames. The inmates milled around the smoking rooms, stocky women in track suits and Nike designer tops. Their arms, necks and faces showed marks, wheals and scars from where they

---

Search me O God, and know my heart today
Try me, O Lord and know my thoughts I pray.
See if there be some wicked way in me
Cleanse me from every sin and set me free.

I praise Thee Lord, for cleansing me from sin.
Fulfil Thy Word, and make me pure within
Fill me with fire, where once I burned with sha
Grant my desire to magnify thy name.

Lord take my life and make it wholly thine.
Fill my poor heart with thy great love divine
Take all my will, my passion self and pride
I now surrender — Lord in me abide

---

had sliced and scratched at themselves for self-harm ran like an epidemic in these units.

I was ushered into the review room as a clinical interloper, and was gruffly acknowledged by the irritable male psychiatrist chairing the meetings. There was huge Maria who waddled in, escorted by two staff. She had been in seclusion for the previous two weeks after she had attacked female staff by squeezing and twisting their breasts with her dirty, long-nailed fingers. She had managed to secrete a biro into the seclusion room and had inserted it into a vein in her arm and infected the wound with her faeces. So savage had been her attacks on staff that she had to be fed, and have her wounds sutured, through a gap between the protective riot shields of the triple 4 squad. Now her frenzy had abated and her face was slack and apathetic. She listened to the psychiatrist advising on medication changes.

I sat on in the review through a succession of other patients. I probably had been deliberately made to wait, because the women's service staff resented my presence as a rival clinician from another service. At last Maeve tramped into the room and plonked herself down with an audible thud. She was an arsonist with an Irish name, for somewhere in her background her family had been travelling folk but she spoke with a soft, Norfolk accent. Her thick, dark hair was cut into a bob and she sat regarding us with pursed lips and occasionally pushed her spectacles back on her broad nose.

"Hello doctors," she said, "I'm not a low grade I am."

"No, we know that, Maeve," answered the consultant.

"Coming to see me about Maxie are you?"

"It's bad news I'm afraid, Maeve," I announced.

"Bad?"

I told her he was dead in as simple and a gentle way as I could.

She pressed her specs back onto her nose and scratched at her dark hair that pressed like a tilted wig onto her brow. Seamed scars writhed with white, corded striations on her wrists as she scratched and scratched. Then she opened her mouth, showing small, white teeth, wedged back, as if having received a great blow in the past at some time, "So, Maxie's not coming back then?"

"No, not coming back," I said.

She sat a little longer with her thighs set apart on the chair then she announced, "Have ter find another boyfriend then won't I?"

"Yes Maeve." We responded in chorus.

Afterwards, I trudged back across the yards, wondering what Max had seen in Maeve. I passed the barred windows of the day units and did not realise that Lynch and Gorman were probably in there, attending the same occupational therapy session and secretly agreeing upon their final plans. We have no idea now how Lynch was to be rewarded, or what Hobman promised him. It could have been by credits, by baccy supplies or a suck in the unit latrines, or by something much more metaphysical. Maybe it was going to be Lynch's way of getting back at me at last — a year after I had fixed his lengthy stay in the hospital — we will never know.

I drove home a few hours later in a chill, misty, evening, while inside the hospital, the staff was gearing up for the regular patient dance at the Blue K. The Blue K was on K block, it contained a mock bar, selling soft drinks for credit tokens, the lights were protected by netting and the large room contained a stage area for Christmas reviews and the monthly film shows for privileged patients.

The lights were dimmed slightly. Two coloured spotlights played on the ceiling and the music started at about 6.30 in the evening. Lynch slouched in to the dance in his denim jacket along with one or two from his unit and about twenty other men from selected villas along with a contingent from the women's blocks. Maeve was not among them. Many just smoked and chatted at the tables while a few jigged about on the parquet flooring to the sound of '80s hits. One patient had appointed himself the DJ. The escorts relaxed and sat at the tables, key chains dangling. This was usually an easy detail for them with only occasionally the need to drag away one of the men if they became over-excited and pestered the women patients. A few couples sat holding hands but mostly each patient group remained apart and cautiously eyed each other.

The evening had gone over half way through its allotted time when Lynch rose and walked up to a women's table as if about to ask one of them to dance. The women stirred, some giggling behind upraised hands. Lynch came closer, then he leaped up onto a table top, pulled out his belt and flailed at an unguarded spot light with the buckle end. As suddenly, he caught a piece of the falling glass, dropped back to the floor and seized a young female nursing auxiliary who had not reacted quickly enough. There were screams from the women patients and the music stopped. Lynch hauled the NA up to the stage with his belt and her key belt chain twisted around her neck in one hand, and a shard of the spotlight glass pressed to her jugular in the other. He was circled by the escorts, but kept them off by swinging his prisoner around with powerful jerks of his broad shoulders. Blood oozed from his fingers. It was not clear if this came from the NA's neck or from his hand. She made a whimpering, muffled sound and her blonde hair was tangled in the brass buttons of his denim jacket. The 444 squad had been summoned by three different radios and the security team came running down the corridors carrying their shields and helmets. In the Blue K the other patients stood away against the walls. Some of the male patients began to shout to Lynch, "Do it! Do it!" while the DJ called for calm over the speakers.

Staff drained from blocks and villas to confront the crisis. Two from the team of five on Maple left that night in response to a general alert.

Hobman watched them go from the second story of the Maple villa landing.

He went down to the nursing station.

"Hot water for tea boss?" he asked, addressing the team leader while he stood at the office door and waved his plastic mug. The remaining staff were distracted and intent on listening to the crisis in the Blue K over the radio and did not acknowledge Hobman. He shuffled further into the office up to the desk saying, "And here's your paper back boss, I have marked a few racing tips."

The staff on Maple had become used to Hobman's constant visits to the office for one thing or another, running errands for them, borrowing the newspaper. They still did not turn their heads as he affected to drop the newspaper onto the floor. He leaned down next to the switch panel on the wall for a moment and flicked off the rear villa door sensor. He picked up the paper again, neared the desk and placed it down. Only then did the team leader look up. He registered Hobman at last with a light-eyed stare, burned out by a thousand night shifts.

"Off you go now, Hobby, we're busy," he barked and returned to listening to the security radio as it fizzed and snatched with messages.

"Sure boss," said Hobman. He then glided upstairs to his neatly-ordered room, put on a black fleece jacket and broke open the back of his large radio cassette recorder taking out from the back of the battery compartment four hooked implements spliced to leather straps. These were filed down eating utensils bent into shape and

231

braided with leather fixings, which he had fashioned in his leather-making classes. He then tied each hook to his forearms facing inward and one each just below his knees, tightly lacing the leather criss-cross. He broke open a large battery that was hollowed out and contained a single brass key for the villa rear door, made from a soap mould taken from an impression of Pinsent's cleaning lady's access key. He picked up a bag of woven cotton, a Greek tourist's shoulder bag with blue tassels brought back from holiday by some patient's relative and appropriated by Hobman. Once his preparations were complete Hobman went back down the stairs, passing Mattie Head without a word. Mattie registered that Hobman was about some unusual business but just said, "Cool Hobby, cool," and Hobman signed silence to him with a finger to his lips.

He leaned over the lower stair banister to see the brightly lit office and the backs of the staff. He checked the patient's smoke room where there was the sound of a football match on television and the deep bell of Nelson Bamangwato's laughter as he chuckled to himself in response to his voices. Then he was at the back door, *click clack,* opening to the chill night, the sensor not sounding in the office. He did not relock as the frail key bent and jammed. He flitted across the villa back lawn and crouched by the dark shadow of a viburnum bush. There was the sound of shouting from the Blue K, whose staff continued to pour into the blocks a hundred yards away. He reached under the bush and drew out a long bundle that had been left there previously. It clattered faintly as he packed it into his deep, soft shoulder bag. He then moved, a quick shadow, across the grass courts, to shelter by the personality disorder unit budgerigar cages. After a pause to check for staff movement he ran over the short grass up to the great thirty foot wall of the black wire fence. No warning came up in security control because for three months previously Hobman, and perhaps other patients, had thrown pebbles through the bars of the windows or from the benches where they were allowed to sun themselves for an hour in the villa garden. The pebbles had fallen on the strip of ground laced with movement sensors up near the wire, setting them off time and again until security switched that sector off, suspecting bird interference, or moles, or perhaps electrical dysfunction.

Hobman went up to the fence, a shadow against the darker black of the four ply mesh, so tightly woven that it would admit no finger holds. He hooked the curved, filed ends of the spoons into the small interstices of the wire and began to climb slowly and steadily, occasionally resting, letting his weight be carried on the leather straps. He reached the sharp-edged top, rolled over it and, as carefully, hooked his way back down then crossed another stretch of grass coming to the shadow of the boundary wall.

He ran quickly along the foot of the curving wall down to a spot where the ground rose slightly next to the medium secure area. He paused and lay down flat as staff scurried past in the mist. Somewhere an alarm for a vehicle lock sounded. He lay just under a camera pole that seemed to point down at him in its arc of movement, but all eyes in security control were on the screens showing the Blue K. Hobman crouched and drew out from his bag jointed pieces of garden bamboo connected by three-way aluminium sleeves, made in the workshops and carried to their hiding place in the villa garden in a cleaner's trolley many months before. These sticks fitted together like tent poles. He leant the structure against the boundary wall to form a shaky ladder with just enough height to get his hand over the slippery cold stone of the rounded parapet of the eight foot wall, then a leg hooked over, and he heaved himself up, rolling and dropping with a soft thump onto the other side.

The lights were turned up brightly in the Blue K. Lynch and his prisoner were pressed up in a corner of the stage by a wall of shields. The other patients had been evacuated back to their wards and Poynton had arrived, furious and wild-haired in his shirtsleeves, staring over at Lynch behind the shoulders and helmets of the security response squad.

"Now, Lynch, be sensible," said the team leader, "Let her go and everything will be alright."

Lynch appeared to be talking to himself. One hand roamed over the body of the NA, while he kept tightening then loosening the belts around her throat with the other hand.

There was a lull in the noise of thudding boots and shouted orders for a moment. The security team could hear him growling, "Lovely, lovely, lovely," to himself.

He threw down his shard of glass and took out a pen from his prisoner's top pocket and inserted it in one of her ears. "I'll ram it," he roared, pressing the flat of his hand to the pen.

Poynton had a brief discussion with his team leaders, "I am not tolerating a hostage situation in this hospital," he snapped, "I want you to take him now."

His team leaders tried to argue with him, concerned for the terrified NA.

"Do it now, use a thunder flash and rush him."

The snatch team lobbed a flash over the shield line then, after the stunning bang had disoriented Lynch, they steamrollered him against the stage wall and the NA was dragged out, sobbing and gasping but relatively unharmed.

"Alright, alright." Lynch's muffled voice could be heard from below the scrum as boots and shield rims hammered down on him. He was double-cuffed ankle and wrists and dragged down the blocks with staff slamming the doors behind him *boom boom boom*. More kicks assisted his passage on up the stairs to Dove ward, where the admissions intensive care staff awaited him.

"Here's your fuckin' freaker," said the security team leader. Lynch was propelled into an observation cell with unbreakable perspex doors where the lights would blaze day and night.

"Lock down and sweep," said Poynton with a sigh of relief.

Hobman was already flitting through the medium secure compound annexe, which stood as an adjunct to the main hospital grounds. He had spotted that this was a weak point in the system when studying the grounds from the upper floor of Maple and had spoken to patients who had used it years ago as an experimental rehab area for the least dangerous. It was now used for restraint training and cell search courses for staff. It had a few villa-type buildings and was not well lit at night. Hobman heard the distant boom of the thunder flash and smiled as he approached the gates.

The wire here was not as formidable as the main fence and he scrambled and hooked his way up. He paused and balanced on the top poles, brought to a halt where razor wire was furled along the top in a thick coil. He reached into his shoulder bag and brought out home-made tin cutting shears with sharply honed blades that he had made secretly in the workshops. *Snip snap,* and one strand parted. He paused on the rattling gate looking for the fifteen minute walking dog patrol but they were not out tonight — all drawn to the Blue K mayhem. *Snip Snap* he cut another strand which whipped back under tension and stung his cheek just below his serpent tattoo. He swayed back, recovered, and then carefully bent the severed ends of wire away, making a gap, and hooked his way through and over. He dropped onto the cindered perimeter track and looked out to the grey expanse of the staff football fields and beyond to the field, the dark hedge lines somewhere in the mist. He untied his fence climbing hooks, left them on the gritty track and moved off into the mist.

Staff poured back to wards and villas chattering about the events of the night. The security team were tired but congratulated themselves on a job well done. They grounded their shields in the yards, lit up fags and recounted the incident to each other. Poynton was edgy, however. "Lock and sweep," he repeated in his reedy voice as outside the mist thickened, and patients were counted off on all units.

On the women's villa Maeve asked of her returning ward residents, "What's going off?"

"One of the sex offenders gone mental," was the reply.

On Maple the TV football match was switched off as the patients grumbled and a count was made. At first there was mild concern.

"Where's Hobby?" asked the team leader.

Then the pace of worry increased. Everyone was locked down in their rooms. A door check found the back door open with the crude key jammed in the lock. No one could understand why the rear sensor was switched off. Events moved on as security control received more bad news. Hobman was not to be found. The ladder was found against the west wall. The dog men reported claw-like implements with straps on the perimeter track. At some stage, Poynton ordered, "Crank it up!"

From its chamber in the boiler house, the great siren started up at 8.15 p.m. It had not been heard in earnest for twenty years. At first there was a whirring, then a steadily increasing shriek, followed by a howl. *SCREE EE WHOO,* echoed through every corridor in the hospital and out over the countryside.

Hobman heard it in shadow and I imagine him grinning. Villagers stirred in the night from their TVs. Pinsent's girlfriend, the villa cleaning lady, heard it in Redford seven miles away. It went on and on, the sound rolling down the river valley and echoing back. The rooks began to leave their nests under its

235

onslaught and the whole hospital cowered under the brutal sound. The night wore on, new sounds took over, the twitter and whoop of police cars setting road blocks to the roads north and south, the thudding of a police chopper scanning on infra red somewhere above the mist line.

Dawn came. Poynton had been up all night and now sat in the security control room. He angrily waved away one of the staff who brought him a coffee and a roll. There was still no sign of Hobman although road blocks had been secured up to twenty miles away. The mist had thickened through the night and the hospital humped under it. There was no patient movement at all. The whole hospital was locked down. Headlights came and went on the long drive. In the car parks there was more movement and lights. Coach loads of searchers unloaded and were briefed. A police incident van distributed photographs of Hobman and the press began to gather. Already the first national headlines ran, "*VAMPIRE KILLER ESCAPES!*"

Hobman at one point had claimed to have drunk his father's blood after killing him. Hobman — Dracu, with his illuminated face and dead-pooled eyes — now reached the nation's breakfast tables along with articles about the easy life that the hospital afforded its patients.

As the morning wore on there was still no news of such a recognisable fugitive. Rings of searchers narrowed on fields, sheds and barns. They tramped through the sticky loam of the bare fields and sieved the larch copses and the bramble thickets of Heaton Camp, but still there was no sign. How far could he have got? More rings were drawn on the maps and the chopper cast its infra-red eye right down and along the reedy banks of the river system. All the drains and culverts were searched. Inside, his files were combed through again for clues and his room on Maple was taken to bits. The team that went to his sister's funeral were questioned. A police guard was put on his remaining sister Nikki and her husband at their house near Brancaster.

The wards and villas seethed with rumours about the escape. Lynch was questioned time and again but gave nothing up. The inhabitants on Maple were broken up and redistributed around the other units in case they had colluded in the escape. Jim Popple appealed to staff to leave him alone. He had been in for twenty years for rape and murder and had become set in his ways on the villa.

"Leave me alone staff wouldja? Gawd I don't want to get out. I don't know if I could account for what I'd do if I got out."

He was moved, nevertheless, as was young Mattie Dread who skipped out with a small box of his possessions, singing, "Hobby's out, the moon will shout."

Nelson Bamangwato also lumbered out to a block ward, as ever with a copy of the *Times* under his arm which he never read. An elderly Dahomeyan, who had come here in the fifties as a student; he had left the severed, enucleated head of his landlady's daughter on the kitchen table for her parents to find. He later told the police "I needed her head for *muti* — for medicine — you unnerstand? I needed her eyes!"

He now keened and moaned, "Kindoke stalks; Kindoke says bad *muti* is heah, evil on the loose, there must be a sacrifice! Spirit needs sustenance, needs something to live on. Papa Legba need something to eat — a sacrifice!"

He clutched a cardboard box of his possessions more tightly and continued to yell, "Kindoke — ancestor spirit. Protect me and all of us."

"Out you go, Nelson!" the nervy staff bustled him out back to the blocks and he trudged off still booming out, "Protect us Lord!"

The searches and transfers went on all day and some staff were reinterviewed several times. Poynton reviewed the results of the room searches and sent off Hobman's writing pad for forensic examination. Late in the day he went back down to Hobman's room on Maple and sat there smoking his umpteenth Royal whilst leaning against the wall, his eyes ranging over the heaps of clothing, the scraps of paper and the shards of his dismantled bed.

★

Hobman waited and watched all the comings and goings that foggy Wednesday. He was not far away — in fact he was only feet away, deep-nested under a hedge by the hospital drive, a dense and prickly hedge where, inside, a fox path had created a hollow that

Hobman had widened by whittling at the twigs with his wire cutters. We now know that, after clearing the medium secure gate, he had not run to the fields but instead he doubled back across the staff sports pitch to the white shape of the old cricket score board that had been unused in many seasons. He had leaned down by a grass roller and drew out from behind it a waterproof rucksack. Then he burrowed under the hedge, dragging the bag after him. Once in his hide he unbuckled it and drew out a roll of camouflaged canvas that made a military bivvy. There was an aluminium foil survival wrap that could block infra-red if you wrapped yourself in it; a torch and a survival knife, with a six inch blade, and a saw back. Deeper in the bag he found packets of raisins and nuts, a can of sardines, two bottles of water, some boiled sweets and a rolled up comic entitled *Daredevil: The Man Without Fear* with an illustration on the front showing a man in a red suit with a crimson face.

Who had left this gear for him? It was later discovered that he had tried to contact Andre, who had been transferred to a hostel in the city, but perhaps he had considered him too stupid and noticeable for the job. No, it had to be Pinsent, who had also been freed on license and who possessed the cool wit to obtain the stuff and arrange for someone to flit through the hospital car parks one night maybe months earlier and leave the bag behind the scoreboard roller. That Daredevil comic was surely a Pinsent touch.

Hobman made himself comfortable that night down in the hide. He pegged up his bivvy with the camouflage side to the exterior and rustled into the alu wrap before the chopper arrived. He slept a little despite the siren's howl. Dawn came and he peered out of a small gap in the hedging to watch the search parties being briefed. He finished one water bottle and peed into it. He ate the slippery sardines with his fingers and passed the time stropping the blade of the survival knife with the little sharpening stone that came in a small pouch on the sheath. He whistled silently as the rooks streamed away into the mist. The search parties struggled into their wet gear and the smell of cooking reached him from a mobile canteen.

The day wore on, the White Lady sung to him, maybe he squinted at the comic, reading it close-to in the narrow nest, reading about the demon hero who transforms himself. The wind picked up as the day turned, driving off the mist and making the poplars sway, shedding the last of their leaves. Deep in his hedge, he rolled in the bivvy and stared out at the flocks of goldfinches feeding on groundsel seeds in the untended bowling courts and he scanned the staff entering and leaving. Perhaps he saw me: it is likely that he did. He lay there on into the night as the searching activity eased off and he may have crept out to ease his cramped limbs, ever mindful of the turning sweep of the car park cameras.

Poynton was exhausted by then, sleeping on a camp bed in the control room and the search parties moved further and further away.

Another dawn came, misty drizzle prevailed and a day of intense coming and going of police cars, of press, and search teams ensued. At some stage in the early afternoon Irina arrived, parking in a corner in the psychology department slot by the hedge. It was the last Thursday in the month.

I got the call in the mid afternoon. It was her ringing my office number from her mobile. Her husky, strained voice was a shock and a miracle. I leaped to my feet in the meeting and Bartram, and his junior medics, watched me curiously.

"Everything alright Jack?" said Bartram.

Of course it was alright, my Irina had rung me at last. I struggled to hear her on the crackly phone.

"Jack, it's me, Irina. I must see you. Come alone. The churchyard, the cemetery in the village. You know it, don't tell anyone."

I left immediately, making a hasty excuse of domestic business to my colleagues. I hastened through the turnstiles looking up at the long glass windows of the control room where figures moved about in a fug of cig smoke. I hurried to my car, past the police Land Rovers and the cars belonging to the press, and pulled out turning eastward at the great gates. There was no one about apart from one police car slowly cruising. I find it hard to remember exactly what I was thinking. It was as if I had suspended conscious thought. An odd prevision, a wariness was there, however, perhaps it was always there with me, and I stopped for a moment scanning the outline of the church on the outskirts of the village. I spotted Irina's small car by the church gate. There was no other sign of movement. She had told me to meet her in the church yard. I remembered that we had strolled there sometimes in the year that we were together, and I had once showed her the gravestones of the hospital dead.

I moved through the worn brick columns of the gates, the latch clacked loudly in the stillness, and I walked around the flank of the old church, my feet swishing in the fallen, crisp sycamore leaves. I stopped in the shadow of the church and called out, "Irina?"

There was no reply.

I called again, slightly more loudly this time, "Irina!"

Then my eye caught movement, nearly fifty yards off on the eastern edge of the churchyard. I saw something, shadows, figures moving against pale stonework and I moved cautiously towards them through the headstones. On that edge of the cemetery there stood a Tudor gateway, once the entry to some great house. Beyond it a rough track wove through orchard land, down to the river where, on the horizon the winking lights of the power station began to show more clearly in the fading light.

As I approached and before I could call out again, I saw a large figure moving that became two figures, closely meshed, moving between the dark pit of the doorway and the shadow of a nearby yew. Then, just once I heard Irina's muffled voice calling, "Jack!"

I rushed forward and made them out at last. It was Irina and behind her a shape, pulling, tugging her back into the shadow. Then I heard his calm, almost languid voice, "And so we begin and end, Dr Keyse."

Hobman.

"He took my car, Jack. I'm so sorry," Irina gasped and I could see Hobman behind her with the glinting arc of the big, saw-backed knife to her throat.

"You know how it is," he said, "you have to follow me. You know that don't you? You see we're off to see the wizard."

He pulled Irina backwards, then he back-kicked at the old gateway door until it gave a little on its reluctant hinges and jerkily opened after more thudding kicks. Irina and Hobman edged into the entry and I followed. We stumbled down the trackway under the black shapes of leafless trees. Hobman forged ahead, occasionally turning and twisting Irina around as he did so to make sure I was following. And, so we stumbled along. I was thinking what I could do, perhaps fall on him but I was fearful of the consequences. They kept moving on ahead in the gloom. It was hard to make out which shape was Irina and which Hobman's.

I remember our footfalls rustling in the sedges and the sound of Irina's gasping breath ahead somewhere. We went further and further from habitation, although I had noticed that a light had come on in a house across from the churchyard when Hobman had been kicking at the cemetery door. I tried calling out to him, "Just wait, Hobman, think what you are doing, don't be stupid, you don't want more hospital time."

The only response was low laughter from him, then he stopped for a moment. I came close to them and could make out that he was still holding the knife up to Irina's neck.

He said quietly, "Come on, come on. You of all people should know my purpose. You do know surely where we are going? The White Sister speaks to you too, doesn't she?"

Then he turned and forged on as the ground grew more marshy and ditches gleamed with water. An icy moon rose and, at last, we broke out onto the bank of the river. It spread widely before us and downstream the red lights winked on the great vats of the power station. We went further along the bank close to the pilings of the road bridge. The river smelt of weed and fear and somewhere a

241

water bird sounded a few warning notes. At last, we stopped by a landing stage that projected into the river which was dimly lit by the lights from the road bridge. Hobman drew Irina down the staging and I followed. I could see her breath emerging in sharp, little pufflets in the chill, dank air. Our feet slipped on the uneven wood which gave a bit under our tread. Below us the river ran darkly, strong and silent.

"What are we doing here Martin?" I called out.

"Bless you brother, not too many questions. Just be glad you are here with me as I feel you have been with me all these years."

He still held the knife but I could make out that his hands dangled at his sides now and he was seemingly at ease.

"The White Spirit, she likes you. I can tell she talks to you. You have been with me since Eaton all those years ago. You remember Eaton when you gave me that nonce, your gift to me do you remember?"

"Yes, I do, Martin."

Then Irina spoke, her voice quivering, "Jack, what's going on?"

"Shush, sister, let brother speak to brother," Hobman murmured.

His shadowy form turned and he seemed to be checking something on the skyline. After a moment I thought I heard the faint twitter of a siren from somewhere in the village nearly a mile away. He turned back to us and unhitched his rucksack, letting go of Irina who swayed about on the slippery stanchions.

"Sit, sister," he commanded and shook out a long roll of material from the bag, which later proved to be his camouflage tarpaulin. Irina knelt there on the staging and Hobman solicitously folded the fabric around her like a cape.

He moved closer to me and we stood facing each other.

"Tell me about you two," he said, gesturing to the shape of Irina. "I want you to tell me about it. I smelled you out didn't I? Both of you by the cupboards at the M Spot."

I faced him and felt his breath on my cheek. He was so close.

"It was love, Martin," I said.

"Don't, Jack," Irina called out, but I reached down and touched her face under the cape. Her cheek felt as cold as stone.

"It's OK," I said.

Hobman remained standing close to me. He spoke again softly.

242

"Yes, listen to him. He knows it's OK. Go on, Dr Keyse."

"Our love had wings, Hobby," I told him. "We met, we conjoined; we swam in each other's flesh. We could not bear to be without each other. We breathed together, our eyes, skin, experiencing our love. It was urgent and immediate — like the way the foxes scream in the night behind the wire. You have heard them, haven't you Martin?"

"Yes, I have heard them." His breath steamed in the chill air as he spoke.

I went on pouring out a confessional, "Our love was elemental, it ached in our bones. Oh, to be with another being like that. And, when it ended, I grieved so terribly. It is so hard to live without that love, isn't it Martin? The wind blows through you, you go on living but not wholly being. Some of us must do without love. We two are brothers in that. We are the unique ones, fated in that way. We live on, keeping true to the past in our own way."

I felt him grip my hand as I went on in my trance utterance, an emptying-out which I can barely remember now, though I can still clearly see his rigid, gleaming face so close to me. I told him everything about Irina and my search for Rachel and somehow in that moment I felt that he had truly understood me.

I know I finished by gesturing to the crouched figure of Irina, "We adored each other Martin."

And I could hear that Irina was sobbing,

"But it ended as these things do."

There was sound then, louder and nearer and he took a few paces past me, and stared along the river bank then came back and said, "Thank you Jack. I appreciated that. For me, it was always Fiona, my lover, my sister, my pride. I blessed the days of our union but hated those who would take her from me — my father, priest-men."

He turned to listen once more then went on, "And why Kress all those years ago, why did you want me to deal with him?"

"I wanted him to suffer for my own loss. I was careless with others. He was a sacrifice, a mistake. It was wrong of me to involve you. Please forgive me. You shouldn't have hurt him like that though."

Hobman replied, "You wanted him gone."

Before I could say more, there was a growing sound of yelping sirens from the road bridge and a lower register of sound, a *whup whup whup* noise, now nearer, now further off. I could make it out distinctly above the columns of the power station. It was a chopper with a searchlight glaring at its nose.

Hobman had seen it but he continued to speak to me as his face turned to the night sky, "No, no, there shall be no bad feeling. We all work through our purposes."

It came on us suddenly and everything was swallowed by light and noise. The chopper thudded over us in a pass then reared up and made a turn to fix on us. There were waving torch beams and the sound of barking dogs somewhere close on the bank.

Hobman turned away from me and was standing looking up. I glanced down at Irina with her pallid face thrown back and, even in the terror of the moment, I felt so intensely tender for her.

I fell on Hobman in that instant screaming to Irina, "Get out! Run!"

I closed with him, wrestling for his knife arm, at the same time hearing a crashing and splashing sound, which I later found out had been Irina leaping into the shallows and floundering to the bank. Hobman was incredibly strong. We grappled but his knife arm coiled and twisted and he flung me off him. He hit me with a smashing impact that came so swiftly that I never saw the blow. He cracked me on the brow with what was probably the hilt of the survival knife, although he could have easily stabbed me. I was momentarily stunned and toppled back onto the slimy wood of the staging. I was aware of more splashing noises and I am sure for a moment I heard Poynton's reedy voice shouting out, then I was lifted in a tremendously strong grip by my clothing. It was Hobman standing over me and he raised me right up and put his mouth to my ear.

"No need for fear any more. We are all spirit brother. I am you."

I could just hear him above the roar of the overhead chopper. He let me fall and I watched him as I sprawled, he walked away down the landing, his back turned contemptuously to his pursuers. At the end of the staging he stood in the shaft of white light from the searchlight. His hair was black and spiky, and his tattoos livid scrawls around the pits of his eyes. He seemed to do a little dance on the rotten boards with his arms akimbo, and the knife flashing in the light.

244

He screamed out above the racket of the blades, "Look I'm a real boy now. No strings!" He turned, put his knife between his teeth and slipped into the river. I swear that he winked at me before he slid away into the water and began to swim while being carried swiftly along by the current.

The chopper drifted above him and I heard a voice calling out, my own, "Come back Martin. I need you!"

The current took him and soon his head was barely distinguishable as the water was ruffled up by the blades of the chopper. He seemed to stop swimming for a moment and raised the hand holding the knife in the beam of the helicopter light. There was the blur of his head, then even that was gone and all that remained was the swift water as it curved away.

PART THREE

The Present

Chapter Six
The Five Steps

Spring came; wildfowl streamed from the lake, flying north again to the Arctic and Scandinavia. The colour of the water went from grey to blue as the light intensified. The lines of police searchers paced the grasslands by the lake, skirted the woods and moved out over the hill, prodding with rods and detectors. They were looking for soil disturbance and they paused sometimes to consult maps and diagrams. Weeks dragged by, the weather impeded progress and the searches were called off for a while due to other alarms — demonstrations, terrorism perhaps. Then they resumed and the area of Clouds Hill was retraced. They hit something by a stand of wind-stunted poplars. It was a place a few yards from the water, the ground laced with sheep tracks. A slot in the stiff, pebbly marl was uncovered and the red soil peeled back. Blue and white banded tape then sealed the area and police landrovers bumped over the tussocky meadows. Sometimes a vehicle went hurrying back to the market town five miles away, its siren yelping. A small digger manoeuvred with the bucket raised and a canopy was erected to flex in the breeze off the water. The press got to hear; people began to gather and the peace of the lake was suspended for a while.

I arrived and watched the search and the excavations, standing among a crowd of press, onlookers and a few hikers that had been swept up in it all. I returned to haunt the hillside later in the summer, after they had all gone and the holes had been sealed up again. They had found some things and took them away. The police called them "remains" — a good word. I imagined bones, cloth rags, felted by time and moisture. I thought of teeth, still with a calcareous stain and I imagined objects holding onto their identity: a comb, a purse frame, keys, shoe soles. I also found a place to rest and think at last. I came drifting back in the nights and found it peaceful there as I lay couched in the grasses, near the huddled shadows of the cropping sheep, listening to the rustle of the poplars and the lapping water on the shore. Sometimes I followed the sheep as they stumbled down to the water's edge and I would look out over the lake.

Rachel and I had come here before when the place looked very different. It was over twenty-five years before, in one of those hot, dry summers of our decade together, maybe in the last year of our relationship. I still have a photo of Rachel standing next to the bike, taken later that day when we reached the coast. We had meandered eastwards towards the sea having decided on a whim to go on a joyride with no real direction. The old 650cc flat twin bellowed down those switchback country roads as I screwed on the throttle and enjoyed the cool wind with Rachel's hand on my hip and insects bouncing off the helmet visor like shrapnel. The road had followed the ridge line of the flat-bottomed valley below us. The roadside grasses were passing in a creamy blur with the speed of our passage when I saw Rachel's gloved hand pointing to the small sign *Barnhaven*. I slowed and dipped down a country turnoff, past woods and a straggle of cottages, down deeper into the valley to the plough lands and the standing wheat. The engine throbbed then gave out a meaty belch as I declutched and stepped down a gear. We cruised to the valley floor, past farms, and the empty-seeming hamlet of Barnhaven. As we approached a copse outside of the village, Rachel leaned over and yelled over the engine noise, "This is fine… stretch our legs a bit."

I stopped at a field gate which was sheltered by ash trees. The wheat stretched away in a rippling, dense mass. I cut the engine, watched the dials drop to zero, and balanced the machine with my boots grinding into the dry, plough soil as Rachel dismounted. I rocked the bike between my thighs to test how much petrol was sloshing in the tank then clanked down the side stand and rested it on a flat stone. I strolled to the deeper shade by the fissured ash trunks, loosening my leathers and pulling off the tight helmet. It was so hot that it made my skin prickle. My boot plates clinked on the pebbles in the dusty soil, and the buckles snagged on loose wheat stalks underfoot. Rachel opened the battered box panniers on the bike and began to arrange a picnic. We sat on the raised roots of the ash trees, looked out at the heat-dazed fields and waved away hover flies. Rachel gave me a coke bottle and I cooled my hands on it. She rolled her bottle against her cheek. Her face was flushed with the heat and from the bright light burning through the helmet visor. Her eyes looked lighter against the sunburnt skin. Her hair was all pressed down from the helmet. We sat and chatted quietly as the engine fins of the bike clicked and creaked faintly and the pipes exuded a burnt-oil smell. We ate sandwiches and looked out over the valley. The sheep on the skyline huddled in the shade and one lone swallow dipped and turned over the wheat. It wasn't a bad place to stop.

Then we heard a growing thrumming roar from somewhere to our right in the valley bottom. We couldn't see it at first and we thought it was a combine like the others we had seen that day. A giant, yellow, road digger came thundering right through a hedge then carved its way through the wheat in front of us. This was followed by another great machine and yet another. We were stunned by this sudden eruption of noise and mayhem. When silence had settled again we walked cautiously over the tracks in the flattened crops to the splintered rents in the thick hedging. There was a smell of sap and of dust in the wrecked hedge line and birds were flitting frantically around their trashed nest sites. Rachel pointed out the notice pinned askew to a pole. It read — *Don't Drown Our Valley.*

We realised then that this was Tuxford Water, although people were yet to call it that. Then it was simply known as "the reservoir". We had heard of it as a *cause célèbre* of the time. The authorities had proposed filling a valley of rich, ancient farmland with water from a dam seven miles down stream. It would take ten years to fill properly. The slender streams, which grew fat in winter, would pour in to form a great lake that would eventually be drawn off on giant sluices, going to slake the thirst of the growing Midlands' cities. We cruised along those doomed valleys that afternoon and watched the diggers ripping down the settlements, Barnhaven among them. Dust blew back onto our helmets, our mood was lowered by seeing something so relentless happening. The old places were erased, the wells were capped and the sheltering copses ground down. The waters were to creep up over the next decade to drown the villages with their two thousand years of habitation. All their secrets were to be submerged: the rich lands full of flint arrow heads from the Stone Age people who had left their barrows on the ridge lines. It would cover the lynchets and the ridge and furrow pasturage and the prime fox hunting lands. The Elizabethan estates and the Victorian lodges were all to go under the water, along with the gate posts and the shale slab that I had leaned my bike against on that day.

We moved on in the afternoon. I cranked the starter, flicked down the helmet visor and the bike throbbed away. I went up the road out of the valley to the ridge then tilted the machine and glided onto the main road, heading east to the coast. Rachel clung to me as I opened the throttle and sped along the flickering hedgerows, out and beyond the rim of recall.

I thought more intensely about Rachel than I had done in years as I wandered there through the grasses by the lake. As the gulls skirled by the lake shore I was reminded of how much I had really missed her over those years. She had given out such a warm, generous and companionable presence and had shown a loving acceptance of my uncertainties. Only after she had bowed out from everything had I really begun to wonder what sort of being had I been with all that time. She remained with me though, like a slow current that twines around a lake swimmer.

★

I had one visitor during the time of my suspension from the hospital after Hobman's escape. It was Bartram. He had come bustling up my driveway with his odd mincing step one cold afternoon in March. He looked quite different out of his usual consultant's bow tie and pinstripes. He came wrapped in a long tweed coat with a heavy, home-knitted scarf and a battered fedora. After unfolding himself from his wrappings he sat drinking tea. He refused my offer of biscuits.

"My weight, you know, Mika is trying to get me to cut down," he said patting his stomach and glancing around at my bookshelves.

Once he was seated, and after a jocular exchange of courtesies, he fixed me with a serious look and said, "Well Jack, you came among us disguised to kill the suitors eh?"

I had forgotten how direct he could be in his strange way and I began to stutter out some sort of explanation but it sounded like an apology.

"No, no, dear fellow, you may tell me what you like in due course. I am not here to question you. It's not to say there haven't been consequences of course."

He took a sip of his tea.

"Well, there have been consequences. An inquiry, internal of course. Poor Poynton has not exactly got the sack but his powers are diminished and there is a sleek young man from the London prison service directing security matters now."

"Poor Poynton," I murmured.

"Yes, he had your interests at heart. We really have him to thank for allowing us to track you and Irina to the river in the first place that afternoon. He got the forensic electrostatic results from Hobman's writing pad that allowed us to read his letter to his sister. And then he got through to Nikki, his younger sister. She told us that at his sister's funeral Hobman had asked her to drop her ashes in the river from the bridge near to the power station. And so we guessed where he was heading. And, as for Hobman, well, we have never found him. I imagine he is in the North Sea now undergoing further transformations."

I felt momentarily guilty about Poynton, thinking of his vigilance and his probing visits to my office after the death of Kress.

"And other than that, things go on," continued Bartram, "The hospital has survived worse scandals. New patients have arrived and some old customers return. Pinsent got recalled from his conditional discharge. Yes, our fish-eyed one, suspicion of involvement in Hobman's escape. Got a recall on his license, much to our delight. He is cooling his heels on a block ward and Lynch, your old friend, has been returned to prison with an additional weight of time after the hostage incident. The wheel turns. The fences are thicker and they have torn down the medium secure area and some of the trees. The poor old rooks are short on nesting sites. The enquiry is still going but little will come of it I expect. *Vulgus vult decipi* and all that. No one will really be concerned at your, let's say, minor deviations from the truth. You followed your own track but we have never felt that you have really let us down."

I wasn't sure what to say.

Bartram tinkled his spoon in his cup and looked at me with a gentle smile.

"And you, how are you Jack? Are you looking after yourself?"

I rubbed the scar from Hobman's knife handle where it had creased an eyebrow. "I suppose I will always carry that mark," I said, noticing how kind his gaze was, almost paternal, although he was barely ten years older than me. "It's hard to explain, it's been infinitely, unspeakably, difficult," I stammered, then felt a welling-up of tears.

"Come on, dear chap."

He put his cup down carefully and advanced towards me and hugged me as I sat, his tweed jacket prickled my wet face. He took me by the shoulders and fixed his eyes on me, "Look, you need to understand. We are all wounded physicians there. We all have our reasons for being there. We miss you. We grew to rely upon you. Come back when you are ready."

I felt grateful, connected as never before with Bartram and the hospital. I was astonished to feel like that, as I had thought I had irrevocably broken with the place or it had done so with me.

"Whatever happens with the Max revelations and the Hobman inquiry, we have a place for you, never mind what security might say, they do not hold all the cards in the hospital."

He patted me on the shoulder then began to squeeze himself into his coat and wrapped the long scarf around his neck.

"You will be alright I am sure. Think about it, won't you? Coming back, I mean."

He pottered out and turned in my drive way as I watched him from the door,

"Oh, and the wife says hello," he called out and waved his fedora in farewell.

★

Little Leanne, Max's niece, had handed me a plastic carrier bag and I had cursorily examined its contents while sitting in my car after the funeral. Later that afternoon, I unpacked the MP3 player and the thick volumes and had a better look at them in my office. My initial impression was that they were merely a collection of cuttings about crime, taken from tabloid newspapers over time, interspersed with a few family photos and Max's scratchy jottings. They formed a dense, compacted mass and exuded a smell of old gum, stale newsprint and an indefinable hospital odour after all those months under his bed at Haven Lodge. There was something repellent about the bulky heap of them, as if they carried some sort of contagion which put me off exploring the contents further. I took them home with me that night, overcame my distaste, and placed them on my desk to take a more careful look at them. There were three children's scrapbooks from a series, made of heavy, soft paper in shades of pink and grey. They were bound with string to which Max had added sections of looped and knotted twine that dangled from the volumes like prayer beads. The stiff pages felt heavy and sometimes they made little cracking sounds when they were turned.

At first glance the subjects seemed to be a jumble. However, I began to see after a while that he had interests and themes. There were many press stories about children and about missing young women and about certain types of offenders. I saw that the Midlands

255

Triangle cases were there, I also recognised the Susan Barber and Kim Newell cases.

He must have gone back in time to old issues of *True Detective* for there was Ruth Snyder and Judd Gray; the infernal Gloucester pair were featured, as well as more recent images of Aileen Wournos. In and around the yellowing clippings wound Maxie's crabbed notations. He had made notes next to the occasional faded photo that seemed to come from his own life. Sometimes there were arrows pointing to images and looping or underlining marks. His scribblings were hard to read and looked almost like shorthand. Sometimes I could make out just a few words like *"this was a good one"* or *"she knew what she wanted"*. Sometimes there were groups of numerals or ragged drawings, in other places just a series of scratchy marks. I closed the thick volumes and hefted the cheap blue and silver MP3 player. It was connected to small headphones, which he had wreathed with knotted string. I donned the headphones thinking that it was a strangely intimate act and flicked the machine on. Max's sister must have downloaded hits from the 1960s and 70s on to it and I quickly put it away again after imagining Max lying there listening to the old tunes on his bed of pain.

Days and weeks passed. I lay up in my place, recovering from my struggle with Hobman. The pile of scrap books and the player remained untouched as I could not bear to look at them. One winter afternoon I finally looked at the scrapbooks once more and picked up the MP3 player. I unplugged the headphones and fiddled with the controls then I noticed a record button and remembered Max wheezing to me, "the things they do now." I snapped the play button on to hear a hissing sound followed by a scuffling clatter then an indistinct woman's voice saying, *"Do yer want proppin' up, duck?"*

And Max's voice replying, *"Nah — leave us a mo' will yer?"*

There was a hissing sound, which I think was a nebuliser, and Max again much clearer.

"Well Boss, we have both come a long way, come a long way. We kept our promises in our own way.

I was always a bad 'un, always. I don't know why. That was just how I was though it all seems like a dream now. The things I did. The things that happened. I think of it now as not quite happening to me but to some bit of me. And sure, I hurt those first little girls when I was nobbut a kid meself as I was hurt when I was small. But the serious stuff later, that was different. A different time.

It was my LeeLee really, she got me doing it. LeeLee. I feel she is here, now, along with the others in the shadows by the black oxy tank whispering in the night. LeeLee, she liked to be called, or ordinary Pegs as I knew her when I first met her. I remember she loved that song. What were it? Yes, 'When Doves Cry'. Played it all the time. Still hear it, especially at night. Her singing it. "Why do we scream at each other? That is what it sounds like when doves cry … Yea they cry … oh they cry."

Pegs, she hated herself so much, she hated anyone perfect. My love was not enough, or mebbe I just could not fill her up enough. I was too like her after all I guess.

And somehow, anyhow, we started and we were a team.

And we would sit in pubs and that and see them going past, and we'd say to each other,

"We can do it to you and to you."

And we would go driving in the works van saying, "If we were choosing tonight it would be her or her."

It was just the taking. It was not the hurting. Taking someone, having the power to do that. To make something happen like that. Doing it together. There wasn't much pain Jack, I want you to know that. We would be sick and sorry later but then, after a while, it would build up again and LeeLee would start on at me and we would begin to play it in our heads again.

When the life is no good, when the loving is no good, there is only anger and shame. That's how it was. Shame also drove it.

And after Pegs was gone, I lost that wanting. It was her game really. That is why I plugged that poor taxi man feller. I were lost. No Pegs, tho' I hated her in a way I needed her.

There was nothing for me after that. Now these last few months have been a blessing really. I feel released from it.

T'resa has my picture books Boss. I'm leaving them for you. Take care of them.

There was then a hiss, a clatter and a clunk and that was it.

The wheezy grating of Maxie's voice was a shock to hear once more and his message to me even more so. Who was this LeeLee? I played the recording again and again, smelling once more the sweet, sick odour of Max's decaying flesh and remembered the dark blue, crudely inked capitals "LL" on his right arm and him saying "What a lass!" I went back to his scrapbooks on my desk and looked carefully among the stiff pages until I found a piece of white card lodged next to an illustration of a teddy bear. On the card, in a naïve woman's hand in dark ink was written the following uneven rhyme:

Love digs deep to forgive so many things you
    Say you can't forget.
Love always takes its jacket off
Preventing you from becoming wet.
Love will always take its time to try and
Make it right for you.
Love will always keep you company doing absolutely
Anything you want to do.
It will also squeeze you tight with a kiss.
Saying, "I apologise, I don't want to argue."
Love will never leave you alone in the dark.
Love is the light to guide you.

L.L. x to M. Always.

This was the first evidence of her presence as I searched again through the heavy scrap books. I turned over the yellowing newsprint clippings and looked at the Polaroid pictures of fields and woodland scenes. That photo of Max on his reform school bed, a press picture of John Straffen being driven back through the gates of Broadmoor with a battered face.

There was a newsprint clipping of Brady and Hindley, then a faded Kodachrome print of woman with short dark hair sitting on a sunlit lawn, thrusting her hand into the mouth of a Doberman puppy with a studded collar. The woman is grinning up at the camera and you can make out the dark shadow of the photographer falling across the grass.

Who was she? This photo, and one other, was as all that I kept back later from the scrap books after giving the rest to the police. Somehow, after Hobman, I felt I no longer had a personal quest to find Rachel. The police took their time looking over the documents. They realised what I had not worked out — that the marks were maps that corresponded to a crude outline of Tuxford Water, and that Max's swirls and arrows and crabbed notations were forms of direction. They also found out about LeeLee — that vacuum at the heart of it all. Little about her came out in the press although Catherine, Rachel's sister, told me some of the detail later. What is known is taken from her remaining family members and from a few public records.

She was born in August, a Leo, a stubborn, pudgy girl. She came from a market town not far from Tuxford Water. She was born Peggy Cumberpatch, one of four siblings, a cuckoo that elbowed her sibs aside. She was not like the others at all, a wilful unhappy child whose waxy skin was scored by her undergarments and who walked with an ungainly duck-like tread. Her father was chronically disabled, due to a head injury in a car accident, and had left the family in her early years. Her ineffective mother made her own clothes, equipping Peggy with shapeless woollen items decorated with bows and hearts and clover motifs that brought derision at school. She talked to her toys a lot and she had a favourite black doll. She was ungainly and her nickname at school was "square arse". She fell on the school swimming pool steps as a teenager and hit her head on the left side of the parietal area. She had no neurological tests after that although she had been knocked unconscious and her front teeth badly damaged, requiring her to wear a plate. She spoke with a slight lisp ever after as the end of her tongue had been bitten off.

Peggy struggled in the world. She groaned at the onset of the menses and was scoured monthly with pain all her life. She was hypochondriacal. She was teased by her peers and struggled for attention from adults. She ate hugely but was a starveling for love. She appears in a few class lists but otherwise scarcely appears in the school record. Her bewildered mother had few explanations for the later researchers. We know that she had a low, husky voice but otherwise there was something about her that did not exist or did not

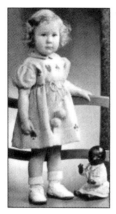

come into being in childhood. As a teenager and adult, she responded to rewards more readily than most people would. Words that were loaded with emotion meant the same to her as any other thus "kill", "sunshine", "love", "dishes", "chicken" "destroy", all had the same resonance to her. At school she conceived a devotion to a sickly boy called Morris. She doted on him and seemed to grieve terribly when he died in a drowning accident. Her mother gave the police her surviving school books showing her experiments with names, at first doing away with her clumsy first name, shortening it to Pegs, then she experimented with Tania, then after leaving school she became Tania Lee then Liana Lee or LeeLee, as she later styled herself. She let Maxie call her Pegs in domestic privacy but we can speculate that she hated the name, associating it with her dumpy, shapeless self, the hairs that bristled on her stocky shins, the crippling monthly belly ache.

At some stage she moved to the city. When did she meet Max? We do not know. What can be determined is that Peggy took out a council tenancy in a dreary estate on the outskirts of the city at the beginning of the decade. Max must have met her and moved in shortly after completing his prison sentence for the first sex offences. What did he see in her? He was drawn to children himself and to the girlish and the vulnerable, yet he had yoked himself to this blocky, dominating lump. Their combination seemed to be one of lethal, mutual subjugation and a melding of a common belligerence. They both possessed a boredom with everyday life. Their bond had perhaps been sealed by thrill-seeking. We think that they began by stealing. They crept into houses, at first contenting themselves with burglary, then staying longer in the homes. Then they cooked food there or lay in the owner's beds, waiting for the people to return before slipping away at the last moment. There were pictures of houses in Max's scrapbook.

They probably felt more alive when taking risks. Sex games also probably pleased them — bondage, subjugation, humiliation. I think of Max passing the time waiting for the home owners to return by endlessly knotting his ligatures. They were savagely resentful of more ordered, happier lives and gradually the idea of playing out their fantasies on a person must have evolved. There were a few clippings from newspaper personal columns in Max's scrapbooks, and we can speculate that they experimented with luring people or perhaps they sent each other out on dates. We will never really understand the mechanics of their phantasy and when I think of Pegs and Max I am reminded of that old nineteenth century definition of psycopathy, a *manie sans delirium*, madness without frenzy, a madness without the excuse of frenzy.

The police had found her name on the council records and had tracked down the estate house that she shared with Max. I went there, after the initial press interest had died down, still on leave from the hospital, and with all the time in the world. It was early summer. A pewter sky radiated a muggy heat and sirens whooped and twittered on the horizons of sound. The estate was maybe five miles from Rachel's old flat, an expanse of cheap, family homes built in the 60s. The houses were beginning to sag and crack, the trees outgrowing their little plots and now hacked back to truncated stumps. Their old house could be distinguished from the others by the blue and white banded tape that sealed it off. It seemed to be vacant, the windows sealed with plastic and the front door standing open. A white vehicle from the police forensic service was positioned outside and a single, bored policeman leaned against the gate post. I peered over the front hedge thinking that Max's works van must have once been parked on that weed-clotted drive. Now a rusting child's tricycle lay toppled there next to a broken splayed folding umbrella. Beyond the back gate I could see heaps of freshly dug earth in the rear garden. A group of young mothers came past pushing prams, smoking and talking loudly. They began to chaff with the policeman.

"Antcha got anything better to do?"

"Found any bodies like?"

"You can dig up my garden anytime you can!"

I walked away to a row of nearby shops, trying to imagine Maxie going out to buy his rolling tobacco. There was the usual Asian corner shop with its wary owner in the doorway, a place for tanning booths, a credit shop and one or two boarded up properties. Lounging youths watched me, their high-crowned baseball caps set at an angle sideways. Some began to whiz past me on roller blades giving me a hostile stare. Swarms of winged ants were massing on the cracked pavements and beginning to take flight in the hot air. I noticed a graffito scratched on a wall — *"dream wiv open eyes"* and I turned away, feeling desolate. This place was rubbed clean by time. There was nothing left to find.

Nothing was left of Peggy either, we know that from the only records we have of her — her last medical notes. She evidently used to have fits of impulsive rage — there are hints of these in Max's writings. At these times she would hit out at him or she would run away and disappear for a while. She used to slash and cut herself and her wrists were whealed with white scars. It was a year after Rachel disappeared and Max must have done something — we do not know what — an argument, a refusal, a minor betrayal of some sort perhaps. Whatever it was, she took an overdose of paracetomol tablets, probably a whole bottle. She slugged it down with brandy from the Asian corner shop. That would teach him. That would show him. He found her curled asleep on the sofa. She roused a little when he shook her awake. She cried and railed at him then she nodded off again. He left her to sleep it off. She had done it before but had never taken so many pills as this time. Anyway, he was too fearful of attracting attention from the authorities to seek help.

It had all seemed to have blown over when she awoke in the morning. He tried to get her to eat something, but she was still nauseous and had a terrible thirst and headache. She even became amorous and attentive to him after asserting her power to damage herself. As the day wore on, she felt a little better and was almost back to her old self but she had a disturbed night of vivid, frightening dreams The next morning the malaise got gradually worse. She found it hard to concentrate and couldn't tell the time right. She became anxious and called on Max for reassurance. The fear and agitation grew worse through the day. He was concerned to see her so muddled in her thoughts and suggested that she lie down and get some rest. He shut her in the spare bedroom and she woke him in the dawn of the next morning calling out, "Maxie, Maxie, where are you?"

He was shocked at last into doing something for she was obviously ill, sweaty and frightened, her skin yellowing. He took her to

Casualty in the work van and the triage nurse whisked her into the IC unit as soon as she saw her, calling to Max, "Why have you waited so long?"

The doctors crowded round her and someone wrote, "*fulminant hepatitis*" on her notes. She had acute liver failure from paracetomol poisoning. In intensive care she was intubated, oxygenated and they filled her with Vit K, but jaundice had set in and she began to slide away. Her eyes darkened to brown holes in a yellow face as bilirubin flooded her body. She developed metabolic acidosis, pressure mounted in her skull and her consciousness wavered. Her mother came weeping to see her strange daughter. Max paced Casualty, unable to cope and yelling at the doctors. She was dead by next morning of cerebral oedema. Her face dark and shiny on the hospital bolster like her childhood doll. There was a brief service at the crem in her home town and her ashes were emptied out from a plastic urn onto the tea roses in the garden of remembrance.

Max had kept his pact with me and had given me a way back to the truth, although there were no survivors from that particular past. The police worked on his scrap books and followed his spidery markings to find that lakeside grave by the poplars on Clouds Hill. Thereafter they worked quickly. It was not DNA that identified her, though they sought it. No, an old-fashioned dental chart brought a match. I first saw the news on a billboard outside a newsagent shop in the city. *Victim Identified* ran the headlines. I had been waiting nearly twenty years for that moment. I stood behind a gaggle of schoolchildren as the bangled wrist of the Sikh newsagent doled out penny sweets into their impatient hands. I carried the heavy, rolled newspaper outside and unfurled it while the morning commuter traffic thundered in my ears. I took a deep breath and began to read.

It was Jayney Kirkman, the fifteen year old papergirl who had gone a year before Rachel. Poor little Jayney, curled in that slot in the pebbly field on Clouds Hill by the lake water. I watched her bewildered parents later on TV. Ordinary people, who held hands in front of the popping cameras. Jayney's sister spoke for the family at the press conference and asked for privacy and understanding. She had lived on, to be nibbled at by the years, while her kid sister remained forever young with her puffed-out eighties hair and big fringe; her room left just as it had been when she disappeared. Her bed was still neatly made up with two dolls propped on the pillow, posters of Wham and Duran Duran on the wall and, on a side table, a domed paperweight that contained a ballerina pirouetting in a snowstorm. The TV news showed the nettle-choked alley from where she had disappeared and original newsreel shots of the police combing the countryside. Then they showed pictures of Tuxford Water. A funeral followed and life rearranged itself while I kept watching.

The police continued to go through Peg's old house in the estate which I had visited. In fact they erected screens and virtually took it to bits after moving out the immigrant family who now inhabited it. They wrenched up the floorboards, pulled out all the fittings down to the plaster walls and probed down to the foundations as well as excavating the garden. They did not find much that corresponded to Max and Peg's tenure although the few items they did find were telling. Some plastic phone cables ties and lengths of flex with distinctive half-hitch knots were found in an outhouse and were similar to those found at Clouds Hill. Examination of the skirting board tack heads revealed carpet fibres that also matched samples collected by the police from the grave. Apart from that nothing much, except the skeleton of a young dog in the garden with the remnant of a studded collar. Oh yes, they also went through the things that Max had given to his sister. One of these items was a small, cheap jewellery box. It contained rings, silver studs, one leaf-shaped earring and a bracelet.

We have no real idea how many more were left to find. Max's scrap book contained a number of pictures of fields and woodland and the jewellery box contained objects that were never matched. The police returned to Tuxford Water a few times and probed here and there, but nothing more was found. Perhaps the lake had crept up over time and covered the sites.

There remained now for me only a night-time scene like a recovered memory. Perhaps I had really known it since Mrs Durrand, the medium's message for me all those years ago. A white ford transit with rust-dimpled sides on the boulevard under the street lights, parked up beyond the Paradise Stores and the bus stop with its metal canopy. Fly posters for student club nights flap and stir as the occasional car runs homeward on the wet boulevard. The rear doors of the van are open and inside the shadowed interior you can just glimpse a tartan blanket, an unzipped sleeping bag, some old sacking and a tangle of flex and cable ties. Max in a white tee shirt by the doors watching the street with his quick, dark eyes. His scalp gleams under the lights and he grinds out a nub end under his foot. LeeLee with the cowed Doberman puppy, scuffling among the fallen plane tree leaves on the pavement, her blunt face moves under the street lights as the shop door jingles its bell. Then she is approaching, her flats going *slip-slap* on the pavement. Her jeans making a slight lisping sound as they drag, then leaning down to pet the dog — she could not pass an animal without making a fuss of it.

I went back to the lake in September and paced the long shore, thinking of that vortex in my life around which everything revolved — that absence of Rachel and how it had affected all my relations with women. How I had stumbled on through life with my companion, the unknowable self, or rather the self that could not endure examination. I had clung to women and I had driven them away. My life had been filled with victims and perpetrators. Sometimes it had been hard to tell one from the other. The pity of it was that I had snatched at love, but my heart had been too full of coldness and regret to make it a lasting thing. I had been such a fool about everything. And yet, what remained with me now were tender thoughts about Rachel, thinking of her as a soft love, an accepting love. If she had a voice I wondered what she would say to me now.

I walked down to the lake shore past the dinghies and their trailers, all covered up for the winter, with leaves beginning to collect in the hollows of their canvas shrouds. A few hardy souls were about, dog walkers, a family playing football on the parched grass. Thistle seeds blew in on the wind across the lake and the young gulls mewled as I went along the edge of the lake that had taken so long to fill. Now, after a dry summer, the level had dropped by thirty feet leaving a long strand of sticky, drying clay. This, that once had been plough land, was now a featureless, flat place apart from where the water had dropped back so far to reveal a tree stump, twenty years drowned, perhaps one of those ash trees under which Rachel and I sheltered all that time ago.

I collected some autumn flowers from the lake verges and boarded *The Tuxford Belle*, a rusty forty seater offering a last end of season cruise around the lake. A crewman took my money as the wind rattled the canvas canopy on the viewing deck. Out in the middle of the lake, they cut the engines for a while and we drifted in silence. I looked out to the tan slope of Clouds Hill and the woodland fringe where Jayney was found then peered down over the rail into the Lethean dark. I leaned over the rail to see my reflection wavering there as the calls of the gulls and terns echoed over the water. It sounded to me if they were calling *Come … come … come.* I tossed my wreath with its sprigs of elder berries and flowers of yellow charlock bound with grasses. It floated for a while, then went down in our wake as they restarted the motors and we went pattering back. As we returned I looked back to watch the silvery, flittering shape of a tern, calling and circling over that place in the water.

★

I went back to the hospital. Where else had I to go? I had an interview with security and received a new key induction for there had been a complete revamp after Hobman's escape. It was comforting to make the long drive once more at the end of summer, passing the shorn fields with the last harvesters grinding up their spumes of dust. The hospital was quiet with many staff still on holiday. No one seemed to take much notice as I walked up the drive, past the red brown scar in the earth where Hobman's hedge had once grown. As I came in, I looked up at the wind vane in the medical superintendent's garden showing St George spearing a writhing dragon and I thought of Heinie's Lambton Worm.

The entrance gate approached and I felt a sense of unease for a moment. Then I turned to go up the steps and once more enter the world of rules and procedures, of magnetic locks, screens and searches. It was a place where I knew that the other staff were talking about me behind my back but I felt that Bartram's power protected me and, besides, I was also sheltered by my new talismans. These were my new tattoos which itched under my shirt. I had gone into the back street place a week before returning to the hospital. The tattooist considered my designs for a while then pronounced, "Cool. No problem."

I watched the marking on his upper arms as he moved his machine over me and the room filled with the smell of hot ink. I admired particularly the legend *No Fear* and the image of a laughing skull with stars shooting out of the eye sockets. His fingers pulled and stretched the skin on my arms. I enjoyed being touched like that as he marked out on my left arm triceps, a sun and moon with winking faces conjoined, with a scroll underneath carrying the words *Omnia Mutantur Nihil Interit*. On my right arm he drew the planetary symbol of Pluto with the letters merged in a helical design and below that the legend *Adsum*. The pain felt sweet as the needle clicked in its silvery snout. Another customer, who had been slouching over image catalogues, came over and squinted at the emerging work. "What's that then?" he asked.

The tattooist leant back and slotted in another charge of ink into the chromed instrument and said, "That's Latin. Very popular now."

"An old poet's words. From his book *The Metamorphoses* — everything changes, nothing is truly lost," I said.

They both regarded me in silence for a moment then the customer tilted his head and looked at my right arm, "I get it. It's Pluto, the new planet. Death and rebirth man — transformation!"

"That's right, mate. Transformation." I nodded assent.

My office looked much as I had last left it when I had received that phone call from Irina in December all those months before. There were heaps of mail and clinical circulars. Some of the drawers were disarranged, probably by Poynton's searchers. I sat at my desk and wondered how I was to work there now and I realised that I would have to find a new way of being in the hospital.

In time I would take up a fresh case load — mainly men but also a few women patients, well-bedded in to the slow stream of the villas. It was soothing to hear the clinking of the keys and to feel the dragging touch of the key chain on the thigh as I walked the corridors. The *riprap* of locks and the dull boom of heavy doors sounded comfortingly familiar, like returning to a childhood home. Staff greeted me in the directorate rooms. Dr Reed put down a canapé from the lunchtime buffet, unselfconsciously wiping her hand on her sleeve then shaking mine, murmuring in her slurred voice, "Good to see you back, Jack." Even the chilly clinical director, Dr Davidson, turned his heavy head as I entered the meeting room and said, "Well, of all people — welcome — and now down to business, colleagues," as he distributed another list of the new admissions and hospital transfers.

It was almost as if nothing had changed. The patients were accepting of me, and somehow I now felt that I had more in common with them than with those on the outside.

Summer ended. Dried wisps of mown grass blew about the compounds. The young swifts swooped round the blocks then abruptly disappeared. Time was doled out by shifts, reviews, admissions panels and tribunals. Families of patients came and went through the security filters. Sometimes at lunchtimes I would go to the hospital swimming pool, something I could never do in the years before. I would strip in the same changing rooms that the patients used, then I would walk over the wet floors, still marked with their damp footprints, and plunge into the empty pool. The water flowed over my blue-black tattoos and I felt free, swimming unguardedly within those walls.

I began to feel more comfortable with those locked up there. I remember walking up to the villas and watching a column of ants on the path thinking that those ants existed here before the walls were built and had simply adapted and continued to exist. I remember particularly Jim Popple, a villa resident, with a round pixie face, a greying scrub of beard and a tear drop tattoo on his right cheek. Incredibly, his own father had been locked up in the place for sex offences thirty years previously. Jim spoke to me in the villa interview room. His small, hairy hands with their long, dirty finger nails rubbed worriedly at his temples. He was in for raping and strangling elderly ladies.

"I'll do it again, mister. I'll do it again if you let me out. Won't I?"

I murmured soothingly to him, "It's OK, Jim. No one is letting you out."

So often in those days I would hear Mattie singing on the C blocks where he had been shifted after Hobman's escape, the sound drifting through the bars out onto the grass courts.

Mattie loved to sing. I had first seen him four years previously, a grinning pied piper, with the other patients following him as he chanted, *We are on the road to nowhere … we'll take that ride.*

He was a cheerful patient and seemingly without malice.

"Jus call me Skitso. Dat's my name here," he had once introduced himself to me.

I recall him wandering into a review with that jerky, springy-kneed gait. He settled into the review room chair as if about to take a nap as we discussed his care plan and he seemed to pay little attention to us. He lay back in his chair, with half-closed eyes, and seemed to be watching the puffballs of cumulus drifting in the sky beyond the barred windows. After the various clinicians had finished describing Mattie's progress we asked him if he had anything to say. He suddenly looked uncharacteristically serious and leaned forward, quickly plucked a pen from the hand of a medical student and snatched a sheet of medical notes. He crouched over the low table and began rapidly writing something then presented the piece of paper to Dr Bartram with a flourish saying, "Dis is my statement!"

It read, *interested only in the Queen Cleopatra now reincarnate as the three gyres in one person with the brown sun Ra of the heavens awaiting the presence of one universal man to redeclare a law long since entombed with the pharaohs …*

We passed the scrap of paper around us and read it in silence as Mattie watched us intently. Bartram's eyebrows writhed in amusement and a staff nurse snorted derisively as he read it. Once we had all finished, Mattie announced, "An' dat law is how to love and be loved in return."

He then danced out of the review room.

Mattie was probably his given name but he may have adopted "Dread" due to some ward joke. Many of the High Secure patients changed their names in that way. He came from South London, a salad of racial genes; his speech was patois with a leavening of Bengali street slang. He was an arsonist, had set fire to some bins in a general psychiatric ward and progressed to high secure, and somehow got snagged up, kept there by his obstinate, gleeful madness.

He had changed little during his time in the hospital, some of his more florid symptoms had leached away to leave just his personality and an ingrained way of being that no therapeutic regime could change.

I waited for Mattie in an interview room in the upper blocks that first September of my return to the hospital. The escorts were taking their time and I stared out from the open window as a cool breeze blew in through the bars. I noticed a lone, stubby oak on its own in the plough land beyond the wire. It was still just alive, standing on a hummock where season after season the plough had ground down around it leaving it exposed with its stubborn roots writhing on the surface.

My reverie was interrupted by the sound of singing growing louder and louder accompanied by the key chink and heavy tread of the escorts.

Is dis love, is dis love, dat I'm feelin? I wanna love and treat you right, evarry day an' evarry night.

It was Mattie come for the review. The escort staff appeared in the doorway and I told them to take a break for half an hour. Mattie sat across from me in the cramped interview room, his eyes flickering around the room as he rubbed his legs which trembled in an akathisic dance.

I asked him about his upcoming tribunal, a three yearly appeal against detention afforded to all patients. We spoke about his offending behaviour and the arson attempts.

He shrugged and said, "I used ta do things an' not think what might happen. Used to smoke skunk, who knows what I was thinking at the time."

I asked him what had changed for him.

He looked out to the sky beyond the window bars, his gaze softened and saddened a little.

"My head is in a different place now, boss."

"What have you learned here, Mattie?" I asked.

"I have learned ta keep the sun shinin' in my soul."

"What would you do if you were let out?"

"Jus' live, man, live."

I asked him who was representing him. "Some lawyer guy innit." He shrugged.

I inquired if anyone was supporting him, family perhaps.

He looked at me with surprised amusement, "Nah, I was in care, doan' know who my fadda was, doan' know where the others are, there's nobody. That's fer real boss."

We sat in silence while I perused his notes and he went on rubbing his legs and gazing out the window.

Outside, footsteps went past in unison, keys clinked, doors boomed and shouted orders echoed down the corridor. My questions eventually dwindled and he shook his head when I asked if he had any questions.

He got up to leave and then I noticed that he seemed to be concealing something in one of his hands.

"What have you got there?" I asked.

He looked frightened for a moment then his face crinkled into a shy smile and he opened his smooth fist to show a dandelion flower glowing an intense fiery yellow in his palm. He must have plucked it from one of the cracks in the concrete in the exercise yards, held it through the rub down searches and had smuggled it onto the ward. His long nails dug into the green nub of it and he spun it in his fingers.

"Me flower, boss," he said and as he stood up to leave he pressed the bright flower head to the skin of his cheek then inserted it behind his ear.

He smiled at me and said, "T'anks fa listnin'."

We shook hands, his eyes on mine, peering out at me shyly through the dangling dreads.

I watched him go down the corridor calling to the guards who were waiting for him, "What up? Ya miss me?"

★

There remains my acquaintance with this city. Night walks with the moon at an angle above the roof lines when the wind sucks at my face; familiar houses yawning in the darkness; yellow lights in front rooms where TVs flicker; shadowed turnings onto streets, where I encounter a fox perhaps, scurrying along the pavement, intent on his business. Plane trees, their leaves in lamplight. Groups of giggling girls going out for the night. They fall silent as I go by, their scent trailing behind them in the night air. I watch lovers passing, grasping each other, trying to meld with each other. I almost envy them, thinking of other faces that once waited for me, smiling faces under lamplight that were once eager to see me. I hear voices, someone calling my name, a woman's voice speaking to me, echoes, rustling of leaves, the flicker of sirens. I stop, listen, then drift on in the shadows, for I am freed from my lovers.

I sometimes see familiar people on my journeys in the city, people from the past. I have glimpsed Louie now and then, walking with a child who has grown up over the years. I would always be able to recognise Louie's straight back and determined step although middle age has encased her. Once I stopped to talk to her as she stood at a bus stop by her workplace and I stared into those same amused, slightly mocking, hazel eyes. She was evidently still working as a nurse, her greying hair scraped back into a bun, an ID card dangled on a blue threaded ribbon and a blue uniform under a beige raincoat. I watched her spark up a Silk Cut and recognised that quick, characteristic whooshing sound she always made when blowing out smoke.

"Well, look who's here," she had said smiling and then she gestured to a pretty girl with a golden mass of hair standing nearby, talking to some friends.

"That's Katie my daughter, had her with Neville. You remember him?"

Oh yes, I remembered him — that face above me in the night.

"We settled down together more or less."

She laughed in an embarrassed sort of way and made a gesture, which I think meant that one surrenders to what one has.

She asked me what I'm doing. I talked a little about the job at the hospital and all the time that I spoke to her I was aware that I should be acknowledging those special things, those profound moments we had together, yet I chatted on, while our unspoken past hovered between us.

Her gaze took in the slice over my eyebrow, Hobman's mark.

"Still in the wars then aren't you?"

"Yeah, I guess so," I replied, then her bus arrived with a groan of brakes.

"Got to go," she said and she leaned forward and in a remembered gesture held my forearm lightly and kissed my cheek, "Take care dear, won't you?"

She gestured to her daughter who detached herself sulkily from her mates and cast me an incurious look before sauntering onto the bus behind her mother. I remained to watch them go. I could see Louie's face through the dirt-smeared windows and our eyes met for a moment then the bus left in a cloud of diesel smoke.

Once, I visited a secure unit miles away. It was a bleak new place with landscaped grounds. I had finished seeing a prisoner for a consultation report and was being escorted out of the unit when I glimpsed a familiar, bent figure with a tuft of grey hair, bobbing between two staff in a corridor. It was Heinie, my old patient from my first days on Eaton Ward. I called to him and the escorts stopped and restively clinked their keys. Heinie stood between them, his beady eyes glittering.

"Hello, Heinie, do you remember me?" I asked.

He clutched at his tattered forelock. His great ears gleamed transparently in the light, the red scar on his temple was vivid. His gaze at first seemed completely blank.

"Yes, boss," he replied mechanically, giving me a brief, cowed glance.

"Tea's up, goin' fer me tea now, boss." His feet shuffled. He looked perplexed and anxious.

"Glad to be out of the hospital are you, Heinie?"

"*Mein herz ist froh* boss."

"Well goodbye."

"Goodbye, boss."

He skittered away, relieved not to be accosted any longer and the escorts tramped off with him.

Then I heard the clear, reedy voice come warbling to me above the sound of keys chinking and the receding footsteps of the staff.

"I'll be seeing you, Father!"

The hospital holds me in its routines and I appreciate its discipline. I welcome the daily trudge along the drive, past the wind vane showing St George eternally spearing the dragon, up to the lodge house with its five worn steps. I set my feet gratefully there, following the trail of staff and patients, for we all go in by one gate and we endlessly tread the long, echoing corridors accompanied by the clank and boom of the great doors.

Many staff come and go but I remember particularly the retirement gathering for Bill Ponds. Nursing and medical staff grouped in the directorate rooms under the print of *The Ship of Fools*. Canapés and soft drinks were passed around and the younger staff gossiped in the corners while the old sweats reminisced together. Dr Bartram gave a little speech acknowledging Bill's length of service  with the concluding encomium, "First and foremost a solid clinician and a support to patients and staff alike". There was a pause as Bill opened a small, wrapped package. It contained an antique, silver, hunter fob watch inscribed *"To Bill from colleagues and friends"*.

Bill began a speech of thanks in his deep baritone but then he faltered. He placed his head in his hands and wept loudly in front of us all.

As Bartram and I walked away to a research meeting, after Bill had recovered his composure, Bartram said, "Freud famously pronounced that the measure of success in life lies in *Leben und Arbeit*. Love and work. That is all there is. When you take a single man's job away — what's left?"

I nodded, thinking that I had spent most of my life rubbing shoulders with these men, spending far longer with them than with any lover and yet we part with just such a banal ceremony at the close of it all.

I only had my work. Irina was gone but she lived on in my heart. I used to see her name on staff lists and, of course, she continued to come to the hospital on the last Thursday in each month. I still felt a cord of connection existed between us and that somehow I was still waiting for her to summon me back once more when her husband had finally gone away. Sometimes, I rang her old number to hear her voice on the answer phone or drove past the old house in the night to gaze up at the roofline and the crooked cherry tree. I once even sneaked in to one of her lectures, on Dyadic Death, to sit discreetly at the back of the audience, watching her figure, listening to her voice. Hobman had drawn us together again and our nightmarish stumbling ordeal by the river seemed confirmation we would be together again somehow. That night, after Hobman had disappeared down the river, we had sat together hand-in-hand in a police car. Later, in the police station at Redford, I had brought her coffee in a disposable cup and our fingers had touched again as she took the cup from me. I tried to speak to her but she had said, "I'm so shattered now. We'll talk later Jack, not now."

The police pressed us, wanting statements. We were interviewed several times that night. A detective later told me that her husband had picked her up from the station.

I came back for questioning many times and was suspended from the hospital.

The police still had many unanswered questions, and they were also occupied dredging for Hobman. There was no inquest as there was no body.

A few weeks later I wrote Irina a letter and sent it to her work address in a psychology unit in another city. In it, I begged her to see me. There was no reply. Weeks passed and I drove cautiously past her house. It looked shuttered and empty. I checked the neuropsychology departmental corridors, based in a teaching hospital twenty miles away. I went to see if she was still there. I slipped past the vigilant secretaries, walking past them with an air of professional confidence and my heart gave a bump to see her name on an office door. But there was no sign of her actual presence nor could I see her car in the staff car park. Summer came, and I had settled to wait. When at last I received a note from her on a card which bore a picture of a kitten lolling next to some chrysanthemum blossoms. I took the meaning of the card to indicate hope and joy.

She gave me simply a time, a place and a date. Enclosed in the card was a map to a psychiatric complex in the city near to her departmental base.

When Irina and I were lovers, I used to prepare for our assignations by playing a recording from *The Magic Flute*, especially the duet between Pamina and the foolish Papageno about love and the hope of a joyful union, the music always filling me with the sense of erotic poignancy. I played it that morning in the steamy bathroom, preparing myself to meet her once more, singing again the chorus, *Mann und Weib und Weib und Mann, Reichen an die Gottheit an.*

Once, years before, I had played the duet to Irina as we lay in bed in my room, and she asked me what the words meant. I told her "Man and wife, wife and man, reaching to divinity". She drew away from me thinking I was mocking her about her marriage but I really did not mean that. I explained that the opera concerned itself with the transformative power of love and that, to me, the words had a tender, ironic yearning and our marriage was one of souls — we were soul mates. She said with a sigh, "You are very sweet sometimes, but you think too much and you draw too many conclusions ... I want us just to be."

We met at The Towers, a disused, midlands psychiatric hospital, a disestablished asylum, close to her new departmental base. Thickets of sycamore and buddleia now sprang up around the crumbling Victorian brick facades. She arrived in a new vehicle, a heavy 4 × 4, which had replaced that little Micra that had carried us so far. I could just make out her features through the tinted windows as she rolled into the weed-filled car park. I savoured the moment of our assignation and watched her from the shadows of a crumbling portico for a moment. She got out and stood by her shiny vehicle with folded arms. A straight, slender figure with her long hair and girlish fringe, sleek in the sunshine. I walked over to her babbling, "So good to see you darling, quite like old times meeting like this."

She unfolded her arms and made a stopping gesture with her hands palm out, "Listen, Jack, I'm not here for a post mortem on our relationship or on what happened with that man by the river. I just wanted to say goodbye once and for all."

The rest of our meeting became a blur.

I unbuttoned my shirt at some stage and showed her that I still wore the Black Madonna medallion.

"Don't Jack. Don't do this to me," she said.

Our meeting did not take long. I remember looking away from her to see pigeons flying in and out of the shattered asylum chapel windows.

"Aidan and I are going away for a while. We are leaving, and I have Anton to consider. I want to have an ending to it all. I don't want to talk about that night by the river. I don't know what there was between you and that man and I don't want to know. The police have wanted to go through it again and again and I really can't bear it. It has been awful."

I asked her if she was happy now and she smiled and kept her eyes on mine as she said, "Yes, I am really happy now. I have got what I want."

I began to beg her to see me — just sometimes.

"Be strong Jack," she said, her eyes moving with distaste.

She leaned forward and dabbed a quick kiss to my cheek and her hot hand pressed mine for a moment. She drove quickly away.

A little later, a green For Sale sign appeared at her house. I went to the estate agent's office and received a brochure entitled Quality Homes describing, "a *delightful converted coach house, carefully and interestingly renovated*", read through all the lists of fittings, "*the entrance door with original transom*", which I had repaired that day of our first kiss, and the "*pampas low suite panelled bath*" where we had bathed together. Sometime later I took off her silver Madonna and coiled it into the glass box with the corn flowers she had given me and I folded her black doll picture away into the box and sealed it up.

Later, much later, I saw her photo on a psychology web site. Her book on Dyadic Death made a small flurry in forensic circles. Many years later, after a long interval I saw her stopped at traffic lights in a car, leaning forward with her sharp profile against a veil of hair, there was a blinding shaft of sunlight and the traffic moved on. Her husband appeared on renowned national advisory committees and I heard his name in the serious press from time to time. Later still, I was drifting through the city one summer afternoon when I stopped to listen to a slight, blonde, beggar girl sitting on some soiled shop steps with bruises over her thin legs, playing the tune *Greensleeves* on a penny whistle. There was a sweet melancholy to the tune and I paused to listen, I caught sight of Irina sitting at the nearby outside tables of a fashionable coffee house. She was accompanied by a young man who had the same powerful features as his father. It was obviously Anton, now grown up. I stood there in the anonymous crowd as the tune *Greensleeves* played over and over and I watched them as they drank their coffee. I wondered if Anton had a subliminal memory of a stranger carrying him, crooning, "*Swing,*

swing together" and showing him the flaring Perseids. The girl stopped playing and I turned to watch her staring at herself in a little pocket mirror with heroin-dazed eyes. I looked back to see that Irina and her son had gone and their table was empty.

Seeing Irina in the street like that, I knew not to speak to her. I had learned to live in the fabric of the present and not in the past. A past that was full of hate which had been a hate for the self, and of loss which had been an estrangement from the self. It was painful but necessary to turn away from everything that I had known and to learn to live in the present moment. It was a discipline that I had at first drawn from work, going up the five steps each day to tread the shadowed corridors and look freshly into the faces of the patients as they streamed past me. And then on weekends or on the occasional day off, I learned to savour the pleasure of days disowned by memory as I walked past the lopsided suburban hedges, noticing the humble offerings of life — sunlight falling on the dusty nettles of the verges, the iridescent soap trails from the Sunday car washers. I had learned to live in the present, for happiness is a release from memory and those everyday offerings around me were the true gifts of life. I savoured them for they helped to wash away the dull ache of the irresolvable past and — who knows? Perhaps one day there could be more than that out there waiting for me.

To live like this is almost to rediscover a self that once was. As once long before, going to a morning lecture with Rachel at university. The lecture was on *Developments in European Thought.* Our lecturer, Dr Knowle, was a minor celebrity, a histrionic, touchy man whose eyes gleamed with emotional intensity when he warmed to his themes. We admired him for his obscure book on modern philosophy where he maintained that something had gone terribly wrong with the European mind. He contended that a sterile objectivism has sheared us away from being within and around things and he called instead for a "deep subjectivity". His lectures were popular and we were moved by his passion even though we barely understood his references. Rachel and I sat near each other at this particular lecture. It was a spring morning. The long narrow hall resounded to our chatter and to the thud of our feet on the floorboards. The doctor made his entrance and began, "Welcome, children of Rousseau, for that is what you are — new Romantics indeed."

His gaze passed over the ranks of long-haired and bearded students. Our noise subsided. He paced the dais in his rumpled corduroy suit and declaimed some lines from the Eighth Bolgia of Dante's *Inferno*, "For those of you who do not have *lingua Tòscana* I translate — 'you were not born to live like brutes but to follow virtue and knowledge'."

He laughed heartily at his own joke and we grinned uneasily. He developed his theme, moving from Rousseau's ideas to Fichte's notion that the consciousness fights an internal battle with its own sense of its finitude. My thoughts drifted. I rubbed at some ink stains on my wrist with a spittle-moistened finger and smelt a waft of patchouli every time the girl to my left leaned forward to scribble something in her notes. I gazed at Rachel, sitting forward to my right, admiring the way she hooked her hair back with one finger in an absentminded gesture while continuing to follow the lecturer.

Movement took my eye beyond the windows where I watched a blackbird hopping in leaf litter under a stand of laurels. The yellow ring around its shiny little eye seemed very vivid against the dark plumage as it turned its head it seemed to look up at me for a moment. The light outside darkened a little and a few raindrops disturbed the foliage. The bird darted away under the bushes. Knowle moved about on the dais, his white shirt front rippling as he acted out his teaching.

"As we move through our day, our consciousness accretes images like soup dishes fitting one into each in a pile, like so."

He mimed being a waiter tottering under a stacked heap of dishes with a waddling, backwards-leaning walk.

We laughed, but on the instant he swung round and stalked among us pointing from one to the other asking, "And how do we get to the truth about what we see and experience?"

"You?"

"You?"

The timid or the dull-witted among us shrugged or avoided his gaze.

"By asking questions?" said a spectacled lad.

"Good, good of Aristotelian! That's a start. We also get to the truth by creatively opposing, by contradicting."

He made his large, white hands into fists and clunked his knuckles together.

"The French have a saying. *Du choc des opinions jaillit la vérité.* The clash of opinions shakes forth the truth. This clash can be destructive or it can be an overthrown by deceit, for existence is so very deceitful my dear, earnest, world-changing Romantics. You tend to see only the world that you really want to see and so, existence has to get round that old gate-keeper consciousness of yours."

He gestured towards us with an ironic smile.

"This journey can be an iridescent, tricky progress. That old fox Hegel said, 'We only get to the truth by a devious and chequered course of development'."

He paused to sweep his hand over the great, balding dome of his head.

"Consider that wonderful word *Aufheben,* that essential movement of things through and towards identity, things that come to be by dissolving and negating themselves."

I watched Rachel's pale forearm under the pulled-up sleeve of her red, cotton blouse and the prominent bluish vein on the back of her hand as she wrote a few notes on a lined pad.

"*Aufheben*, an irregular transitive verb meaning to annihilate, to cancel, to abolish, yet also to promote, to raise, to lift up and transmute."

Outside the spring shower quickened to a brief drumming crescendo, then slackened. I watched the laurel leaves bouncing under the impact of the drops then the movement slowed, as the shower passed and the leaves flickered in a dipping motion as they shed the rain in a stately metronomic beat.

"*Aufheben* is uniquely a word and an idea that encompasses both a movement and a result. It is a word that has been hijacked by ideologues, but it belongs to everybody for it exemplifies the pulse of life apprehended by the mind."

Knowles concluded, and his hands fell to his sides in a theatrical gesture that signified exhaustion and completion.

We shuffled our papers and exchanged glances. The university clock tower bonged out the hour and Knowles waved us out.

"Remember dear things; remember the absolute goal lies in the journey itself."

Rachel and I sought each other among the knots of departing students. The rain had passed and the laurel leaves continued their dipping motion, except when a breeze swept through and brought about a sudden coarse pattering of drops all around. We agreed to go for a walk between lectures and went down to some ornamental grounds surrounding a lake on the campus. We stood in a patch of early spring sun, on the rain-scoured gravel path, under the lime trees in bud and I took out my Instamatic for a picture.

Rachel sighed, "Why now?"

"Because it is now," I said.

She endured my need to take the picture, the sunlight gleaming in her hair and her eyes fixed on the skyline. I sensed that she was impatient with me as if I had not understood something.

We walked on, our hands clasped.

I said to Rachel, "I'm not sure if I get the *Aufheben* thing. It's too abstract."

She laughed and pulled herself away from me.

"It's easy. It just means 'to lift up' — look."

She went to the edge of the path where lilac, rain-toppled, crocus blossoms lay in the wet grass. She stooped and picked a flower, raised it to me and brushed my lips with it.

"*Aufheben!*"

★

All the days we could have had Jack. But which were not to be.

I used to think that it was your fearfulness that undid us, for fear drives away love. At least, I thought it was fear. Maybe it was just unbelief. You were a man who had no belief. Whatever others found true you found so hard to accept. You always sought after knowledge, wanted to look at things and you knew the names for everything, yet you did not see my signals, my gifts, my truth.

And I have lived a hundred lives since you left me — for that I thank you.

What did you teach me? You taught me ... patience and suffering.

For there is a terrible shameful loneliness, the betrayal of abandonment, something I should have prepared for in some inner heart for only a fool could not see that there was an inattention about you and there was a wind that blew through all the cracks of our little house.

But I did so love being with you in the early days, playful, happy, for happiness is a forgetfulness. Holding you as we rode on the bike and in all our early ways.

I called you Mecki. The hedgehog — impudent little bristly fellow of my childhood, my doll Mecki, with your sticking up hair and cautious brown eyes.

I don't really remember our lovemaking now, just you, your presence over time, kindly, well intentioned, clumsy, always waiting, and cautious as if for some sickening blow to fall.

I remember you in our hotel room in Pisa, reading, falling asleep over your book, the watchfulness going out of you, then me sleeping too. Rain drumming on a skylight awoke us, you drew me to you and we lay there safely embracing as the rain thundered above us. Or crouched in student lodgings, trying to dry our washing and keep warm over a tiny gas fire while mice scuttled in the shadows and we both wept with laughter when you melted my knickers on the gas mantle. You were fun and you awoke something protective in me for there was a vulnerability about you. I wanted to look after you but you would not allow that.

You would allow me to do so little for you, though in a sense you were a demanding presence.

And I knew that you would protect and avenge my hurts for you had that sense of honour and a harsh pride — but what good is that? You cannot live on that.

I did so love you and my heart was open enough to love others after you had gone though I could never quite let you go for you kept returning like a familiar traveller on the far shore.

You come to me still, in the silence of the night or in the speaking silence of dreams.

A presence, indicating something, standing by thresholds ...

Come to me again, in dreams of the past,

Come to me, lean low, murmur and say, "Vergissmeinnicht !"

★

282

I went to see Catherine for the last time one evening in September. We had kept in touch and agreed to meet following the inquest on Jayney Kirkman. We met at a hotel not far from Rachel's old flat. I drove there as if to an assignation. The city paused after the day and drew breath, the young girls going out on dates, waiting at bus stops, their abdomens curving under their short crop tops, the parks with their yellowing plane trees outlined against a milky sky. Catherine sat waiting for me in a panelled alcove of the bar of the old fashioned hotel. She rose to greet me as I approached, tall like her sister, her hair now shorter and with blonde highlights. She wore a grey linen jacket with a lime-coloured blouse. Her red-painted toenails peeped out from designer sandals. Her eyes held mine as she talked of her daughters, grown up now with boyfriends of their own and of her husband, Ray, who was on reduced hours and heading for early retirement.

I asked if she was content. Yes, she said, speaking with that familiar slightly shaky tone as if about to break into laughter.

"We go cycling now as a family and we are doing up the house a bit. And you?"

Well, that was more problematic. I skated over my life and my work in the hospital and asked if she had seen anything about Hobman's escape in the press.

"No. I no longer read things like that," she said.

She no longer wanted to follow the cases of the missing either, although everything had got stirred up again after the Clouds Hill discoveries when the police contacted her again and showed her a few things they had found in that bleak estate house. They showed her items, that Max had given to Theresa, in the jewellery box and some of Rachel's possessions still stored from the original investigation. Once the inquest was over, they allowed her to take some things that she thought she recognised and which she wished to retain as keepsakes of her sister. Apart from that, she wanted an ending to it all, although she told me that sometimes as a family they went to Tuxford Water.

"Yes. I do too," I told her.

She gave me back Rachel's red leather address book, which I had originally bought her in Italy and which had been retained by the police all this time.

I gave Catherine in return some copies of my photos of Rachel.

And that was it. We made our exchanges then parted. She came up to me to kiss me on the cheek in farewell and for a moment I put my hand to her hip bone in a remembered gesture.

★

It was at about that time that Bartram and I let Mattie Dread go.

Each patient at the hospital was given an independent tribunal, every three years, in order to determine their continued detention. Very few such hearings resulted in any change to their situation. Mattie Dread was due for such a tribunal and Bartram and I summoned him for a preliminary review. He entered the review rooms with headphones to a walkman clamped to his ears. He sat on one of the shiny, plastic chairs and sang falsetto,

Let's get.

Let's get.

Bartram signalled to him to take the headphones off and he slid them back to hang around his neck. We could hear the tinny music and he continued rolling and jerking his head to the beat. He leaned forward and drummed his long fingers on the low table that held the medical notes and sang,

Everybody get into it

Get stupid

Let's get retarded ha!

Let's get retarded in here!

We tried to talk to him but he said, "Whatever you say Bossmen." and put his headphones back on and resumed drumming on the plastic sides of the chair and sang again,

Let's get, ooh hoo

Let's get cookoo

Ow wow ow!

Retarded yeah!

He then gazed at us with a benevolent look and lifted one earphone off an ear and said, "I leave it all in your good hands. I believe in you doctors!"

His rich, deep laugh rolled round the room and we couldn't help smiling in return.

"What are we going to do with him?" said Bartram after we had dismissed him. The whirlwind had departed with the sound of "*Oo hoo cookoo*" diminishing down the corridor.

Psychology said that there was no insight.

Nursing grumbled about him.

Bartram said, "I have the feeling that even after a hundred years of treatment here he would still be exactly the same!"

I walked with Bartram down the blocks afterwards to the canteen past the trudging lines of patients returning from workshops and therapy rooms. Bartram said to me as we walked, "Perhaps we have to give up our structures, to give them up to change. Perhaps we are the first to really understand that or the last — I really can't quite decide. I see us as precursors in a strange way — antennae here, the antennae of the race!"

He laughed and clapped me on the shoulder, "Behold — *Ab uno disce omnes.* From one person learn all people!"

He gestured to the stream of patients as they came past, some whispering or croaking out their greetings, their faces lit up by the porthole vents, their eyes glimmering, drawing my gaze towards them.

Why did we let him go so readily? In the past he would have been winnowed and filtered through the villas until he was a husk of a creature fit to be processed out to medium secure. Perhaps we had become weary of being guardians, maybe Mattie's residual joyfulness had called to us. Bartram had once said to me, "You know Jack I feel sometimes that we are all hiding here in the hospital, that we simply would be noticed too much in the outside world."

Maybe in that way we were sending Mattie out as our envoy, our explorer.

Bartram and I both wrote reports recommending his discharge. I met him a few weeks later as he was escorted through the open air courts to the tribunal room. The air was fresh and still after autumn rain with just a hint of wood smoke and damp earth from the fields beyond the wire. Leaves came drifting off the birches and poplars within the enclosures and a machine came buzzing along the paths to suck them up, for the hospital disliked untidiness.

I sat with Mattie in the waiting room to the tribunal chambers. His solicitor looked up from the copies of our reports and shook his head with amazement.

"You clinicians have made it very easy for me today."

Mattie was cheerfully gazing about as if at a new world. He had plaited beads into his hair for the occasion. He turned to me and asked, "Are you a believa doctor? Do you believe?"

I looked back at him and just then his eyes looked suddenly serious and penetrating and his hair was shot through with a reddish aura from the autumnal sunlight slanting through the reinforced window glass.

"Yeah, I guess so Mattie. In my own way," I replied.

"Good, so do I!"

He smiled warmly at me before we were summoned by the clerk to the tribunal.

"Let's do it," said Mattie.

We briefly passed through an open air court to get to the tribunal room. As we swept down the path with the escorts Mattie reached down and plucked a handful of grass from the side of the path.

We assembled before the three man tribunal, which consisted of a bluff, red-faced, retired psychiatrist, a probation officer with a world weary air and a High Court judge, out of his robes, in a blue Saville Row suit and a neatly pressed three cornered handkerchief in his breast pocket. He dictated the proceedings with crisp authority. Mattie's solicitor addressed the judge and asked for an absolute discharge on the grounds that his client was not insane, nor dangerous.

A dance of arguments then ensued with the panel questioning Bartram and I and Mattie's solicitor also weaving in his points. We willingly conceded that Mattie did not pose a demonstrable risk to the public.

All the while Mattie remained silent, staring down at the clump of grass that he twirled in his fingers.

"What is it that you have there, Mr Dread?" the judge eventually enquired.

Mattie showed the tribunal the vivid swatch of verdure.

"What is this, sah? It is grass or some might say the flag of my nature for green is a hopeful colour. Or mebbe these leaves are little children of all vegetation? Or the hair of my ancestors perhaps? Or again just the sign of sameness for it grows around black folks as well as white!"

"I see, Mr Dread."

The judge looked momentarily uncertain. In an attempt to recover his poise he asked, "Perhaps you can let us know what your plans are if we decide to release you from your detention order?"

"Takin' it easy, sah!" replied Mattie.

They agreed to release him in the end although it was unusual. He took his discharge immediately and declined help with funds for bus fare or even a lift to Redford station.

"I'll be fine. I'm just walkin'!"

Bartram and I stood together in the lodge house that autumn afternoon and watched him go down the five steps with his black knapsack, his dreads bobbing as he bounded away with a springy tread. He never looked back and we watched his figure disappearing down along the hedge line and through the drifts of fallen poplar leaves, then he turned at the gates with their pineapple-topped finials where we, at last, lost sight of him.

Author's Note

In a sense we are all waiting for someone to come back from the past, bringing a lost happiness, and this book describes that state of being. Writing it has been like carefully fashioning a mask to fit a face whose features I could just barely make out. It has been shaped by twenty years work in mental health services, where I have learned so much more from patients and from staff, but I must insist — this work remains firmly fiction.

I owe much to individuals — particularly to the Three Graces at the inspirative heart of the novel: to C.D.O. for kind permission to use materials in this book, to S.G. for all those wild times and to A.M.S. who remains *in pectore*. I also owe a debt to the late Roger Poole — an inspirational lecturer.

Warm thanks to Derek Thomas for early purgation of the text and to Antonia Owen for her advice. I am grateful to Paul Tribe for lending his image and to Ross Bradshaw for taking a chance on this frail barque and for his editorial work. Last and first, I thank Sharon for helping with this book and with so much else.